T0000215

ADMIRAL AND COMMANDER

BAEN BOOKS by CHARLES E. GANNON

THE CAINE RIORDAN SAGA
Fire with Fire
Trial by Fire
Raising Caine
Caine's Mutiny
Marque of Caine
Endangered Species
Protected Species
Killer Species, forthcoming
Misbegotten (with David Weber), forthcoming

OTHER BOOKS IN THE TERRAN REPUBLIC SERIES
Murphy's Lawless (with Griffin Barber, Kacey Ezell,
Kevin Ikenberry, Chris Kennedy, Mike Massa & Mark Wandrey)
Watch the Skies (with Kacey Ezell,
Kevin Ikenberry & William Alan Webb)
Mission Critical (with Griffin Barber, Chris Kennedy & Mike Massa)
Admiral and Commander (with Chris Kennedy)

THE VORTEX OF WORLDS SERIES
This Broken World
Into the Vortex
Toward the Maw, forthcoming

THE RING OF FIRE SERIES
1635: The Papal Stakes (with Eric Flint)
1636: Commander Cantrell in the West Indies (with Eric Flint)
1636: The Vatican Sanction (with Eric Flint)
1636: Calabar's War (with Robert E. Waters)
1637: No Peace Beyond the Line (with Eric Flint)

JOHN RINGO'S BLACK TIDE RISING SERIES
At the End of the World
At the End of the Journey

THE STARFIRE SERIES (WITH STEVE WHITE)
Extremis
Imperative
Oblivion

To purchase any of these titles in e-book form,
please go to www.baen.com.

ADMIRAL AND COMMANDER

CHARLES E. GANNON
& CHRIS KENNEDY

ADMIRAL AND COMMANDER

This is a work of fiction. All the characters and events portrayed in this book are fictional, and any resemblance to real people or incidents is purely coincidental.

Copyright © 2024 by Charles E. Gannon and Chris Kennedy

All rights reserved, including the right to reproduce this book or portions thereof in any form.

A Baen Books Original

Baen Publishing Enterprises
P.O. Box 1403
Riverdale, NY 10471
www.baen.com

ISBN: 978-1-9821-9333-1

Cover art by Kurt Miller
Space vessel model by Thomas Peters

First printing, April 2024

Distributed by Simon & Schuster
1230 Avenue of the Americas
New York, NY 10020

Library of Congress Cataloging-in-Publication Data

Names: Gannon, Charles E., author. | Kennedy, Chris, author.
Title: Admiral and Commander / Charles E. Gannon and Chris Kennedy.
Description: Riverdale, NY : Baen Publishing Enterprises, 2024. | Series:
   The Terran Republic series
Identifiers: LCCN 2023053513 (print) | LCCN 2023053514 (ebook) | ISBN
   9781982193331 (trade paperback) | ISBN 9781625799562 (e-book)
Subjects: LCGFT: Science fiction. | Novels.
Classification: LCC PS3607.A556 A66 2024 (print) | LCC PS3607.A556
   (ebook) | DDC 813/.6—dc23/eng/20231117
LC record available at https://lccn.loc.gov/2023053513
LC ebook record available at https://lccn.loc.gov/2023053514

Printed in the United States of America

10   9   8   7   6   5   4   3   2   1

To the readers of the Murphy's Lawless arc; it is thanks to you that this tale can be told at all!

—CEG

To Sheellah.

—CK

55 Tauri at Periapsis

├──┤ = 1 AU

Jrar System
4 AU

Periapsis of Binary
8.5 AU

Shex System
5 AU

▸ Both systems shared original planetary accretion disk so are on the same plane.

▸ Orbital direction of planets of both systems are counter-clockwise.

▸ Orbital periods in 24-hr days
Kulsis: 1024
R'Bak: 369

▸ Return to comparable periapsis value: ~1100 24-hr days, or 1466 18-hr (R'Bak) days

orbits 1&2 too small to show clearly

── = transit of ~11.2 AU
(incl. all curvature/vectory changes b/c not straight line)

PART ONE

Approach

Chapter One

Spin One

"*Ugh!*" Major Kevin Bowden let the air out of his lungs in a rush as the seven-gee retroboost ended. Finally, he could breathe normally again. "It's been a while since I was at that kind of acceleration, and you get out of practice *fast*."

"We RockHounds don't do it often enough to get used to it," Malanye Raptis said. She smiled. "It is wasteful of resources."

Bowden returned her smile. "Yes, but it was worth it." The thermal signature had been brief and not pointed in the direction of any of the surveyors. "We did it!" he declared, and held up a hand for a "high-five."

Raptis cocked her head and looked at Bowden's hand.

"It's a—" He looked at his hand for a moment, then he put it back in his lap and sighed. "Never mind. I'm just happy we made it back." He glanced out the bridge windows of the hijacked Kulsian corvette. The RockHound packet and the stolen Kulsian lighter had maintained formation, and he caught a few glints of reflected light off the nose from the tugs that had been sent out to help recover them. No one—neither RockHound nor SpinDog—had ever piloted a corvette before; common sense dictated it be pulled in carefully.

"I'm relieved, also," Raptis said. She chuckled. "I never expected this to work."

"Which part? Stealing a Kulsian lighter, getting a Kulsian

3

corvette to think we were damaged so it would approach us, or commandeering the corvette and bringing it back here undetected?"

"Each step was improbable; to have accomplished all of them... well, it strains belief."

It was all part of the plan, not that Colonel Rodger Murphy had shared any more of it with Bowden than he needed to know. Bowden's part had been to assist in the hijacking of the corvette that would be used as the template for replicating a whole squadron of copies to stop the coming Kulsian fleet.

"Yeah," Bowden agreed. "And I'm not looking forward to that part of the debrief where we go over losing half of Tapper's boarding teams and damn near everything else." Several of those who'd made it back were still too badly wounded to move. Not only had that taken up a disproportionate share of the available living space, but they'd have to be carried off carefully, necessitating a hard dock when they reached the main SpinDog habitat, *Spin One*.

"But yet we succeeded." Raptis's voice was full of wonder. "Somehow."

"Yeah, we did." Bowden winked at her. "But I'm willing to bet that this was the easy part."

"The... *easy* part?"

Bowden nodded. "Now we have to get the SpinDogs to all work together to copy a bunch of ships, and both the SpinDogs and RockHounds to agree on a plan for how to arm and fight them. And then we have to take on the Kulsians."

"I'd rather fight the Kulsians than try to get the primae and Legate to agree on anything. It's probably safer." Raptis laughed. "Will Murphy be doing that or someone else?"

Bowden winced. "Murphy had Tapper brief the ship takedown; I'm willing to bet that the after-action report is going to be my job."

Raptis reached over and patted him on the shoulder as the tugs began latching on to the ship. "You have my most sincere condolences."

It didn't take long for the tugs to attach and maneuver the corvette into the bay, despite its size and the spin of the core-hollowed asteroid that held the habitat.

Feeling suddenly sluggish in the 0.85 gee equivalent, Bowden shut down the comparatively massive corvette. "Come on," he said. "Let's go see if they need any assistance with the casualties."

"They will certainly need someone to show them how to put the ramp down."

"There's a ramp?" Bowden asked.

"Of course," Raptis said. "How else did you think we would exit the ship? Through the boarding tube?"

"Well, I—" Bowden stopped before he embarrassed himself any further. *The more I think I know about operating spacecraft, the less I find I actually do.* The boarding tube was on the corvette's main deck, almost four meters above the floor of the hangar—or, as the SpinDogs insisted, the docking bay. The bottom hinge of the ramp was a meter closer, but even at 0.85 of a gee, that was still quite a fall. And for the casualties...not good at all.

Raptis led him back to the cargo deck and through the various people who'd been on the mission in various capacities. They appeared to be just standing around—or lying, in the case of the casualties on their improvised stretchers.

"It's right here," Raptis said. She shooed a few people back and slapped a large yellow control button. A two-meter-wide section of the deck hinged down, becoming a boarding ramp that reached the deck of the hangar.

Bowden looked at the people waiting to debark and shook his head. *How is it that they know how to leave the ship and I don't? Probably because they haven't spent all their time on the bridge of it trying to learn how to fly it.* Aside from sleeping, he couldn't remember much time not spent at the controls. Sometimes, he'd slept there, too; they'd had only three qualified pilots to get the three ships back to *Spin One*.

The ramp touched down with a clang, and Raptis stepped back.

"All ashore who's going ashore," Bowden said, motioning to the ramp.

Horace Chalmers, one of the team that had infiltrated R'Bak Downport, raised an eyebrow at Bowden's distinctly maritime order as he helped his friend Jackson to the ramp. The small African-American sergeant's thoroughly bandaged head appeared mummified; he was still recovering from a fractured cheek and several other lesser injuries he'd sustained while capturing the lighter they'd used as bait.

Bowden watched Chalmers move slowly down the ramp as still-ambulatory members of Tapper's boarding teams began carrying stretchers toward it. Major Mara Lee and the SpinDog healer who'd helped her with the birth of her child—Naliryiz—were near the bottom, along with some of the Terran medical personnel. Between that group and the rest of the SpinDog onlookers, three other Lost Soldiers stood facing away from the corvette, hands near their holstered pistols. *Hopefully that's just a precaution and not indicative of some new inter-Family tensions.*

"Medics!" Major Tapper called. "Get a doctor in here *now!*"

Bowden turned back as Harry Tapper and Sergeant First Class Marco Rodriguez set down the stretcher. The man on it—a small, Vietnamese sergeant named Pham—was struggling to breathe. His mouth opened like a fish out of water, but nothing went in or out beside a small trickle of blood.

"Hold on, buddy," Tapper said. "You made it this far. Just hold on." Pham pushed against the restraints in a reflex to grab at his chest and spasmed. Harry kept his eyes on his soldier but bellowed, *"Medic!"*

Bowden spun back toward the ramp. The troops going down had run into SpinDog security types who had flowed around the medical team toward the corvette; they were apparently under orders to secure the vessel immediately. The cries from inside the ship energized the growing jam into a frenzy of motion; the groups in the docking bay jostled and squeezed past each urgently as those near the ramp tried to sort themselves into upward and downward lanes.

"Clear the ramp!" Bowden roared, pointing at Korelon; as Tapper's respected XO, he could expect prompt obedience. "Get our people down to the deck!" He scanned the front ranks of the crowd in the bay, found Mara Lee's eyes, and pointed behind her at Naliryiz. "And get *her* up here now!"

Mara nodded sharply, took the healer by the arm, and rushed toward the ramp, elbows out. In a command voice that couldn't be missed, she yelled, "Out of our way!" Naliryiz was already ahead of her.

As she did, Korelon was ordering everyone on the ramp—regardless of which direction they were going—to jump down over the sides, leading by example.

The ramp cleared as the two women stormed upward. Seeing their approach, Bowden raced over to Tapper, who was still talking earnestly to Pham.

"Stay with me. Help's coming."

Pham stilled.

"No!" Tapper yelled. "Stay with me. Damn it, stay *here!*"

"What's going on?" Mara asked as Naliryiz bent over the small Lost Soldier, hands already at work.

"We were taking him off, but he started struggling to get air into his lungs," Tapper replied. "A second later, he stopped breathing altogether and jerked. Looked like he had a heart attack."

"A heart attack?" Naliryiz asked as she moved her medical sensor to Pham's chest and listened to its hardwired earbud.

"He grabbed his chest like he was in pain."

"What can we do to help?" a medic asked as he arrived, trailed by two orderlies.

"Help him breathe," Naliryiz replied. "He did not have a heart attack. More likely he has a blood clot that has reached his lungs."

The medic put a device over Pham's face with a rubber bag attached, and he began squeezing it.

"But he was wounded almost a week ago," Tapper said with a frown. "No sign of anything since. And now it hits all of a sudden?"

Naliryiz nodded. "Your hard counterboost probably caused the clot to break loose. We must get him down to surgery. We can help him, but there isn't much time." She looked at the medic. "You—keep doing that." She looked back to Tapper and one of his men. "Pick him up. Quickly. Let's go!"

The group sped down the ramp and were soon lost in the crowd that closed behind them. Bowden kept hoping for another glance as they made for the hangar exit; no such luck. He turned back to the remainder of the team in the ship. "All right," he said, "nothing else to see, or do, here. Time to turn the ship over to the replication experts."

Colonel Rodger Murphy almost stumbled when the current of the crowd moving in the corridor abruptly changed from feeding into the landing bay to flowing out of it. Over the suddenly struggling heads and shoulders in front of him, he heard Mara Lee shouting, "Out of the way! Make a hole!"

Murphy pulled several SpinDogs back against the bulkheads, nodded for his adjutant to do the same. Janusz Lasko, the big Polish submariner who was also his bodyguard, frowned but complied: he didn't like obeying any order that made him less able to protect his commander. In contrast, Murphy's first "security overseer," Max Messina, had always "failed to hear" any directive that impeded his mission: keeping the colonel alive. An annoying habit, but also the hallmark of a professional.

It was that very same, and very large, veteran of the Vietnam War who now pushed out of the crowd like a one-man flying wedge, almost staggering when he hit the open space Murphy and Janusz had cleared. With a nod, he pounded past, sweeping his arms to push any leaning gawkers back against the walls.

Right behind him, Tapper, Rodriguez, and Korelon hustled forward with a stretcher. The feet-first occupant was small: Pham, the senior NCO of the small group of North Vietnamese Lost Soldiers. He had various SpinDog monitors and tubes connected to his chest. Securing his head and watching his vitals, Naliryiz was half bent over him as they moved, oblivious to everything except her patient.

The crowd started backfilling the wake of empty space behind them . . . but more angry shouts cleared them back: Chalmers pounded past, arm around Jackson, whose head was a large, lopsided knot of bandages and medical tape.

"And where is Yukannak?" Janusz muttered. Like many large men, he was notably good-natured, which made his bitter tone all the more significant. Yukannak, a Kulsian collaborator, had betrayed the team shortly after the lighter launched from R'Bak Downport. And if the usually mild Polish torpedo loader wanted a piece of the traitor, then it was a surety that many less peaceful types would be after his scalp. Or possibly more personal parts of his anatomy.

"Yukannak won't be coming through here," Murphy answered.

"Why not, sir?"

"Because I ordered him taken directly to a maximum security cell."

Janusz nodded sharp approval. "Let the dog lick his wounds alone."

"I'm not locking him up to punish him."

Lasko frowned. "Then, why, sir?"

Murphy looked back at the man who was almost a full head above his own six feet. "To keep him alive. We still need him."

Janusz's eyes shifted to look over his commander's head. "But—isn't *that* him?"

A pair of survivors from the SpinDog boarding team hustled yet another head-swathed figure forward.

Murphy recognized the man's light build. "Vat?"

The only response from beneath the con man's bandages was a mumble-punctuated groan as he was half-carried away.

"That is Lieutenant Thomas?" Janusz wondered. "But there was no report that he was injured when they seized the lighter."

"He wasn't," answered the broad-shouldered man who followed along behind.

"Report, Sergeant Roeder," Murphy ordered sharply.

Tapper's medical specialist started, peered around Lasko, straightened. "Beg pardon, sir. The lieutenant wasn't part of the fight to grab the lighter; he'd already been drugged by Yukannak. But he got cocky when he interviewed one of the Kulsians from the corvette."

"He got 'cocky'? In what way, Sergeant?"

"Didn't want restraints on the prisoner, but then leaned into him hard and personal. I wasn't there, but scuttlebutt said it was about his dirtside girlfriend's uh, unusual sex play. The Kulsian went ballistic."

Murphy raised an eyebrow. Vat knew only one Kulsian: Yukannak. Furthermore, most of the intimate information Vat had gathered while at Downport involved members of the gay community. How he'd discovered useful sexual—or possibly romantic—leverage to facilitate the interrogation of an unknown Kulsian crewman was unclear. "And how did Vat get so badly injured? Did he send away the guards?"

"No, sir, but the Kulsian lost his shit so quickly that the guards didn't dogpile him before he reached the lieutenant."

"And they couldn't pull the prisoner off before he rearranged Vat's face?"

"That's easier said than done when weightless, sir. And the Kulsian had great zero-gee skills. Our guys . . . well, not so much."

Two more of Tapper's boarding team appeared around Roeder, a prisoner held between them, nursing a bandaged hand. When they'd passed, Murphy muttered, "I take it that was the interview subject?" Roeder nodded. "I'm surprised that he's still alive." Vat had a sharp, often vengeful temper.

The sergeant obviously thought the colonel was referring to possible payback from the guards. "That Kulsian wouldn't be breathing now, except that Lieutenant Thomas gave direct orders that under no circumstances was the prisoner to be offed—er, seriously injured."

Murphy glanced at Roeder. "Why?"

Roeder shrugged. "Don't know. The lieutenant said the guy was a 'ringer.' Which were the last words he spoke before I had to immobilize his jaw." The sergeant sounded grateful that he'd had a medical imperative to muzzle Vat for the trip back to *Spin One*.

"Thank you, Sergeant. Carry on."

"Sir, yes, sir."

Like Murphy, Janusz stared after Roeder's receding back. "Colonel, what is a 'ringer'?"

Murphy shook his head. "A person of special, even crucial, value."

"But how would this common Kulsian crewman be a . . . a ringer?"

"That," Murphy said with a nod, "is precisely what I intend to find out."

Chapter Two

Spin One

As Murphy entered his briefing room, ops center, and HQ all rolled into one, his staff officer, "Pistol Pete" Makarov, glanced in the direction of the colonel's office. "You have a visitor, sir. Major Korelon."

Murphy nodded his thanks and, without breaking his stride, entered his sanctum sanctorum, hand extended. "Welcome back, Korelon'va."

The RockHound officer was already standing. Either he'd remained that way since arriving or had jumped to his feet upon hearing Murphy's voice. "I am sorry to intrude, Colonel Murphy, but I am scheduled to depart *Spin One* within the hour." After shaking hands—a Terran gesture that did not come naturally to RockHounds or SpinDogs—he bowed sharply: the local equivalent of a formal salute. "I wished to express my gratitude."

Murphy waved toward a chair. "For what?"

Korelon shook his head at the offer to sit. "For your help, your patience, and later, your support. You had little reason to trust that I would serve well under Major Tapper after our, eh, unfortunate first exchanges."

Murphy smiled at the euphemism. "Are you becoming a diplomat now, Major? I don't think I've ever heard an imminent knife-fight described so tactfully."

Korelon smiled back. "In fact, my new assignment involves just such a shift in my duties. Legate Orgunz has indicated that I am to once again be a liaison."

Murphy shook his head. "Then why are you departing? That's the role that brought you here in the first place."

The other nodded. "Indeed, but I will no longer be performing that role on *Spin One*. Rather, I am being sent back to the outer system."

Murphy frowned. "Have you been pushed out of your position here? If so, I will speak with Legate Orgunz. Your work has been extremely helpful to—"

"No, Colonel. You misunderstand; I have chosen to return to the stations and outposts of my people. I am, to use your geocentric phrase, returning to my roots."

Murphy glanced around at the well-fabricated bulkheads and the many comforts and amenities they implied. "That will be...quite a change." By comparison, the dwellings of the RockHounds—small habitats bored through slowly rotating asteroids or holes cut into hangar-sized rocks—were extremely austere.

Korelon smiled. "My time here on *Spin One* has been pleasant, but that is part of the problem. In coming here to be an advocate for my people's interests, I have drifted away from their ways, their daily tribulations. That must end."

"But then how shall you continue your work as a liaison?"

The RockHound shrugged. "I shall do what I did here, but in reverse. If we are to unify as a greater people—as the free spacefaring families of the R'Bak system—I must now be a liaison not *for* the RockHounds, but *to* them." He glanced at the entrance. "I appreciate that you have much to do, Colonel, given our return. So I shall not take up any more of your time."

Murphy raised a pausing hand. "Major, before you leave, a question or two. Specifically, I'd be grateful for any light you can shed how and why one of your prisoners attacked Vat during questioning."

Korelon frowned. "You are referring to the Kulsian drive tech who emerged from an access panel after we took the corvette, I believe? If so, that is almost all I know about him. Which was clearly Vat's intent."

"He felt it necessary to withhold details from *you*?"

"Not just me, Colonel: from everyone. Even the mission's

commanders. Vat insisted that any further information about the prisoner be reserved for your ears only."

Murphy felt his eyebrows rise. "Only mine? Do you have any idea why? Or what happened during the interrogation?"

Korelon smiled ruefully. "No, but the prisoner remained furious for several days." He shrugged. "Apparently, the lieutenant made several unflattering remarks about a woman the drive tech mentioned."

"Mentioned during the interview?"

"No, I believe the lieutenant learned of her while reviewing the prisoner's personal effects."

Personal effects? "Do you know what those effects were or where Vat secured them?"

"I am sorry to report that only Vat himself could answer those questions, sir. He was adamant that they remain secret until he spoke to you."

"Did anyone else see those personal effects before the interview?"

"Just one of my men: Markaz. He accompanied Lieutenant Thomas during the search of the corvette's staterooms and bunks. Most everything was on disks and chips, but the drive tech kept a sealed folder hidden in the false bottom of his footlocker."

Murphy reflected on what a lowly Kulsian drive tech would feel necessary to conceal from his fellow crewmembers. "Who was Vat's guard when he questioned the Kulsian?"

"There were two, but Markaz was in charge of security. Again, at Lieutenant Thomas's request." Korelon shook his head. "Markaz was deeply troubled that he became distracted. He submitted himself to me for disciplinary action."

"Wait: he was distracted? By what?"

"By the lieutenant's peculiar questioning, and that it became quite... personal."

"Personal in what way?"

Korelon's jaw became rigid. "I am not familiar with your codes of military justice, nor am I certain that Markaz's perceptions are accurate. I am therefore reluctant to share anything that might place the lieutenant in an awkward position."

Murphy shook his head. "Protecting the lieutenant's honor is commendable"—*particularly since he's a Terran, and hardly your favorite*—"but this may prove to be a counterintelligence matter of the highest importance. So I must insist: what did Markaz report?"

Korelon shifted his feet. "The lieutenant suggested that the woman was nothing more than a promiscuous piece of"—the RockHound faltered—"was a dalliance of no consequence, sir."

Murphy felt the hazy puzzle pieces of Vat's interrogation snap into sharp focus and almost fling themselves together. "And Markaz is sure that was what caused the prisoner to attack?"

Korelon nodded. "And with such suddenness that Markaz, one of my senior troops, was taken entirely off guard." Korelon waited, grew uncomfortable as Murphy reflected on the details. "Sir? If that is all...?"

"It is, Major. And thank you for coming by to tell me of your plans. It has been an honor to work with you."

Korelon stood straighter, eyes wider: not in alarm or anger, but surprise. He bowed again, but it was deeper and he held it for at least two seconds. "The honor has been mine, *Ektadori'u* Murphy." When he straightened, he saw the puzzlement on the Terran's face. He smiled. "Ah. You are not familiar with that title."

"I am not," Murphy admitted.

"An *ektadori'u* is one who does not lead by rank alone, but by their wisdom, their presence, their example." Korelon's smile became rueful. "It is not always easy to be an *ektadori'u*, though, for one may be masterful yet not have commensurate rank. That is often...upsetting to those of higher station or rank."

Murphy smiled. "That situation," he murmured, "is not unknown among my people."

Korelon grinned, started to move away, but as if remembering something, turned back. Very carefully, he came to attention and delivered a perfectly acceptable human salute.

Murphy returned it with crisp precision, but lowered his hand more slowly, casually. "Godspeed, Mr. Korelon. Don't be a stranger. There's always a meal and a drink waiting for you in Lost Soldier country."

The RockHound grinned and slipped out of the colonel's office.

When Murphy heard the office's outer hatch seal behind Korelon, he called to Makarov. "Pete, I've got a question for you."

The Russian major's head tilted into view beyond the coaming. "Sir?"

"Are you familiar with the SpinDog title ektadori'u?"

Makarov, a professor of linguistics before the Soviet Army had dragooned him into becoming a translator, frowned uncertainly. "Give me a moment, sir."

"Fine. I have a recording to make. I'll let you know when I'm done."

"Very good, sir," Makarov mumbled as he pulled Murphy's door closed.

Murphy sat at his desk, called up the computer's video recording program. It was no better than what he'd used sending messages back home from Mogadishu. When it finally signaled that it was ready, he tapped the ACTIVATE key.

"This communiqué is per authorization protocol code: Salsaliin. Vat, you should have been given this recording by my adjutant Timmy Uggs. When you receive it, Major Makarov should have been present as a witness. If that is not how this recording was presented to you, it means secure protocols have been breached and you must not reply to this message.

"However, if it was delivered according to the aforementioned protocol, instruct Uggs and Makarov to leave the room while you write down the location of the personal effects of the interview subject who attacked you. Place that note in a sealed folder, ask Major Makarov to reenter, and pass it to him without discussing or mentioning the contents."

Murphy ended the recording and copied it to a ubiquitous and unmarked SpinDog micro disk. "Pete?"

His office door—actually, a light-duty hatch—opened instantly. "Here, sir."

Murphy held out the disk to the Russian. "Today, after duty hours, I want you to buttonhole Timmy and visit Vat in sickbay. Timmy is to give him this recording. Follow Vat's instructions: they'll be coming from me. He will give you something that is eyes-only to me."

"Yes, sir. If you are still interested, I now have the full definition of ektadori'u."

"Oh: right. Go ahead."

"Roughly, it means 'he or she who commands.' But not in the typical sense of being dominative. Rather, it refers to what one might call 'natural authority,' a person who is innately masterful or persuasive."

"And distinct from any consideration of rank."

Makarov's stare was almost offended. "Sir, why did you ask me for the definition if you already knew it?"

"I didn't, really. It's how Korelon said farewell. He didn't share any more than that."

Makarov's eyes widened. "Sir, I do not believe you understand the full significance of his calling you by that title ektadori'u."

"Well, he said it can cause resentment among higher ranks who aren't as respected."

"It signifies a great deal more than that, sir. It is also an oath."

"You mean, an oath of service?"

"No, sir: more than that."

"Damn it, Pete: among the Hound-Dogs what could be *more* important than an oath of service?"

Makarov was shaking his head. "It is an oath never to fore-swear you." When Murphy's expression did not illuminate with understanding, he added, "Not many terrestrial languages have an equivalent, sir. To be called an ektadori'u is an oath never to harm or bear false witness against the person so titled—so long as they have not fallen from that high standard."

Murphy frowned. "So if Legate Orgunz ordered Korelon to kill me—"

"Korelon would refuse. And accept the consequences."

Murphy shook his head. "Damn, that's a pretty messy arrangement."

Makarov nodded. "That is why I said it is so significant; it is, as you say, potentially very messy. That is why it is so very rarely conferred. It also means that if you are unable to respond to a personal challenge, the person who named you ektadori'u will stand as your second. Or, if a challenger vastly outmatches you because of age or infirmity, Korelon would serve as your champion, in the medieval sense of the word."

Murphy frowned. "Sounds like something I should keep between Korelon and me."

"Pistol Pete" shrugged. "Perhaps, but I suspect he must share it with certain others. For instance, I imagine Korelon must at least inform those—such as Legate Orgunz—to whom he has already given an oath of service."

Murphy nodded. "Yeah, it's probably common courtesy to give your boss fair warning: 'Don't order me to kill this guy, because I won't.' Keeps the high-ranking folk from being publicly disobeyed."

"That makes sense, sir—but it is only my *suspicion*." The Russian rose, frowning.

Murphy knew the look. "What else, Pete? Spit it out."

"Sir, you asked for the closest equivalent term in our language. I would say it is 'commander,' but there is another word—almost forgotten, now—that is almost as accurate: 'hortator.'"

Murphy suspected he'd blinked. "Come again?"

"Hortator, sir. It is Latin, sharing a root with the word 'to exhort.' Historically, hortators urged on citizen galley rowers or horses in chariot races. But over time, it came to mean a person with a natural ability to convince others to undertake important actions or endeavors. Partly due to their oratory and strength of personality, but also by dint of their integrity and example."

Wonder if Korelon would still call me ektadori'u if he knew I was genetically defective and closing in on the end stage of multiple sclerosis? Given the Hound-Dog mania for eugenic perfection, it was doubtful. "Thank you, Pete. By the way, here's the chip to take to Vat. After you have his reply and have brought it to me, you are to move him to a separate room and arrange for a round-the-clock guard. Staff that detail from the group Vat led while saving that town way out in the Hamain. It was called, uh..."

"Ikaan-tel, sir. Also, it may be nothing, but while I was chasing down the definition of hortator, a very odd inquiry came in, someone looking for Korelon."

Murphy looked up. "Who?"

"Oddly, not his own people. It was a representative of the J'axon Family. When I reported that Korelon had just left, the person asked me if he had missed his packet back to Pakir Station."

Murphy considered. "And then?"

"Then they disconnected without thanks. Quite rude."

Murphy nodded and stood slowly. "Major Makarov, I want you to do the following, as quietly and casually as possible." "Pistol" Pete Makarov's eyes widened as Murphy reached into his desk and produced two spare magazines for his sidearm. "First, do you still have access to the security feeds for all the traffic bays and their access corridors?"

"Yes, sir. The permissions for observing today's mission return have not been rescinded yet."

"Good. Review all the camera feeds. You're looking for any that are not functioning or have been shunted to show an endless loop of empty corridors. While you're doing that, stay alert for anything out of the ordinary."

"Such as?"

"Such as anything *not ordinary*, Pete." *Chrissakes, a little initiative, please!* "If you notice anything suspicious, contact me on the secure line, encryption protocol three." Murphy moved for the exit.

"Sir, if I may: what is this about?"

"Possibly nothing, but Korelon didn't tell anyone he was coming to see me. So someone could be keeping an eye on his whereabouts or—"

"Or whoever is following him might also be attempting to keep track of you. But why?"

Murphy shook his head. "I'm not sure, but I know a few places where I can find out—assuming I can go there without being observed. Which is why, if you get another of those strange inquiries, you tell them I'm in my office listening to a classified debrief."

Makarov swallowed. "Yes, sir. Shall I tell Janusz where you are going?"

"Absolutely not. Keep him here, guarding the main hatch. Conspicuously. In the meantime, page Max Messina and tell him to be standing by. I may need him to meet me wherever I'm headed."

"Which is where, sir?"

"We'll know that when I get there—or if you see something suspicious on the monitors," Murphy tossed over his shoulder as he left the ops center.

Chapter Three

Spin One

Murphy returned Max Messina's nod as the large man gracefully slipped out of an accessway near docking bay three. The Lost Soldier checked to either side, tucked his .45 into the shoulder holster under his jacket, stepped next to Murphy.

Who asked, "Did Makarov manage to contact you?"

Messina nodded. "The major read me in on what he saw and what you need. I hang back here. I only go in if you call for me. Or Makarov sends me the go-code."

Murphy nodded. "Any questions?"

Max sighed. "Just one. I'd expect this kind of stunt from some of the hardliners still angry about Dolkar's execution... but Family Otlethes?"

Murphy shrugged. "I helped Primus Anseker uncover some of the accomplices behind the attempts to sabotage Bowden's mission. Today's celebration of its success gives him some extra political clout."

Max glanced toward the docking bay and shook his head. "Bad use of clout."

"That's why I'm here." Murphy secured the flap on his own pistol's holster. "Lethal force is the last resort, Max."

"Roger that, sir."

Murphy nodded his thanks and entered his override code into

the control panel for the official personnel entrance to docking bay three.

When Murphy had been summoned to witness the trial that deposed Dolkar, primus of Family Kormak and condemned him to death, economy had determined the method of execution. Rather than sending him out an airlock, Guild-mother and Breedmistress Shumrir, of the Otlethes Family, had the traitor euthanized so that his "consumables" could be recovered.

Apparently, this day it was more important to send a very public message than to harvest biological resources from the eleven people kneeling less than a meter away from the inner bay doors. Flashing lights painted spinning orange and red whorls upon the plexiglass pressure barrier between them and the gathered witnesses, signifying that the much larger docking bay beyond the inner doors was open to space.

As Murphy entered, only a few of the heads that turned remained facing him; he was a regular visitor to the facilities of the Otlethes Family. So he was somewhat surprised to feel a hand on his arm, pulling him to one side. He resisted until he saw the fingers around his bicep: tapering and finely boned. Decidedly feminine.

Naliryiz leaned toward him as she drew him away from the closing personnel door. "What are you doing here?" she muttered.

Murphy sighed. "Trying to keep your people from killing themselves."

"What do you mean by that?" she hissed, guiding him toward the small observation gallery. "The only people who are going to die today are those who almost killed us all!"

Murphy shook his head. "That's not how I hear it." He jutted his chin toward the captives. "It's unclear how many of them had a choice, or if they even knew they were aiding and abetting Kemalis's sabotage."

"Is there such a difference between a traitor and his accomplices?" asked a familiar male voice behind him.

Murphy turned, speaking as he did. "With respects and regards, Primus Otlethes, there *is* a difference." *Almost as great as the change in your demeanor.* He and the primus had been sipping celebratory tumblers of Stolichnaya barely two hours before the corvette had been brought into docking bay one.

Anseker Otlethes crossed his arms. "I do not see the logic of your assertion, Sko'Belm Murphy. Since the abettors were approached surreptitiously, they knew what they were asked to do was wrong. Furthermore, they expected to benefit from their actions. The only difference between them and Kemalis is that they did not have to carry out the sabotage themselves. If anything, that makes their crime worse than those we've already executed; they lacked the courage to put their own hand to the task."

But Murphy's thoughts had snagged on the words "already executed." *If this doesn't stop now* . . . "For a moment, let's leave aside the details of their culpability. Let's focus instead on their greatest, intrinsic value to your interests. I propose it shall not be realized by executing them."

Naliryiz started moving them away from the small group that was gathering in the gallery. "Then what *is* the intrinsic value of these eleven?" Her question was barely more than a murmur; their voices had begun attracting attention, and this was a time for unity in action, not debate over the measures to be taken.

"Their value," Murphy answered quietly, "is in their survival."

"You would have us show mercy?" Anseker asked. "I appreciate that our ways are different, but this is not merely unwise: it is nonsensical. If you allow a traitor to live, you only encourage others to rise up."

"Perhaps," Murphy replied, "but firstly, in the course of aiding your investigation when Kemalis's betrayal was first reported, I spoke to persons who know some of those you have lined up." He nodded toward the eleven naked figures; two had already soiled themselves. "Everything indicated at least half of them did not cooperate willingly but succumbed to leverage, to threats against themselves and their family."

Anseker shrugged. "If one is to be involved in affairs that determine dominion, then one must pay the price for that participation. It does not matter why they elect to do so."

Murphy's eyebrows rose. "Does that include saving one's children from death—or what might be worse? That was the most common threat, from what I heard."

Naliryiz's violet eyes shifted to her primus. "Is this true?"

Anseker's gaze did not change, but his mouth stiffened. "There have been mutterings," he allowed. "But to substantiate such claims would consume time that we dare not spend. Any further contemplation of sabotage must be dealt with now, both firmly and swiftly."

Murphy sighed. "If only that issue was so easy to address. And with such finality."

Anseker looked like he was trying to decide whether to be worried or impatient at Murphy's hanging tone.

It was Naliryiz who broke the silence. "What do you mean? Because it is clear that you are not speaking about future actions by the eleven gathered here. After this day, they shall no longer be able to abet traitors, knowingly or otherwise. Their faces are known and their loyalty is suspect; no saboteurs would risk including them in covert schemes."

Always the fastest study and the sharpest knife in the drawer, eh, Naliryiz? Murphy nodded, made sure his feelings for her did not show on his face or in his eyes as he turned toward Anseker. "It sounds as though you've already executed individuals against whom you had ironclad evidence of direct participation."

The primus nodded.

"Then even those who might desire your downfall will not dare cry out against their deaths, for fear that their own honor will be smeared by supporting proven oathbreakers and traitors.

"However, if you execute these eleven whose guilt has *not* been so concretely established, how many blood oaths might be sworn against you? How many might accuse the Otlethes of being more concerned with swiftness than certainty, when deciding the fate of others?"

When Anseker struggled to find a reply, Murphy used that silence. "On the other hand, I think there is a path that would result in few blood oaths being sworn—so few that they could not give rise to deeper and wider trouble."

"Even so, we have this matter in hand, Sko'Belm Murphy," the primus answered in a tone that was admirably firm and yet, had a hint of invitation in it.

Murphy nodded. "Clearly, you do indeed have this matter in hand. But since you do, why not explore another alternative, if it only costs you a minute to do so? An alternative that does not compromise either your display of resolve and dominion in this or any other circumstances?"

"Go on."

"So long as it is understood that nothing I say is binding

upon you, there is no harm in allowing me to speak to the condemned. In fact, allowing me to do so with all these witnesses present demonstrates your surety of control."

"And what would you say to the eleven?"

"That you have allowed me, as your ally, to ask them questions and, depending upon their answers, offer them an alternative to spacing." Anseker began to frown. "That alternative—and its consequences—would be my affair and my affair only, and yet subject to your approval in every particular."

Anseker's lips tightened and his eyes flicked toward Naliryiz, who nodded. The primus leaned forward. "If any problems arise, for any reason," he muttered, "it will be on you and on your men."

Murphy shook his head. "My men have no part of this, but you may do anything you wish with me if something goes wrong. I shall not protest. Nor ask for you to reconsider. Is that assurance enough?"

Anseker's eyes were both hard and intrigued...and perhaps keen with new admiration. "You have my permission." He waved for the guard who was standing watch next to the pressure barrier to admit Murphy.

He tried not to feel the eyes on his back as he made his way across the deck of the inner landing bay. He walked slowly, hoping that it made his approach appear both confident and somber. In fact, it allowed him to concentrate on each step, alert to any unsteadiness that might arise if his multiple sclerosis ambushed him.

He reached the pressure barrier, nodded to the guard; the far portside section retracted. Once he stood surveying the condemned, it whispered closed behind him.

All eleven faces were looking over at him. In some eyes, there was hope: in others, fear. And in a few, revulsion and hatred.

"You know who I am?"

All the heads nodded.

"And you know that Primus Anseker of the Otlethes Family is watching from the gallery and can hear every word spoken?"

More unanimous nodding.

"And you know why you are here?"

One struggled to rise as she spoke, but her restraints prevented her. "I know what I am accused of, but I dispute it!"

Another simply muttered. "I am no traitor."

Murphy shrugged. "Here is what I know. Some of you are traitors. Some are not—or at least, were ignorant of the intents of those who threatened you into complicity."

Many vigorous nods answered him.

"However, it is impossible to know which applies to each of you, and time is short. Primae at war can brook no uncertainty regarding the loyalty of those sworn to them. However, as I am an outsider, and so neither a primus nor a possible aspirant to such dominion, I do not have the same responsibilities or needs. My honor is not at stake, here, and so, my freedom of action is greater.

"But it is still tightly constrained. So what I am able to offer is this: If you swear a year's oath to me, and your primus agrees, I shall hear your response to the charges of treason that have put you in this place."

Murphy waited for Anseker's objection. None came. He began walking down the line. "I make no promise other than this: that my people and I will do our very best to learn what part, if any, you played in the sabotage of which you stand accused. Our customs and legal forms are different from your own, and we have neither the time nor the inclination to educate you in their particulars."

He reached the end of the line, turned, folded his hands behind his back. "If you wish to accept our judgment, nod as I pass you." He resumed walking, back the way he had come. By the time he completed his walk, nine had signaled their agreement, although one was shaking so badly that the man had to resort to a stuttering "Y-yes." The other two simply spat on Murphy's boots. He did not pause or even glance at them; he kept walking, nodding to the guards that he had finished.

As the plexiglass pressure barrier closed behind him, Murphy saw Anseker motioning for a sidebar at the far end of the gallery.

Naliryiz joined him on the way, but remained silent until they stood with the primus. "Bold," Anseker said. "Do you have any preferences regarding how to deal with the pair that spat on your feet?"

Murphy shrugged. "They didn't choose to commit to me, so it's not my business. But I'd advise that, whatever you do, you take them out of the bay, first."

Anseker's smile was wolfish. "So, you feel sending them out a regular airlock will be sufficient?" Naliryiz glanced at the primus in surprise, and possibly, with a hint of disdain.

Murphy's answer was another shrug. "My only suggestion is that it shouldn't be public."

"And the others: how do you plan to proceed with determining their guilt? Polygraph?"

"Only to start with. A person can fool equipment. But there's a way to assess their veracity on the back end."

Naliryiz frowned. "I'm not sure what that means: 'on the back end.'"

Murphy smiled an apology. "We'll start by having them pledge their year's oath upon something that they swear means more to them than their own lives. If they don't have anything in that category, that's both a difficulty and a good sign."

"A *good* sign?"

Anseker nodded. "Yes. Because it may jeopardize their ability to take the necessary oath. So logically, if they had something that meant more than their own life, they would swear on it. If they didn't, they would lie. But if they could do neither—"

"—then they are probably telling the truth," Naliryiz finished for him, nodding. "And at considerable risk to the parole they've taken."

Murphy nodded. "And once the oaths are in place, we'll require that they follow an order that requires them to lie. Bearing false witness, for instance." Murphy smiled. "What we're looking for is a flat refusal."

Naliryiz saw the pattern. "Because if they are willing to lie when they made their oath upon something more important than their own life, it means their oath is worthless." She crossed her arms. "So again, those who refuse are trustworthy enough for the charges against them to be investigated closely."

"And to serve us under their parole for a year." Murphy held up a hand against Anseker's predictable objection. "Which will include a stipulation that we are prohibited from giving them any orders that would place them in opposition to any SpinDogs or RockHounds."

The primus shook his head. "You are strangely ready with solutions, Sko'Belm Murphy. Particularly in the face of a surprising betrayal. Are you always so calm when dealing with misfortune?"

Murphy shrugged. "There were so many ways someone could

sabotage the mission that was likely we wouldn't detect it ahead of time. So it wasn't that surprising, and it's been almost a week since we heard. But frankly, I'd say it was a stroke of good fortune, not bad." When Anseker looked askance at him, Murphy drove home his point. "So, if the traitors hadn't tried—and failed—to sabotage the mission, how long would the ringleaders have remained hidden, preparing to strike, perfecting their cutouts and compartmentalization? How long would it have taken to uproot them all, if you ever could? And if they were still operating when the Harvesters arrived, what would have kept them from revealing the spins, and maybe our fleet, by radio?"

"Your explanation makes the mission to take the Kulsian ship akin to irresistible bait," Anseker muttered.

"Well, the mission to seize the corvette had too many requirements and moving parts to keep it a complete secret. And it was a target that Kulsian sympathizers could not afford to ignore, given your ability to replicate it."

Naliryiz frowned. "But you did not plan the operation to also reveal the traitors in our midst—did you?"

Murphy kept his shrug nonchalant. "On my world, we have a saying: It's always best when you can kill two birds with one stone." He bowed, departed, left both the healer and primus staring in his wake.

Evidently, he'd sold the "Terran mastermind" fabulation pretty well.

Chapter Four

Spin One

When Murphy heard a sharp knock on his stateroom's hatch, he presumed it was Janusz about to check in before he turned the CO's security detail over to whoever had the spot in the overnight rota. But when he swung the portal open, Naliryiz stalked in, narrow arms crossed in a way that made it look like she was hugging her lean low-gee body for warmth.

He smiled. "Well, hello to you, too."

Usually she responded gladly to even his most predictable—not to say hackneyed—attempts at banter. But not tonight. She stared up at him from beneath her very straight, very severe brow. "What you did today was very brave."

"Well, I just—"

"It was also very foolish."

"Was it?"

"Do you hold your life so lightly?"

"No," Murphy sighed, "but I don't really know how much of life I'm holding on to, anymore, do I?"

Naliryiz's face went very pale.

Damned if every one of their talks didn't come back to the multiple sclerosis. "Look: it's just hard, cold numbers. Putting my life up as collateral for those eleven people kept you all—SpinDogs and RockHounds both—from stumbling into a range war right when we need everyone pulling in the same direction, not running headlong against each other. This way, we *all* get to do the work necessary to have a fighting chance against Kulsis. Otherwise, the Otlethes Family—and any allies that continued to stand with them—would have been struggling against a mounting wave of fear and resentment over a mass execution that was likely to have been labeled The Day of Spacings. Or something equally grim and accurate. I just took the necessary steps to defuse that."

She shook her head. "Yet, if one of the RockHounds violates the terms of their parole..." She couldn't bring herself to speak the inevitable endgame aloud.

Murphy nodded. "If one of them violates their parole, I die." He shrugged. "And with any luck, I'll become a martyr." He shrugged. "If chanting my name—whether the people doing it like me or not—helps everyone hold it together long enough to repel the Harvesters, then once again, you continue to exist."

"Yes, we do...but without *you*." Her eyes were imploring him to survive, and many other equally impossible things.

Murphy found a natural smile. "Odds are I won't last that long, anyway." He fought against the curve of his lips becoming brittle, felt himself losing. "Anseker and his cronies thought I was bargaining with a full life, not the last bits of one I'll soon be quitting. Hell, if I go out with my boots on, maybe they'll never find out just how genetically inferior I really was."

Naliryiz opened her mouth to speak, but her eyes grew bright and, lips clamping tightly, she exited his quarters without uttering a word.

After all, what was there to say?

The next knock on the coaming that housed the hatch into Murphy's quarters was slower, heavier. Almost certainly Janusz.

He opened the hatch and discovered he was both right and wrong. His Polish bodyguard peered around the coaming sheepishly. "Colonel, you have visitors."

"Visitors?" Murphy swung the hatch wider.

Three men stood behind Janusz, two wearing the black uniforms of RockHounds serving in an official capacity, the other garbed in the mishmash of clothes and gear that marked him as a salvage jobber from the far reaches of the system.

Murphy glanced at Janusz, who shrugged. "Come in, gentlemen. Janusz, you can wait outside."

"Actually," said the older of the two in black uniforms, "it would be more convenient if your armsman waited at a distance." He shrugged in response to Murphy's quizzical look. "We mean no imposition, but our words are for you alone."

Janusz looked worried as Murphy gestured him out of the stateroom and invited his guests to sit.

The three looked around at each other before the oldest shook his head. "It would not feel right to be seated as we speak, Colonel Murphy."

So, since you want to do this standing, maybe you mean to shoot me fair and square to my face, after all. "You have me at a disadvantage, gentlemen. You know my name, but I do not know yours."

"And for now, let it remain so," the younger uniform-wearer intoned with a solemn nod.

The older one agreed with a single inclination of his head. "Yes." He looked up into Murphy's eyes. "My people are in your debt, Colonel Murphy."

"For what?"

"For intervening before seven of our kin could be slaughtered, and then again, for standing as the bond of their parole."

Murphy shook his head. "You owe me no thanks. Had the situation been reversed—had they been SpinDogs lined up for execution and you ready to send them into space—I would have done the same."

"We know, and that is the greater half of our gratitude. Let us speak plainly. You are much prized by the SpinDogs." He saw the dubious look on Murphy's face. "Well, most of them, at any rate. So logically, your path to power depends upon grooming that relationship: to both ingratiate and become indispensable.

"But you did neither. You defied them—or at least, convinced them there was a better path. Which, at the very least, suggests you are wiser than they."

Murphy frowned. "I'm sorry to disagree, but that doesn't mean I am wiser. As you say, the SpinDog families hold the power. They cannot afford to be seen as flawed, or weak, or both. I am an outsider. I am free to suggest alternatives without being disgraced or damned."

"Still, you risk being thought weak."

"Or foolish," added the one in utility-motley. He sounded like he might be expressing his own opinion.

Murphy shrugged. "Had all eleven people been spaced without a full hearing, without any consideration of the blackmail or circumstances that brought them there, do you think it likely that the SpinDogs and RockHounds would have been able to work together to do what they now must: build the fleet that is our only chance of survival?"

Their response was peculiar; they nodded, but at each other rather than in response to him. The younger, salvage operator lagged behind the older two, but finally joined them with a grudging shrug.

What? Am I being... tested?

When they'd come to whatever silent consensus had been established among them, they glanced cautiously at the door. Not fearful, but secretive. *What? Are they going to show me a secret handshake?*

"Your solution was timely and wise, Colonel Murphy, but it does not set all dangers of division to rest. There is still an appetite for vengeance in the bellies of those who feel a parent or child or sibling was wronged during the recent power struggles. There are probably those who might be even more eager to work for the Kulsians, more eager to settle the blood debt than survive—either individually or as a group."

"They don't have power," the other one in black muttered, "but they exist within every Family. Both in these spins and on our stations."

"And our outposts," added the third and youngest.

Murphy crossed his arms. "There will need to be a determined and unified counterintelligence effort to ensure that such individuals do not—cannot—make contact with the Harvesters when they arrive."

"Aye," said the younger of the two in uniform, "but how can that be, when we are disdained by those on the spins?"

"You do not know all the injustices we suffer," added the young salvager.

"I *am* aware of them," Murphy corrected gently.

"Aware of many, perhaps, but not all." The two in black glanced furtively at the younger one, whose eyes evinced slight exotropia when he turned his head quickly. As a child, Murphy had heard such persons called "wall-eyed"—a condition that was, luckily, absent among the Lost Soldiers. Their "pedigree" was already suspect among the SpinDogs, for whom such physiological—or genetic—defects were unknown.

But thanks to the twice-traitorous Yukannak, Murphy had learned why they were present among the RockHounds: their Breedmistresses were less proficient. Probably because they either lacked adequate training or were themselves less genetically optimized to conduct Reifications: the semimystical means whereby the SpinDogs read and groomed their Families' genecodes. Guildmother Shumrir had forbidden Murphy to ever mention or ask about Reifications, but questioning Yukannak had not been within the scope of her prohibition. He revealed that Reification was not only known on Kulsis, but drove much of its Overlords' interests in what they called R'Bak's "pharmaflora."

As the two uniformed RockHounds averted their eyes from their salvager companion, Murphy saw an opportunity to demonstrate that he did indeed understand the full dimension of the inequities they suffered: specifically, children born without the benefit of genetic screening. But if he showed himself too knowledgeable...

Hell, this can't be any riskier than staking my life as bond for nine parolees. "Do you refer to the impediments your Breedmistresses encounter when conducting Reifications?"

Their eyes widened. "You know of this?" said the oldest.

Carefully, now. "I know enough to know I have much more to learn."

The other chewed his lip. "Still, you understand why, among themselves, the SpinDogs call us 'lesser beings'—and believe those slurs."

Which, judging from your own faces, you half-believe yourselves. Murphy merely shrugged—which they could interpret however they wished.

Again, the three exchanged glances, but this time, whatever consensus they reached was far more definitive. "We shall meet again," the oldest said, straightening. "And that you may know we are in earnest, we leave this with you." He produced a tube from his pocket, handed it to Murphy, nodding for him to open it.

Murphy extracted a rolled sheet of paper and unfurled it: a

drawing. Well, more of a schematic, annotated in a script that had a faint similarity to classical Ktoran—and so, was indecipherable. Reading and writing had not been included in the Dornaanis' time-compressed language lessons. "What is this? Or perhaps, more importantly, where does it come from?"

The younger of the uniformed pair nodded at the schematic. "Better that you should ask *when* it comes from, Colonel Murphy." He smiled at Murphy's surprise. "We understand that your Lieutenant Thomas, the one you call Vat, has become quite fluent in our language. See what *he* makes of this writing."

Noticing that the salvager was observing the exchange only in occasional, reluctant glances, Murphy played another hunch. He nodded at the fellow. "Was it you who found this?"

The young man started, looked away. "No. It came down to me."

"His great-grandfather discovered it one hundred and twenty-four of our years ago," the middle-aged one in black supplied. "While conducting deep salvage."

Conducting deep *salvage?* "Where?" Murphy asked.

The old one shook his head. "That is something you cannot be told. It is something you must see."

Murphy heard his hanging tone. "I would very much like to visit that place."

The senior of the three smiled; his teeth were so yellowed they did not even reflect the bright light of the stateroom. "We suspected as much." The salvager tugged at his elder's sleeve, pointed at his own strangely ornate watch; the older one nodded. "We have stayed too long as it is." His deep bow was copied by the other two. The salvager opened the hatch, looked out, nodded up the corridor—to Janusz, no doubt—and swung it wide for the other two.

As the oldest stepped over the threshold, he paused and glanced back. "I see why Korelon named you ektadori'u, Rodger Murphy. We shall be in contact, so that you will be able to prepare."

"Prepare for what?"

"To see what few have seen. It will require a week. Tell us when you believe it possible for you to be absent for that long. We will see to the rest. Be well—and be *very* careful—Colonel Murphy."

Chapter Five

Spin One

It was several days before the few white spaces on Murphy's day-planner overlapped with any of the equally scant ones on Kevin Bowden's schedule. As the former fighter-jock slid into the chair across from his desk, Murphy once again considered telling him about the strange visit from the RockHounds. But he kept coming back to the same reason not to: Bowden was going to have to work so closely with both them and the SpinDogs that he'd be under a constant microscope. If he did or said anything that even faintly suggested information derived from the back-channel contact with Murphy, that could make Kevin's job that much more complicated. Or maybe impossible.

"So where do we start with the replication process, boss?" Bowden asked brightly.

"Firstly, I have now been multiply corrected regarding that term."

"'Replication'?"

Murphy nodded. "They consider that 'our' term, even though it is their technical and legal label for it. They prefer autofabbing. Or even fabbing, for short."

"Okay, then that's my new vocabulary word for the day. Frankly, I don't care what it's called. Just that we get it going ASAP."

"The good news is that the prep work is already underway.

The engineers are already going over the corvette in detail, as well as the schematics and repair manuals they found on it. Their guess is about two weeks before they've got enough data to feed into their replica—autofabbers to start producing the simplest components. But—"

"But the SpinDogs and RockHounds aren't coordinating with each other." Bowden's smile was unsurprised. And rueful.

Murphy nodded. "Hell, that's just half the problem. The Spin-Dog Families won't cooperate with each other."

Bowden nodded. "None of them have ever done anything like this before. Everything with them is at arm's—or dagger's—length. This requires shoulder-to-shoulder teamwork. Not their strong suit."

Murphy nodded. "I don't envy you your job, Kevin."

Bowden blinked. "*My* job? Sir, you're the one who's got the real pull with the primae—"

Murphy kept nodding. "Which is exactly why it *can't* be me working as both cheerleader and chief cat-herder to get the corvette into production. As it is, I am always at the ragged edge of representing a challenge to their dominion."

Bowden smiled sourly. "Yeah, they hate it when any of us are right."

"Indeed they do, but me most of all, because I'm the closest thing to being their peer."

Bowden nodded. "And if you're right too often, you look like a more dominative leader than they do. Yeah, okay: I get it. But there's another challenge in store for us—well, me, I guess."

"There are many. Which are you referring to?"

"That we're not repl—damn: autofabbing—the corvette directly, but a modified version of it. I've continued to identify more system upgrades that we'll want to borrow from the schematics the Dornaani left us. Most of them are also simpler to manufacture. But—"

"But, once again, the Families will feel we're making their technology look inferior."

"Sucks to be them," Bowden answered, "and now, me, too—since I'm the one who has to convince them that including those systems is actually *their* idea. Anything else, sir?"

Murphy lifted an eyebrow. "In a rush, Major?"

Bowden smiled. "Not me, sir, but Harry Tapper is. He was already waiting outside when I walked in."

Murphy smiled. "Typical. SEAL time."

"Beg your pardon, sir?"

"Kind of a mantra among the frogmen, as I understand it. Being 'on time' means being someplace 'fifteen minutes before fifteen minutes before' you're actually due there."

Kevin rose in the direction of the door-hatch. "Well, hats off to them. I'm going to gather my staff. Should be interesting, since they don't know they've volunteered for the duty, yet."

No sooner had Bowden left than Harry slipped in sideways; the hatchway was that narrow and his shoulders were that wide. "Grab a seat, Major."

Harry sat, face carefully neutral. "Thank you, sir. I read your white paper on a social contract for all us Lost Soldiers."

"You are being far too kind, Harry. 'Social contract' is a very grand term for that very loose collection of ideas. Which is why I dubbed it a Homeland Manifesto."

"And if I didn't know you better, sir, I'd say what you just said is an awkward attempt at false humility. Frankly, it's a very good start. But I do have one major problem with it."

Murphy leaned forward. "Good. What is it?"

"The date, sir."

Murphy frowned. He'd expected Harry Tapper to be full of insightful suggestions, stubborn insistences, helpful revisions. But—"What date are you talking about, Major?"

Harry leaned forward, too. "The date at the start of the whole document, sir. According to that, you started writing this almost a full Terran year ago!"

"And...?"

"And why the hell didn't you tell me? Tell *all* of us? Why did you just let us go merrily along, reminding us of oaths sworn to changed or even dead nations whenever we balked at yet another crazy mission that was equal parts desperation and death wish?" He leaned back, tagged on a belated, "Sir?"

Murphy sighed. "Firstly, drop the 'sir,' Harry. Right now, we're just two soldiers who are putting aside our ranks to speak as citizens of some as-yet-to-be-determined nation or province or territory of our own design.

"Secondly, let me answer your question *with* a question: When, in your considered judgment, would have been the right moment to mention that I was considering a social contract for the Lost Soldiers?"

"Right away, sir—er, Murph."

"I prefer 'Rodg,' but whatever. As to 'right away,' what should I have said? That although one of the individuals who dropped us here swore the same oath of service to the same nation that most of us had, we were cutting ourselves loose from that? Hell, Harry: in those early days, that connection to Earth was the only tie that bound us together as something other than an armed rabble. And we couldn't risk appearing—or acting—that way. If we had, the SpinDogs would have exploited that disunity to dominate us. They would have picked us apart through a nuanced combination of threats and bribery. And probably burned us up as foot soldiers as quickly as they could, since they certainly wouldn't have welcomed us into their gene pool."

Tapper's frown was displeased: whether with Murphy's reasoning or his failure to anticipate it was unclear. "Okay, so not right away. But sooner, much sooner, than now."

Murphy gestured beyond the bulkhead toward the universe of infinite possibilities. "I could cite a dozen reasons at every major inflection point why it would have been ill-advised. However, there was a constant, a criterion that we hadn't yet met: indispensability to the SpinDogs. They wanted the technology that the Dornaani AI has managed to dole out in penny packets. If they could have pushed us aside—while we were standing next to open airlocks, probably—to get at that data, they would have. The danger of losing all that technology was the stick that kept them at bay."

Tapper squinted. "And the carrot?"

"Us. Our understanding of that technology and the best ways to wield it, from the most specific tactical applications to its most sweeping strategic implications. Yes, we were singing for our supper—long enough for both the SpinDogs and RockHounds to realize that we were collectively the goose that had laid an unprecedented number of golden eggs: both technological *and* operational. And that's what finally happened the moment the corvette you grabbed was safe in *Spin One*'s docking bay."

"So, now we're more like black swans," Harry said with a shrewd smile. "I could still come up with a few quibbles over your timetable, Murph. But I can concede this without reservation; you got us here, and we're talking about building a life. So it's just Monday Morning quarterbacking to pick at the particulars. Especially since I'm not sure I could have played it as close to the chest—and the limits of our capabilities—as you did." He scratched his ear. "Which is why I'm still trying to figure out why you've shown me your Manifesto first. From your seat, I've looked like a bit of a bull in a china shop."

Murphy shook his head. "Only because you needed what this Manifesto promises; something to really live—and therefore, really fight—for. And now that it's time to set forth the shape of the society in which we're going to live, I know that you'll bring the same professionalism and determination you've brought to the battlefield to this nation-building exercise."

Tapper rolled his eyes, smiling. "Murph, you're making me blush, but I'm still not going to the prom with you."

Murphy grunted. "No loss; you probably can't dance worth a damn. But back to business. There's a catch."

"There always is."

"For now, don't talk about this with anyone other than Makarov."

Tapper frowned. "Why?"

"Why else? The SpinDogs. If they got wind that we were thinking of how to build a separate nation—"

"They wouldn't be happy. Might panic and start thinking about how to rein us back in."

Murphy nodded. "We'll expand the discussion group slowly. In the end, we need to hear from everyone. We're not about to create a pluralist society by executive fiat."

"Yeah," Harry mused, "that certainly would make it the fruit of a poisoned tree. Okay, for now, I'll keep it to myself. But then, how do we reassure the other Lost Soldiers who are feeling like we're risking our lives for no good reason?"

Murphy smiled. "See? You've just given yourself your first job. Think about it and tell me what you come up with. And Harry?"

"Yes, Murph? Or are we back to 'sir'?"

Murphy shrugged off the question. "I want to thank you for making sure that the survivors of the corvette's crew got back here alive. I know there was a lot of...sentiment for a different outcome."

"You do have a way with words, sir. But don't thank me; thank Korelon. My guys weren't the problem and we had a clear understanding of the intelligence value of prisoners. But the RockHounds were pretty ready to paint the bulkheads red. Korelon kept them in line."

"In no small measure because of your cult status among the survivors."

"Whatever you say, sir. Anything else?" Tapper had already half stood.

"Yes: Stella and your children. They are going to have first priority for relocation, if that's what all of you wish. But if you do, I'll need to know which of the two choices you settle upon."

"Thank you, sir."

"It's the very least I could do. Don't make yourself a stranger, Harry."

They exchanged lazy salutes, after which Murphy wandered over to the still-open door. "Mack," he mused, using another of Makarov's nicknames, "you heard all that, yes?"

"I did, Colonel. Should I have shut the door?"

"No, I wanted your opinion. Assuming we actually survive to found a community of our own, do you foresee any pushback from the Families up here?"

"Do you mean the departure of the Lost Soldiers from the spins, or the locations you're suggesting for us to live?"

"The latter. I know the Families will be relieved to see us go. And it takes a lot of political pressure off our allies, in particular."

"I agree, sir. As to the locations, I doubt there will be any dispute over us founding a community on the second planet, sir. V'dyr is of no value to them, and frankly, is not entirely hospitable to us. Of course, that is its virtue as well: it is a shirtsleeve environment that no one else is using. Except the Kulsians, and then, only during the Searing."

"And the protectorate on R'Bak itself?"

"Well... I am less certain about that, sir."

Murphy synopsized his reasoning. "No skin off the backs of the Hounds or Dogs. They're not going to be looking to live dirtside for a long time, if ever. And they need reliable interface with the surface."

"Agreed, sir. But the Families are always alert to agreements or conditions that could change the balance of power. And while your proposal would certainly ensure reliable interface with the planet, I suspect that some primae would not be comfortable allowing us to be in control of R'Bak Downport."

Makarov had a point—a good one—but it was one Murphy had already considered. "I suspect you're right about the primae's reactions. But if they won't or can't get their own hands dirty holding on to Downport, they've only got two alternatives. One: they cut their own deal with whoever is in power at any given time and deal with the inevitable caprice and chaos of wrangling a stew of satraps and blackmarketeers that almost distrust each other as much as they do off-worlders. Or, two: the primae strike a bargain with us and thereby secure a reliable conduit for all their needs."

Makarov smiled sourly. "And if this were a perfect world, populated by perfectly logical persons, they would obviously choose the latter. But it is not a perfect world."

Murphy grinned. "Thanks for the tip." He moved toward the main hatch.

"Sir, do you need an escort?"

"No, I'm staying in Lost Soldier country. I'll be in Interview One if you need me."

Chapter Six

Spin One

Mara "Bruce" Lee and Naliryiz were already in Interview One's observation room when Murphy arrived. The latter did not meet his eyes immediately.

Mara, on the other hand, joined him near their side of the one-way mirror, jerked her head at the figure behind it. "So this is the 'ringer'?"

Murphy studied the handcuffed man: a medium build that had been raised in full gee. His severe features were probably fairly attractive to women, although they were mottled by fading bruises: reminders of the beating he'd taken after being pulled off Vat. "I believe that's our man. Won't know until I talk to him." He glanced at Naliryiz. "I take it you are here as witness for Primus Anseker."

"I am."

"And Legate Orgunz?"

Mara raised an eyebrow. "He replied to the invitation with— and I quote: 'I do not need to send an observer if Murphy is the source of the report.'" The chopper-jockey raised her other eyebrow. "No surprise?"

Murphy shrugged. "Most of the people about to get spaced a week ago were RockHounds."

Mara shook her head. "That doesn't wash, Murph. This kind

41

of trust...damn, what did you do? Summon the Sea of Galilee and then walk on it?"

Murphy smiled at her. "You'd have to ask Orgunz." Which was no less than the truth; even if the RockHounds' visit signified a big uptick in his popularity with their Legate, it still wasn't prudent, or safe, to reveal.

Naliryiz joined them at the observation panel. "Why is this Kulsian a 'ringer'?"

"Well, it's not *him* exactly. But I believe he's the key to getting accurate information out of Yukannak."

"I do not understand."

Murphy nodded. "After we destroyed the inter-system transmitter and the coursers scattered to find refuge with the satraps, we started looking for any of them who'd be sources of accurate information about the surveyors and the Harvesters. Problem is, most of the coursers are just raiders; plenty of violence and energy, not much in the way of brains. We found only one who was useful."

Naliryiz nodded. "Yukannak. Who betrayed the team that seized the lighter from Downport."

"Yes. But from the start, it's been difficult to tell just how much disinformation he mixes in with the intel he shares."

Naliryiz studied the man in the austere interview room. "So he may be able to tell you when Yukannak is lying." Her violet eyes returned to Murphy's; he forgot where he was for a split second. "But why would he be any more reliable than Yukannak? Why would he be willing to betray his own people?"

Murphy nodded. "That's what we're here to find out." He turned his sidearm over to Mara. "Major, we do this by the book."

"Then you should have Janusz or other dedicated security here, not me."

"There's a problem with that: nothing the subject says can leave this room. I'm making an audio recording, but that's it."

"Why all the skullduggery, Murph? It's not like there's anyone waiting to get word of his whereabouts and send in an extraction team. And good luck to them, if there was one."

Murphy smiled. "All true, but I'll sleep better knowing that the only people who are aware of this subject's value are people who I know personally and who have a history of being able to keep secrets. So humor me, yeah?"

Mara shrugged. "Knock yourself out." Naliryiz started. Mara rolled her eyes. "Just another of our stupid expressions. Go ahead, Colonel; I've got your back."

As Murphy entered, the Kulsian drive tech looked up warily, then looked away: sullen and resolved.

Murphy recognized the expression from Mogadishu and a few other less well-advertised places where the US brought prisoners of particular interest. There, the process was typically one of wearing the prisoner down, asking innocuous questions to get any responses at all. That typically proved to be the edge of the wedge that split a subject's silence wide open.

But in this case, time was very limited. The three individuals in Interview One could not routinely gather together without being missed elsewhere. And the more frequent those absences became, the less easy—and less plausible—any false explanations would become. So the only way to keep the debrief—and its subject's importance—confidential was to act quickly. Consequently, rather than wearing him down, Murphy had to use the equivalent of shock therapy.

He crossed his arms. "Lanunaz, I'm not here to talk about you. I'm here to talk about Benreka."

The drive tech started violently, then became panicked. "Why do you all want to know about Benreka? Is she in trouble? Is she safe? I swear: if any of you bastards have hurt her—"

"Lanunaz." Murphy said it loudly but calmly, as if he was passing down a sentence on a murderer.

Lanunaz's mouth snapped shut.

"Lanunaz," Murphy repeated more casually, "let's start with the obvious. You are in no position to make threats or demands. Yes, we are interested in Benreka. More importantly, like you, we want to ensure that she remains safe."

The Kulsian frowned, fretted, started to reply, stuttered into silence. *Clearly out of his depth.* "It's all a trick," he finally muttered, looking away.

And thank you for the opening, Lanunaz. "Let me prove that the last thing I want to do is trick you, Lanunaz. Not because I'm a nice guy—I'm not, although I'm not a bad guy, either. But I do have a goal. And I'm pretty sure it's very similar to yours."

"And what is my goal?"

Murphy shrugged. "To be with Benreka. Of course."

Lanunaz swallowed.

"The only thing I have in common with your first interviewer is that I've read all of Benreka's letters to you, Lanunaz. And it's clear that you have very serious feelings for each other. That—and only that—is why you're useful to me."

As was often the case, frank and pitiless admission of the interviewer's interests had a very sobering effect upon the subject. The exchange had just become faintly transactional. It baited over eighty percent of prisoners out of the deepest holes of silence, and Lanunaz was clearly not a hardened criminal who knew the ropes. Better still, Murphy had told the unvarnished truth, which subjects usually detected.

"What do you want?" Lanunaz asked.

Murphy heard that question as if it was a deadbolt being thrown back. "We want you and Benreka to read some documents."

Lanunaz frowned, tilted his head as if he suspected something had obstructed his ear. "Read documents?"

"Read documents," Murphy confirmed. "I'll explain."

And, like a suspicious but eager schoolchild, Lanunaz leaned forward, attentive but uncertain he would understand what came next.

"The first interviewer revealed that we have control over a significant slice of R'Bak's surface, particularly in the Ashbands, the Hamain, and the Greens. You know where those are, I presume."

Lanunaz nodded cautiously.

Of course you do, since Benreka is a scouting surveyor. "During the campaign to control those regions, we captured a relatively high-ranking Kulsian prisoner: a *wa'hrektop* who'd been made a silci by the J'Stull satrapy. He'd fled to Imsurmik just before we seized it. He has provided us with general information as well as revealing your forces' communications and operating protocols."

Murphy was careful to appear unattentive to Lanunaz's expression, but peripherally saw what he had hoped to: utter disinterest. No hint of outrage or even disdain that a fellow Kulsian had decided to help the Overlords' enemies.

"Unfortunately, this informer is not entirely reliable. That's where you and Benreka come in. From now on, we're going to pass any of what he tells us through the two of you. We want you to simply tell us where he's speaking the truth, lies, or has left out important caveats or additional facts. Do you understand?"

Lanunaz nodded. "What I *don't* understand is why you think we won't mislead you, too."

"Well, firstly, you and she won't be together when you go over his reports."

"What? You said—!"

"Lanunaz, I said we want to ensure Benreka's *safety*. I said nothing about the two of you being together. At least, not until we have secured control of this system."

"Then how—?"

"Lanunaz: just listen."

Lanunaz seemed to swallow his lips.

"Our informer is from the less privileged classes of Kulsis, but he still hopes to ingratiate himself with the forces of the Overlords. He believes that by misleading us, he can claim he tried to remain loyal to them. That way, they may at least allow him to live, maybe even reward him." Murphy paused and studied Lanunaz carefully. "But you don't have any such hopes, do you? In fact, you have every reason to hope that *we* come to control this system—since that's the only possible way for you and Benreka to be together, isn't it?"

Lanunaz's mouth had sagged. "How do you know?"

Murphy shrugged. "What she didn't write in her letters to you is there between the lines. And it's in line with what our informer told us about Kulsis: a lot of arrogant people with immense prejudices."

Lanunaz looked away; not just his face, but even his neck had become a bright red. He was silent for three full seconds. "How do I know we can trust you?"

"*Know* you can trust us?" Murphy shook his head. "I have no way to prove that. All I can do is be as forthright as possible. That's why I won't paint any pretty pictures for you. We obviously don't trust *you*; that's one of the two reasons we're keeping you and Benreka apart. Each one of you is leverage to ensure the cooperation of the other."

"And the other reason?"

"Without any way to coordinate what you report to us, we'll know if one or both of you are lying as well."

"So, when you've got all the information you need, how do we know you won't just kill us? Cover up your tracks?"

Murphy sighed. "Look, this is going to be a long process. Even once you and Benreka are reunited"—Lanunaz sat up sharply—"we'll still need insiders' views of Kulsian society, habits, and thought."

"By then, you'll probably have others with new information, so you *could* just kill us, at that point."

Murphy shook his head. "But *why* would we? Besides, we want to minimize the number of sources we have to manage, hide, and protect. Also, the more we recruit, the greater the odds that one of them will have a change of heart, escape, and alert the Overlords to all the information we've been gathering about them."

Lanunaz glanced away. "What you say is convincing, but it's not a guarantee."

Murphy just waited and let him do the math. Unable to trust his captors and without any leverage of his own, he had only two choices: accept or decline. And given what life on Kulsis had taught him to expect, he probably assumed that choosing the latter would incur swift and grim consequences.

Lanunaz sighed. "How do we start?"

"Two things. First, you help us get Benreka to safety."

"What? She's in danger?"

"No, she's in the field with other surveyors."

"Is something wrong?"

"Not yet, but that will be changing. Very soon. That's why we need you to tell us her current unit or location. Either will do."

Lanunaz swallowed, pushed back from the table. "No. You're just trying to scare me, to get me to tell you where you can grab her. Kill her! Maybe that's what you're *really* trying to do!"

Murphy told himself that in Lanunaz's place, he might not be thinking very straight, either. "I'm not trying to scare you, but yes, *of course* we have to have her in our custody. But *killing* her?" Murphy shook his head. "Benreka is a low-level survey officer without any special clearances. Why would anyone go to all this trouble to kill her?"

"Ransom," Lanunaz snapped without doubt or hesitation.

Murphy, who'd thought the deal was sealed, started—and damned himself for dropping his guard. "Her parents are . . . are that wealthy?"

Lanunaz studied his "interviewer" with surprise and then a bit of malign satisfaction—before realization softened his expression. "So you really *didn't* know her parents are rich. Which means—"

"Which means we are doing this for the reasons we say."

Although if Benreka's family is that well connected, she could prove a better intel source than we dared hope for.

Lanunaz nodded. "Okay, I can help you find her. You said there was a second thing?"

"You were a technician on one of the most advanced Kulsian corvettes."

"*The* most advanced," he corrected proudly.

Murphy nodded. "So you clearly have considerable knowledge about your ship and the surveyor flotilla in general. So we want to know if, when the Harvesters enter the system, they'll follow similar protocols."

Lanunaz put up his hands. "I was just an engineer's mate on the nuke drive. I wasn't around for any meeting with the bastard officers. Fate and filth: they didn't even want me in the same room with them."

Murphy nodded. "That's fine. We're not looking for specific plans, just day-to-day operations and anything that came up in conversation. And in the pre-mission brief."

Lanunaz frowned but nodded. "What do you want to know about first?"

Murphy waited for Timmy Uggs to close the office hatch behind him before resuming his perusal of the highlights from the transcript of Lanunaz's review of Kulsian space operations. Given what he'd revealed about Harvester fleets, Bowden's production and battle planning would become much more focused and, if not easier, at least less tentative.

Normally, there would still be a two-year window before the Harvesters arrived. That agreed with what the Families had observed and Yukannak had reported, but Lanunaz was unable to speculate on how much recent events—the unexplained loss of the coursers and now, a prize corvette—might accelerate their timetable.

The actual mission time between Kulsis and R'Bak—or more accurately, the primary star Jrar and its binary second Shex—varied based on where planets of both systems were in their orbits. Being a drive tech, Lanunaz was able to speak confidently about the transit time given the current distances: just over one hundred days. That included plenty of margin for errors or mishaps, as well as lots of extra reaction mass for unexpected maneuvers.

However, if the Harvesters were launching sooner, it was also logical that they would want to travel faster; Lanunaz estimated that, at best, they could cut the travel time in half. However, that would come at the expense of reserves and flexibility.

That, in turn, was likely to impact where and how they refueled, but Lanunaz confessed ignorance of how that might change given the exigencies of the present situation. Typically, the Harvesters had plenty of time to array themselves as needed throughout the Shex system, the long, ponderous cargo frames and larger vessels setting up automated fuel gathering facilities that they would tap before returning to Jrar. But if they were coming sooner and faster, they would probably not be able to follow their standard procedures, some of which required considerable time.

One reason was that although Shex's two outermost planets— gas giants, both—were excellent fueling stops for typical Harvester fleets, they were unfriendly to hurried efforts. Apparently, as the gas giants came closer to the punishing rays of Jrar—a much larger and brighter F-class star—their atmospheres became supercharged tempests. More importantly, the frozen volatiles on their satellites either liquefied, or—in case of the farthest orbit— vaporized. This was not limited to surface ice: any water bound beneath a moon's rocky surface outgassed, sometimes explosively and always unpredictably. Ironically, scraping or mining the ice that reformed toward the end of a Searing was far preferable to risking the impact of hull-crushing chunks spewed out by geysers.

The same timing impacted skimming gaseous hydrogen from the upper atmospheres of the gas giants themselves. Perilous even during the most quiescent conditions, the constant heating generated wild, immense storms that made any attempt at fuel scooping not merely more difficult, but almost suicidal.

Neither system had asteroid belts but retained dense ecliptic disks that could not accrete into planets due to the binary pair's frequent and close periapses. Despite the doubling of debris, actual collisions remained rare even at the height of the Searing, but the abrupt increase in gravitic forces initiated a period of increasing meteor showers. It also explained why, according to the Dornaani who had carried the Lost Soldiers to 55 Tauri, there were unusually high concentrations of debris at almost every planet's Trojan points.

Lanunaz had also remarked that there were a surprising

number of wrecks at the far edges of the Shex system on what he called "long-cycle vectors." He explained that these were so-called death ships: craft that had likely been on outbound trajectories but were damaged before they could fully escape the star's gravity. Typically, such ships lost internal pressure, temperature, or both, killing the crew before they could effect repairs.

Murphy set aside the collection of bullet-pointed sheets. Bowden could make good use of them, and more in the weeks to come. But unfortunately, the most pressing question was one that no one, probably not even the Kulsians themselves, could answer with certainty:

How many weeks before the Harvesters arrived?

Chapter Seven

Spin One

"We need to talk."

The fork traveling to Major Kevin Bowden's mouth stopped in mid-flight, paused, and returned to his tray. Bowden's eyes came up to find Colonel Rodger Murphy looking down on him.

"Hi, sir," Bowden said. "Is this a 'drop what you're doing; we need to talk right now' kind of thing, or more of the 'when you're done eating come on by my office' sort?"

"There is nothing more important than this topic."

Bowden glanced at his tray with a half smile. "Good thing I wasn't attached to any of this, then." He bussed his tray and followed Murphy back to his office.

"Please see that we're not disturbed," Murphy said to Makarov as he passed through the anteroom outside the office.

Makarov lifted an eyebrow at Bowden, who could only return a shrug. Bowden entered the office and closed the door. He turned, and Murphy waved him to a seat. Bowden sat on the front, leaning forward. "What's up, sir?"

"It's game time," Murphy said without preamble. "The Harvesters are en route."

"Shit." Bowden winced. "We're not ready." He took a deep breath and let it out slowly as he shook his head, adapting to the news. "Okay," he said with the next breath, "how much time do we have?"

51

It was Murphy's turn to shake his head. "Not long. Not as long as we expected, certainly. Looks like they'll be here in about a hundred and ten days, give or take a few."

"*That's it?*" Bowden exclaimed. "We were supposed to have—"

"Over two hundred days," Murphy muttered, cutting him off. "I know. It's worse than our worst-case scenario. But now, it doesn't matter what we were *supposed* to have. All that matters is that we make the most of the time we *do* have. And that, according to all of my sources, is about just over a hundred days before we have to be in position."

"Any idea of what changed or—more importantly—why? That might go a long way to determining what the best way to fight them is."

"Actually, I am starting to get a little insight into it, based on some comms intercepts we've received. Part of it, of course, is that we're a victim of our own success. Our initial advances on the planet—and particularly *your* success in blowing up the transmitter—kept them from sending preliminary reports back to Kulsis, like the advance team of 'coursers' normally would have done. Still, although the Kulsians may not know what's happening here, they're definitely aware something's going on that's out of the ordinary.

"We know the surveyor missions to the southern hemisphere are larger and more frequent than normal, and that they've been poking around trying to find out what's been going on up north. So far, though, the word they're getting isn't coherent enough for them to believe that there are actually 'off-worlders' with 'helicopters' killing their allies and deposing a lot of friendly satraps."

Bowden tilted his head. "So what do they believe?"

"They really aren't sure, but their best guess—and their biggest fear—is that there is some sort of small pirate force that is preying opportunistically on unaccompanied shipping."

Bowden frowned. "If they think that there is a pirate force here..."

"They're going to respond by sending a larger fleet with a higher proportion of security vessels," Murphy agreed with a nod. "The good news is that—even though they're coming heavier than normal—it doesn't appear they're coming loaded for bear. I'm betting that's because they can't envision a scenario in which they will have an honest-to-God fleet battle on their hands."

Bowden pursed his lips. "But we're talking about a lot of ships, still? All coming hard?"

"That's what the comm traffic indicates, yes." Bowden smiled. "Why? What is the smile for?"

"'Fly off,'" Bowden said with a twinkle in his eye.

"What does that mean?"

"My first cruise, I got to be part of the fly-off when the carrier returned from overseas. I was the junior guy in the formation, which meant that, out of the ten-plane formation, I was the guy all the way out at the end.

"We launched late due to some issues with one of the catapults, so we had to buster to get down to Oceana in time for our scheduled fly-in. We really poured on the power, kind of like the Kulsians are. Rather than make a fuel-efficient transit, they're burning a lot of extra gas."

"Okay, you're right, the fact that they're up on the power curve means that they'll burn more gas. What does the large formation have to do with it?"

"So, as the junior guy for fly-in, I was at the end of the formation. Ever play crack the whip as a kid?"

"No," Murphy said. "I must have missed that."

"The short story is that any small motion made at the center of the formation is amplified as it goes down the line, with individual ships jockeying to stay where they're supposed to be. By the time you get to the outside of the group, the last ship is having to make huge power adjustments to stay where they're supposed to be. It's easy to fly formation with two ships, or even four, but the more ships there are, the harder it is on everyone, and the more fuel you burn just to maintain your position.

"So, if they were already going to be lower than normal on fuel when they got here, due to the faster transit..."

Murphy smiled. "A lot of them are going to be *really* low on fuel when they get here."

Bowden nodded. "The lead ship will probably be okay, but the outriders—their smaller warships, in all likelihood—are going to be running on fumes when they get here."

"And we can use this to our advantage."

"You bet your ass—" Bowden cleared his throat. "Sorry, sir, you bet we can."

"Good. Put together a battle plan based on this info. We're going to need to brief the Hound-Dogs—"

"I'm sorry," Bowden said, interrupting. "Hound-Dogs?"

Murphy chuckled. "There was a submariner from Tennessee who was trying to make a point, but one of the Dogs kept interrupting him. He made some comment about 'All y'all Hound-Dogs,' and it just kind of stuck. The fact that they both hate it—like any good call sign—has made it stick like vac-suit repair tape."

Bowden gave him a half smile. "You know, I kind of like that."

"Well, they don't, so watch who you say it around. Especially when you brief them on your plan."

Bowden winced. "And when am I doing that?"

"In a few days, if it can be arranged, or maybe next week. We need to get their buy-in so we can maximize what little time we have."

"No worries; it'll be a piece of cake," Bowden lied cheerfully. Given how his stomach was suddenly feeling, it was a blessing he hadn't finished his meal.

Chapter Eight

Spin One

"I'm going to need your help," Bowden said to the collection of people he'd slowly accumulated, and genuinely come to think of, as his staff: SpinDog Burg Hrensku, RockHound Malanye Raptis, and Captain Dave Fiezel, a former USAF F-105F pilot. "I have to brief the Families, potentially as early as the day after tomorrow, on how we're going to stop the Kulsian force that is headed our way."

"Do we know what we're facing?" Fiezel asked. "We kind of need to know that in order to develop an answer to it, don't we?"

"We don't know exactly yet, as it's still a long way out, but based on the message traffic and comm hits we've intercepted, it appears they're already on their way here, and they're coming in heavier and sooner than expected."

Burg narrowed his eyes. "How soon are they expected and what size force?"

"I just spoke to Murphy, and he's estimating that they'll be here in about a hundred and ten days, plus or minus a couple."

"That soon?" Fiezel asked. "I thought we were going to have almost double that."

"I thought so, too," Bowden said. "Unfortunately, we both thought wrong. All of the trouble we've caused to far has obviously raised some hackles and has them worried about what's going on here."

"How worried?" Raptis asked. "How many ships are they sending?"

"Intel is guessing somewhere between sixty and seventy, probably led by a strong force of corvettes with a bunch of smaller outrider vessels to screen them and a number of cargo ships to bring back the harvest."

"But we don't know how many of each yet?" Fiezel asked.

Bowden shook his head. "It'll be a while before we get any sort of visual confirmation on what's coming." He shrugged. "We'll have to set up our plan based on seventy ships, probably about eighty percent of which are combatants. Call it thirty corvettes and thirty smaller ships with enough weapons to join a fight."

"That's a lot of ships," Burg said. "Even with all the Families pulling together—that's SpinDogs and RockHounds both—we'll be lucky to have"—his face scrunched up as he did some calculations—"twenty-five or so corvettes to meet them."

"With a hundred and ten days?" Bowden asked. "The Otlethes have already started replicating them, along with their allied Families. If we get everyone going—"

"We don't have a hundred and ten days," Raptis said. "We probably have less than a hundred."

Burg nodded.

"Why's that?" Fiezel asked.

"If Bowden is right, that we must surprise them to succeed, then our ships must be in position before the Kulsians arrive. If all our vessels are still running around when they approach, they will not only foresee our attack, but might have clues to the shape it will take."

"Right," Fiezel said. "So how long do we really have, then? At what point will they be able to see us?"

Burg shook his head. "It's not that easy. Yes, they are probably pointed at us right now. They're actually driving toward where we'll be when they arrive, but that's beside the point. In any event, the bows of their ships are generally pointed in our direction as they boost toward us at whatever the best acceleration is for the slowest ship in the group. They will do that for a while, then they may coast for a while, but as they reach the local area, they will have to turn around and conduct a long braking burn." He smiled. "That will be the time during which we may be able to move our ships to wherever we need them."

"*May* be the time?"

Burg shrugged. "Just because their bows are faced away from us, it does not follow that all their sensors are. And although their own exhaust will significantly degrade their ability to see our thermal signatures, they have other means at their disposal. To say nothing of the possibility that, when they are approaching, they may deploy independent sensor platforms that could maneuver away from their exhaust cone and get a clearer picture of what we're doing." He frowned. "We will have some time to maneuver to where we need to be, but not more than a few days, maybe a week."

"Depending on if and when they deploy those sensor drones, we will have a little longer than that," Raptis said. "The SpinDogs don't operate at the far reaches of the system like we RockHounds do, and Burg has forgotten one point: there is a lot of debris out there. And as the two stars come closer together, the junk from each system bangs together more frequently, creating an area that is dangerous to fly through, especially for a fleet the size of the one the Kulsians are sending."

"Right," Bowden said. "The Kuiper Belt and the Oort Cloud." All three people looked at Bowden quizzically. "That's what we called them on my planet in my time. Basically, there's a region of icy and rocky debris that orbits on the outer edge of the system."

"Exactly," Raptis said. "But whereas they are slow-changing around single stars, in a close binary system like ours, they are always changing. And in the eighty-eight years since the Kulsians were last here, it is dangerously different. They will not wish to risk entering it."

Bowden nodded. "As most of the debris is concentrated on each star's ecliptic, that means they'd have to go either up or down to avoid it."

"Correct. This will add distance to their travel, more course corrections, and multiple retroburns. All of which equals lower fuel reserves when they finally arrive."

"I've never done a retroburn after a flight that long," Bowden said. "How long do you think their burns will be?"

"It's hard to know," Raptis said, scratching her head. "It will depend on how hard they boost at the start, and their velocity when they have to dip back down into the ecliptic. If they don't scrub off the energy they put into both those vectors, they either go flying over or past the planet. Or both."

"And it will also depend on how efficient they want to be, right?" Bowden asked. "If you had all the fuel in the world, you could boost to halfway, flip over, and boost just as hard and long to stop yourself. I don't suspect they will have the fuel to do that though."

Burg shook his head. "No, they don't. They must calculate their burns so they have some fuel reserves when they get here. Enough to land on the planet or make sure their fuel collection facilities are up and running." Burg shrugged. "How much is 'enough,' though, is a matter of debate. It is impossible to know how much the Kulsians will have when they arrive, but it won't be much, especially if they are making the transit faster than normal."

"That's my thought, too," Bowden said. "We need to use that against them. Perhaps get them in a battle of maneuver, where they drain themselves dry."

"If that is a factor," Raptis said, "then it might be better to wait until they make orbit or—even better—until they start their descent to the planet. Climbing back out of the gravity well will be an even larger drain on their reserves."

Bowden nodded. "Okay. That's the answer for 'when' we hit them. The other question is how do we best take them under fire to maximize our strengths?"

"What strengths do we have?" Burg asked. "We're going to have a lot fewer ships."

"True, but we are operating close to our supply base, so unless we do something stupid, we're not going to run out of fuel. We have the ability to mass our ships so that—even if we're outnumbered—we achieve at least a local superiority in numbers. Our best bet will be to concentrate our fleet and strike the rear or side of their formation. We'll have the fuel for a sharp hit-and-run attack, but if they maneuver to engage, they'll be spending fuel that they need to conserve to reach their objectives."

"We're probably going to want to hide behind R'Bak or its moon," Raptis said, "or both. Some Families will probably be more comfortable with one or the other. We could maybe hide ships in the asteroids at the Trojan points, too."

Burg shook his head. "The SpinDogs will never go for that, since it would get the Kulsians interested in looking there. If they were to find the Spins or Outpost..."

"Yeah, let's not do that," Bowden said. "We don't want to give the Kulsians *anything* for free. We want to make them earn it." He took a breath and let it out slowly. "Okay. That's the basis for a plan, anyway. What else can we be doing?"

"We need the fabbers who are better at creating large structures to focus on making the corvettes' hulls," Burg said over steepled hands. "Shift the rest to the systems that go into them, with the best reserved for manufacturing the improved systems from your blueprints."

"Okay, but why relegate some to just building the hulls?" Fiezel asked.

"Because if duplicating the Kulsian systems are as much as they can handle, that's a waste of time."

"Why?"

"Because the Kulsians have shit for equipment," Burg said.

Bowden raised an eyebrow at the epithet.

"That's what you would say, right?"

Bowden nodded.

"Anyway," Burg continued, "a great deal of our equipment is better than what we've found in the Kulsian corvette. This is particularly true when it comes to the blueprints you brought with you; those systems are not only more advanced, but simpler to operate and maintain. So why would we want to reproduce Kulsian dung when we can outfit the ship with our own—or even better—equipment?"

Raptis frowned. "Not that I am eager to praise the Kulsians, but I do not know if it is fair to say that their systems are 'crap.' However, their designs *are* overengineered without providing any additional redundancy or reliability. So they take up more of a ship's volume and energy. However, their performance is comparable to our systems, and they are more experienced at building ship-to-ship weapons."

Fiezel nodded. "And despite all the talk about how lousy all the local computers are—both Kulsian and SpinDog—Makarov has a different take on it. Being Murphy's one-man staff, he gets to look at a lot of technical briefs in detail. And, not too surprising, it turns out he's something of a computer whiz. According to him, the local software is not only well-designed but, to use his words, 'surprisingly elegant.'"

"So why does it suck?"

"Because it's got to run on analog systems, which really limits what it can do."

"You just won the understatement-of-the-year award, Dave."

"Makarov would agree with you. He kind of sympathizes with the SpinDog programmers, says the code feels like it was written by 'drones wearing straitjackets on their brains.' Has the same impression of their technical folks, from engineers all the way down to maintenance: competent or better, but shackled to IT and electronics that we'd consider three generations behind their hardware."

"All good points," Bowden said. "I think Burg's suggestion to introduce a level of specialization into the autofabbing tasks is a good one, but we'll need to bear in mind that it does increase the chance that we could run into interoperability issues. It's going to be tricky enough to make our machinery fit and work together with what we keep of the Kulsians, but now we're adding the need to ensure that our different autofabbers are all pulling in the same direction."

"Which brings us to the greatest challenge in this entire process: making sure the Families do not hold back advantages for their own ships." Burg's chuckle was dark. "None of them have ever willingly shared their best equipment with another. Or are likely to now."

"Even if it's to defend their habitats?"

"Even then."

Bowden rubbed his chin. "Do you think you could talk them into letting us have it?"

"Probably not." Burg held up a hand, stopping Bowden's next question. "Nor will you be able to get them to do it, nor will Malanye, nor will even your Murphy."

"What about...?" Bowden thought for a moment. "We're going to want them built all the same, so if we tell the Families that everyone has to build them the same, they'll give us their best, right?"

Burg and Raptis looked dubious. "I suppose it is possible," Burg said, "but I find it highly unlikely."

"Well, we have to start somewhere, right?"

Burg nodded but remained doubtful.

"So we put together a baseline and I talk to all the Families and see what I can get them to pony up."

Raptis tilted her head. "'Pony up'?"

"See what they'll bring to the table, since their offspring will be flying them."

Raptis shrugged. "If you say so."

"I do." Bowden nodded. "And, while I'm talking to them about the template we're building for the corvettes, I can also pre-brief them on the plan we have for fighting the Kulsians and get their buy-in."

"Did you hit your head while you were stealing the corvette, Boss?" Fiezel asked.

"I don't remember doing so. Why?"

"Because either your brain got bruised or you've been away from here for so long that you've forgotten how things work. You seem to think that if you can get *some*one to agree, eventually *every*one will agree. And then live up to their words."

"I know how things work," Bowden said, "but we're not just talking about their safety: this is about survival. Don't you think that's enough to bring everyone together?"

"Nope."

Burg shook his head. "No."

Raptis chuckled.

"So *you* think there's a chance?" Bowden asked.

"No. I don't think you have a—how do you say it, 'a hope in hell'?—of getting agreement. I just found it amusing that you thought it possible. There are Families that say no to ideas simply because other Families said yes. And what makes it even funnier, and sadder, is that you're only considering relations among the SpinDogs. Getting consensus among the Families of my own RockHounds is going to be even harder."

"So you're telling me I shouldn't bother?" Bowden asked. "That it's impossible?"

"No, I agree you should ask. A miracle may happen. However, I think you need to temper your expectations. I suppose that it is not beyond the bounds of reality that everyone will agree with you . . . but I have never yet known it to occur."

Chapter Nine

Spin One

Bowden surveyed the conference room three days later with bags under his eyes. The run-up to this meeting had not been promising; he'd failed miserably in all the areas that his staff had predicted he would. Worse, most of the Family heads wouldn't even talk to him, so he had no idea where they stood in regard to his basic plan. The only thing he'd made progress on—with Murphy's help—was to get most of the Families to undertake autofabbing the corvette hulls while the others shifted their efforts to churning out non-Kulsian subsystems, which was—at least—a bit of a start.

Between the autofabbing nightmare, looking at different performance options in light of tactical ramifications, and trying to talk with all the various factions on the spins to coordinate them, Kevin hadn't gotten much sleep, and it was beginning to show. Adrenaline could only keep you going so long.

The seating in front of him reminded him of his ready room on the carrier; space was at a premium, so the seats were packed tightly together. Unlike the carrier, though, the seats were hard metal and bolted to the deck, with just enough room for the thinner Hound-Dogs to slide between them. The only objects in the room that weren't gray were the green plastic seatbacks and matching headrests, which he found an odd choice. *They need an interior decorator*, Bowden thought with a smile.

Although the facility could seat dozens of people, most of the seats were empty, with only five taken in the front row and a few Lost Soldiers in the back. Two men and a woman wearing the Spin-Dogs' gray coveralls sat on the left end of the front row, matched by a solitary figure in the black coveralls of the RockHounds on the right end. Where the SpinDogs' uniforms were heavily decorated, Legate Orgunz's uniform was simple; only the Legate insignia shone from his collar points.

Murphy—for obvious reasons—sat in the exact middle between them, careful to give no sign of favor to either side. Unlike other meetings Bowden had attended, there were none of the aides and sycophants who normally followed the Family heads around.

"Honored Legate"—he nodded to Orgunz—"Honored Elders"—he nodded to the three on the other end of the row—"Boss"—a smile at Murphy, "thanks for coming. I'm Major Kevin Bowden, and I'll be going over the strategy we intend to use to defeat the Kulsians."

The SpinDogs looked pained at that pronouncement, and Orgunz looked grimmer than normal. Bowden smiled warmly. *This is going to take all my salesmanship skills.*

He flipped over the top page of the large tablet of butcher-block paper mounted on the easel next to him. An astrographic chart was revealed. Kevin gestured toward it with a large pointer. "As I'm sure you're all aware, we are currently at periapsis, where the two systems are at their closest point of approach. Because of this, and a number of other factors, the approaching Kulsian fleet will arrive sooner than normal. It is also far larger than any previous force of Harvesters."

"Most of this is your fault," Orgunz noted.

Bowden smiled. "There's no doubt that our operations here have contributed to that, but they have also given us a unique opportunity."

"And what is that?" Orgunz asked.

"If you'll bear with me for a moment, I'd like to outline a few factors, and then I will discuss that opportunity."

"Quickly," one of the male SpinDogs said. "Our time is at a premium."

"Of course, Elder J'axon. I will be as brief as possible." Bowden turned back to Orgunz. "As you noted, Legate, our operations have provoked this response. They have also successfully kept any word from getting back to Kulsis that suggests that we are the ones frustrating their plans...So, while the Kulsians know that there have been several very atypical events in this system, we believe they don't know the full details or scope of them.

"Our comm intercepts suggest their leading hypothesis is that a pirate force is operating from bases on the system's fringes. They're also wondering if the initial loss of their coursers was due to a coronal mass ejection or some other kind of solar event with hard radiation and electromagnetic flux. They haven't ruled out a plague, either. Bottom line: they still don't know what's happened, and the surveyors haven't been able to find answers. So the Kulsians are sending a lot of ships to search for and eliminate the problem, and they're burning hard to get here as soon as possible. And that gives us a singular tactical opportunity."

Bowden glanced around the compartment. "Since most of you are pilots, this may be familiar to you, but for those who aren't, any large number of craft traveling in formation requires that the individual ships burn a lot of extra fuel to keep them where they're supposed to be. This is especially true for the ships that are on the periphery of the formation; they are frequently forced to jockey their throttles to maintain their position relative to the other ships. The bigger the formation, the more fuel-inefficient it is."

Bowden pointed to the diagram. "As you can also see, at periapsis, the two Kuiper belts—"

"The what?" Elder J'axon asked.

"Sorry; that's our term for remainders of the planetary accretion disks surrounding both stars beyond the farthest stable orbits. At periapsis, 55 Tauri's two stars' respective 'junk rings' come into contact, causing considerable vector changes in that debris. So, in order to safely navigate here, the Kulsians will have to travel 'up' out of their ecliptic plane to avoid the junk-ring collisions taking place between the two systems.

"So, you have a large force, coming hard, that has to travel farther than normal. When they get here, they are going to be low on fuel."

"Perfect," Orgunz said. "We can strike them on arrival, and they won't be able to maneuver. Our habs will be safe, as they will never get a chance to see them."

The SpinDogs looked conflicted, wincing as they nodded. They clearly agreed with the RockHound's statement, but the act of doing so seemed physically painful to them.

"Well, yes, we could do that," Bowden agreed, "but I have a plan that I think will better maximize our assets."

He flipped the page. "As you can see here, I am proposing we hit them as they reach R'Bak. This will give us a number of advantages. First, just prior to arriving, the Kulsians will have continued braking, and they will now be at the very end of their fuel. If we wait until their ships start to descend, climbing back out of the gravity well to engage us will completely empty their tanks. Having the combat in R'Bak's orbit will also allow us to use our microsats for intel and targeting, and we can hit them from a variety of hiding points, driving wedges into their formation that will scatter them and allow us to outnumber them locally, even though they outnumber us on the whole."

"I disagree," J'axon said. "If I were that low on fuel, I would want to go to the gas giants in the system to refuel before arriving at R'Bak. It only makes sense for them to do so."

"As much as I don't want to admit it, I believe Elder J'axon is correct," Orgunz said. "There is nothing worse than being out of fuel. It leaves you without any choices." He nodded. "They will definitely go to the gas giants to refuel first. Our best bet is to either strike them on system arrival or to hide until they leave again. Or at least until they disperse, so we can outnumber them locally, as you have recommended."

"Although scooping the gas giants' atmospheres or scraping their icy moons are both possibilities, I respectfully disagree," Bowden replied. "First, the Kulsians have never done so in the past, so it is unlikely they will do so now: there's no evidence they have the equipment for either option. Second, if you look at the astrographics, the two gas giants will be out of place for them to simply stop there. Instead, they would have to go past R'Bak to get to them, burning even more fuel."

Bowden shook his head. "Getting water from the moons is an energy-expensive process that wastes their most precious asset— time. Remember, we are already near periapsis. Shortly after the Harvesters arrive, the systems will be starting to diverge again, so the more time it takes to complete their mission here, the farther—and longer—their trip home.

"Looking at their operational patterns from past trips, when the Harvesters arrive, they head to R'Bak to refine water into deuterium and tritium and then lift it to orbit. Only once they've accumulated sufficient fuel stocks do they send out a special team to the moons to set up automated plants for generating the fuel they'll use during the return trip. I saw their processing machinery on one of my training flights; they leave it in place from Sear to Sear. It will take time to refurbish the equipment, time to get it working, and still more time to start generating fuel." Bowden shrugged. "They aren't going to do that first. They're going to do what they're here for: harvesting resources. Once that's in their hands—and only then—will they start worrying about the trip home."

Murphy leaned forward and looked down the row at the SpinDogs. "Primus Anseker, what do you think?"

Anseker glanced toward Murphy with a raised eyebrow, and Bowden realized Murphy was calling in a favor—one that wouldn't be easily repaid. And Bowden had better not screw this up because the Lost Soldiers' reputation would be shit. He chuckled to himself. *Of course, I won't have to worry about the wrath of the SpinDogs if the attack goes poorly; I'll be too dead to care.*

After a moment, Anseker nodded. "I think the Terrans' plan has merit. The Kulsians will be disorganized and out of fuel as they descend to R'Bak. That is the time to hit them."

The primus raised a pausing finger as mutters began to rise around him. "There is another highly decisive factor that has not been widely shared for reasons of security." He waited for, and got, expectant silence. "As you were briefed before the surveyors arrived, the Terrans' alien translator now flawlessly decodes Kulsian signals. But it affords us an even greater opportunity when we engage their Harvester fleet. In analyzing their signals, the translator has also delineated very predictable patterns in their frequency switching when sending short range, ship-to-ship radio signals."

Anseker smoothed a wrinkled sleeve nonchalantly. "Within a week, special jamming platforms will arrive at loiter points between our star and the Kulsians'. When the battle commences, their radio communications will be significantly degraded, possibly unreadable."

"Do you mean to say," Orgunz muttered reluctantly, "that they may not even be able to inform their Overlords of our existence or the battle?"

"Possibly, but I am not depending upon that result," Anseker clarified. "Sko'Belm Murphy rightly cautions us that any sending of an inter-system signal—forbidden by the Death Fathers—will alert the Kulsians that their Harvester fleet is in grave peril. They might also use different frequency patterns for such emergency messages. But if they do not, it is likely that the Overlords will be unable to extract much useful information from the fragments of intact code that might reach them." Anseker turned to glance at the other SpinDog primae. After a moment, they nodded their approval.

Anseker turned back toward Murphy. "The SpinDogs will support your plan. I will expect you to keep me well informed of your progress."

"I will, Primus Anseker," Murphy said, completing an exchange that was pure theater for the benefit of the other leaders.

Orgunz sighed and shook his head. "I am not convinced that this is the best way to proceed. It is certainly not the safest. Still, if everyone else is comfortable with Sko'Belm Murphy's claims, the RockHounds give their support, as well."

Anseker nodded at the Legate, glanced back at Murphy with a strange look in his eyes. "I am curious about how these plans build toward our long-term goals."

Murphy nodded and stood to address the room. "At the moment, we are under the thumb of the Kulsians. Just as this system always has been. I intend to change that. This battle—if prosecuted correctly—will allow us to savage the Harvester force, inflicting losses so great that the Kulsians will be unable to dispatch another viable force during the present Searing. Any fleet approaching after that would be at an immense logistical disadvantage, given the rapidly increasing distance they'd have to cover, whereas we could use that time to build even more ships.

"But even if they do mount another offensive during this Sear, we will still have additional time to replicate more ships to meet them, as well as any ships and or matériel we might capture in the upcoming battle. It is also my intention to immediately seize Downport as well. That way, they will not have that as a base of operations, either, should they return.

"Finally, and most important, we will have proven to the secondary powers of Kulsis that the major powers there are not invincible. By showing that they can be beaten, we embolden the insurgencies there and sow political and economic discord that may do our work for us." He smiled. "The best possible outcome? That they will not be able to return until the next Searing. But our primary objective is simply this: that we win the coming battle."

Chapter Ten

Spin One

As Murphy approached the last, and private, room in the Lost Soldiers' sickbay, he nodded for the guard—a Brit that the Ktor had scooped up during World War II—to move down the hall.

"Is he awake?" Murphy asked, returning the other's palm-out salute as they passed.

"Yes, sahr!" the guard replied in a Yorkshire accent thicker than the pudding of the same name. "And as narsty as ever!"

Murphy lowered his hand. "Then don't move too far away. He might bite."

"Yes, sahr! So I'm told, sahr!"

Murphy smiled as the Tommy turned smartly and took up his post farther along the corridor. He forced his lips to remain curved as he sighed and opened the hatch.

"How's the patient?" he asked brightly as he entered.

"I'm dying," Vat replied in a flat, hopeless voice that was muffled by the slightly diminished wrappings around his head.

Murphy scanned the room for signs of emergency equipment and monitors but there were none. "You're dying?"

"Yes."

"Of what?"

"A broken heart."

Murphy cocked an eyebrow. He couldn't see enough of Vat's face

69

beneath the bandages for clues as to how much of his woe was an act versus actual. "I wasn't aware any of your injuries were fatal."

"Well, they're not: not the ones you can see," Vat almost spat. That's what's so cruel about it."

Murphy managed not to roll his eyes. "Okay, I'll bite. What are you dying of?"

"Like I said: a broken heart," Vat lamented. His near-wail was mostly theatrics, but not entirely.

Murphy played along. "And why is your heart broken?" To his knowledge, Vat's time on R'Bak Island had not resulted in any enduring romantic involvements or, as Vat preferred to call them, entanglements.

He answered with some genuine heat. "What's broken my heart? My broken face, that's what. Have you seen what these space-breathing SpinDog bastards call plastic surgery? When I come out of these bandages, I'm still going to look like the Elephant Man. But with scars."

Murphy crossed his arms. "I'm sure that's an exaggeration."

"I'm glad *you're* sure," Vat grumbled in a huff. "I've seen some of their work."

"You're not impressed?

"Impressed? Hmmm...how do I put this? To say I'm terrified would be to understate the fact that I am totally and utterly shit-scared of what I'm going to look like for the rest of my now-cursed life." He sighed. "I mean, I was never Adonis. But I was in the running. Well, some people thought so."

He stole a look at Murphy. "What about you? Did you think I was handsome?"

Murphy rubbed the close-cut hair at the back of his head. "I gotta tell you, Vat: Not the sort of thing I've had time to think about."

"Yes, but if you did?"

"I still wouldn't have been thinking about it," Murphy admitted. "To put it succinctly—"

"I know, I know," Vat interrupted. "I'm 'not your type.' I get it. But work with me here a little bit, huh? I'm trying to put a good face on this. To coin a phrase." His half-concealed head swiveled in Murphy's direction. "Look, why the hell are you here bothering me, anyhow? It's been, uh, weeks, I guess. Why the sudden concern?"

"I've been here before, Vat. You just don't remember."

Vat sighed. "So you came in to look at me when I was still under general anesthetic."

"Yes."

"Which time?"

"*Both* times."

"Yeah, I'll bet."

"You can ask the guards."

"Yeah, like they'll tell me the truth. They're on *your* payroll."

"Vat, we don't *have* a payroll. Although we're working toward fixing that."

Vat muttered something, released a long, unhappy sigh, and fell silent.

Murphy just waited. Although Vat's injuries hadn't been dangerous, the various facial fractures proved too severe to knit without corrective surgery. Unfortunately, wiring broken bones was not within the scope of SpinDog surgical practices. While effective, they sacrificed aesthetics and precision for reliable outcomes. He could hardly blame Vat for dreading what the mirror might show him after his second round of corrective surgery. But at least he was off the pain medications: another area in which SpinDog medicine was excessively focused on reliable outcomes. Although Vat had been conscious most of the time, he had been in no condition to think, let alone talk.

"You still haven't told me why you're here," Vat grumped.

"I wanted to see if you could help me read something."

"*Read* something?" Vat snarled. "You weren't in school the day they went over 'I before E except after C'?"

Murphy raised an eyebrow. "I'm going to pretend I didn't hear that," he said quietly. "I'm sorry you're still in pain. I'm sorry you're worried about how you're going to look after the bandages come off. But I'm not so sorry that I can let that kind of insolence slide."

Vat nodded soberly. "No, I don't suppose you're ever *that* sorry. Or can afford to be. I also wasn't aware that you had problems reading."

"I'm not talking about any of *our* languages."

Vat sat up, flinched when he stopped; he'd moved a little too quickly for whatever sutures and pins were still holding his face together. "So this is, uh, a local language?"

"Mostly, I think. But even that's just a guess."

"Okay," Vat said crossing his arms, but doing so slowly, carefully. "This is just no fair. You come in here, where I can't get away from you. And then you start trailing bait in the water, knowing that I'm going to snap after it." Through the peepholes in the gauze, Vat's eyes flicked over toward Murphy. "Just do me one favor: no foreshadowing, no slow reveals, no plausibly deniable vagueness. Lay it out straight for me, okay?"

"Okay," Murphy agreed. "So, here's what we've got." He laid out the SpinDogs' subpar equivalent of photocopies across the overbuilt gurney that was Vat's bed.

Vat stared at the collection. "What the hell is this and where did it come from?" He leaned over it, eyes widening.

"We don't know what it is. That's the problem. All I can make out is that there are at least four or five different character sets." Murphy handed him the notes he'd made. "It came from vaults deep underneath Imsurmik. There's more: lots more. And not everything is on paper. There's parchment, hide, even tablets: some stone, some clay."

"Whoa!" exclaimed Vat. "Who do you think I am? Indiana Jones?"

Murphy shrugged. "Why not?"

Vat looked up from under his mostly covered brow. "You know my ability with language is more by ear and instinct than anything else, right?"

"I'm aware of that. But I also know you're smart as hell. And when you put your teeth into something, you hang on like a bulldog. So: will you bite?"

Vat was already looking back at the papers. "I've already bitten."

Murphy nodded. "Good. Then I can give you this." He handed out the tube that the RockHounds had brought him.

Vat stared at it. "You promised no slow reveals or surprises."

Murphy shook his head. "I couldn't give you this until you were committed. This doesn't come from beneath Imsurmik."

Vat's eyes rolled up to find Murphy's. "So where does it come from?"

"I'll tell you when I find out. It was left with me, but it's meant for you."

"Damn, Colonel, can you just drop the mystery-theater bit?"

"Not this time. It was brought to me in confidence. For good reason, I suspect. If you look at it, you'll see what I mean."

Vat opened the tube, extracted and scanned the drawing and its annotations. He crumbled. "Thanks a lot. A bona fide mystery. The kind that keeps you up at night. Just what I needed: insomnia *and* work while I'm trying to recover."

Murphy shrugged. "Personally, I think that's how Indiana Jones recovered so quickly from all those beatings he took in the movies. You know, the healing quality of laboring in the service of a noble cause."

Vat looked up and sighed. "Colonel, could you let just one more really snarky insult slide?"

Murphy smiled and shook his head. "No, I can't. But maybe this will be a consolation."

"Yeah, what?"

"I'll bet if you have a scar, it'll be on your chin, right where Indiana Jones's is." Murphy crossed his arms, considering. "This way, you'll be able to add the adjective 'rugged' to your self-proclaimed 'good looks.'"

Vat snickered. "Sometimes you're almost funny, Colonel."

Murphy nodded, exited, but after a moment, leaned back to peer around the coaming.

Vat was poring over documents, comparing them while absently rubbing his chin.

Right where Indiana Jones had the scar.

Chapter Eleven

Spin One

Murphy nodded to the guard who'd followed him into Interview One. The soldier moved so that his back was against the door.

A thin man was sitting cuffed at the table: Yukannak. His head had been shaved and his left eye and jaw were bound with tightly cinched bandages. Almost half his right ear was missing, the ragged rim indifferently stitched. Murphy had a momentary flashback to the first time he saw *Frankenstein* as a kid.

He stepped forward, placed himself in front of the table's center. Yukannak did not look up. "You know our term 'bullshit,' don't you?"

Yukannak opened his mouth slowly, carefully before answering. "I heard your men say it all the time. When we were in Downport." He sounded as though he was talking around a mouthful of marbles.

Murphy nodded, pulled the thick folder from under his arm and tossed it on the table: the complete transcripts of Yukannak's many interviews. "Well, that's what this is: bullshit. All of it."

"I understand your anger because I seem to have betrayed—"

"Don't even start with that," Murphy laughed, waving away the Kulsian's words. "There's no question that you were looking for any opportunity to sabotage the mission and serve up the team on a platter to your Overlords. But that's not why you're here."

Yukannak glanced up, a hint of interest in his eyes.

Murphy tapped the thick sheaf of papers. "This is why you're here. To correct all the lies you've told us from the start."

"Colonel Murphy, on the off chance that there were some inaccuracies, you surely understand that I would not have—"

"Not have lied? Not have occasionally seeded in misinformation? The subtle kind that we wouldn't detect or you could claim was a superficial distinction, but would be quite noticeable to a native Kulsian? Which, when added together—all the small errors in slang, idioms, history—would send a very clear message: 'I am misleading the enemy as much as I can.'"

Murphy shrugged. "Oh, I get why you did it. You were thinking ahead toward your 'liberation.' You'd be able to point to that misinformation in the hope that the Overlords back home would forgive you for cooperating with us at all. Maybe they'd even buy the story that, in order to undermine our efforts, you had to appear to be genuinely cooperating with us. Which was the smart play, because if things had gone otherwise—if *we* came out on top—you could spin it around and plead that what might seem like lies were just inaccuracies that never impacted our operations."

"Which they never did," Yukannak murmured.

Murphy shook his head. "You're persistent, I'll give you that. Although right now, I suspect you believe that's the only card you have left to play. Problem is, it's become worthless. Maybe you've lost track of time, but the surveyors have been on R'Bak for quite a while. Which means there are now a lot of other people there who are just like you: skilled, knowledgeable, tasked with getting shipments ready for the Harvesters. But unlike you, some of them are genuinely helping us."

Yukannak shifted his jaw slightly. "And you still have your own people on the planet, with so many surveyors abroad? You are very brave indeed."

Murphy smiled. "That's prudent, calling our actions 'brave' instead of what you really mean: 'foolhardy.' But it makes no difference to me, particularly since we don't need to be on R'Bak to work with our friends there. And no, we're not so 'brave' that we use radio—which you Kulsians would find within days."

"If that," Yukannak muttered.

Murphy didn't bother reacting to the Kulsian's proud but futile emendation. "So here's what you need to think about right now,

Yukannak. We know you've lied to us all along. Hell, we expected that, and I don't even blame you; we're the enemy, after all. But before you went dirtside to help our team in Downport, you accepted my parole. And you didn't just break it, you shattered it. Betrayed my men. Damn near killed some of them. Kept lying while you did." Murphy leaned back. "And yet, here you are."

Yukannak stared at the transcripts. "So," he sighed, "you have found genuinely disaffected persons among the surveyors. One or more from the southern hemisphere, no doubt. And they will indicate where I have lied."

Fortunately, Murphy had prepared for the interview by presuming that the Kulsian would deduce why his enemies believed he'd amend his earlier statements honestly. "You can hypothesize to your black heart's content, Yukannak. Doesn't matter to me. All I care about are these." Murphy pushed the transcripts at him. "Get started."

Yukannak stared at the stack of papers and frowned. "If you do indeed have someone who can tell you where I have . . . been less than fully forthcoming, why do you need me to do it?"

Murphy smiled. "Oh, I wouldn't waste time trying to trick you, Yukannak. You're the expert liar, here, not me. But if you don't believe there are Kulsians helping us, there's an easy way you can prove it to yourself."

Rather than lean forward, Murphy leaned back. "Just leave one error in place. Please, do that. I'd like it; I really would. Because you see, I'm authorized to speak with you but not to . . . well, 'discipline' you." He leaned back. "The SpinDogs insisted they be left in charge of that, as well as your care."

Yukannak wasn't able to keep his Adam's apple from cycling rapidly.

"It's up to you. Although it might prove helpful if you cooperated."

"Helpful in what way?"

"I understand you've complained that your injuries did not receive adequate treatment. So just leave one lie in place. I'm sure the SpinDog medtechs will show their appreciation by 'examining' your injuries. In minute detail.

"And you don't have to make a hasty decision. Take as long as you like. But if you want your SpinDog warders to give you something to eat, and if you want the temperature in your cell to remain above five degrees Celsius, and if you want more than half a liter of water per day, then you'll want to start correcting these transcripts."

Mara and Naliryiz nodded at Murphy as he closed the door to Interview One behind him.

"He's already started," the healer said.

Lee smiled and shook her head. "I've got to hand it to you, that was some pretty nice work, Colonel."

Murphy shrugged and sat. "Helps when you hold all the cards." *And a subject who knows there are a bunch of SpinDogs just itching to "clean his wounds" with a bit of exploratory knife-work.*

"Still, looks like we won't have long to wait," Mara added, watching Yukannak flipping through the pages. "Where did he lie, according to Lanunaz?"

Murphy leaned back, waited until he controlled a tremor starting in his leg: in recent weeks, doing so had not only become more difficult, but took longer. "There weren't a lot of blatant falsehoods. Mostly lies of omission."

"About what?" Naliryiz slid into the chair next to him, letting her weight push it much closer than was common between professional peers.

Murphy did his best to ignore her proximity. "Yukannak said that the lack of Harvester activity in the southern hemisphere and the northern part of the Greens was due to disinterest. There's some truth in that, but there's another factor: they're more difficult to control.

"Because they're both less affected by the Searing, they retain most of their vegetation and almost all of their water sources. That leads to more stable communities and political structures, which means it's harder for the Kulsians to apply their favorite strategy: bribe and back the most cooperative satraps. That's how they take over regions: divide and conquer. And because both areas also remain reasonably well-forested, the coursers and surveyors take heavier casualties when they move around there."

Mara nodded. "When I was teaching helo pilots at the northern edge of the Greens, you could always see canopy somewhere nearby. A small force willing to cross that region in stages could do so just by moving from one point of concealment to the next. Is it the same down south?"

Murphy tilted his head in partial confirmation. "Not as much cover, but a lot more arable land and bigger cities, largely because the Harvesters never have made durable inroads there. The nation— or maybe confederation—of Peregryn has been able to maintain a united front against most incursions, and whatever toeholds the Kulsians make never survive from one Searing to the next."

Mara frowned. "Why?"

"Weather," Naliryiz answered before Murphy could. "During the Searing, trans-equatorial travel is extremely hazardous. Jrar's approach injects an immense amount of energy into R'Bak's oceans and jet streams. The resulting storms and floods are frequent and often catastrophic. In-atmo flight is not much safer. So any landings the Kulsians make in that area cannot be supported by air or sea links, only direct planetfalls from space."

Murphy nodded. "And even when the weather improves, there still isn't much travel over the equator. Not just because the temperatures and weather are still awful, but because there isn't a lot of motivation for merchants from either north and south to take the risks. The north's trade is dominated by the satraps and the goods they covet: Kulsian technology and pharmaflora. The south is more inwardly focused, occupied with providing enough food and goods for its much greater population."

Mara folded her arms. "Okay, but how are Yukannak's misrepresentations about this any more than...well, little white lies?"

Murphy smiled. "Because he used those little white lies to conceal a much bigger one. Specifically, why are the Kulsians more focused on R'Bak's northern hemisphere when the south is generally wealthier?"

Mara nodded. "So, his important lies were what he concealed about *Kulsis*."

"Exactly. And it was easy to hide because there are a lot of misleading similarities between R'Bak and Kulsis. Although R'Bak's is much worse during the Searing, both have punishingly hot equatorial belts that are dangerous to cross. Kulsis's political and cultural environment is far more organized and secure, but beneath the surface, it's every bit as tangled and diffuse as the satrapies and tribes in this system. They, too, maintain distinctions and prejudices that seem arbitrary or ridiculous to an outsider.

"However, there is something that unifies almost all Kulsians in the southern hemisphere: their feeling that the north is inhabited by a bunch of hierarchical and autocratic oppressors. In the north, the opinion runs the opposite direction: that the south is a dumping ground for the disorganized, the desperate, and the inferior."

Mara raised an eyebrow. "The 'inferior'?"

Murphy nodded. "That's the party line among the great powers. The strongest of them, the Syfarthan Combine, controls the rest of the north through a set of pacts, treaties, and marriages."

"Sounds feudal," Mara grumbled.

"It does, except it's even more complicated and convoluted: I couldn't follow Lanunaz's explanation of all the class distinctions. Their pecking order is so bizarre and petty that it would be funny, if it wasn't a matter of life and death. Literally."

Naliryiz nodded. "Still, it is easy to see why the Kulsians instituted the 'satrapy' model on R'Bak. It is the likeness of their own society, writ upon the beings of another world."

"The *lesser* beings of another world," Murphy amended. "Which arises from the same presumptions that lead the Overlords to define the people of the south as *inferior*."

Mara crossed her arms. "Look, I know they must have inherited the Ktoran insistence upon dominion, but what's the rhetoric they use to convince themselves that everyone else is their inferior?"

Murphy shook his head. "The best way to ask that question is in reverse: What makes the people in the north believe they're *superior? That's* the critical piece that Yukannak left out of all his descriptions, because it explains why the Overlords are so laser-focused on harvesting the resources in the north, and particularly the Hamain." Murphy sighed. "Ironically, we had all the pieces of that puzzle in front of us. Hell, it was all but spelled out in the database Vat put together while he was on R'Bak Island."

Naliryiz frowned. "What kind of database?"

"A list of the resources and trade goods that the surveyors always look for. Of where previous Harvester missions had concentrated their efforts. Of what their cargo priorities were." Murphy laughed at himself. "We just thought it was the pharmaflora. Although, to be fair, pharmaflora *was* the second-highest priority on the Kulsian agenda. But it was a *distant* second."

"A distant second to *what*?" Mara almost shouted.

"To the pods that allow the families of the north to maintain their genetic advantages."

Mara started. "What are you talking about?"

"According to Yukannak and Lanunaz," Murphy began, peripherally aware of Naliryiz's widening eyes, "the way that Breedmistresses determine optimal pairings—the genetic matches with the fewest potential defects and greatest potential advantages—is something they call breedsensing. It's genetic knowledge that transcends mere observation. It involves, well, sensing the patterns of genetic material and how those can be combined to produce desired outcomes."

"'Sensing'?" Mara echoed helplessly. "What the hell does that even mean, Murph?"

"It means they can examine genecodes with a sense beyond the five we know. That sixth sense is the product of a state they call Reification."

Naliryiz's eyes were so wide they trembled. "Murphy! You swore not to ask about that word! All the Families present at Primus Dolkar's execution witnessed your acceptance of that condition!"

He turned toward her. "Guild-mother Shumrir's exact words were, 'You are not to ask *us* about it.' And I have kept my word; I have never asked any SpinDogs, or even RockHounds, about it." He gestured toward Yukannak. "But that promise did not include Kulsians. Nor any other path by which I might have come to learn more about the word. Which, in this case, was not entirely intentional."

"Well," Lee asked, "so what about me, now that I've heard the word? Do I have to pretend I never did?"

Murphy glanced toward Naliryiz. She continued to stare, unblinking, at Murphy: fearful, intrigued, possibly impressed. But also...slightly aroused? *No: ridiculous.*

He turned back toward Mara. "You haven't promised anyone you won't ask about Reifications. So if anyone has a problem, they can come to me. But frankly, we couldn't avoid the topic any longer."

"Why not?"

"Because the pods the Kulsian breedmistresses use for the most delicate Reifications are the Harvester's top priority resource on R'Bak. Every Searing. No fail."

"They're that valuable?"

Naliryiz's voice startled Murphy; it was not merely low, but husky. "Reification is a...a more expansive state of awareness. It is *not* limited to breedsensing. So yes: the pods—they are called Catalysites—are very valuable. For those who crave dominion, possibly they are the most valuable objects that exist."

Mara shook her head. "Okay, fine. But they've got a whole planet of their own on which to grow them. Why come here to grab a few more?"

"Because," Murphy said quietly, "Catalysites do not grow on Kulsis. At all."

Chapter Twelve

Spin One

Naliryiz rose slowly, her body very still, as Murphy explained. "Before I came out of the interview room, I scanned ahead to the corrections Yukannak had made about Reification. I suspected he hadn't told me everything, but I wasn't prepared for the full story.

"Catalysites do not ripen until they've gone through height of the Searing in the high desert beyond the Hamain." He turned to Naliryiz, anticipating the question about to leave her mouth. "Yukannak doesn't know—and maybe no Kulsian does—the crucial variables in that process. The radiation of the two stars at the right range; the humidity; the microbes in the air and the soil; the magnetic fields: Kulsians have tried to replicate all the variables in every possible combination. Without luck."

Mara almost spat her summation. "So they come here every Searing to get these Catalysites or the master race on Kulsis stops being the master race. Is that about it?"

Murphy shrugged. "That's how it started."

"There's more?"

"Yes. There's economics, Mara. There's the relationship between scarcity and value. The Overlords not only adapted to sending Harvester fleets here every eighty-eight years, they realized that any family that hoped to keep an 'elevated' genecode would want—would *need*—to be a part of that effort. If they didn't do the actual gathering themselves, by helping, they could at least audit the process. Because there's no honor among thieves—particularly those who are also autocrats.

"So now, the Overlords who control the Harvesting have leverage over every family that wants a share of the Catalysites: that wants to remain 'superior.'"

Mara's eyes narrowed. "Otherwise, sooner or later, they'll get sent down to the southern hemisphere to join the rest of the defectives. Christ, it makes me want to puke."

Naliryiz stood over Murphy. "Why?" she asked, holding Murphy's eyes.

He stood. "Why what?" he countered, moving his gaze to someplace—anyplace—other than a meeting with her own.

"Why did you not tell me you knew of this?"

Really? How can you even ask *me that?* "If you mean not telling you when I learned what Reification is, I wasn't about to put you in a position where you'd have to decide between keeping my secret or telling Anseker—as your oath requires."

"But why keep it a secret at all?"

"It was the only way to be sure that it didn't lead to an inquiry involving dozens of ego-bruised Families that might then paralyze our efforts to defeat the approaching fleet. And until now, I didn't know how much of Yukannak's story I could trust.

"But if you mean the secret that R'Bak is Kulsis's only source of Catalysites, I just learned that when I flipped through his corrections in the interview room."

"I must report to Anseker. Immediately," she breathed. But she didn't move.

Murphy nodded. "I understand. There will be more interviews with both Yukannak and Lanunaz. Do you wish to be present?"

"Is that what *you* wish?"

Murphy waited until he was sure his voice and his words would be perfectly calm and perfectly professional. "I'd be glad to have you as the Otlethes Family's witness, if it's convenient for you."

Although nothing in her face changed, somehow Naliryiz looked as if she'd just been punched in the gut. She nodded, turned, and left.

Two seconds after she had, Mara let out a long, loud sigh. "Wow. Really turning on the charm there, huh, Murph?"

"We've been over this, Lee."

"Apparently not often enough. Sir. Look: if you can't be with her officially, and you still won't take a chance to be with her on the sly—"

"Think of what that would mean, Major. Undisclosed meetings would be playing at the brink of political suicide."

"Well, then at least you could have said something encouraging about the three of us getting together again." Mara waved at the overhead fluorobars. "You know, 'I'll look forward to seeing your smiling face and violet eyes again!'"

"Impossibly corny. Besides, I can't say anything remotely like that, not until the Harvesters are defeated and their wrecks are floating in our wake."

"For Chrissakes, why?" Mara was almost shouting.

"Because Anseker has enough to worry about without one of his senior staff—and relatives—being seen with me."

"I did say, the *three* of us, Colonel. Completely public."

"And completely misreadable."

"Look, Murph, no offense, but I don't think anyone is going to 'read you' as the *ménage à trois* type."

"Lee, can you be serious for a moment?"

"Sure...as soon as you can be clear. What, exactly, would there be to misread if the three of us were seen together publicly?"

"In a single sentence? That Family Otlethes was cozying up with two of the most influential Lost Soldiers, even to the exclusion of their own SpinDog peers."

"Would anyone really see it that way?"

"Maybe not without a few helpful whispers, but you can bet there'd be plenty of muckrakers making the rounds. Unrepentant RockHounds. Secret Kormak sympathizers who still want to topple Anseker. Every primus wanna-be who worries that the Otlethes Family is becoming too 'dominative.' In short: that the balance of terror, which the SpinDogs call a balance of power, is in danger of becoming a unipolar state."

Before she could object, Murphy put up a hand. "Look, Mara, you're the only person I can speak to about any of this. About Naliryiz, about my MS, about the best way to respond when it finally catches up with me. So cut me some slack, okay?"

She bit her lower lip—whether in reluctance or regret, he couldn't tell. "Sure, Murph."

He stepped closer. "This isn't just about me, Mara: this is about you, too. About the bag you'll be left holding when I'm no longer around." She started to step away; he held her with his eyes. "I'm not being paranoid or dramatic. Think it through. If something were to ever happen between Naliryiz and me, it would have to be completely aboveboard. There's no way it could be a dalliance, and SpinDogs don't 'date.' And there are too many cynical locals who'd immediately think, 'Well, who knew? Murphy was a honeypot to get a second seat at the Otlethes' family table.' And that's why I have to keep my distance until and unless we find an answer to my... my condition.

"Can you imagine the reaction if she and I were together and then it came out that I have multiple sclerosis? That I have a disease that renders me incapable of self-control, let alone 'dominion'?

"We—none of us—would have a leg to stand on. The Otlethes would have to disown me and, to save face, they'd have to say they were tricked. And then what would happen to you? And your daughter with Ozendi? Is Anseker supposed to shield you? You, around whom there will always be this question 'Did she know Murphy was defective? Did she keep the truth from Naliryiz, too? And isn't that a betrayal of the whole Otlethes Family?'"

Now it was Mara who looked gut-punched, but he had to press on to one, final point. "Lee, if you haven't thought about this yet, you should start. At some point, I won't be able to conceal my condition. And I can't let it take me slowly. If I do, that would make all the Lost Soldiers look weak, flawed, like a rootless bunch of 'lesser beings.'

"So, there's going to come a time where you'll probably have to go in search of me. If you want my advice, you should *fail* to find me. That way, no one will ever have to tell a lie about the... the particulars of what you might actually encounter." He made his eyes as hard as he could. "But if you actually disregard my advice, if you *do* go searching for me, you have to select a very small number of people to help you. People that you know intimately. People that you would trust with your life—because that's probably what you're doing. And if you choose wrong, that could be the end of you and all the Lost Soldiers."

She nodded, eyes hollow. "I... I understand, Colonel." She

saluted, waited for his return. When he lowered his hand, she walked quickly out of the observation room.

Murphy sighed, tried to keep his shoulders straight as he took a long stride to the door to Interview One and opened it.

Yukannak was motionless, staring into the opposite corner.

"Sir?" asked the guard next to the table.

"Take the prisoner back to his cell, Corporal. We're done, here."

Chapter Thirteen

Spin One

Bowden smiled at his staff, who'd responded to his summons to meet met him in the assembly bay. "I couldn't tell you until the ink was dry, but the SpinDogs and RockHounds both decided our plan was the best and decided to put it into action."

"Really?" Burg Hrensku's eyes widened. "I have to admit to being surprised that they agreed. On anything. So, what happens, now?"

Kevin nodded toward a pair of large delta shapes filling the cavernous space before them. "The hulls of the first two corvettes have been replicated and they're going through the outfitting process. In a few days, we should know if there are still basic interoperability issues or if we're ready to kick the autofabbing process into high gear. That said, we still have to figure out how best to equip them. We also need to start gathering the people who are going to be flying the ships." He took a deep breath and let it out slowly. "And then we have to train them on our combat doctrines and their roles within it."

Hrensku chuckled. "Is this going to be like how you trained us to fly together to assault the transmitter on the planet?"

"Just like that, yes."

Hrensku smiled. "You know then, not everyone will like it or want to do it your way."

"I'm aware." *Herding all those cats is totally going to suck.*

Bowden smiled. "I'm also aware that my strategy was successful in destroying that transmitter—against pretty long odds—and that I was put in charge of this assault by the heads of the Families, so the ship captains had better listen to me."

It was Raptis's turn to chuckle. "You have been around the RockHounds long enough to know the likelihood of that."

"Okay, so it isn't actually 'likely.' Still, we will have to convince them—or as your primae like to say, 'bend them to our will.'" Bowden nodded. "I'm counting on you to tell them that I usually know what I'm doing."

"Sometimes," Fiezel said.

Bowden frowned. "You're not helping."

"Didn't say I was trying to." He nodded to the Hound-Dogs. "They know you well enough by now to know that you're full of shit, sometimes, too."

"He is correct," Raptis said with a nod.

"Okay, well, if you're done giving me a hard time, make sure you save some of that spirit for your actual enemy. There's a big fleet of ships coming, crewed by people who'd like to see us dead, and we all have jobs to do. Burg?"

"I am going to go round up the pilots, or at least as many of them as I can."

"Dave?"

"I'm going to see what we can put together for a simulator, such as it might exist in a culture that doesn't value computers."

"We value computers," Hrensku said.

Bowden chuckled. "You do? For what?"

"They help hold papers in place on our desk when there is a breeze!"

The group laughed while Bowden shook his head. "Shouldn't you go be about that, then?"

The two men walked off, still laughing.

"And what is my job?" Raptis asked.

"I'd like to go over some of the tactical maneuvering with you again. I think I understand how it works, but I want to be sure I'm not missing anything."

"Can we get something to eat while we do so?" Raptis asked.

"Yeah, I'm starving." Bowden started walking across the assembly bay in the direction of the refectory, but stopped suddenly as he came abreast of them.

"What's wrong?" Raptis asked.

"Those corvettes," Bowden said, pointing at the first output of the Otlethes Family's considerable replication facilities.

"What about them?"

"Do you notice anything about them?"

Raptis shrugged. "They are new and shiny, as they ought to be, having just been fabbed?"

Bowden shook his head. "They're new and shiny, and *different!*"

"Different?" Raptis shrugged. "They are not exactly the same, but they are far more alike than they are different. They are very strange to look at. For RockHound craft, they are too similar; they have no personality. You can't tell whose craft it is or what they are doing."

"But they're not supposed to be *similar*; they are supposed to be *exactly the same*." He pointed at the closest one: a pair of small sensor booms emerged from the lower fuselage, just behind either side of the cockpit. *But remember to call it the "bridge."*

Raptis made a sour face as if the concept was not merely distasteful but alien. "Why is it important that they be exact?"

"Because we got the best technology I could convince the Families to give to model them from. Either there is additional technology we didn't incorporate—which would have made the model better—or one of them is intentionally inferior." He sighed. "Or, more likely, both."

Raptis pursed her lips in thought. "I see what you are saying. The thought—the concept you are articulating—is...foreign for us, but I suspect you are right. The answer probably *is* 'both.' I suspect—as we warned you—that the Families will reserve some of their own best technology for the ships their members will be flying, while providing the 'average' technology for the ones they donate to the general fleet."

"Even if it means we lose to the Kulsians?"

Raptis shrugged and motioned to the corvettes as evidence that the instinct she was articulating ran very deep indeed. And if the Otlethes would do it that way, everyone else was bound to, as well. Still, Bowden had to know, so he strode over to a technician who was connecting wires under the wing of one of the craft. "Excuse me?" Bowden asked.

The tech looked up. "Yes?"

"I was just curious," Bowden said pleasantly. "I notice that, while similar, these ships aren't exactly alike. I thought they would be."

The tech lifted an eyebrow as he smiled and nodded at the ship he was working on. "This one is for our family." He pointed at the other. "That one will be used by . . . I don't know. It is one for the fleet."

"I see," Bowden said, nodding. "So, this one has some additional capabilities that the other doesn't?"

"Of course. This one has a much better radar system and optics package."

Bowden turned to Raptis. "We were right. It *is* both."

Bowden walked into the anteroom outside Murphy's office. Makarov looked up and Bowden indicated the door behind him with his chin. "Boss busy?"

"Is that Bowden?" a voice called from within the other office.

"Yes, sir," Bowden replied.

"Come on in."

Murphy nodded to the chair in front of his desk as Bowden walked in. "Sit. I've got two minutes before my next meeting. What's up?"

Bowden fell into the chair. "I found out why we can't have nice things."

One of Murphy's eyebrows rose. "You what?"

"I found out why we can't have nice things. I was just in one of the hangar bays. There were two corvettes fresh out of one of the Otlethes' fabbers."

"And . . . ?"

"One had a better radar and optical search system; the other had the systems that are included in the template we created."

Murphy shook his head. "Disappointing." Then he chuckled. "Not surprising, but certainly disappointing. I take it that they were holding back their best technology from us when you finalized the design package?"

"It seems so."

Murphy cocked his head. "So what are you going to do about it?"

"If I'm going to fight all these ships, I need to know what exactly I'm commanding. Therefore, with your permission—and as much as I hate doing so—Dave Fiezel and I are going to drop what we're doing, and walk through *all* the various fabbers on and around *Spin One* to see what we really are dealing with when it comes to configuration control. We don't have the time to do it... but we don't have the time not to, either." He sighed. "For good or bad."

"What do you need from me?"

"Permission to go see the Otlethes' autofabbers. None of the Families are going to want me to see what they're doing; up until now, I have been banned from seeing anything that deals with the process. If you can get Primus Anseker to let me see theirs, though—which I know has a problem—then I ought to be able to get the others to let me do so. Hopefully."

"If you think one necessarily leads to the other, you haven't been paying attention to how things are done around here."

"I know." Bowden sighed. "But it's a place to start. Once Anseker shows me theirs, I'm hoping he'll lean on the others to do so, too."

Murphy smiled in commiseration. "Hope is a pretty poor plan of action."

"It is, but I doubt you'll allow me to threaten to shoot anyone."

"Despite the fact that I've wanted to do so myself, many times, no. I will not."

"Will you at least talk to Anseker? We have to nip this in the bud, or we're going to have a fleet of ships with specs so different that we won't be able to depend on them."

Murphy stared at him a moment and then nodded slowly. "It won't be easy, but I'll give it a shot." He grimaced. "Not like I don't already have enough on my plate. Well, desk."

Bowden smiled as he frowned at the stacks of folders and binders. "I've gotta ask, sir... what is all this anyway?" *And why the hell is it keeping you from being a hundred and ten percent involved with building our own fleet?*

Murphy rubbed his eyes. "Everything that needs to be in place for our planetside operations."

Bowden stared. "Our what?"

"Our ground campaign. To take R'Bak."

"Sir, I thought that was something we'd do *after* defeating the Harvesters."

"Yes, but it has to be relatively soon after. If we give them more than a few weeks' breathing space, the surveyors will try to collapse back on Downport. So that means we don't just need to interdict it, but *take* it. And R'Bak Island.

"The only way to do that is to know where the surveyors have staged to and so, where they'll be folding back from. Problem is, they're in small groups scattered to hell and gone. So that means combing through accounts of the places they've routinely visited in the past. Not just towns and regions, but anchorages and rivers, too. Because those aren't just watercourses for the surveyors; they're landing fields. They've got a lot of seaplanes and even amphibian and triphibian vehicles.

"Then there are all their ships, mostly freighters. If they were all moving, and we weren't already over-tasking the Dornaani microsats, it might not take a lot of effort to locate them all. But at this point, they spend most of their time in ports, waiting for the surveyors to come back with news of trade commitments and soon, caravans of local goods. So once again, we have to get ahead of the challenge by picking through whatever local reports or rumors or chronicles might contain references to not just the regular ports but the secret or temporary ones that are only used during the Searing. And then we have to build a recon target list for the microsats to cycle through to watch for changes."

Only when Murphy finished was Kevin aware that he was holding his breath. "Yeah, but what about the surveyors who can't fall back on the Downport? There have got to be a lot of them in the outback?"

Murphy nodded grimly. "And now you're starting to see why this pile is so big." He rubbed a hand down the length of his face. "Same process, except harder. While you were flying around down there, I'm sure you saw that there are barely any roads worthy of the name."

Bowden's only reply was a grim chortle.

"My feelings exactly. So all we can do is watch choke points— fords, passes, oases, river junctures—and work out a signaling system with the indigs that does not require regular radio transmission or reception. And again, the only way to get ahead of the surveyors' movements is to sift through any accounts for paths they've routinely used in the past when they scatter out to drag in cargos for the Harvesters."

Bowden knew it was cruel to ask, but he couldn't resist it. "And do you have plans for the rest of R'Bak, sir?"

Murphy rubbed his eyes savagely. "Don't even, Major. This is why I get headaches." He chuckled, which struck Bowden as strange because it didn't sound entirely like he was joking. "Plans? Yes. Resources? No. Which is why the plans remain pretty vague. The single biggest problem is that anything beyond our current theater of operations requires replication of additional standard equipment—which is presently and indefinitely sidelined until your fleet no longer needs one hundred and ten percent of the total autofabbing capacity of the Hound-Dogs.

"But there are some preparatory initiatives I'm setting in motion. Mapping the tunnels that run under the entirety of the Hamain and beyond. Outreach to communities at the periphery of our present AO, both for intel and finding staging sites into whatever lies beyond. And tracking whinaalanis."

"Tracking whinnies, sir?"

"Yes, Major, because they seem to have a better knowledge of both the tunnels and remote water sources than the indigs do. Now: any other questions about my minute-to-minute nightmares?"

"Uh, how do you prioritize it, sir?"

"Simple. Everything is top priority." Once again, Murphy didn't sound like he was entirely joking. "Next question?"

"When do you sleep, sir?"

Murphy chuckled. "I'll sleep when I'm dead, Kevin. Now get out of here. We both have way too much work to do before either one of us can afford the luxury of dying."

Chapter Fourteen

Spin One

"Just you," said the SpinDog who had come to meet Bowden in the Lost Soldiers' conference room. He jerked his head at Fiezel. "He stays here. You alone may visit our facility."

"But I thought—"

"You can come or not," the man said imperiously. "It matters not to me. But no one else. The primus was quite clear on this."

Bowden turned to Fiezel. "Sorry, buddy. Back to the simulators for you."

Fiezel shrugged. "Not like I wanted to see the piece of junk, anyway."

"Right." Bowden smiled. *It's tech-related and something that didn't exist even in* my *time, much less during the Vietnam War. I'm sure* you *didn't want to see it.*

"Follow me," the SpinDog said. Without waiting for an answer, he turned and walked through the self-closing hatchway without holding the pressure door for Bowden.

"Don't worry, I got it," Bowden muttered. If the SpinDog heard him, he didn't acknowledge it; if anything, he lengthened his stride, and Bowden had to quick-walk to stay up with him. Not surprisingly, the autofabbers weren't anywhere close to the occupied section of the asteroid; instead, the SpinDog led him on a hike that was well over a klick and had his shins hurting from the rapid pace. Bowden finally decided the man was trying to confuse him on the directions for how to get there, because Bowden was fairly certain that they passed through the same section of tunnel twice.

And, if the SpinDog was trying to get him lost, he succeeded. Bowden struggled on, though, with no idea of where they were or how to get back. He was almost to the point of either asking for a break or a slower pace when they reached a guarded hatch.

A SpinDog stood on either side of the entry, and when they saw Bowden approaching, both drew pistols. Bowden stopped, although the man—whose name he still didn't know—didn't. He walked up to them, muttered something, and one nodded toward Bowden. His indifferent guide turned, rolled his eyes, and motioned him forward as one of the guards opened the hatch.

Sounds of machinery running and metal hitting metal filled the passageway as the SpinDog went through the entryway and waved him through. Bowden stepped into the space, and his eyes widened; it was almost half the size of the hangar bay he'd landed in. A good portion was filled with machinery, leaving an open area not much larger than the partially assembled corvette that sat in it. Even with all the people crawling over it, Bowden didn't need more than a quick glance to see the ship was destined for someone in the Otlethes family; it was outfitted with all their superior equipment.

"Obviously that craft will be piloted by someone from the Otlethes Family."

"Yes," the man said proudly. "It is mine. It has all the best equipment on it. I will teach the Kulsians not to try to claim dominion over the Otlethes Family."

"That's the best equipment you have? Radar? Optical tracking?"

The man nodded. "Everything is the best, from the motors, to the control systems, and all of the weapons systems. They are all top of the line, as befits a member of the Otlethes Family."

Well, at least now I know where he gets his attitude from. Now how am I going to break this to him and get him to go along with it?

Bowden forced himself to smile as an idea came to him. "I'm glad your ship is the best, and I hope you kill a lot of the Kulsians with it."

"I will be at the front of the battle; they will not escape my wrath."

"What about your wingman?"

"Who?"

"Your wingman. What—" Bowden paused. "Let me start over. I think we got off on the wrong foot. I'm Major Kevin Bowden."

"I know. The primus told me to meet with you."

"I figured. The problem is, I don't know who *you* are."

"How is it possible that you do not know a member of the leading family?"

Bowden shrugged. "Mostly because I'm not from here, and I've been gone a lot. You know the corvette that you're using as the template?"

"Yes? What of it?"

"You may not be aware, but I'm the one who brought it back."

"Oh." The man's eyes got a little bigger, and his bearing took on a minimum of respect. "I knew it was a Terran, but I hadn't heard who." He gave Bowden a small nod. "I am Teseler, Anseker's oldest nephew."

"It's nice to meet you," Bowden said, trying to swallow his reflexive dislike of haughty people. "So, Teseler, my question stands. While you are killing Kulsians, what about your wingman?"

"What of him? I don't even know who it will be yet."

Bowden tried to keep the smile off his face. "I see. Have you heard about the fleet the Kulsians are sending?"

"No."

"It's big, bigger than normal." Bowden waved a hand at the machinery ringing the bay. "Even with all the Families producing ships as fast as they can, the Kulsians will outnumber us."

"Then why are we fighting them? We should hide. It has always worked in the past."

"We're fighting them because your primus has decided we should." He shrugged. "And numbers alone don't guarantee victory in battle."

"It is a good start."

Bowden nodded. "It is. But we will have better ships, flown by better pilots, who are fighting with a better strategy. We can be victorious, but we must have all those things to do so."

"I don't understand. My ship is the absolute best we can build."

"I understand that. What about other ships you've built? The ones that will not be flown by members of the Otlethes Family?"

"What about them?"

"If they are substandard, they will fall to the Kulsians easily, leaving you even more outnumbered. Ultimately you, too, will fall."

"I will make sure I fly with other Otlethes. They will protect me."

"Maybe...and maybe not."

Teseler bristled. "Are you questioning the honor of an Otlethes?"

Bowden held up a hand. "Not at all." He smiled. "Let me ask you something. Have you ever been in a fight where thirty or forty ships fought an equal number of enemy ships?"

"Of course not. We've never done anything this stup—er, desperate before."

"I have."

"You have? When? I have never heard of such a thing."

"Back on Terra, I was a pilot of an atmospheric fighter. There were many times where we had huge battles of that many craft, all trying to kill each other." *Of course, they were exercises, but he doesn't need to know that.* "And in all of them, one thing is certain—the person you start off with on your wing is very unlikely to be there at the end."

"I have heard your people have no honor."

"No, that's not it. When you get that many people in a big furball, it's hard to—"

"Wait. What is a 'furball'?"

"Sorry. That is a Terran term for when battle is joined between a large number of ships, and they are going all over the place." He demonstrated with his hands.

"I can see the combat being shaped like a ball, but where does the fur fit in?"

Bowden chuckled. "You know, I have no idea how they came up with that word. It seems really stupid now that you mention it." He thought a moment. "The term may have come from the term dog-fighting, and dogs—they're animals on Terra—have fur, like the batangs do down on R'Bak." He shook his head. "But forget that. All that matters is what it refers to: a situation where you have so many ships flying around that it's easy to get separated from your wingman and end up with someone from another group."

Teseler's brows knit as he tried to imagine what that many ships maneuvering in the same space—each trying to get an edge over the other—would look like. Finally, he shook his head. "With that many ships all flying around that close, how do you keep the enemies separate from your allies?"

"It's hard," Bowden admitted. "And it will be even harder for us doing it in space where we won't be able to see our enemies as easily as we could when I was doing this in atmosphere." He paused. "We have procedures that help us identify friend from foe, but it will probably take the absolute best equipment we can put on the ships to make it work."

"Not all of the ships have the best equipment, though."

"And you want the guy on your wing to have substandard equipment? He might not be able to protect you if he does. Worse, what's to keep him from mistaking you as an enemy and firing upon you?"

Teseler opened his mouth, but then he shut it before he said anything. He tried again with the same outcome. Bowden watched him with a small smile.

Finally, the SpinDog sighed. "I understand what you are getting at now and why you want all the ships to have the best equipment. But it's not that easy."

"Because that means giving away some of your secrets to the other Families that might not have had them."

"We will lose advantages over them once this is done."

"Hold that thought," Bowden said. "Let me put it to you another way. I don't care how the ships are armed, so long as they are armed the same. If you don't want to share your technology, I'm okay with that, but you have to take it off the ship you're flying, too."

Teseler's brows knit again. "Why would I do that? It makes no sense. Why would you want me to fly with inferior equipment that has a smaller chance of killing the enemy?"

"Because I'm going to be in charge of this. I need to know how all the ships are armed and how they maneuver. I won't have time once battle is joined to figure out what everyone's capabilities are before giving them orders; I need everyone to operate the same way. If that means all the ships have inferior equipment so that they can be the same, I'll accept that as the price I have to pay so that I can achieve platform uniformity."

"Platform uniformity?"

"It means that I can task any ship with any mission without having to determine whether that hull has the right equipment or engines or whatever. I need everyone to have the same systems and performance so I can direct them to where they're needed without delay."

"I am needed at the front. It is the place of honor."

"And what happens if someone takes us from the side by surprise?"

"Well, they just—" He stopped and tried again. "I could just—"

"Fly through the formation to deal with the new threat?" Teseler nodded. "It won't work. Not only will you mess up our formation, but now who's going to fight the people in front of us if you turn aside? All our ships, wherever they are in the formation, have to have the ability to defeat the threat. Otherwise, we'll lose them unnecessarily...and there isn't a single ship we can afford to lose."

Teseler frowned as he worked it all through his head. Finally, he said in a quieter voice, "I don't like it, but I see the need to put our best equipment on every ship. The primus is going to like it even less when I tell him."

Bowden smiled. "Perhaps it won't be as difficult as you think. Do you have the best of every kind of equipment?"

"No." Teseler shook his head and looked at the deck. "The Usrensekt Family has far more efficient engines than we do. They use less fuel and can fly for longer periods. We have very good optical trackers, but the Trzgarth Family's are better."

"Guess what?"

Teseler looked at him glumly.

Bowden smiled. "You're going to give, but you're going to get those things in return, because I'm going to them when I'm done here, and I'm going to make the same arguments. Do you suppose they would rather fly on inferior craft any more than you would?"

"Their honor would demand they have the best."

"Just so," Bowden said, happy to have the SpinDogs' arrogance work in his favor for once. "We're going into combat. They should have the best ships so we can maximize our chances, but you should have them as well. I need the best ships that we can build, and I need them to all be the same. Does that make sense?"

"Although I wish it were not so, it does. Perhaps when you go to talk with the Usrensekt, you will let me come with you."

"I might, but why do you want to come with me?"

"I know the person who is in charge of their autofabbers, and their family is allied with ours. He has long desired our radar system, just like we have desired their engine efficiency, but we have never been able to come to an agreement on a trade. If I'm there to offer our radars in trade for their engine technology, that may ease the discussion." He smiled. "It also will allow the discussion to happen much sooner than if you have to go through the primus of the family."

"That would be helpful," Bowden said. *And the more "things" we have to offer from the start will make it easier for the other Families down the line to say yes when they're approached.* Bowden smiled. "When are you available to do that?"

"The sooner I can get their engines on my ship, the sooner I can become familiar with their operation. I can be ready now. Are you?"

"I am," Bowden said, ignoring the grumble in his stomach. He'd already missed lunch and now stood to miss dinner, too. *But if we can get buy-in from both the Otlethes and Usrensekt Families . . .* "Let's go."

Chapter Fifteen

Spin One

Teseler led Bowden to the Usrensekt Family autofabbers, housed in a rock-carved space nearly as big as the Otlethes Family's. The journey to get there seemed a lot straighter and less arduous than it had to get to the Otlethes' fabbers. Whether that was because Teseler now considered Bowden someone he wanted to work with or because the two locations were just physically closer, Bowden wasn't willing to guess. Either way, it didn't take them long.

It also didn't take them long to come to agreement. With Teseler extolling the virtues of a common ship template, where everyone got the "best of the best," Teseler's counterpart in the Usrensekt Family—who was never actually introduced to Bowden—agreed to the plan.

Feeling pretty good about his efforts so far, Bowden called a staff meeting.

"What did you find out?" Bowden asked.

Hrensku looked around the refectory and dropped his voice. "I found out that many of the SpinDogs do not trust you. Does that count?"

Bowden frowned. "Don't trust me? For what reason?"

Hrensku nodded toward Raptis. "You spend too much time with RockHounds."

Bowden shook his head. "I also spend time with you, too. Doesn't that mean anything?"

"It means you are trying to ingratiate yourself with me to steal the SpinDogs' secrets."

Bowden sighed. "Did you get anything of *value*?"

"A little. I found out there is some technology we didn't have. I made notes." Hrensku handed over several sheets of paper.

Bowden glanced at the top page and smiled. "I already got the first two."

"What? How? I didn't think it would be possible to get the engine technology from the Usrensekt Family. They have held that secret for . . . for as long as I have been an adult. Many Families have tried to acquire that knowledge, but no one has been able to pry it from them."

Kevin shrugged. "I got Teseler to help me explain the situation . . . and the benefits of cooperating."

"Teseler . . . *helped* you?" Hrensku's eyes bulged. "Despite his primus backing this plan, I never thought the Otlethes would give up their radar system—not the best one, anyway—as it gives them too great an advantage finding salvage in the outer system. It is even better than what the RockHounds have."

Raptis nodded. "It is."

"How were you able to force them to donate their technology? What did you threaten them with?"

Bowden chuckled. "That's the funny part. I didn't threaten them at all. For Teseler's part, I just showed him how beneficial it would be to have wingmen with technology as good as his own, so they could better protect him while he was killing Kulsians and being a big hero. The fact that he stood to gain everyone else's technology if he shared his only sweetened the deal."

"You can lead a horse to water, but you can't make him drink," Fiezel noted.

"What is a horse?" Raptis asked.

"It's an animal people ride back on Terra," Bowden said. "The saying means just because you show someone that something is in their best interest doesn't mean they'll choose to accept it if you force it on them. So I didn't try to force it on Teseler; I let him come to the conclusion on his own."

Hrensku nodded. "And because he thought it was his idea, he was more ready to accept it."

"Not only that, he was ready to help me explain to others

why it was a good deal." Bowden looked at Malanye Raptis. "What about you?"

"My results were about the same as Burg's," the RockHound replied.

"The RockHounds have been holding out on their best technology?"

"No. They do not trust you because you live on *Spin One* with the SpinDogs and are therefore under their thumb."

"But I'm not—"

"And yes, they were holding out on a number of technologies which even I was unaware of. Apparently"—she lowered her voice—"there is a source of some high technology, a place that some of the leading Families have access to. It's probably salvage from battles that were fought in the system previously, but I wasn't able to find out where or what it was."

"How do we get access to it?"

"You would have to talk to Murphy and get him to talk to the Legates; I was unable to find out any details on it." She passed him a handful of papers. "I did, however, find some interesting things we can incorporate into our template... if you can get the owners to donate them."

Bowden turned to Fiezel. "What about you? Don't tell me the Terrans don't trust me, too?"

"Naw, I trust you just fine," the former Air Force officer said. "Most of the folks do, too, aside from you being a navy puke."

"Great," Bowden said, deadpan. "What'd you find?"

"I went through all the stuff the *Olsloov* left behind for us. There's an awful lot of stuff that—if we could use it—would really let us kick the Kulsians' asses."

"But...?"

"But some of it is beyond the capability of the locals to autofab, whether that's because it uses materials they don't have, or it's too arcane for them."

"Too arcane?" Bowden asked.

"Basically, it's too high-tech. The SpinDog folks I spoke to wouldn't consider making it."

Bowden shook his head. "Think you could change their minds, Burg?"

"Probably not," Hrensku said, looking at the deck. He looked up and his eyes met Bowden's. "I understand—having worked with you—that *some* computer technology is safe, but most of them have *not* worked with you and will be less trusting of it. They will not want to make it, much less install it in their ships."

Bowden turned back to Fiezel. "What did you find that we can actually use?"

"Well, we probably can't put it on every ship, as some of the captains will refuse to use it, but we have the capability to use the Dornaani microsat net to provide real-time links to our missiles and other command-and-control functions. We can also use them to gather intel and have them pass it to our command platforms via spectrum-jumping lascom."

"Well, that's something, anyway."

"It is." Fiezel smiled. "And it's beyond anything that the Kulsians will have, which will give us an advantage."

"I'll take it," Bowden said. "As greatly outnumbered as we're going to be, I'll take every advantage I can get."

"Like I said, though, some of it is going to be too whiz-bang for a lot of the SpinDogs and most of the RockHounds."

"Some of my people would probably accept that type of technology," Raptis said, "assuming it was not *too* computer intensive." She pursed her lips. "Reetan Taregon and Festal Lantrax, for sure." She sighed. "Of course, nothing is as easy as it ought to be."

Bowden raised an eyebrow. "What is that supposed to mean?"

"It means that, although they would probably be the most trusting of the technology, they would be the least trusting of everything else. They rarely come to the spins as they don't like the people here, and they never have anything positive to say about the Lost Soldiers."

"Oh, goody," Bowden said. "Is there anyone who likes us?"

"Besides yourselves?" Hrensku asked with a laugh. "There are a few, but not as many as you would like. Not as many as I would like, either, if the truth were told." He clapped Bowden on the shoulder. "I think you're a passable fellow, but being seen with you gives me a bad reputation."

"You, too?" Bowden asked Raptis.

"Probably even more so among my people," the RockHound said. "The SpinDogs see Lost Soldiers on the spins all the time and are more used to your presence. The RockHounds do not see you as often and therefore find it harder to trust you."

Fiezel chuckled. "Assuming we can find some pilots that will listen to you, Kevin—and that we can get all the goodies from the SpinDogs and RockHounds so we have decent ships to fight from—how do you intend to make this hodgepodge of shit work?"

"It was after your time, but let me tell you about this little concept we had that was called AWACS."

The second day's shilling started out well, and Bowden was able to convince several of the minor Families to ante up the limited technological improvements they had. For all three, it wasn't much...which was probably at least partially to blame for why they *were* minor Families.

They also had a much smaller autofab capacity. Where the Otlethes had eleven units and the Usrensekt had ten, these Families only had one or two, and not all were spacious enough to build corvettes. However, many of their replicators were highly efficient, capable of producing those subsystems and components that were the most complicated and took the longest to complete. Bowden knew that they had the most to gain by receiving access to the best technologies, so was not surprised when they accepted...almost eagerly.

That streak of positivity ended when he approached the entrance to the Trzgarth Family's autofabber. Although Teseler led Bowden to its outskirts, he refused to accompany him to the entrance. His description of the relations between the Otlethes and Trzgarth Families sounded rather like those ascribed to the Hatfields and the McCoys.

The wide bulkhead-rated portal was—like all the autofabbers Bowden had been to—well guarded. The two men standing outside reached for pistols when he approached, kept them trained upon him even after he had stopped and held up his hands.

"What do you want, Terran?" one asked.

"I'm here to speak with whoever is in charge of your auto-fabbers."

"They don't want to talk to you."

"Even if I can get them the Otlethes' radar and the Usrensekts' engine technology?"

"You're lying."

"I'm not," Bowden said. "I'm here to bring those things in trade to your...well, to whoever is in charge."

"I will let him know," the same man said, "but if you are wasting his time, it will not go well for you."

"Understood," Bowden said, suddenly feeling a great deal less sure about this sales strategy. "I am telling the truth."

"Wait here."

The man went through the hatch and returned with another man about five minutes later. Just the way that he looked down his nose at Bowden let him know this was going to be a tough sell. *But having the best optical tracker is worth it.*

"Hi!" Bowden said, trying to keep a friendly tone to his voice. "I'm here—"

"My man told me what you said. What is going to cost me?"

"Well, is it possible to go somewhere and talk?"

"We are somewhere, and we're talking. Do you really have the Otlethes' and Usrensekts' technology to trade?"

"Not with me here, but yes I do. The thing is—"

"What do you want for it?"

"I understand you have the best optical tracking technology of all the SpinDogs."

"We do, and you can't have it."

"Well, I—"

"What else do we have that you would take in trade?"

"Nothing. We're trying to put together the best template possible, so that when we meet the Kulsians in battle, we'll be able to beat them. The other Families are contributing their best technology to this effort. Will you not do the same?"

"No, we won't. There's no way the Otlethes are going to get our trackers. Ever. We would delete it from our systems to keep them from having it."

"Is that your final word? Is that what the primus would say?"

The man puffed up his chest. "I speak for the primus. We will provide the ships that we have agreed to produce, but we will not give our best technology to anyone else. Especially you."

Bowden squared his shoulders. "I see. Well, in that case, you might as well stop making the corvettes, because you won't be allowed to participate in the attack with us."

"You would turn down our assistance?"

"Yes," Bowden said, "I would, and I am. Everybody else has agreed to share their best technology and is doing what they can to prepare for the fight. I have already said that nonstandard ships will not be allowed in the fleet. You can either join us and get everyone else's technology or you can let us do the fighting for you."

"Not at the cost of giving you our optical tracking systems."

"That's fine, then." Bowden turned and started walking. He made it three steps before a gun fired from behind him and the round ricocheted off the tunnel wall near his head. Bowden spun to find the man holding one of the guard's pistols, pointing it at him.

"That was a warning shot," the man said. "Don't turn your back on me, ever again, and do not come back. If you do, you will die."

Chapter Sixteen

Spin One

Captain Tyree Cutter moved slightly to the side as Murphy peered over his shoulder. "So this is the bigger version of the comms pattern you got operating near Imsurmik before you left?" The colonel studied the high-resolution photograph from the Dornaani micro-satellite.

"Yes sir," Cutter answered, once again drawn in by the extraordinary precision of the image. It was a far, far cry from the grainy photos in the briefing packet with which he'd waded ashore at Omaha Beach on D-Day +5.

He pointed to a lonely stone on an otherwise empty expanse of volcanic rock. "It's a pretty simple code, actually. First we check to see if there's a stone on this sheet of rock, or this one over here. There's a third slab just out of frame. But between the three locations—A, B, and C—we get seven different code signifiers. Three are when the locals simply put out single rocks, three more codes signified by pairs—AB, AC, BC—and one last code that is all three rocks."

"Could you get more codes by adding more variables? Shape or color of the rocks, perhaps?"

Cutter shook his head. "No, because too many things could cause a false or uncertain signal. Sun could bleach a rock, rain could darken it. You just don't know."

"Still, I'm sure you've got more than seven signals?" Murphy asked with a smile.

"Sure do, sir. These first seven just indicate which code to use when reading the real signals that are in these six ravines on a nearby tableland." Cutter pointed to a different image: a half dozen dark gashes cut through a barren plateau as if it had been raked by the claws of an immense monster.

Murphy nodded. "So, there are stones positioned in there as well?"

"Yes, sir. Each one's meaning changes based on which of the seven 'code sets' is showing back here." He nodded toward the first photo. "Gives us hundreds of different messages to choose from."

Murphy leaned back, crossed his arms. "What about using time as a further variable? You'd probably have thousands of discrete signals, that way."

"You would, sir. But notice how long the shadows are in the ravines. It's not as bad a problem back at the three code indicators, but even there, irregularities in the surface make early or late-day imaging uncertain."

Murphy nodded. "And these ravines don't get much sun at all, from the look of it."

"Exactly, sir, which means that, even for the Dornaani satellites, being able to tell if there's a smaller stone on top of a bigger stone, or in the middle of a very uneven shelf, can get pretty tricky."

Murphy studied the various close-ups of the ravines. "I imagine you can only send short messages, though."

"Well, sir, it's based on the traditional ways that the people of our ground commander, Tanavuna, would leave messages for each other when they're out ranging across the Ashbands. The signals aren't individual letters, spelling out words like Morse code, sir. Instead, the locals use ideograms indicating the status of the person or group that left it behind—mini-sitreps, if you like."

"So these signals are limited to what is happening in Tanavuna's area of operations?"

"No, sir. The patterns in the ravine include location and time indicators. So if Tanavuna gets a report from elsewhere, he can signify where it came from, when, and what the friendlies in that location reported." Cutter leaned back. "With this, we can keep tabs on almost the entirety of the Hamain. A lot more, once they start swapping intel through the crystal sets we left behind. We'll be able to get almost daily reports on where the enemy is located, in what numbers, and what they seem to be doing."

Murphy nodded. "Excellent. And can we send messages to Tanavuna?"

"That's a lot harder sir. But we do have a squelch-break system in place. Pretty much the same thing you used to communicate with Jackson and Chalmers on R'Bak island, before they grabbed the Kulsian lighter."

"So Tanavuna has a special crystal set that he monitors for our messaging on a given frequency?"

Cutter nodded. "The frequency is a mathematical derivative of the local calendar date and our Earth—er, Terran calendar date. So it not only changes every day, but it never repeats."

"So assuming that network of crystal sets is operating, how broad a reporting area does this give us?"

"It covers the entirety of the Ashbands and some of the Hamain. We have some agents on one or two of the other islands, of course, such as those you left behind with the emergency shuttle. We have also have quite a few well-trained agents in the Greens. What else were you thinking of, sir?"

"I'd like to see if we can expand your reporting pattern."

"How so?"

"I want Tanavuna to take a team and scout out other ravines that might be useful for signaling."

Cutter leaned forward so his elbow was on the table, chin in his hand. "Where would you like him to start?"

Murphy scanned the nearby map, focusing on the wastes that bordered the high desert: the Hamain. He pointed to a red pin at the edge of it: a battlefield marker. "Here."

Cutter managed not to show any surprise. "Why there, sir?"

"We already have contacts on the ground, there. It's a community where Vat intercepted a satrap-operated balloon in the weeks before we took out the raiders' homemade inter-system transmitter. In the course of assisting the village—Ikaan-tel, I believe—the locals grew to trust us. Vat was there when their matriarch died and helped them through that transition. He also trained them on some of our weapons and left enough behind for a small militia.

"After he left, we ran a few helo flights in there to drop off some of the simple devices we had autofabbed to help the locals get through the Searing without having to migrate or move to the satrap-controlled regions. We included one of those crystal sets, too, in case the surveyors came calling.

"So there's a reasonable amount of goodwill there. Possibly enough to convince some of them to work as scouts or just simply report if they spot surveyors or other hostile forces. Which is why it would also be useful to learn more about that region and the high desert just beyond. If we ever have to conduct operations there, it would be helpful to know our way around."

"Will do, sir," Cutter agreed with a nod, although why anyone, surveyors included, would go to such a desolate spot was hard to fathom. "So in addition to finding some good signaling spots farther out in the Hamain, what should we be asking them to show us?"

"Water sources."

"Well, sir, we can already see those." He pointed at the map and shrugged. "Not that there are a lot left. They're just dry wadis, now."

Murphy shook his head. "I'm not talking about the water sources we can detect on our own." He swept a hand at all the images. "We've been using the micro-sats to track whinnies."

Cutter frowned. "Not sure I see the connection, sir."

"We're watching to see where they get water. Bo Moorefield and others who've spent a lot of time around whinnies have noticed they often avoid drinking at rivers or other open-water sources. Sometimes they prefer isolated springs, or, using their climbing ability, go to higher sources. So if we can identify the places they expect to find water during the Searing, that could be crucial information for our own forces and allies over the next several years."

"Yes, sir." Cutter scratched the stubble on his cheek. "And you want Tanavuna to lead this?"

"I do, Captain."

"May I ask a question, sir?"

"Of course."

"Why Tanavuna? We have indigs who are from communities much closer to this...eh, Ikaan-tel. Already known to the folks there, possibly. Certainly speaking the same dialect."

"Yes, and with that may come entanglements we want to

avoid—such as if we have to stage out of Ikaan-tel. It could start rivalries as each family or group tries to put forward their own friends, maybe relatives, to help us. Instead, I want someone who speaks their language and shares a lot of their traditions and experiences, but is not part of the village's matrix of relationships. Someone who's more disposed to report candidly and act objectively. Clear?"

"Absolutely, sir. I'll send Tanavuna the message as soon as we've got a gap in the surveyors' satellite pattern. Which may be a little while."

"Excellent. But there's one additional thing, Captain. The codes and the whinnie-tracking: that stays between you and me."

"Why, sir?"

Murphy shrugged. "Anybody who knows where the whinnies' water is would know where to look for us or our operatives, should we need to use this information. So I don't want to take any chances that it could fall into enemy hands. Same thing with the codes. That's why, when you go planetside, you're going to carry this information to Tanavuna personally."

Cutter straightened abruptly. "I'm going planetside, sir?"

Murphy smiled. "I've watched you moping around since we left R'Bak." He paused. "You miss them—your men—don't you?"

"That's why I asked to be left behind, sir. But...I thought the surveyors would see us if we approached R'Bak, much less landed on it. What's changed?"

Murphy shrugged. "Firstly, we just recently confirmed that one of the surveyors' satellites has 'failed.'"

"Failed?"

Murphy smiled. "Well, it seems there was a flurry of space gravel that just happened to intersect its orbit, which we just happened to have calculated and tracked thanks to one of the Dornaani microsats. Makes a pretty show for everyone on the ground, too: lots of shooting stars. And the Kulsians can make all the wishes they want...for all the good it will do them."

"You started your explanation with the word 'firstly,' sir. Is there another new wrinkle in the situation?"

"Yes. One of the reasons we could get away with the space gravel is because a lot of it is naturally inbound right now. We've only recently learned how much the Searing increases the amount of space debris that comes in-system. More of the junk beyond both stars' outer planets gets displaced by the gravitic tug-of-war between the two stars."

Cutter smiled. "So the weather report calls for increasing meteor showers, eh?"

"It does, Captain. Which is how we're going to get you dirtside."

Tyree looked down his long torso. "I'm a little bigger than space gravel, Colonel."

"As are plenty of meteorites, Captain. And you'll be riding one of those."

"Uh...what? Sir?"

Murphy chuckled. "Actually, the small ship carrying you will be hiding behind a large rock we pushed in that direction. When it starts heating up, any Kulsian sensors that focus in too tightly will experience the equivalent of whiteout: too much heat and too many fragments to see clearly. That's when you'll be deployed in a landing pod that resembles a lifting body. A lot safer than the drop pods that Harry Tapper and others have used."

"And it's been tested, right?"

"Yes, and if we didn't have full confidence in it, we wouldn't use it."

Cutter nodded but couldn't push down the anxiety that kept rising up. To date, nothing cobbled together for the Lost Soldiers had been without some flaws: flaws that had been overcome because of the expert humans using them. "Uh, sir... you know I was with the Thirtieth Division in Europe? Not a paratrooper?"

Murphy smiled. "I'm quite aware of that, Captain. I won't promise you a smooth ride, but I will promise you a safe one, particularly since the surveyors have almost all their satellites working on dirtside observation."

Cutter tried to appear reassured and was pretty sure he failed miserably. But it wasn't just how he was returning to R'Bak that was troubling him: it was why. "Sir, I know you wouldn't go to all this trouble just for me to be a code-courier. What's my real mission?"

Murphy nodded. "We'll talk about that a bit later. In a fully secure environment. Right now, I need you to brief Makarov on the codes and give him a copy. Also, you and he should come up with special signals for your status, in the event of emergencies."

Cutter wasn't sure what sort of emergencies Murphy had in

mind and was even less sure he wanted to find out. "Very good, sir. When do I leave?"

Murphy smiled. "How soon can you be ready?"

"I'm ready right now, sir."

The colonel laughed. "I'd oblige you if I could, but it will take a little time to prep your ride, take your measurements for the drop pod harness, and wait for a window that offers an approach vector that stays within R'Bak's planetary shadow and over the horizon from Downport." Murphy did some mental math. "You think you can wait two weeks, Captain Cutter?"

Tyree couldn't hold back a smile at the thought of seeing his men again. "Just barely, sir."

Chapter Seventeen

Spin One

Bowden returned to his staffroom shortly after meeting with the Trzgarth Family.

"What happened?" Fiezel asked. "You look like you saw a ghost."

"I tried to meet with the Trzgarth Family."

"You did that . . . alone?" Hrensku asked. "You are a braver man than I."

"I take it that things didn't go so well?" Fiezel asked.

"The Trzgarth scion shot at me as I walked away," Bowden said, "if that's any indication."

"You're lucky to still be living," Hrensku said. "T'Barth is an excellent shot. If he meant for you to be dead, you would be."

"Well, here's to small favors, then," Bowden replied. "However, the Trzgarth Family is officially 'out' of the attack force."

"What do you mean by 'out'?" Raptis asked.

"I mean that I told them if they aren't going to play by our rules, they're not going to play at all. I told them to stop building corvettes, because I wouldn't let them in our fleet."

"What happened to not forcing the horses to drink?" Hrensku asked.

"I didn't get a chance to show him how good the water tasted. He was antagonistic from the start, didn't care what I said, and told me there was no way we were ever going to get their technology." Bowden shrugged. "We'll use what the Otlethes have. From what I hear, it's nearly as good."

"That's what I always wanted to take into battle," Fiezel said. "Something that's 'almost as good.'" He sighed. "We shot down a lot of fighters in Vietnam that were almost as good as ours. They never had a chance."

"True, but even the second-best that the SpinDogs and Rock-Hounds have is probably better than the Kulsians'."

"How do you know?"

"Because the Hound-Dogs have successfully hidden every time the Kulsians have come. They've made themselves invisible. That implies a higher level of technical sophistication when it comes to sensors in general." Bowden sighed. "Would I like to have the best? Sure. And there's still a chance we will."

Fiezel laughed. "I thought there was 'no way we are ever going to get their technology.'"

Bowden winked. "While there's life, there's hope." He looked up at a knock on the door to find Major Pyotr Makarov staring at him.

"Murphy wants to see you, *now*," Makarov said.

"What'd I do this time?"

"One of the Families is really pissed at you."

"That would be the Trzgarths."

"It's not a surprise, then?"

Bowden chuckled. "Let's just call it a lucky guess."

Murphy frowned when Bowden made it to the door of his office and waved him in. Not knowing whether he was in trouble or not, Bowden approached the desk, saluted, and said, "Major Kevin Bowden, reporting as ordered, sir!"

The frown deepened as Murphy returned the salute, then he grunted and motioned to the chair. "You've had a busy morning, I hear. The head of the Trzgarth Family would like to have you tossed out of an airlock. He was too pissed off to tell me why, though—beyond telling me that I needed to rein you in." Murphy stared at Bowden. "Care to tell me *why* I need to rein you in?"

"The scion of the Family—T'Barth—didn't take kindly to being told that I wouldn't have his ships in the fleet."

"I see. And you did that...why?"

"Because T'Barth told me in no uncertain terms that they would never give us their optical tracking technology for the corvette template."

Murphy rubbed his chin. "The rumor is they have the best optical trackers."

"That's not a rumor; that's a fact."

"I would think you'd want them."

"I do. Very much."

"So what are you doing to get them?"

"Not a damned thing."

Murphy didn't say anything; his lifting an eyebrow was eloquent enough.

"Seriously," Bowden continued. "First off, he wouldn't talk; all he did was yell at me. And if the Family won't talk, I can't show them how it benefits them to participate in the project. I also won't use nonstandard ships in the fleet; I can't. I've already gotten a number of Families to agree to pony up their best gear. If I let the Trzgarth Family get away without providing their best equipment, everyone else is going to withdraw theirs. That, we can't have. And finally, I have too much going on already to waste my time trying to appease a spoiled Family." Bowden held up a hand when Murphy started to talk. "And, at the end of the day, I don't have to. If they're not going to conform, I'm not going to let them play. Eventually, one of two things will happen. Either their honor will demand that they be part of this, or the leading Families will squeeze them enough that they'll change their minds."

"They're making a big deal about you keeping them out. There have been threats...mainly directed at you."

Bowden smiled. "I won't go anywhere by myself, then, and I'll stay out of dark corridors."

"This isn't a joke. The Families play for keeps, and they aren't above assassinating someone if they think they can get away with it." Murphy clenched his hands sharply, almost as abrupt as a spasm. "I speak from experience."

Kevin nodded. "They've tried to kill me a few times, now, too, but there's nothing I can do about it. I'll try to keep myself safe, but I *can't* let them get away with this. They're either all in, or they're out."

Murphy looked down at a paper on his desk. "They apparently

have one of the biggest autofabber capabilities among the Spin-Dogs. Losing that will cost you a number of ships."

"I'd rather be without them than have someone that won't follow orders. If I let them get away with this, they'll never do what they're ordered to in a fleet battle. Never."

"What do you need from me?"

"At the moment, nothing." Bowden tilted his head. "How many Families are there in the SpinDogs?"

"That's a good question."

"I hope you have a good answer, sir. It would make my life a lot easier if I knew how many people I had to coordinate with. Maybe a point of contact with each. Some idea of which ones—like the Trzgarth—hate our guts, so I know to tread lightly around them or find someone else to talk to them for me."

"Unfortunately, I don't. If you needed an exact answer, I would say about thirty. With the way ties shift among the different Families, I could give you an answer today, and tomorrow it would no longer be correct. And that's just the ones who're big enough to have a seat at the table...assuming you were ever able to get all of them to sit at a table together. There are also lesser Families under their umbrellas that accept the main family's primus as their own. And not all the big Primae even recognize those smaller clans as true Families."

"But if I got through to their primus or the primus's representative, they would direct the lesser Families on how to use their autofabbers, if they had them."

"Probably." Murphy chuckled wryly. "I keep forgetting you haven't spent much time here. The Families—like most of the things here—are fluid. Just because something exists today doesn't mean it will tomorrow—relationships first and foremost among them."

Bowden nodded. "Yes, sir. That's kind of what I got from the SpinDog on my team. About the only thing they can agree on is their hatred of Terrans."

"Some of them are okay with us." Murphy shrugged. "Assuming you don't get us all killed by the Kulsians, anyway."

"I'm trying my hardest, sir, despite how much they're fighting me on it."

"Well, go get on with it, then. Time's running out. I'll have Makarov get you the latest list of Families, and I will send someone else to join your team."

"Who's that? What's his specialty?"

"Keeping you alive. You can assign him whatever tasks are prudent, but his main job will be ensuring you don't get killed."

"That may be the hardest job of all," Bowden said with a sour chuckle.

All the humor went out of Murphy's eyes. "Yes. It may well be."

The next few days went by like a whirlwind as Bowden tried to track down and get agreement from all the Families and the local RockHounds. Where he could, he sent Hrensku and Raptis to talk to them, so as not to have to overcome the innate distrust of having a Terran make the offer. In some cases, it worked, in other cases, the SpinDogs' and RockHounds' innate distrust of each other was such that even having a local make the presentation wasn't enough. Then it was up to Bowden—and his new tag-along, Szymon Kaminski—to convince the Family to join the effort.

Kaminski was a Polish submariner who had spent all his time in the engine room and looked like Popeye after a can of spinach. Ironically, most of Bowden's conversations with him were in the SpinDogs' language—courtesy of the Dornaani language programs—as he didn't speak English well. Bowden didn't need him to talk during his presentations, though. All he needed him for—and what the brawny machinist's mate did best—was to stand behind Bowden and glower.

With Kaminski in tow, Bowden didn't have any more issues like he'd had with the Trzgarth Family. Not everyone was cheery and gracious—far from it—but most of the people he met with weren't outright abusive. By that point, the word was getting around from Teseler and the Usrensekt scion about what was going on, helped along by Hrensku.

By the end of the second week, he had the agreement of all the SpinDog and RockHound Families he cared about... except the Trzgarth Family and two of their allies.

"What do you think, Boss?" Fiezel asked at their end-of-the-day meeting.

"I think I misjudged how much a person could hate someone they don't even know," Bowden said. "With everyone else falling into line, I really thought that the Trzgarths would bite the bullet and join us."

Raptis's brows beetled. "Why would you bite—?"

"It's one of his sayings," Hrensku said. He'd flown with Bowden long enough to have heard most of the incomprehensible Terran sayings. "It means to do something you don't like."

"But biting a bullet isn't that bad. There are many other things that I'd want to bite down on far less than a piece of metal."

"Don't blame me." Hrensku held up his hands. "I didn't make it up."

"Are you done?" Bowden asked.

Hrensku looked at Raptis, who shrugged. "Yes, I think so."

"Good."

"So, what are we going to do about the Trzgarth?" Fiezel asked.

"I'm going to sleep on it tonight and talk to Murphy tomorrow. Maybe he knows someone who can lean on them. Otherwise, we lock down the template and start building the ships in earnest. We don't have time to screw around with assholes who don't play well with others. It's time to start completing the corvettes, training the pilots, and getting ready for battle."

"What did you find out?" Murphy asked the next morning.

"I found out that, sadly, I was right. We gave all the Families what we thought was our best template for them to fab us a fleet of corvettes that we could use to take on the Kulsians."

"And...?"

"And the results are better in some places and far, far worse in others."

"Explain."

"As we knew, some of the Families were holding out on us with their tech. Most of these were RockHounds who had tech that they used out in the black, but never brought to any of the habs, so no one knew it existed. Since it was the best they had, though, they're using it on their personal corvettes—the ones they won't bring within sight of a habitat, so we wouldn't know they exist—to give them an edge over everyone else."

Murphy nodded, and Bowden continued. "When I realized that, I had my folks concentrate on the ships that Family heads were building for themselves. We collected the new tech and have distributed it out to the other people fabbing corvettes for us."

"Except for the Trzgarth."

"Yes, sir. Except for them. They remain holdouts."

"Even without them, I can't imagine that was easy."

Bowden chuckled ruefully. "It wasn't. There was much wailing and gnashing of teeth. Malanye Raptis had to keep one person from knifing me when my back was turned; I'm glad I took her along as my liaison. The SpinDogs may not like me, but the RockHounds have a new level of hatred for me." He shrugged. "Still, that was accomplished to the best of our abilities, and we raised the base-line tech level of the fleet quite a bit. We started out *believing* we'd gathered the very best systems for the hulls, but now, we're damn near certain of it. Aside from the Trzgarth, that is. The problem comes, not surprisingly, when you start looking at computer systems across the fleet and the energy storage issues we might have."

"Let's start with the computers. What's wrong with them?"

"What's wrong?" Bowden laughed. "What's wrong is that they don't exist here. The Families have never fabbed most of the 'high-tech' systems before"—he used air quotes—"and they don't really understand them. At all. And when I say high tech, it's only because what they had prior is laughable. There was a far better computer system in the Hornet I used to fly than currently exists in the best ship of their fleet. Hell, the A-6E Intruders in my airwing had better computers, and they were designed during the Vietnam War and operated at four hertz!"

Bowden shook his head. "The bottom line is that we're trying to slave twenty-first-century tech to something that's barely the same as what we had in the 1960s. And it *just won't work*. The digital systems won't talk to the analog systems, and most of the locals don't want the digital stuff on their ships in the first place.

"The biggest issues we're having are with the Arat Kur systems you got for guidance and tracking, as well as the targeting computers and their interfaces with precision painting lasers. If we could get all of this working on every ship and networked across the fleet, we'd have such an advantage over the Kulsians that we could meet them anywhere and kick their asses. Hell, we could take a fleet of just a few ships to Kulsis and kick their asses there."

"But you can't."

"No, sir, we can't." Bowden shook his head. "Not even close."

Murphy chewed on the inside of his cheek a second, then he looked up and smiled. "I see the twinkle in your eye. You have a solution."

"I do. Not a perfect solution, but good enough for government work, as well as our purposes here. Which may or may not prove to *be* government work."

"Don't keep me in suspense..."

"AWACS. Like what we had back home."

"An airborne warning and *control* system." Murphy nodded. "I take it you mean for targeting purposes?"

"Yeah, but it would be a bit of a lash-up between multiple platforms. The important thing is that it can send sensor data to command hulls that can distribute that information to all the others." Bowden rubbed his chin. "If we could work out fire coordination on a few platforms, we could manage the battle across the entire fleet, especially for long-range targeting. That would allow us to mass our fire and ensure our weapons go where we want them to." He shrugged. "We really need this, too, because not enough of them are getting the hang of those weapon systems. It's a digital world, and yet, they're all still thinking analog."

Kevin rolled his eyes. "Hell, what am I saying? Most of *our* guys are still thinking analog, especially the ones from before our time. The difference is that they *want* to get their hands on the new tech and experiment with it. The Hound-Dogs act like anything with a real computer is a plague-carrying tarantula."

"What do you have in mind for your AWACS model? I imagine that this is going to affect how you do everything, won't it? Both tactics *and* strategy?"

"It will, sir. We were building sets of squadrons—and we're going to continue to do so—but now each squadron isn't just a group of like-capability ships—it's built around one or two ships with unique and crucial capabilities."

"Something like the old carrier battle group?"

"Exactly. When we went on cruise, we had one asset with the decisive capability—the carrier. However, just like the carrier battle group, there's no redundancy in that capability, which means a big portion of the other assets' time is spent defending it."

Murphy frowned. "So we need more than one AWACS asset per squadron. If they're going to have the decisive capability we need, we can't have them be single points of failure; we need at least two fully C4I-capable platforms per maneuver element."

"We don't have enough to do that. And it's 'squadron,' sir."

"Whatever you say, Admiral."

Bowden raised an eyebrow. "Admiral?"

Murphy stared off theatrically, as if trying to recall a distant memory. "What did you navy pukes call the person in charge of a fleet? I know the CO of a ship is 'Captain,' regardless of rank... but what's the title of the person above him?"

Bowden sighed and looked down. "Admiral," he muttered.

Murphy smiled. "The bottom line is that I like your plan, Admiral, and I think it will work. We're no longer on defense; we're on the attack, and we need to think and act that way. Having only two fully capable ships per maneuver el—per *squadron*—will be hard enough. But if we've got only *one* per combat group, any plan you make will either be way too constrained because you're protecting that asset or doomed to failure because that asset is way too vulnerable. There's no happy medium. If you have two platforms, though—"

"—then I have some flexibility." Kevin nodded. "Risk is more scalable and less absolute." He pursed his lips and gazed intently at Murphy. "It all comes down to one thing, though."

"Which is...?"

"Whether we can get those ships built in time. Because I've been to the fabbers and the Families. They tell me that they're building as fast as they can, and integrating the new technology is going to take even longer than the ships they're building now. It's going to be close, and having the Trzgarth involved—along with their fabbing capabilities—may make the difference."

Murphy's jaw clenched. "I guess it's time for me to step in and see what I can do."

"I'd appreciate it, sir. There's only so much I can do from the grass-roots level. I really thought they'd cave by now, but—"

"Spite is a powerful thing."

"Yes, sir. It is. And I need those ships or I'm going to get my ass kicked."

"We can't have that, because their next stop would be here at the spins."

Bowden nodded.

"What did you say was the other issue?"

"Power storage, sir. You have to remember that the Hound-Dogs have never considered attacking the Kulsians. Not only does this mean they're not mentally prepared to be the aggressors—and we'll have to teach this out of them—but this generation of ships has some serious issues in power generation and storage."

"Let's face it," Bowden said with a smile. "Attacking someone, especially with lasers, uses a *lot* of power, and the capacitors, cables, and power buses they have aren't sufficiently robust enough to generate and distribute the power required to blow through the armor we can expect to face."

Bowden winced. "Right now, we can tickle them with our lasers, but if we want to actually drill holes through their sides, we either need to fix this or get the Kulsians to remain in place long enough for our underpowered equipment to burn through. Even rolling the ship would be enough, probably. We'd just make a scorch mark around their ships. They'd probably never even know they were hit."

Murphy nodded. "And the solution is...?"

"Generating additional power is out for now. The corvette we captured had a small auxiliary fusion plant that appeared to be the backup in case its primary nuclear reactor was damaged or broken. I'd love to fab a whole pile of these, but it's a bridge too far. We don't have time to get them up and running, and trying to implement them across the fleet"—Bowden shuddered—"I'm afraid we'd go into battle and half our ships would either go dark or spontaneously turn into small, brief stars."

"Don't tell me what we can't do. Tell me what we can."

Bowden nodded. "I wanted to use lasers for point defense, with a secondary use as an anti-ship weapon, but we're going to have to swap them out for railguns. We can still use the lasers for very close-in work, but that's about it."

"Goods? Bads?"

"Well, our power systems are better able to handle the strain of a railgun, mostly, but our accuracy goes to shit. With a decent targeting system, which we have, a laser really can't miss. We just can't put out enough power with the available collimators to damage a warship at any sort of range. The railguns can damage them, but we have to be closer to get the hit rate we want. We can still fire from longer distances than the Kulsians, but a maneuvering target will be a lot harder to hit."

Bowden sighed. "If we beat back this bunch of Harvesters, the next won't stand a chance against the Hound-Dogs' fully matured fusion plants and upgraded weapons systems come the next Searing. Hell, we could probably go after the Kulsians in their own system in a half dozen years."

"Let's concentrate on *this* year, though, shall we?"

"Yes, sir," Bowden said. "I am." He grimaced. "Which is why we're yanking out the big keel-following lasers we were hoping to use as ship killers and replace them with a railgun. We'll swap it on the template so that the new ships being fabbed have them, and we'll upgrade the others as we can."

"And for point defense?"

"I'd like to use smaller lasers for that; when it comes to hitting fast targets, nothing beats the speed of light. But we still haven't settled on a design that is small enough *and* packs enough of a punch."

Murphy nodded. "It seems like you either have a working solution for each of your weapons or are drilling down toward one. I'll see what I can do for assisting with the Trzgarth."

"Thanks, sir. I'd appreciate it."

"Don't thank me yet. From what I've heard, this may not be possible, but I'll do what I can."

Chapter Eighteen

Spin One

Murphy heard the hatch to the observer's gallery of the departure bay open. Without turning, the jaunty footfalls told him who'd entered.

"Didn't know if you were coming, Kevin."

"I wasn't going to, until I realized I could buttonhole you and get the latest word on whether the Trzgarth Family have agreed to play ball."

"I'm still waiting to hear from them. Good to see you had time for this, though."

"You wanted all the command staff for the send-off, I was told. Otherwise, I'd be lounging by the pool we don't have," Bowden lied cheerfully. He craned his neck to check the rest of the gallery. "Is Tapper here?"

"No. He's on Pakir Station, conspiring with Korelon to ensure our survival."

"You mean, making sure the RockHounds keep to their tech-sharing agreements?"

"And autofabbing quotas." Murphy sighed. "Probably best that he's not here, though."

"Why's that?"

Bo Moorefield's voice provided the answer from behind them. "Harry's family is down there. Stella, and his son—and maybe another, by now?" He joined the two at the observation gallery's

133

railing, glanced down at the duffel bag he'd almost stepped on, saw the name tag, looked up at Murphy. "Going somewhere, sir?"

Murphy nodded at the wedge-shaped craft sitting in the center of the bay, techs pulling hoses and diagnostic leads from various ports behind the cockpit blister. "I'm hitching a ride with Cutter." He looked down the rail.

The captain tipped an imaginary hat at the brass lined up to his left. "Sirs."

One of the techs trotted over toward him. "Captain?"

"Yes?"

The SpinDog offered the briefest of nods. "We must get a baseline on your flight suit's biomonitors. It will take but a moment of your time."

Cutter nodded, ambled toward the ramp down to the flight deck. "They just won't salute, or say, 'sir,' will they?"

"Not if they can inhumanly help it," Bowden quipped.

Murphy chuckled. "Inhumanly help it. I hadn't heard that one yet."

"Saved it special for you, Colonel."

Bo glanced from one to the other, smiling. "Are you two always like this?"

"Always," Murphy grinned.

"From first coffee to nightcap," Bowden almost crooned.

Bo put up his hands. "Okay, this is too much like a stand-up routine."

"Yeah," Mara Lee chimed in as she entered where Bo had. "Give it up for tonight's opening act: 'Admiral and Commander.'"

Bowden rolled his eyes. Murphy effected a world-weary sigh... but, how had he become "Commander"? If Makarov had let slip that Korelon referred to him as *ektadori'u*...

"You haven't heard that yet, sirs?" Lee asked with a wicked smile. "I understand you are particularly fond of *your* part of that marquee," she gushed at Bowden.

"Oh, I am. No pressure from it. None at all."

Lee glanced at Murphy. "I guess 'Colonel' was too plain vanilla, sir. On the other hand, 'Sko'Belm'? That *was* a mouthful."

"Sounds like a detergent. Or a ski-outfitter," Murphy groused, playing along—and hopefully burying any thread that might connect the title "Commander" to its RockHound equivalent.

"I hate to talk business, Boss," Bowden said with a grin that suggested he relished doing so, "but how did Anseker react to all the last-second subsystem replacements? Did you get charbroiled, or just spend a quick minute on the grill?"

"Sorry to disappoint, but neither. He anticipated it."

Bowden stared, glad and disappointed all at once.

"It seems the SpinDogs are quite familiar with how often—and suddenly—changes may be needed for autofabbing templates. And in a project as ambitious as yours, they've been surprised there haven't been more. Specifically, they'd briefed their weapon engineers to be ready for you to jump back and forth a few times. The only downside is that they expected it to occur earlier in the process. So of course they are all snarling about last-minute revisions—because after all, they have to complain about *something*."

Moorefield crossed his arms. "Yeah, particularly where Terrans are involved. Because we're so very special."

"Speaking of us special Terrans, Bo, I wonder if you could help me get a little more insight into whinaalanis."

"Sure, sir. What is it you'd like to know?"

"Well, to start, why we're the only ones they'll allow to saddle and ride them."

Bo shook his head. "Wish I knew that myself, sir. For every fact I put in my campaign summary, there were a dozen speculations: all perfectly reasonable, all completely without supporting evidence."

Murphy nodded. "I'm proposing approaching the topic a little differently. We've been asking targeted, mission-specific questions."

"That's all we had time for, sir."

Murphy nodded again. "Yes, but now we could ask broader questions."

Bo frowned. "To what end, sir?"

"To understand them more completely, which might be the key to understanding why they're so fond of us."

Moorefield rubbed the back of his neck. "I'd hardly know where to start, sir. Particularly since the closest whinnie is two orbital tracks away from here."

"Which could be a blessing in disguise. You're an old hand with horses, Bo. Is the best way to understand them by studying data in a lab, or working with them?"

Bo laughed. "I see your point." He put his hands on his hips, reflecting. "But damn, I was so close to them for so long, I'm not sure I can stand back far enough to come up with any questions.

They just seemed eager, and naturally suited, to become our...
well, our friends."

Murphy smiled. "Okay, so I'll start you off: were they fond
of any particular foods?"

Bo smiled back. "You mean, the way horses like apples and
carrots? I see where you're going. I'll have to think about that."

Murphy nodded. "Please do—as well as any other basic questions that strike you. Is there any treat they liked as much as
horses like sugar cubes? Did the riders working up in the Greens
see them going after different foods up there? What kind of plants
did they avoid? Did they keep space between them as they slept,
or were they all huddled up? Did they prefer to spend the night
on high ground or low ground?"

Bo was staring at the deck. "I get where you're going with
this, sir. Not sure that it will help figure out why they treat us
differently, but it couldn't hurt. I'll look into it, get together with
some of the others who rode them—which was almost half of the
Lost Soldiers who served under me down on R'Bak." He looked
up as Cutter returned, wearing a SpinDog flight suit. "Looking
ready for action there, Tyree."

"As ever, sir."

Bo put out his hand. "Good luck, Captain. Wish I was going."

Cutter glanced at Murphy, who nodded. "Well, a little silver
birdy tells me you're next."

Bo looked sideways at Murphy. "Whenever that is."

Murphy shrugged. "Not entirely up to us; the Kulsians get
a say. But Tyree's right—you *are* next. Once Kevin has finished
destroying the Harvester fleet, we'll have to take Downport."

Bo smiled, pleased, shook Cutter's hand one more time and
backed away. "Guess I'd better start thinking about how best to
take R'Bak Island, then."

As he exited, Mara crossed her arms. "Well, I know Bo's
going to need air support. And probably vertical envelopment.
And sustainment."

Murphy grinned. "Which means that you should start thinking about coordinating air assets for the attack."

"Getting a look at the OPORD would be a good start, sir."

"Major, right now, I don't even have a fragmentary CONOPS
to scribble on the back of a cocktail napkin. But in the meantime,
make a wish list—and a worry list."

Lee was frowning. "Gonna be hairy. Won't be much time for pilots and crews to get back up to speed." She glanced at Murphy.

Murphy shrugged. "I agree, which is why you won't have to wait for the OPORD, Major; you're going to help Bo scratch it together."

Mara nodded, turned, and reached out toward Cutter. "You take good care. No heroics."

"Never crossed my mind, ma'am."

"From what I've heard, that's *all* that crosses your mind. Just make sure they're the kind you can tell us about later." She nodded and followed Bo.

Murphy pulled a folded envelope out of his pocket and handed it to Cutter. "This is a letter from Vat to a villager in Ikaan-tel. Tanavuna is to deliver it personally. Her eyes only."

The infantryman nodded slowly, pushed open his flight suit, and slipped the envelope into the breast pocket of his uniform blouse. "I read you loud and clear, sir."

"And before you zip up that shiny onesie you're wearing, here's something for you." Murphy produced an ancient pack of cigarettes from inside his own, more basic flight suit. "The smoke with the dented filter has a waterproof lining on the inside of the paper. It contains the intel you'll need to contact and coordinate with the emergency shuttle and team we left behind on R'Bak, should that become necessary. There are no instructions, just a value and a data string. The value is your unique seed to be used with the data string, which you'll recognize as the equation you established for the visual comms system's progressive change in squelch frequencies. If you lose that cigarette, it's wildly unlikely that anyone could make sense of the information."

Cutter nodded even more slowly than before, put the pack in the same pocket as the envelope. He smiled. "Can I zip up now, Colonel?"

"You had damn well better!" declared a voice as the hatch to the crew ready room opened. The speaker—a woman with the tight haircut of a RockHound but an improbably stocky build for someone raised in micro-gee—nodded at the craft sitting in the bay. "Unless, of course, you want to stay here to breathe vac. I'm Hadraysa—'Captain,' to you—and we're on a tight schedule." She glanced at Murphy. "Korelon sends his regards."

There it is; the first of the code phrases the RockHounds sent. "I missed Korelon the last time he was on *Spin One*."

"That's because he was avoiding you!" Hadraysa completed the required exchange with a convincingly brusque laugh. "Get your gear aboard. Jabrael will help you secure it."

Jabrael, a silent Hound-Dog of uncertain origins, nodded and waited.

Bowden put out his hand to Cutter. "Try to come back in one piece, Captain."

"Always uppermost on my mind, sir."

Murphy nodded back toward the hatch of the observation gallery: two dockhands were waiting. "Better get out while there's still oxygen in this barn."

"No convincing needed!" Bowden replied, already halfway through the hatch. "I'll update you in a few days, Colonel."

Actually, a few more than that. Which Bowden would learn when a message popped up on his system in an hour, directing him toward a letter explaining Murphy's absence, albeit without detailing it in full.

With all his command staff gone, Murphy fell in alongside Cutter as he walked to the surprisingly compact delta-shaped craft with its nose aimed at the bay doors. "Tyree, do you get seasick?"

"Only in the boat heading toward Omaha Beach, sir."

"Then you'll be fine. I think."

"Fine for what?" Cutter said sharply.

"The final stage of your landing. The ride down should be easy; the lifting body and ablative shielding is designed for a smoother descent. The final drogue chute detects your attitude to ensure you almost glide down to the water. But for safety's sake, it will put you down anywhere between two to five klicks offshore."

Cutter had heard it all before and was obviously wondering why he was hearing it yet again. "Yes, and...?"

"Satellites show a storm rolling in near your landing footprint. Current predictions say it will miss you, but the water might be...well, more choppy than we anticipated."

"Can't we delay the drop?"

Murphy shook his head. "Remember how hard it was to find a window to get in behind the rock the Hound-Dogs boosted, which would also put you at the optimal insertion point? Well, it would take almost three weeks to put together all those elements again."

"Great," Cutter muttered as Jabrael pointed how to best enter the spacecraft.

Murphy heard the anxiety that had crept into the captain's voice. "There's no chance the pod will sink, it's got its own guidance to motor you to shore, and you'll have a rudimentary periscope to stay oriented. But it could get rough. So, even if you feel the pod graze the bottom and you're eager to get out, don't pop the hatch until you're firmly grounded. A green light will come on when the sensor is satisfied the pod is immobilized."

"Sounds foolproof, sir," Cutter drawled sardonically. "Care to come along for the ride?"

"I am, Captain."

Cutter stopped, one long leg inside the ship. "Seriously, sir? All the way to R'Bak?"

"Well," Murphy drawled, "not dirtside. But until you're dropped, yes." He smiled. "This way, before I head to *Spin Two*, we have plenty of time to review the details of your mission."

"Roger that, sir," Cutter sighed. He sounded as if he was scheduled for a root canal.

Murphy followed him into the ship, the techs sealing the hatch behind them.

RockHound packet Darkseek, R'Bak orbit

There was a slight bump when Cutter's pod detached from Hadraysa's small ship. "And he's away," she declared.

Other than the pilot's very low, streamlined canopy, there was no way to see outside. So Murphy could only imagine the tapering, flattened pod beginning to glow as it descended, nose-up, toward the black nighttime expanse of R'Bak's Great Eastern Ocean.

"How long to...well, wherever we're going?" Murphy called up into the cockpit. It was too small to think of as a "bridge."

"You'll know that when we arrive," Hadraysa called back with a sly smile. "And we won't be moving toward it for a while yet: we have to follow with the debris that skipped off the atmosphere until we're safe away from the inhabited parts of the planet and have its mass between us and Downport. Then a few puffs of our attitude thrusters will nudge us into the shadow of one of the midget moons. Once there, we can burn hard."

Murphy settled back, glad he'd brought reading material.

It promised to be a long journey.

Surveyor packet **Kunsheft,** V'dyr orbit

Le'Bal Trenks, Senior Wa'hrep of the surveyor commerce packet *Kunsheft,* opened the narrow hatch of his vessel's small bridge. *More like a cockpit,* he thought, squeezing around the back of his XO's seat. His second officer, Saldazn, was typical of most G'Talls: an overachiever and far more capable than his rank suggested. That was the fate of those who had a parent from the ungroomed bloodlines of the southern continent. And Trenks was happy to be the beneficiary of Saldazn's abilities: those with his own pure parentage were typically reluctant subordinates.

"Status?" Trenks demanded as he lowered himself into the slightly more spacious pilot's seat. "And why is the damned blister cover still closed?"

Saldazn nodded sharply "Regulations, sir. Rad spike is still too high. Regarding status, I am completing calculations to alter orbit to bring us to our planetfall point, Lord."

"Lord": just hearing that made Trenks feel a bit more alert, a bit more alive. A G'Tall like Saldazn wasn't strictly required to affix that honorific, but the navigator/sensor operator had learned quickly enough that whatever made his captain feel happy made his own life that much more pleasant. "Any projection on the rad levels?"

"They are fading, Lord. I suspect we shall be able to withdraw the blister shields within the hour."

Within the hour? So sixty more minutes of staring at the dull gray covers? Trenks managed not to sigh. Not that looking at V'dyr was much better. It had a fair share of gray in its cloud-cluttered atmosphere: only two orbits out from Shex, the hot world's scant water was overwhelmingly captive to a ceaseless cycle of vaporization and torrential downpours. "And have you found any traces of the lost ships?"

"None, Lord. The wreckage of both the lighter and the corvette appears to have deorbited. While I have detected some pieces, that is all they were. Just pieces."

"Do you find it odd that there is nothing remaining of the corvette?" Trenks asked. "Because I do."

"I will admit that it is strange. Even if they were crippled, both craft deorbited very quickly," Saldazn replied. "Of course, if they were docked, then it is quite plausible that both were destroyed by the same occurrence. A catastrophic engine failure, an impact by uncharted debris spawned by this Searing: either incident might not only reduce them to junk, but push the remains toward V'dyr."

Trenks nodded reluctantly. "Which would also explain why they had no time to send a radio message, alerting the worker crews on the planet. But still, those on V'dyr might have seen the debris burning as it fell."

Saldazn shrugged. "Yes, but with the workers restricted to the temperate—well, survivable—poles, the wreckage might have fallen at middle latitude they could not see. And even if its descent was within their field of vision, they might have dismissed it as more of the new meteorites from this Searing or missed it entirely if it was daytime."

He swept his eyes over the sensor feeds again, as if some new contact might appear in one of them. "But I do agree, Lord; it is still strange that there are no traces at all. Given its size, there should have been something left of the corvette, at least."

When Trenks remained silent, Saldazn asked, "What are you thinking, Lord?"

"I'm thinking this may be proof that there are others in the system who wish us ill."

"Do you think it is these 'Others' that are rumored to have come to R'Bak? Maybe they are now operating around this planet, as well?"

"No, I do not think that there are ghosts or old wives' tales in orbit around V'dyr," Trenks said. "I do, however, think it is possible a group of reavers has gone rogue and may be hiding out nearby. Perhaps they are trying to cut their own deals with the locals."

"With respect, Lord, we have not seen any sign of that on R'Bak."

"That does not mean it has not happened out here, though." Trenks shrugged. "If they were able to get a corvette full of the local drugs back to Kulsis, they could sell them for a fortune on the black market. That might be enough to finance...many things."

"I see," Saldazn said. "What do you intend to do?"

Trenks scoffed. "With this undersized cargo vessel? I will tell you what I do *not* intend to do. I am not going to go looking for trouble. We would be no match for even a poorly armed and led corvette. They would reduce us to dust before we even got close."

Trenks shook his head. "No, this is a problem for the Harvester fleet to solve when it gets here."

"So we are going to leave?"

"We are going to continue with our mission," Trenks said with a smile. "However, that doesn't mean we can't make it easier for the fleet when they arrive. Prepare four of our snoop platforms. We will leave two of them in orbit here and send two back toward R'Bak."

"The cost of that..." Saldazn muttered.

"The cost of *not* doing it might be worse," Trenks interrupted. "I do not want the missing corvette to reappear suddenly and catch us unaware when we are loaded. And if the platforms generate some intel on the pirates, we may stand to be reimbursed for their use, as well." He shrugged again. "As long as they help us leave without being attacked, they are worth the expense."

"It will be done as you say." Saldazn was turning toward the satellite deployment controls when the automated long-range optics scanner pinged.

"What is it?"

"A flash, Lord. Very distant."

"Where?"

"R'Bak, apparently descending from near orbit."

"More junk from the new Searing?"

Saldazn pursed his lips. "It was too brief and too distant to be certain, Lord. If so, it was somewhat atypical."

"In what way?"

Saldazn pointed at his sensor board, even though Trenks could not read it from where he sat. "The flash was not only bright, but the object causing it continued to glow. Meteorites typically burn up very quickly, if they are as small as this light output suggests."

Trenks waved a dismissive hand at Saldazn's sensors. "I have seen that before. Fragments of a nickel-iron asteroid may burn up that way, particularly if there is an unusually high concentration of metal at its core. It lasts a bit longer and may be a bit brighter when it comes apart. Unusual, but not an anomaly.

"Now lay in that course to the polar insertion point. I want to be loaded and heading back to R'Bak in two days. The sooner we get away from what might be a pirate's hunting grounds, the easier I will sleep."

PART TWO

Maneuver

Chapter Nineteen

Kulsis

Ebis'qupoz Kurop't Barogar resisted the urge to fling his packet down on the reflective surface of the glistenwood table that ran the length of the Syfarthan Combine's secure meeting chamber. The faces around it were mostly those he'd met with previously, but were now either expressionless or sheepish. The latter was not only gratifying but proper: Barogar had warned them the price of their inaction would be to return here, but under far less salutary conditions. He'd been all too correct, as was proven by the new faces at the table.

Barogar surveyed the haughty representatives of the Overlords of Kulsis. Six months ago, they still had not deemed the silence, and presumed loss, of the coursers sent to R'Bak worthy of their attention. But clearly, they deemed it worthy now. No less than three representatives from the Syfarthan Combine were present, and the expressions on their faces—and so, all the others'—indicated that they no longer considered the irregular events in the Shex system a mere "nuisance."

But nothing signified the dramatically increased priority so much as the presence of Imgeffa, Prime Guild-mother and Matriarch of the Syfartha Family, who nodded at him. "On behalf of the Overlords whose representatives are gathered here, we thank you for your tenacity in this matter, Ebis'qupoz Barogar." She squinted around the table. "Would that all those charged with oversight of Harvesting in the Shex system had your dedication and foresight."

Barogar acknowledged her praise with a long, respectful nod. Although not an Overlord herself, she was the greatest living Breedmistress and a power unto herself—particularly among those whose Families were highly reliant upon breedsensing. "I am honored to appear before you, Matriarch Imgeffa, and gratified to be summoned back to this high council."

She smiled at the word "gratified." Half a year ago, he'd been ridiculed for wasting the time of the collected *eqzarqu*, who collectively set protocols and handled disputes arising from Harvesting operations. Now, it was they who had to endure his oblique but unmistakable gibes.

Imgeffa nodded. "I hear your words and what simmers beneath them, Ebis'qupoz Barogar." She leaned back; for a moment, her face looked every bit as worn as one hundred forty-one years had made it. "I have also heard and read how the eqzarqu of this chamber synopsized your last appearance before them. But there are inconsistencies between their summary and the latest intelligence we have from the Shex system. So I will trouble you to present the situation as you perceive it, loyal son of Kulsis."

Barogar managed not to preen. "It would be my honor to do so. As I am a military man, I am not skilled in grandiose language and flattery, so I hope my blunt report will not offend."

Imgeffa's turned a small, icy smile upon the eqzarqu. "Trust me, Ebis'qupoz, bluntness will be most welcome."

He nodded. "The urgency of what brings us together now—the loss of one of the two surveyor corvettes fitted with an experimental auxiliary fusion plant—arises from what came before. Since that may not have been communicated in full, I present it now.

"Less than a week after our coursers arrived in orbit around R'Bak, we lost all contact with them: an unprecedented occurrence. Opinions were divided over the cause. One hypothesis was that a slow-moving plague on the planet had been carried up to the courser ships before it was detected. However, those of us with field experience doubted the viability of such an explanation. Frankly, there is no record of any pathogen that our personnel could have contracted from a local population that showed no sign of such a plague, then remained dormant in the coursers long enough for them to carry back to their ships, and finally emerged and spread so quickly and fatally that no one on those vessels got a chance to send word of it.

"Several learned persons in the Syfarthan Combine's operations braintrust floated a rival explanation: that Shex had experienced an immense coronal mass ejection, or CME. They conjectured that the electromagnetic pulse would have destroyed all the coursers' electronics, including their radios and both microwave and laser line-of-sight comms.

"However, that hypothesis was even more problematic than the notion of a plague. A CME would almost certainly have appeared on our sensors here in the Jrar system, as we were nearing periapsis with Shex. This would be true even if the CME propagated on a vector facing directly away from Jrar. Furthermore, the majority of our ships are hardened against solar storms and keep spares of all comm systems off-grid and in Faraday cages for just such occurrences.

"A third, unsought conjecture arose among experienced ship commanders: that there had been a schism among the coursers, with those loyal to the Overlords being overcome by rebels—who, wisely, remained silent and began operating as pirates."

High Lord Makatayth, technically the most senior representative from the Syfarthan Combine, frowned. "But it was your own command staff who discounted that third explanation. And you yourself dissented, claiming that the bush-beaters were not capable of such a coup."

Barogar strove to keep his tone respectful. "I did not dissent, High Lord. I merely pointed out that the schism hypothesis presented unresolved quandaries." Not the least of which had been political practicality; the captains' thesis had been phrased with more force and certainty than the facts had supported at that time. In response, the eqzarqu had quashed it swiftly, more concerned with its reek of successful revolt than its logistical improbabilities.

Makatayth leaned forward. "And do these quandaries concerning the bush-beaters remain?"

"They do," Barogar affirmed, barely managing a deferential nod. "A coup among the 'bush-beaters'"—*ridiculous not to call them what they are: reavers*—"would be almost impossible to keep silent. Mutiny, per the Overlords' directives, is one of the very few occurrences that warrants inter-system radio communications. Keeping such treason quiet would require rank-and-file coursers to have control over all comms, both spaceside and dirtside. Control protocols preclude that. The only alternative would be if the mutiny was led by the coursers' officers. But in that event, they could simply have maintained normal comms; we would have had no way of knowing they had rebelled until the surveyors arrived."

"Who found no evidence that our loyalty-screened cadre had mutinied," Makatayth pointed out preemptively. "And whose flotilla we dispatched to Shex with all haste." He turned to Imgeffa. "As I hope the summary indicated, when the matter was put before the First Lords' Council, we authorized Ebis'qupoz Barogar to increase the security complement of the surveyors he rushed to Shex."

A wild exaggeration, but I dare not contradict: only state the facts. "I fast-tracked an early surveyor flotilla with two primary frames carrying eight independent ships each, along with a few dozen packets and smaller interface craft. The flotilla's total complement was eighteen hundred personnel, with one hundred forty-two more security specialists than usual." *Which was the most you'd allow, Makatayth—you lying sack of devolving genes.*

Imgeffa frowned. "I have heard that this increase in security ships and combat-capable landing teams came at the expense of prospecting and resource collection experts. Is this true?"

Barogar nodded sharply. "Yes, Matriarch. I am partly responsible for that decision."

"Partly?"

He nodded again. *Fate and filth: please don't ask me to name names...*

The Matriarch either saw or intuited that pressing for more details would send the meeting into a downward spiral of blame-trading. "I presume, then, that the surveyors actually essential to the job of preparing shipments for the Harvester fleet were over-tasked?"

"They were, and not just because there were fewer such personnel. The security forces were ordered to discover what had happened to the coursers, but the situation they found was so unexpected and difficult that they often commandeered equipment and personnel from the scouting and gathering task forces."

Imgeffa leaned forward. "Explain."

"The barbarian tribes had revolted at roughly the same time our coursers arrived. The satraps in the lands we call the Greens have been unseated or are either under siege or isolated from each other. Our stronger and more important allies that lie farther south, in the Ashbands and the Hamain, have also been reduced. Most that remain give conflicting reports of the causes and events of this uprising. The surveyors' security detachments not only found themselves in uncertain conditions, but often unwelcome."

"Unwelcome?" Makatayth exclaimed indignantly. "Why do our forces tolerate such responses?"

"Because they lack the numbers to punish them," Barogar replied flatly. "Some teams have been lost without a trace. And many satraps are now uncertain who it is more important to appease: us or the barbarians." The silence that followed was satisfying: *Finally, they are perceiving the severity of the situation.*

"Upon receiving these assessments, I discontinued any further investigation into the disappearance of the coursers, particularly in the lands currently controlled or contested by the savages. As it is, we have barely enough security personnel to protect our scouts and gatherers, upon whose work a successful Harvester fleet depends." *And which finally brought you back to this table.*

Makatayth leaned forward. "And is there no sign of unrest on R'Bak Island?"

Barogar, feeling himself an equal in the room, finally sat. "None that has been reported."

Imgeffa heard the nuance that Makatayth predictably missed. "Not having report of something does not mean it does not exist." She ended on a hint of a smile.

Great lady, you could not help me more had we scripted it ahead of time. "You are correct, Matriarch. Indeed, it is an incident on R'Bak Island—at Downport, to be precise—that may finally point to why the coursers went silent and vanished without a trace."

"You refer to the seizure of a lighter, sometime after it lifted?"

"Yes, and the detailed and knowledgeable planning that preceded it. And probably the loss of the corvette several days later."

Makatayth frowned. "But the corvette was assisting the lighter, responding to its distress call."

"So they believed."

Imgeffa squinted. "You suspect it was a ruse?"

"I do."

"To what end?"

Barogar shrugged. "To attack the corvette."

Makatayth scoffed. "That would be suicide. The only way a lighter could destroy a corvette would be by triggering a catastrophic containment breach in its own engine."

"I did not say the lighter's purpose was to destroy the corvette, but to *attack* it. With the intent of taking it."

"And who would have the nerve—or the training—to even conceive of such a plot?" Makatayth balled up his fists, their image doubled by the glistenwood table. "Ebis'qupoz, you promised us sober, well-reasoned analysis—"

"And that is exactly what you are getting, First Lord. If you will hear it out."

Imgeffa grinned before anyone else could reply. "I, for one, am intrigued to hear the Ebis'qupoz's hypothesis."

Barogar nodded his gratitude toward her. "There can be little doubt that the lighter was stolen to facilitate the seizure of the corvette. The preparations were meticulous and subtle. Unfortunately, the surveyors' initial investigation provided few additional facts."

"Why so?"

Barogar shrugged. "Those that were questioned revealed little."

Makatayth's fists rose slightly. "And have the surveyors' commanders forgotten that torture is the most effective tool in such circumstances?"

Barogar decided not to correct the First Lord, who obviously had never learned that a subject in the throes of agony—and certain that more is imminent—will say anything to stop the pain. "Those interrogated were not withholding knowledge. They simply did not have any. Those suspected of helping the hijackers infiltrate the spaceport were either dead or missing. Most of the latter probably fled as soon as they completed their role in the operation. Several of those had mercantile connections in the city, but mostly within its black market."

Imgeffa frowned. "But we have excellent contacts inside the black market, do we not?"

"We do, but most of those are accessed through our allies: the satraps and other legitimate powers who tend to be durable over time. But the black market itself is not a stable or a predictable entity. Given the constant churn and change between Searings, we are lucky if, in any given city, two such organizations' origins reach back as far as the prior Harvester fleet. And it did not help our current investigation that weeks passed before the corvette's loss was confirmed."

One of the less cowed eqzarqu asked, "Why was it not reported immediately?"

Barogar let his eyes drift toward the fellow. "The corvette was a silent asset, Eqzarq. In layman's terms, the surveyor's senior commander knows it is on patrol, but not its exact location. And the captain of the corvette was the senior naval officer in-system."

Makatayth scoffed. "And is there no contingency for either side to initiate communication if needed?"

"The corvette can, but not the dirtside authorities. Access to a silent patrol vessel's coordinates for line-of-sight communications is rightly considered an unacceptable risk to its security. Conversely, neither ground nor space platforms have ever had a sufficiently urgent need to send a message to such craft."

"And why was such security deemed necessary, since there has never been a single spaceside threat in the Shex system?"

Barogar nodded toward Makatayth. "I agree, First Lord: our doctrinal complacency on that matter is what led us to this pass. On the other hand, imagine what might have occurred if the extraordinary effort and subtle conspiracy used to seize the lighter could have been exerted to gain access to secret codes revealing the location of the corvette—had such codes existed."

"No matter! A corvette is more than a match for any pirates, no matter how sly!"

Barogar paused a moment, making sure he neither smiled nor frowned as he asked, "You and your peers keep using the word 'pirate,' High Lord. Why do you insist upon that term?"

Makatayth started. "What other term suits, Ebis'qupoz? If the lighter was indeed used to lure in and take the corvette, they cannot simply be thieves. As you pointed out in the report you sent as the reason for this meeting, they were not merely capable pilots. They navigated to a precise position just off the second planet so that the lighter was in its detection and radio shadow when the corvette commenced rescue operations. Such skills are not acquired through a few quick dirtside lessons on a simulator; it was the work of experienced pilots who were already familiar with both craft."

Barogar nodded. "I agree."

"You ought to: you wrote it!"

"Yes, but pirates are not defined simply by the skills they possess, but their motivations and, particularly, the way they solve problems. And you may trust me on this: in neither regard do these perpetrators behave as would what you call 'pirates.'"

Makatayth seemed ready to object, but Imgeffa gestured him to silence.

"Firstly," Barogar began, "what motivates pirates? The promise of wealth, yes? And certainly, a corvette is a valuable ship.

"But to whom would they sell it? The illiterate locals on R'Bak who are still uncertain whether electricity is a natural force or magic? Or interested parties here on Kulsis, presenting it for auction in the Great Bourse or a spaceside shipyard? As if anyone involved in the trade or sale of vessels doesn't know that the Overlords would publicly flay anyone who engaged in such business? Or that they would fail to richly reward those who reported it?

"And where would these 'pirates' spend their ill-gotten gains? Here, where we track every form of value with great precision? Or R'Bak, where it might buy them all the uncut gems and raw pharmaflora they could want—but without any way to trade it for anything they value?"

Imgeffa let her gaze make a slow circuit of the faces at the table. Most averted their eyes. "Continue, Ebis'qupoz Barogar."

He rose. "These are compelling reasons not to label these ship-thieves pirates, but they are not the most decisive. Because whatever their reasons for seizing the corvette, we must also ask: how do they live? Presumably, pirates make their homes near their hunting grounds. In space, this means locations where they may come and go subtly, without leaving fiery trails as they depart from or return to planets.

"But therein lies the problem. For even if we assume that they have automated plants to liberate oxygen and moisture from moons or asteroids—and that is a sizable assumption—we must answer this: how do they mean to eat? And if they know our Harvesters are coming, how do they mean to hide for the two or three years that we gather wealth from R'Bak?"

When no one offered an answer, he provided the alternatives. "There are two possibilities. One is that they are both motivated and convinced that they can lay aside the many tonnes of food required to live a life no pirate would tolerate: hiding motionless for up to three years. Or they do not live in space after all—which takes us further away from what we think of when we speak of 'pirates.'"

One of the less outspoken, but also less cautious, of the eqzarqu muttered, "They'd have to have been preparing for years before the Searing, to lay in enough supplies. And yet, no one saw them do so? There are no reports of planetfalls of launches? Of interactions with communities who have surpluses to trade?"

Imgeffa nodded sharply. "I am convinced. These are not pirates. But then, what are they?"

Barogar shrugged. "An enemy force that has remained hidden. Until now."

Chapter Twenty

Kulsis

"An enemy force?" Makatayth snorted. "From where?"

Barogar stared him down. "Where else? Where we ourselves came from, fleeing the Death Fathers. What were we before our Exodate became the masters of this world? Another, smaller Exodate could have arrived at Shex since the last Searing." He shrugged. "Or these enemies could have come from Kulsis itself."

"You mean, the descendants of those who failed to return with a prior Searing?"

"It is impossible to speculate until we have more information. However, over the centuries, there have been numerous missing ships, convoys, freighters, and groups of scouts and gatherers. If some of those losses were in fact desertions, and if some of the ships or other vehicles were not damaged but spirited into concealed locations, a considerable population of such exiles could exist. And if they were able to maintain a reasonable body of knowledge and significant repository of technology, they would have the run of the Shex system in our absence." He shrugged. "It could continue indefinitely, so long as they were careful where and when they interacted with the locals."

Makatayth's dubiousness was at least partly feigned. "Do you believe they could truly become so self-sufficient that they would never have to reveal themselves to satraps who would report them to us?"

"If they have aircraft or spacecraft, they could intercept single ships or distant caravans or even sweep up remote villages across the face of R'Bak a dozen times a year...and there would be no one left to report. And even if some eyewitnesses escaped to tell the tale, would such an account persist twenty, or even ten years to reach the ears of our next group of surveyors? So, if they began curtailing their activities even fifteen years ago, would our current Harvesters have any chance to hear of them now? And if they did, would they believe the reports or dismiss it as tales told by ingenuous barbarians?"

Imgeffa was frowning even as she nodded. "This presumes that such a community could persist even though none of its present members could still be alive from the prior Searing. Many complex skills—such as piloting—could be lost, or at least degraded. And would they dare to persist going to and from space, for fear of inspiring legends that might last among the barbarians?"

Barogar nodded. "My own wonderings precisely, Matriarch. But if the community keeps using its most crucial vehicles—and so, skills—in the interludes between Searings, they might very well retain a high level of aptitude. And there are details in the current surveyors' reports which suggest just that.

"For instance, none of the coursers' satellites were still in orbit when the surveyors arrived. Given the conjectures of a CME, it was—dubiously—theorized that they might have been disabled while they were all correcting their vectors to maintain stable orbits. But if we presume a hidden community of spacefarers, it is far more likely that they destroyed the satellites...because it would be foolish for them *not* to do so. After all, they would have to assume that any orbital platform might have recorded them ambushing and destroying the coursers. For the same reason, they would make every effort to ensure that any incriminating debris burned up in R'Bak's atmosphere."

Imgeffa rubbed her seamed and wrinkled chin. "If they retain the ability to come and go as they please, from R'Bak to space and back again, they could conceivably be hidden anywhere. But they would be wisest to choose places where they have air, water, and food, and yet are unlikely to encounter either barbarians or us." Her hand stopped beside her jaw. "The second planet, V'dyr: could that be their refuge?"

"It is a possibility," Barogar admitted, admiring the elder

stateswoman's nimble mind. "But the portion of the surface where humans may survive are relatively small regions at both poles. However, the surveyors always send work crews there to assess if there are enough valuable resources to justify the effort of gathering and boosting them to orbit. Those teams have never seen any sign of other visitors."

She nodded. "What about R'Bak's equator? It is acceptably temperate when the Searing passes, is it not?"

Clever old girl. "That is a most charitable characterization, but yes, there are places where it is more tolerable: islands and an isthmus that links the largest northern and southern continents. But that is a great deal of territory to assess."

Imgeffa lifted her chin. "I am not sure that I would be convinced by your thesis, Ebis'qupoz Barogar, were it not for the timing of the uprisings in the Ashbands and the Greens. Tell me: what do you make of this unprecedented chaos among the satraps upon whom we most depend, other than those who watch over Downport in our absence?"

Barogar nodded. "It does speak to and support the idea that our adversaries have not only considerable familiarity with the planet but with the way we operate there. Their timing and targets—including the destruction of what may have been an almost-completed makeshift signaling device—suggest careful and purposeful planning."

Makatayth finally sounded more involved than defensive. "Yet it also seems to indicate that concealing their existence is no longer as high a concern for our enemies. The uprising, the interdiction of the coursers, the seizure of the corvette: these are all bold, overt acts."

One of the eqzarqu leaned forward. "Yes, but they may also be driven by the need to compensate for having overstepped the margins in which they may operate safely. Specifically, if enough coursers survived to actually begin constructing an inter-system radio, all the subsequent actions may be part of an attempt to erase any definitive intelligence regarding their existence."

Makatayth nodded. "Well-reasoned. Creating the uncertainties we grapple with now may have been their object. We *believe* that what was left of our coursers *might* have been trying to put together a signaling platform, but we do not know. We *believe* the tribes of the Ashbands are better led than ever before, and *may* be better armed as well because it is *possible* they seized the caches we left behind—but again, we do not know."

Barogar crossed his arms. "No, we *know* they are better armed. Much better." He spun a photograph toward the center of the table. The faces tilted forward, assessing the image: a battle rifle of some kind.

"This looks quite dated," Makatayth sneered. "Possibly weapons for reserve units garrisoned in the south."

"Except that weapon is not one of ours," Barogar insisted. "The weapon is unique. It is actually quite well designed. Wooden furniture with a twenty-round magazine. It is without factory marks and uses a round with admirably flat trajectory, accuracy, and lethality. They have been found in barbarian hands in every region where there has been an uprising. Reportedly, the units equipped with them are more disciplined and adhere to prudent move-and-fire tactics, although there is no way to assess the accuracy of that claim."

Makatayth sniffed. "And how many of these unusual weapons have been reported? A few hundred?"

Barogar shook his head. "Many thousands."

Imgeffa's comment sounded strangled. "That implies a significant industrial capacity, if true."

Makatayth nodded at her caveat. "As you say, Matriarch: 'if true.' Every Searing, the surveyors report the panicked yammerings of satraps that are less motivated by their promise to provide truthful information than to make themselves seem blameless for failing to meet their quotas." He waved away Barogar's photograph and his many other documents. "Regardless of their station, R'Baku are all lesser beings, and so, inveterate liars."

Which Barogar found amusing; the First Lord was renowned as the most accomplished prevaricator among the seasoned deceivers of the Syfarthan Combine's High Lords' Council. "The High Lord's reference to lesser beings may not simply refer to R'Baku, in this case."

Imgeffa's eyes cut quickly in his direction. "Do you refer to those on our own planet?" Barogar nodded. "You promised to speak bluntly, Ebis'qupoz: do so now."

"I shall, but with this caveat: What I have presented thus far has all been deduced from proven data."

"And what you present now is pure speculation?"

"Yes, Matriarch."

"I am eager to hear it."

Remember you said that. "I have given thought to how such a community as I have projected could continue to expand, particularly when it comes to recruiting new members from subsequent Searings. And only one thing makes ready sense."

Imgeffa saw it before he had to utter the dread words. "They are dissenters. And so, disproportionately from the south, from Waadtheru."

"But how would that be?" Makatayth almost shouted.

"How would it not, First Lord? The Harvester fleet disproportionately recruits from Kulsis' own southern continent. Where else is life so miserable that skilled persons will risk their lives for as many as five or six years with the Harvester fleet or those groups that precede it?"

Makatayth sucked in his breath slowly. "They are the majority of our surveyors."

"And almost the sole source of our 'bush-beaters,'" Barogar added archly. "All lesser beings. Sent to a planet of lesser beings."

Imgeffa articulated what no one else dared. "So, you are proposing that the origins and coherence of our enemies and R'Bak is rooted in our own planet's separatists and dissenters? That their motivations are not so much piratical or mercantile as they are political?"

"It is a possibility, Matriarch."

"It is a wild supposition! As you say, it is not based upon facts!" Makatayth's voice had risen a pitch. As the most senior overseer of Harvesting operations, his name would figure prominently when the historical trends of casualties were analyzed. Because it would reveal what Barogar had discovered while preparing for the briefing: a massive preponderance of the "missing, presumed dead" casualties from the first Searing onward were natives of Waadtheru. The land where lesser beings were sent. The place that got its name from a shortening of the phrase "to live beneath the boot."

Imgeffa's glance at the First Lord was one she might have reserved for a turd in a soup bowl. Having silence him, she asked, "Why would they show themselves now, Ebis'qupoz Barogar?"

He shrugged. "They may be growing too numerous. They may have found the corvette to be too tempting. For all we know, it could be an attempt to cover a mistake, or a rogue operation that became too weary—or greedy—to live in hiding any longer."

"So, they either planned the uprising or felt the need to raise it to cover their other actions."

"Or, if they are indeed descendants of deserters from Waadtheru, it could be a means of striking at us the only way they can: taking away the Overlords' assurance of dominance."

The Matriarch's neck tightened into a mass of desiccated cords; she suddenly seemed more mummy than living woman. "You mean, they intend to strangle our supply of Catalysites, to eliminate our capacity for Reifications, for breedsensing." She seemed to be saying it to herself, as if that was the only way to make such a horror real.

"Yes, but that might not be their only, or even their key, objective anymore. If our Harvester fleet is a failure, it is their success. It signifies that the cornerstone of this chamber's power—the wealth that comes from the harvests—has been undercut. What follows cannot be predicted. It certainly would encourage lesser families and dissidents. That in turn could lead to internal disputes over rival policies for managing the emerging crisis.

"And of course, there is the financial dimension. What we cannot adequately secure for trade, the deserters on R'Bak can. And if the savages perceive that, which among their satraps and chiefs will continue to fear us more than the local masters of technology? Masters who will be deadly to them for eighty years, whereas they would feel our wrath for only eight." Barogar shrugged. "In time, there may come a Harvester fleet that arrives to find that the deserters have removed all the pharmaflora and gathered all the Catalysites."

"Or destroyed them." Every face turned toward Imgeffa, horrified as much by her words as her tomb-like voice. "There is logic behind such a strategy: If the Overlords can no longer gather Catalysites, it is likely they would cease to bear the expense and risk of sending a fleet. But there is also vengeance: since they are irremediably lesser beings and cannot use the Catalysites to groom their own genecode, they shall destroy them. Out of sheer spite."

"And we have no target to strike?" Makatayth asked as if just awakening to that fact.

Barogar managed not to sneer. "We cannot determine that until we arrive. Which brings us to the most important part of our meeting."

Imgeffa was struggling to remain composed. Speaking apparently helped. "We must settle the composition of the Harvester fleet."

"Yes. It must be changed to address this situation. Oddly, our adversaries have made our decisions somewhat easier."

"How so?" muttered the quiet eqzarq.

"In most of the regions from which we typically take resources, we now lack adequate security for gathering them. Consequently, we must focus on controlling the sites where we find our priority harvesting items. Areas that contain only secondary and tertiary resources shall be ignored."

"That's a seventy percent cargo reduction!" Makatayth almost moaned, no doubt anticipating the full scope of the impending fiscal disaster. "Just how does that *help* us?"

"It gives us the freedom to craft a flotilla structured for offensive operations, as well as planetside and spaceside searches. We shall be optimized to find the sources of these disruptions and exterminate them in such a way that no one will ever think of trying cases with us again."

Imgeffa nodded stiffly. "And how do you mean to do that? They were hidden before. They are no doubt hidden now."

"That is true. And to maximize the odds of finding them, we must address another weakness of our fleet: the time it requires."

Imgeffa's eyes sharpened. "It must leave sooner. The more time we spend debating small matters and picayune points of personal interest, the more it is likely that our enemies have hidden themselves." The eyes that bore into Barogar's were those of a raptor with one last kill in it. "So: you intend to arrive before they believe we could."

He nodded. "We must launch this fleet with all possible speed."

"How quickly can it be done?"

"Sixty days, maximum."

"S-sixty days?" Makatayth stuttered. "I know something of logistics; we could barely get enough ships in place in that time. Many of them are still being outfitted for the mission."

"Yes, First Lord, but that, too has become simpler. You were outfitting the landers and cargo haulers for a multipurposed mission with a far longer duration. Now that we are resolved to collecting a greatly reduced volume of goods, we can carry more weapons and fuel in their place."

"And if there are hardships? If supplies are insufficient?"

"Then we shall exert dominion and seize what we must. Happily, I will have no shortage of forces with which to effect that."

Barogar stood very tall, looked around the table. "Do not forget: our enemy had the cooperation of many thousands of barbarians. It was they who have rebelled and taken towns, even cities, in the Ashbands and Greens.

"A lesson once understood by the R'Baku is clearly in need of firm reteaching. I am not speaking of the cullings of the past. Or of the fiscally prudent restraint in conducting them. This time, it is the Harvester fleet's blunt, brutal necessity to terrify every tribal savage into revealing whatever they know, or see, or simply suspect regarding our foes. They must know, by bloody example, that their lives depend on being as complete and unstinting in their cooperation as possible, and that any who show the faintest hesitation shall join the others in the festering midden heap of corpses we shall leave in our wake."

Imgeffa's eyes had brightened. "It sounds as though you have a plan, Ebis'qupoz Barogar."

"I do, Matriarch, and I mean to execute it with great vigor."

She raised a cadaverous, cautioning finger. "I heard the emphasis you put on the word 'execute.' Be careful not to be so bloody-minded that you do not raise the entire planet in revolt against us."

"I assure you, the R'Baku shall not become rebels."

Because if I have to kill every last one of the savages to prevent it, that is exactly what I will do.

Chapter Twenty-One

Shuqdu Station

Without preamble, Hadraysa turned her head so that it was pro-
filed against the fine dusting of stars showing through the bridge
canopy. "This will be your one chance to see Shuqdu Station,
Rodger Murphy."

Murphy closed the book he'd been reading, hearing the tone
of invitation in the captain's voice. He pushed himself gently
toward the cockpit-sized "bridge," drifting toward the navigator/
comm operator's seat just behind her.

"Secure yourself," Hadraysa instructed. It had taken a while
to become accustomed to her brusque manner. From what little
she'd shared, she was from a sect of RockHounds whose dedication to equality and self-reliance bordered on a religion. They
only used a title on a first meeting, refused to follow a Legate's
orders except on a case-by-case basis, and almost all eschewed
life on stations. Instead, they inhabited small outposts, often no
bigger than two or three nuclear families. Her sole crewmember,
Jabrael, was mute, extremely introverted, but very capable. It was
quite possible that he was autistic and so, another example of the
breedsensing inequities with which the RockHounds contended.

As Murphy strapped into one of the two rear seats offset to
either side of the pilot's, she glanced at his book. "Still reading
that make-believe story?" Another way in which her sect was

reminiscent of some orthodox religious groups: fiction was deemed an idle distraction from the serious work of living a productive life. "What is it called?"

Murphy smiled. "*Treasure Island.* It's about pirates."

She snorted. "I am surprised you trifle with such distractions, Rodger Murphy. They are beneath the interest of a commander."

He smiled. "We think otherwise. In addition to being entertainment, stories can be useful."

"How so?"

"To relax. To experience how others lived and thought in times past. To ask and ponder questions freed from the prejudices of the time in which one lives."

She sighed. "Yours is a failing not uncommon among notable commanders. The same depth of thought that makes you excellent leaders also makes you more likely to be philosophers. Regrettably."

He laughed. "I think that's the first time anyone ever called me a 'philosopher.'"

She half-turned to show him a broad smile. "Then perhaps there is hope for you yet. Now, attend: can you see the station up ahead? Low at the center of the canopy?"

He had to squint to make out the long, cigar-shaped rock that grew as he watched. Only when Hadraysa puffed the attitude thrusters to bring them in line with its long axis did Murphy notice it was spinning, and then only because the change in viewpoint revealed the movement of the shadows on its rough surface. "It will be nice to stand in some gee-equivalent again."

"It's barely point two," she remarked. "And you might find it a bit disorienting. Shuqdu is actually tumbling in all three axes, but the yaw and pitch are so gradual that only the most experienced RockHounds can see it with the naked eye. But inside, it's just enough to trick your inner ear and your eye. It takes getting used to." She shrugged. "Of course, you won't have the chance."

"So I'm not to see the station."

"You are not." Her tone indicated that had been decided well ahead of time.

Murphy noticed that they did not seem to be headed for the ten-meter aperture that seemed to be a cleft leading to Shuqdu Station's primary docking bay, but a smaller patch of darkness just above it. "We're not even heading to the main interface, are we?"

Hadraysa nodded approvingly. "You have good eyes...for a

philosopher. No: we will berth at a smaller facility which has ready access to one end of the launch tube."

"Launch tube?"

"A railgun that runs the length of Shuqdu. It can send out ships in either direction. It's a good way to get into the deep black before engaging thrusters. The Kulsians would have to be looking straight up our exhausts to spot us. And even then—" She halted abruptly, as if she'd been about to reveal something she shouldn't. "Lean back, Rodger Murphy. The final approach involves some tricky piloting. The quick changes of vector can be unsettling." One last grin. "Particularly for philosophers."

The same three RockHounds who had visited Murphy in his quarters on *Spin One* were waiting for him as Hadraysa escorted him out and then returned to her ship without so much as a glance in his direction.

"We are honored that you have come here, Colonel Murphy," said the oldest. "You may call me Ogweln." He gestured to the middle-aged RockHound, who smiled. "You may call my associate Fvaranq."

Murphy nodded to both, glanced at the young salvager, who still avoided meeting his eyes. "And how may I call you?"

Ogweln shook his head. "He prefers not to be addressed by any name."

So, personal choice? Another sectarian restriction? A security firewall? There was no way of knowing and no tactful way to ask, so Murphy simply said, "I see and shall comply."

The salvager glanced at him briefly and offered the faintest of nods.

Murphy accepted his duffel from Jabrael, who he had not heard approach and who left before he could say thanks. "So what now?"

"We commence our journey. But we must ask you to wear a blindfold from here on, Colonel Murphy. You may remove it when you are in our craft and in a compartment without a view of the exterior. We hope you shall not be inconvenienced or insulted by this requirement."

Murphy smiled. "I half expected it, Ogweln."

"Excellent. We shall be joined by three others. We shall go to a blind compartment aboard the ship once we are underway, that you may meet them properly. Now, if you will allow us to take your bag, we shall cover your eyes and begin our travels."

Deep Space, Shex system

Five days later, Fvaranq called Murphy from the other side of the hatchway of the four-bunk compartment that he shared with the rest of the crew. "Colonel, are you awake?"

"I am," he answered, looking up from *Treasure Island.* The only sign that Murphy was an honored guest was that he had a bunk of his own. The other six shared—or were, as the navy had called it, hot-bunking. A two-person stateroom was reserved for Ogweln and the ship's captain, who also elected not to share her name.

Fvaranq opened the hatch slightly. "We have arrived."

Murphy set aside his book and reached for the hood that had served as his blindfold when outside the stolid gray bulkheads hemming him in.

"You will not need that again until we begin our return." Fvaranq glanced at *Treasure Island,* noted the bookmark. "You have almost finished the story."

Murphy nodded. "I read it once before, when I was a little kid—uh, child."

"Why read it a second time?"

"I see it differently, now." Which was only part of the truth. The other half was that comparatively few books had made the trip into the future with the Lost Soldiers. Their Ktor abductors had either not bothered to take any along with the other cargo they had stolen or had purged any that had been unintentionally included. The sum total of the Lost Soldiers' lending library on *Spin One* was comprised of whatever had been buried at the bottom of the backpacks of the infantrymen among them.

Murphy stood into slight resistance. Fvaranq nodded at his rapid adjustment to the momentum. "We will conclude braking any moment now. Come: we should be strapped in when we tumble."

They made their way to the bridge: a four-seat module with a canopy shaped like a low-slung geodesic dome. The shields were down, not just against rads but to eliminate disorienting the pilot as the craft went through a one-hundred-eighty-degree pitch to face their destination.

"Secured?" asked the pilot as soon as Murphy's five-point harness fastened with a clack.

"Aye." Murphy had adopted the term during the journey out with Hadraysa. On their own ships, many of the more orthodox RockHounds became irritated if passengers did not adopt basic shipboard vernacular.

Without announcing the maneuver, the captain tumbled her ship sharply. Murphy's stomach seemed to rise up, its contents threatening to continue on that vector.

He had just finished gulping back a good portion of his breakfast when the canopy shields retracted: it was as if the triangular segments were scales of an insect folding back upon each other with brisk, geometric precision.

Murphy blinked. They were drifting toward what appeared to be the jagged ruin of a wall or building, dim in the weak rays of distant Shex, the shadows faintly doubled by the glow from Jrar.

"Flammarion effect," Murphy muttered, recalling the word from either a science class or an old science fiction novel: he couldn't recall which.

"A what?" Ogweln murmured.

"The doubled shadow that occurs in binary systems."

"Hmm. Interesting," the captain mumbled. Her tone suggested the last thing she'd expected to hear out of the mouth of a Lost Soldier was a space-relevant term. "And that is all you have to say?"

Murphy shrugged. "For now, yes."

"Well," she sighed, "I lose that bet."

"You do indeed," Fvaranq chuckled. "Care to double it?"

"Buying you one drink is more than I can easily tolerate. I'll not risk two."

Murphy glanced between them. "What was I expected to say?"

"Something about the size of the wreck before us."

Murphy looked at it again. "A wreck? As in, a ship?"

The captain chortled. "That drink might yet be mine, Fvaranq."

"We'll see."

Ogweln waved them to silence. "So, did you or did you not anticipate that our salvage included such large wrecks as this one?"

Murphy shrugged. "I didn't have any preconceived notions about your salvage operations. Or rather, I put them aside after you visited me."

The captain's tone was testy. "Fvaranq! Did you give him a hint when you were on *Spin One*? Why you conniving, station-hugging—"

"Be still," Ogweln murmured. The captain halted in mid-complaint. "Tell me, Colonel: if you could have asked us one question after we visited you, what would it have been?"

Murphy stared at the object toward which they were slowly drifting: he couldn't see where any of its sides ended. "I would have asked, 'Just whose ships are the RockHounds salvaging?'"

Ogweln smiled. "Well, our own, of course. As you have no doubt deduced, we can never leave a wreck or a crippled craft adrift, lest the Kulsians detect it. They would learn of our existence. And if it was crippled in such a way that it left debris, they could conceivably track that vector back to us."

"And I assume the shipmaster who conducts the retrieval is paid a fee in lieu of having salvage rights?"

"Or an equivalent value in goods." Ogweln's smile widened. "But you are still not asking what you truly wish to ask, Colonel Murphy. Your set lips betray the deeper question behind them. Do not be oblique. You have my word; we may speak directly here. And if you ask a question I may not answer, I will say so."

Well then, here goes. "Salvaging ships from this system is a zero-sum game; you are simply regaining what you already built. Real profit from salvage would mean you have to be salvaging *Kulsian* ships.

"But that has its own risks. The Kulsians keep close track of every hull that each of their three waves bring here: coursers, surveyors, and finally, the Harvester fleet itself. If a vessel goes missing, is damaged, or malfunctions, sooner or later, they'll start a search at its last known location or along its last known vector. But if they can't find it with medium-range radar—because they follow the same limits set by the Death Fathers—then they may look for it during the next Searing.

"So if one or two go missing? They can dismiss those as anomalies. But more than that?" Murphy shook his head. "Taking their wrecks *away* is ultimately almost as dangerous as leaving yours to be *found*, because either one shows the Kulsians they're not alone in this system."

Ogweln nodded. "Very well-reasoned, Colonel Murphy. So,

you have deduced that the RockHounds carry out very few salvage operations."

Murphy shook his head and smiled. "Actually, no; I think the RockHounds are always searching for more derelict hulls. And they must be unusually valuable, if they are rare and hard to find."

"Like this one?"

Murphy shook his head as their ship bumped softly against a modular docking ring that the RockHounds had affixed to the side of the structure. "No," he said, "I think this is something else."

Ogweln's smile was almost coy. "Time to find out."

Chapter Twenty-Two

Deep Space, Shex system

The frosted interior of the derelict was high and vaulted, like a cathedral rimed with ice. It left Murphy with a momentary sensation of standing at the entrance to a crystal temple, forbidden to—and so, forgotten by—mere mortals. And that impression was reinforced by the change in the demeanor of the RockHounds after they'd entered the still-pressurized section of the gargantuan wreck and removed their helmets.

Upon arriving at this desolate place in deep space and the wreck that was thermally one with the darkness around it, the boisterousness that had prevailed since departing Shuqdu Station had begun quieting. The RockHounds became calmer, their exchanges shorter and less frequent. Finally, they settled into a silent trek through the frozen relic, their diminished pace hinting at something like reverence. Among the oldest, their upward glances at the glaciated masses around them were a strange mix of an anticipation and dreadful awe. And as they pressed deeper, Murphy understood why.

They began passing ruined machinery and controls that lacked the typical switches and levers and toggles of the technology they knew. Instead, there were smooth surfaces and great empty vertical rings surrounded by railings, as if something—a hologram?—might have been displayed there. Overhead, even conduits and internal struts seemed to follow graceful lines, though they hung and tilted like the skeletal remains of cubist giants who had witnessed the death of their own ship. Eventually, everything they passed echoed a technology as foreign to Murphy as what he'd seen in the almost surreal interior of the Dornaani ship *Olsloov*.

Arriving at a towering intersection, Ogweln gestured to the groined vault that the ice had formed overhead. "As I mentioned on *Spin One*, we found this just over one of your centuries ago. It has been here for many times that long. Except for the area we enter now, its power has failed and the temperature of the hull merged into background. Despite the small heat still within, it cannot be found with thermal scans."

He moved with slow familiarity toward the only source of light in the area, other than what they held in their hands or were affixed to their helmets. Touching it, several previously unseen lights flared to life, revealing that the intersection did not merely join several passageways or even chambers, but three caverns that snaked their way through a still larger structure choked with debris.

"What was this?" Murphy asked his guides.

Several of them shrugged. "Likely it was a rotational habitat," Fvaranq murmured, "like the ones inhabited by the SpinDogs but made from metal and what appear to be composites."

The salvager shuffled past, his steps labored. "Probably a generation ship," he mumbled. "This would have been the rotational core."

"Not a ring?" Murphy asked. Not that he was especially versed in the technologies and architectures of space habitats, but he'd seen smaller rings used to provide equivalent gravity as well as the slow rolling spins.

"Rings," Ogweln offered, "were typically discrete containers arranged into, or upon, a torus that rotated around a hub. But this seems to have been a multichambered tube. If so, it dwarfs any human construction of which I am aware."

"This way," muttered the shuffler as he slipped sideways through a thicket of wreckage. Following, they emerged into a high corridor that ran out like a strangled tributary from the icicle-draped monument to both human engineering ambition and impermanence.

✧   ✧   ✧

They navigated many half-choked passages, some so broken that they had been severed and separated, compelling the group to lower themselves down from one askew section to the next. After much clambering in and around the gaps of the three-dimensional jigsaw puzzle, they came to an unusually intact door, larger and heavier than the mightiest bulkhead access points they had passed.

The two youngest in the RockHounds' team reacted to Ogweln's nod by manning a massive hand crank on the left hand wall. Putting their full strength and weight into the windlass-like device, it groaned and began to turn very slowly. Murphy moved toward them, intending to assist, but Ogweln extended a blocking arm. Apparently this duty was the specific charge of those currently performing it.

It took almost half a minute for their labors to produce a visible gap between the portal and the darkness unveiled as it slowly retracted sideways into the bulkhead. Another minute and the gap was large enough for them to pass through in single file, although Murphy and Fvaranq had to turn sideways to fit.

Between the ruin around him, the solemn demeanor of his companions, and the sepulchral vastness of yet another dimly seen chamber disappearing upward and outward into complete darkness, Murphy was glad for the glow of their helmet lights.

His first impression was that of a checkerboard array of rectangular altars, stretching away from him in every direction. But as he remained still, taking it in, Murphy noticed one or two lights scattered among the long, dark objects. As his eyes became more accustomed to the dark, he saw that what he'd thought of as altars were more akin to serried ranks of sarcophagi.

But when Fvaranq found and activated the chamber's lights, Murphy decisively revised his judgment. Yes, the chamber was certainly a resting place, and every bit as cold as the grave, but not so final. In fact, quite the contrary.

Murphy swallowed. "Are these all—all cold cells?"

"We call them sleep cylinders," Fvaranq corrected. The others nodded.

Murphy shook his head. "I have questions... *many* questions."

Ogweln nodded. "Of course you do. We knew you would. That is one of the reasons we chose to bring you here: that you might see this and know such things have existed. Or at least passed through this system." He gestured for Murphy to follow. "Come: we dare not remain here long. We shall speak again once we have returned to the ship and are on our way."

Fvaranq sealed the hatch to Murphy's bunkroom. He joined Ogweln opposite Murphy, and gestured in the direction of the immense hulk they'd left behind. "Without revealing anything specific, it is well beyond Shex's outermost orbit. There are other such wrecks, although none so large. But all of them are places where we may hide. Or, in the event of a long war, sites from which to observe or mount ambushes on enemies, arriving out of what they mistake as deep and empty darkness."

"If they are that far out from Shex," Murphy mused, "then during the Searing, they must also come unusually close to Jrar. Probably within ten A.U. That also means they could function as hidden staging areas from which forces can deploy into the enemy's home system, or launch warheads or kinetic impactors toward Kulsis." He paused. "Or R'Bak." They nodded somberly. "All of which is very valuable information...but that's still not why you brought me out here."

Ogweln may have smiled. "So. You have puzzled it out."

"I think so. It's not simply that you're looking for Kulsian wrecks for salvage. You're combing the deep black for whatever was left behind by the waves of Ktoran exiles who came to this system before you. And who may have raided, or even fought wars against, each other. Just like we will against Kulsis."

Fvaranq glanced at Ogweln, whose nod seemed to signify grudging approval. "I have not corrected any of your conjectures because, in general, they are accurate. Moreover, your perception is not only swift but unsurprised, so I must ask: When did you begin considering the possibility of derelicts that dated from the earlier Exodates?"

Murphy shrugged. "Shortly after arriving in this system. I might have become a historian instead of a soldier, and I'd learned enough to appreciate that every war leaves both social and physical wreckage. So I've been hoping that if you did come across salvage from the, eh, Exodates, that you might have gleaned some technical insights from them that could be useful to us now. Simply the repair schematics from such a ship as that one would be invaluable."

Fvaranq frowned. "If we had such, do you truly believe we are too ignorant or lethargic to use them before now?"

Murphy shook his head. "No, but you might not reveal them to the SpinDogs. Which might be why you contacted me so surreptitiously: that you keep this knowledge as a bargaining chip. Besides, there are some diagrams and references that might now be unfamiliar to you, but recognizable to us."

Ogweln crossed his arms with a frown. "You speak of computers?"

Not only computers, but we can start there. "Yes. For the most part."

"Then I must disappoint you, Colonel Murphy. Exodate wrecks—if that is what we stood in—have even fewer such devices than Kulsian ships. These great vessels came directly from the Ktoran Sphere, so for those who built them, the edicts and lethal resolve of the Death Fathers was not legend, but reality."

"But repairs—heck, just maintenance—is too complex to do from memory. If there weren't simple data storage systems, then they must have had microfiches or paper manuals."

Fvaranq sighed. "Such records were usually casualties of the battles that, quite literally, ripped these to pieces. Merely finding salvage that faintly resembles the hull from which it came is a great rarity. And what combat—or scuttling—did not eliminate, the ravages of space usually have."

"But you have found a few such references?"

Ogweln nodded. "A very few. And they, along with what we find when we board—but do not *remove*—Kulsian wrecks are why there are several technological areas in which we hold an advantage over the SpinDogs. The past Ktoran outcasts and the present Kulsian Overlords are both the products of immense industrial complexes, that in turn gave rise to the economies and populations needed for true research and innovation."

Ogweln shrugged sharply. "We have no such capabilities. We may only improve upon what we glean from their wrecks. But there has never been anything among those rare finds that holds the promise of unforeseen discoveries. If there was, you may rest assured that the Legate would have brought them forward before the present cooperative autofabbing commenced."

"So then . . . why *have* you showed me your"—*what, holy of holies?*—"greatest secret?"

The two RockHounds exchanged glances before Fvaranq explained. "At the outset, there was one practical consideration. Specifically, we heard that you—the Lost Soldiers—arrived in sleep canisters. We thought that you might be learned in their construction. Or that the mysterious Dornaani might have left such schematics with you, either when they departed or in one of their subsequent automated tranches." When Murphy regretfully shook his head, they nodded. "We concluded as much long before we extended our invitation. But it was never the definitive reason for it."

Ogweln leaned forward. "You risked yourself for us. On a day when it was revealed that several of our kin helped Kamara betray the mission to secure the corvette, and more were on the edge of execution, you interceded." He leaned back. "You put forward your life—and with it, those of your Lost Soldiers—as bond for theirs."

"Anseker would not have harmed me."

"No, he would not have. But he was not who you had to worry about."

When Murphy frowned uncertainly, Fvaranq picked up the explanation. "Anseker's fortunes have risen along with your star. But he has many peers who wish it was them, or wish you'd never arrived, or wished the Kormak Family had prevailed in its attempt to exterminate the Otlethes Family. Publicly straining your relationship with Primus Anseker not only risks his aura of preeminence, but your own life." When Murphy shook his head, Fvaranq shrugged toward Ogweln. "He does not understand."

"I think I do, actually. Having challenged the primus's judgment, I make it more likely that someone will risk assassinating me. Either because they believe Anseker will no longer investigate so deeply or harshly if I were to be slain, or that his position might actually be more secure without me around as a perpetual...well, nuisance."

"That is correct. As is your conjecture why we have not shared all our technological insights and sources, but that we can foresee a time when it will be necessary."

Murphy nodded. "Your secrets were your insurance, even if you couldn't develop them yourselves. If the SpinDogs ever became too aggressive, too 'preeminent,' you could have taken one of their emissaries to the derelict and threatened to destroy it all if their actions became overtly or slowly genocidal toward your people. And that would have given them great pause, because they stand the best chance of analyzing the technologies and employing them.

"But now, with a lethal threat to all of you, you anticipate having to share both the knowledge and the locations of the deep space relics. Either as havens from, or a means to strike back against, the Kulsians. Or both."

Ogweln nodded. "And now, it can be accomplished—with you as our intermediary." Murphy blinked, began to protest, but the old RockHound raised a stilling palm. "It could not be otherwise. You have seen how we who live in space are divided into two camps. The fracture lines are so sharp that it is impossible to believe that any product of that divided world can be objective. Or, if one actually could be, no one would have believed them capable of an unprejudiced view and fair dealing.

"Then you came from the stars and not only lack any intrinsic alliance to either side, but have acted as a Justiciar who saved our families, though we are held to be the lesser beings in this system."

Murphy frowned at the unfamiliar word. "A justiciar? Like a judge?"

Fvaranq leaned forward, very serious, and the emphasis he put on the word was unmistakable. "A Justiciar is a judge chosen by the acclaim of the people. More like an advocate."

"Or a Legate?"

Ogweln nodded. "They have many similarities. They are positions that are not always filled, for they are not always needed. And even then, there are not always persons worthy of the titles. Consequently, the title of Justiciar has lain unconferred for many, many generations now." He smiled. "We are resolved that the time has come to confer it, once more. But I am not now asking you to decide whether you would accept the title, Colonel Murphy. It is a profound decision for anyone to make, let alone an outworlder. Best reflect upon it during the journey back to *Spin One*. Regarding which: it is time to secure for thrust."

Chapter Twenty-Three

Spin One

Bowden looked around the bulkheads of the compartment with a skeptical look on his face. "You think this is going to work?"

Dave Fiezel shrugged. "It's the best I could do in the time I had with the tools and technology I had available."

"Well, we'll do what we can with it," Bowden said with a wince. "It's not like I was expecting a full-motion, surround-sound experience."

"A what?"

"Never mind." Bowden smiled. "I wasn't talking about the tech in the first place; I was talking about this." He swept a hand toward the seated men and women. One half—the group on the left—was wearing gray coveralls, and the other half was wearing black. A line of empty seats separated the two groups. "What is this? Kindergarten?"

"Naw. Then it would have been the boys separated from the girls," Fiezel said. "Here it's the Jets separated from the Sharks." When Bowden's eyebrows knit, he added, "*West Side Story*? Didn't you ever see it?"

Bowden shook his head. "Don't know what you're talking about."

Fiezel laughed. "And they say the Air Force has no class."

Bowden turned and walked to the front of the room, then he

signaled for everyone's attention. "Thanks for coming," he said once the group was quiet. "Look around. What do you see?"

"SpinDogs and RockHounds," a man wearing gray coveralls said.

"*RockHounds* and *SpinDogs*," a man in black coveralls replied.

"You're both wrong," Bowden said loudly when it looked like the two groups were on the verge of calling each other names. "What you see is the team of people who are here for a common cause—to defeat the Kulsian force that is coming for us."

Some muttering broke out, and Bowden spoke over it. "It doesn't matter *why* they're coming, or who's done what to whom in the past. You can blame me and the rest of the Terrans if you want, and I'm fine with that. We're not going to bicker or argue over it. Nothing in the past is changeable, so it doesn't matter how we got to where we are. The only thing that matters now is that the Kulsians are coming, and they're going to kill any of us they can find."

Bowden smiled. "Some would say, we should run and hide from them. That's what you've always done before, and it's worked for you in the past."

Several people, especially those wearing black, muttered in the affirmative.

"That's not good enough anymore. What right do the Kulsians have to take your things? To rape your women and children, and to steal all the medicinals of the planet below? A friend of mine—Major Mara Lee—needs some of those to safely have children. Should we suffer because the Kulsians think they can simply take them from us? How long has this gone on? The Kulsians stealing from you?

"I think that it should end, and that it should end *right now*. And, more importantly, that's what your leaders—the heads of both the SpinDog and RockHound Families—think, and they have chosen to fight this time. We are going to meet and defeat the Kulsians in battle. Best of all, we have a onetime opportunity. We know they're coming, but they don't know we exist. Not yet, anyway. They know that something's happened to their reavers, but never in a million of their nightmares would they expect what they're about to run into. Us—SpinDogs and RockHounds— working together to kick their asses.

"I know that you have not traditionally always been the best of friends"—several in the front row, of both sides, voiced their agreement—"but it is time to put those things aside, because the only way that we beat the Kulsians—the only way we *can* beat the Kulsians—is to work together. As you're well aware, we are currently building a fleet of ships to meet the Kulsians in battle. They will be the best-armed ships you will ever have seen, and a number of them are going to have new technology you may be uncomfortable with. If that is the case, you either need to find a different ship or learn to like it.

"Make no mistake, though, we need the new technology. We know the Kulsians are coming and that they will outnumber us. But as I said, we will have surprise on our side, and we will have technology that is better than theirs. We also will do something else they won't—we will operate together, which will give us a synergy they don't have."

"'Synergy'? Is that a new type of weapon?" a man in black asked.

"No, synergy is what it's called when the interaction of two or more things produce a combined effect greater than the sum of their separate parts."

"The Terran means *jashgaz*," a SpinDog translated wearily.

"Then why didn't he say so?" grunted the RockHound.

Bowden raised his voice. "It *means* combining what you SpinDogs"—he waved at the gray half of the audience—"and you RockHounds"—a wave toward the men and women in black—"with everything the Lost Soldiers bring to the table. Put all that—and all of *us*—together, and that's going to result in a lot of dead Kulsians."

He directed a hard stare slowly around the now-attentive faces. "But that is all based on one thing: You need to listen to what I'm telling you and follow my instructions. The Families put me in charge for a reason—I am familiar with how to use the new technology I am going to show you. If you follow my lead, we will be victorious."

"You are going to be on the ships with us?" a man in black asked.

"When I used to fly back on my planet, we had a man called the CAG who was in charge of our group. Doesn't matter what that stands for; it's only important to know that CAG was the leader of our air wing. Whenever there was a big flight—a dangerous one going up against our enemies—you could count on the fact that CAG was going to be in one of the first planes to face the enemy." Bowden nodded to the man in black. "And you can count on me to be there, too."

The man nodded and sat back, obviously satisfied.

"Now, we don't have a lot of time before they get here," Bowden said, "and we don't have all our ships finished in any event, so some of the training is going to have to be done with a thing we call simulators."

Bowden motioned toward the screens set up around the room. "We have these screens set up here and in other rooms nearby, where you will operate as if you are operating your ship."

"They don't look like the displays in our ships, though," a man in gray said, turning up his nose.

Bowden smiled. "No, they don't, as I mentioned to our head network guy, Captain Dave Fiezel." Bowden nodded to Fiezel in the back. "They do have two things going for them, though."

"What's that?"

"We have them here, and we have them now," Bowden said with a smile. "We can't use them to simulate everything I'd like to teach you, but between the lectures I'm going to give you and what we can do with them, we will practice the maneuvers that we'll use to defeat the Kulsians. Yes, it will be a little different in your own ships as you work with your crews, and we will have the fog of war, but this will give us a baseline ability to coordinate our actions. And, best of all, the Kulsians can't see us practicing on the simulators."

"Go back a second," the man in black said. "What is this 'fog of war' you mentioned?"

Bowden forced himself not to sigh. *Like I told Murphy, I knew that one of the two major issues was going to be training them to be warriors. The indigs of R'Bak were mentally equipped to take the fight to the enemy. The Hound-Dogs? They've spent centuries hiding from the Kulsians. But going out to meet them in battle is as foreign a concept as going to a drive-in to watch Star Wars. There was so much military thought that he needed to teach them—human history was replete with warrior-sages' advice from Sun Tzu to Carl von Clausewitz—if he only had the time. Maybe given a few years...*

"The fog of war," Bowden finally said, "is the inability to know what's going on around you once battle is joined. If you had all the information, you could make perfect decisions. On the battlefield, though—or in space, where we'll be fighting—it is impossible to know everything. The Kulsians will try to hide their motives and capabilities from us, for a start. Comms will not work periodically, which is something that always happens even with the best technology. And—as hard as it is to know what the enemy is doing—sometimes you won't know what your allies are doing, either, which makes it hard to predict—and coordinate—everyone's actions."

Bowden smiled. "And that's why we're going to use the simulators to the greatest extent possible. If we can all figure out what we're supposed to do in a given situation, and how we're going to operate together, that will give us some clarity. Knowing you can count on your friends to act a certain way will help remove some of the fog of war." His eyes roamed the crowd. "So who's ready to give it a shot?"

The crowd mumbled and muttered, with nothing like the enthusiasm he'd hoped to garner from them. "Okay, take five minutes to get a drink or whatever else you need, then we'll make some selections and get started."

Swallowing his sigh, again, he walked to the back of the room.

"What did I miss?" he asked his staff. "I hoped to get them all excited, but I failed... pretty miserably, it seemed."

Burg laughed. "On the whole, I thought it went pretty well."

"Really?"

"Absolutely," Raptis replied. "There were no challenges for duels, no fistfights, and the only one I heard called any names was you."

"What names?"

"It doesn't matter, but the general consensus seems that they're at least willing to try, which is more than I expected," Burg said. "The Families must have leaned heavily on them, and the Primae have given you their support."

"They have?" Bowden asked. "I didn't feel very well supported."

"That's because you are an outsider," Raptis said. "The man in black who asked all the questions? That was Reetan Taregon, son of one of the leading Legates and probably the person most acknowledged as the best pilot in the RockHounds. Most Rock-Hounds believe that they are individually the best pilot they know, but most will agree that—if it isn't themselves—it is Reetan."

"The man in the gray asking questions?" Burg asked. "That was Targ J'axon, who is the son of one of the leading SpinDog Families. With a Taregon and a J'axon here, they have implicitly shown their support for you."

"And it's not just them," Raptis said. "There were a number of other leading Families represented."

"There was also a nephew of Primus Anseker in the back of the room," Burg said.

"There was?" Bowden asked. "Teseler?"

"No, it was the other brother's son. You've been seen with Teseler, so sending one from another line of the Family implies complete faith in you."

"Which one is he?"

"His name is Stendil, but he isn't here any longer," Burg said. "He left when you called for the break, probably to go report back to the primus on who was here and how the first meeting went. You may not have noticed him, but all the SpinDogs will have, and most of the RockHounds, too. If they know Primus Anseker is watching—even through one of his relatives—they will do their best for you."

"You have their attention," Raptis added. "Just make sure you don't lose it."

Chapter Twenty-Four

The Hamain, R'Bak

"I don't like it," Benreka said, studying the small camp at the base of the long, sandy slope.

"You never like anything," Nilzwurn replied, eyes hidden by the rubber eye shields of the surveyor binoculars; they were optimized for the heat and dust of R'Bak.

The other four surveyors in the team chuckled. It was a customary response to bickering between their commanding officer and his executive officer, who was also the only woman in the group. But that didn't mean all of the laughter was good-natured.

Those who were from Kulsis's northern hemisphere evinced their region's typical, if contradictory, tendencies toward both leader worship and misogyny, even when the contradiction between those two cultural reflexes was not only sharp, but ironic.

That was certainly the case in Nilzwurn's scouting team, even though Benreka was from the north continent herself. She was not merely the source of almost all their long range plans, but clearly the superior tactician, as she'd proven time and again in their engagements with the barely seen Sarmatchani insurgents roaming this particular stretch of scrub-desert.

No doubt Falhoolp and Oblonil would have pointed to the fact that two-thirds of the time, her tactical solution had been to withdraw before becoming more heavily engaged. But they would have been less eager to reflect upon how, when following her advice, they'd suffered almost no casualties in what would have been fruitless combats, one a meeting engagement and the other an improvised ambush.

"I tell you," Benreka persisted, "that just doesn't look right."

"What? What's so strange?" Nilzwurn groused with a shrug, taking his eyes away from the binoculars. "A Sarmatchani crone with three whinaalanis."

"Three whinaalanis that have been unloaded."

"Why wouldn't they be?" Falhoolp chimed in from behind. "The barbarian hag has clearly decided to take lunch. So, she means to stay for a while."

Benreka was about to point out that unloading some of her wares was one thing, but the woman's decision to remove the creatures' harness and tack was anything but common. Particularly not when there was still travel left in the day and it was barely past the height of the light orange sun the locals called Shex.

Nor did Benreka bother to point out that the woman was not the kind of Sarmatchani they'd been encountering up until now. She had the longer robes and lighter sandals of the tribes that lived near the fringes of the high desert of the Hamain. The Sarmatchani who alternated their hunting between the scrub hills and the flatlands to the west had gear and garb that was a compromise between what worked best in both those environments.

In lieu of sharing her observations, Benreka decided to remain slightly apart from the rest of the group, which was usually fine with them—particularly in the wake of one of the all-too-frequent leadership spats. The men tended to gang together afterward, snickering as if their cliquishness was a show of solidarity with their much bedeviled—*or would that be henpecked?*—leader.

"Falhoolp," called Nilzwurn, "you stay here on overwatch."

"What for?"

"To protect us against the phantom tribesmen that Benreka's imagination might conjure."

More chuckles. Oblonil either found it amusing enough to warrant a full-fledged guffaw, or was trying to score points with Nilzwurn.

Benreka gathered her legs beneath her. "I'll go first."

The men stared at her.

"Why are you suddenly in a hurry to see the faces of the Death Fathers?" Nilzwurn asked.

She sneered. "I'm not. But we don't want her running off."

"Again," Nilzwurn said, "why not? She leaves all the gear and gets away with her skin." Falhoolp grinned at that. There was no way this old woman was going to get away alive and he knew it.

Benreka played along. "She's out here on her own with three whinaalanis. That's unusual enough. It usually takes at least one local to control each whinaalani. But for some reason, they like her or are willing to listen to her. Whichever it is, that's item of interest number one. The second and greater item is why she feels so safe here."

Nilzwurn frowned, probably because he hadn't thought of that, and of course, wasn't quick-witted enough to come up with a pithy rejoinder. In this case, however, that pause gave him enough time to actually see the value of Benreka's point. He nodded at her. "Okay. You take the lead."

"I'll tell you when to come on down," Benreka tossed over her shoulder as she rose slowly above the ridgeline.

"Wait a minute, I—!" objected Nilzwurn, but she was already striding down the slope, hands raising slowly to show that there was nothing in them.

"Nervy bitch," Falhoolp muttered.

As Benreka continued toward the old woman, she had a brief temptation to turn around to see whom Falhoolp's rifle was trained on at that particular moment. She doubted it was the old woman.

Who stood, staring at Benreka. At the same instant, the whinaalanis squirmed and leaped away, moving toward lower ground just a dozen meters beyond where the lizard-train had stopped for a midday meal.

Benreka hastened forward, calling, "Your mounts!"

The old woman looked behind, almost bored, and shrugged: utter resignation. She made no move to reach cover or to follow her whinaalanis. She simply waited for Benreka, who could hear Nilzwurn behind her, jogging to catch up. Either he didn't want to be left out of the encounter or, for some reason, his instincts had kicked in enough to tell him that his executive officer's behavior was not merely unusual, but suspicious.

Behind them, Falhoolp let out a string of frustrated curses at the whinaalanis. They had once again demonstrated their species' reputation for surprising intelligence; as they fled, they remained beneath the contours of a small ledge just a few meters beyond the woman's stopping point.

That provided the topic with which Benreka began what she hoped would become a genuine conversation with the woman. "This is a strange place to stop, Mother," the Kulsian said, using the local term of respect for those of great age.

The woman snorted out a bitter laugh. "I am a mother no longer and certainly no mother of yours."

"Then what is your name, that I may call you as you wish?"

The woman seemed to contemplate deflecting that question as well, but ultimately shrugged. "Issikoffa," she spat. "You may call me Issikoffa."

"And why did you stop here, Issikoffa?"

"One place is as good as another."

"Is it?" Benreka looked around at the loose tack, scattered packages, and small crates. "You chose ground lower than you might have," Benreka remarked, glancing back toward where Falhoolp waited with his rifle and eternally-ready trigger finger. "But you remained near the lip of the lower land."

"And is that so unusual?" Issikoffa asked, a gray eyebrow rising.

"On its own, perhaps not. But it's also strange that you untacked all your whinaalanis, as you might at the end of the day."

Issikoffa sighed. "So I am now an object of suspicion because one of my whinaalanis ended last season lame and needs more time to rest without a burden during the day?"

"It is a rare thing that humans love whinaalanis so much that they will risk losing all their gear and goods when the sun is still high and their camp can be seen from afar."

Issikoffa's laugh was mirthless. "And with observation you introduce your actual intent, yes?" She waved at her packs in disgust. "Take what you came for."

"We came to ask questions, as well, Issikoffa."

"Oh? And what could Kulsians possibly need to learn from a dirty old barbarian woman in the wastes?"

Oblonil, who'd come up behind Nilzwurn out on one flank, sneered. "Your words, not ours. Barbarian."

"I didn't need to hear your words," she said, spitting in his direction. "It is easy to read the thoughts of such as you."

Benreka heard Oblonil curse as his feet moved into double time, closing rapidly.

Nilzwurn stilled them with a single word: "Halt. Answer the question, old woman: what are you doing out here?"

She lifted an eyebrow at him as well, then glanced at her wares. "I would have thought it was obvious."

"You're a long way from any community. Closest is that damned village I can't pronounce. Nuffer... er, Nafif..."

"Nuthhurfipiko," supplied Benreka, eyes on the woman.

She seemed surprised by the smooth pronunciation.

Nilzwurn nodded. "Yes, that one. It's at least two days away from there. More, moving by whinaalani. You're a long way from any of your people, hag."

The woman shook her head. "You speak with such certainty, off-worlder." Then she glanced up malevolently under one brow. "How do you know 'my people' are not all around you, even as we speak?"

Nilzwurn shook his head. "I know because we have eyes that watch from the sky, Issikoffa. We're the only things for miles around."

Benreka glanced at him. It was a good bluff. The locals had little understanding of space. It was likely she didn't understand that just because there were satellites in orbit, it didn't mean that every part of the planet was under constant observation. Hells, the surveyor teams rarely knew if one of their platforms was overhead at any given moment. Whatever had removed the coursers—possibly a splinter group among them—had eliminated a number of satellites in the process. And just recently, two more had failed: one a victim of micro-meteoroids, the other an electrical malfunction.

Issikoffa sat on one of her packs. "Well," she said, "since you've called my bluff, you might as well get about your business." Her eyes left Nilzwurn and drifted toward Benreka, where they remained—suddenly and mysteriously intense beneath a slight frown.

It may have been the peculiar nature of Issikoffa's attention that gave Benreka the acute situational awareness that had her hitting the dust the instant after the first rifle report echo-cracked over the sandy expanse.

It was a flat, sharp sound: not one a surveyor weapon, but neither was it one of the local flintlocks or matchlocks. Instead, it sounded very much like one of the weapons they'd heard about since landing and which had killed one of the original team members at such extraordinary range that its report had been distorted by attenuation.

But there was no *wheeet!* of a near miss nor any dusty impact. Either the shot had gone unusually wide or—

"Falhoolp?" Nilzwurn shouted at the slight rise now seventy meters behind them. "Falhoolp!" His second cry didn't have the rising tone that asked for a reply; it was one of urgency, even fear. As Nilzwurn was waving the other two surveyors who'd just begun descending the ridge the ridge to drop, Oblonil was diving down, unfettered by having a command rank or any consideration higher than brute self-preservation.

He was prone in the dust when the crackle of distant rifles arrived at almost the same moment as their bullets. The rounds kicked up grit, knocked over packs, dropped one of the upslope surveyors with a gaping red wound in his chest, and rolled Nilzwurn in the dust as he grabbed at a through-and-through thigh wound.

Benreka's response was to lift up her weapon high enough to be seen and throw it aside. She became aware of Issikoffa looking down on her as if she might have been a wayward dog: a vast improvement from the gaze that, moments before, had regarded her as a subhuman enemy.

The meeting of their eyes was broken by a swift blur that came from behind Benreka and tackled the old woman off the crate upon which she'd sat with strange, foreboding serenity: Nilzwurn. Staggering on his bloody leg, he rolled up to his feet, holding her close to his chest, face looking over her oddly relaxed shoulder. He'd either dropped or tossed away his rifle; his other hand was pushing a revolver tightly against Issikoffa's temple. The hammer was back and his finger was white upon the trigger.

"She'll die if you shoot!" he yelled into the wastes.

Oblonil, glancing at the two corpses splayed on the slope behind them, rose into a tight running crawl and joined his commander.

"What are you thinking?" Benreka asked, baffled.

"I'm thinking that with me using this old crone as a shield, and the two of you covering our withdrawal, we can get back to the vehicle and get the hell out of here."

Issikoffa clearly understood enough Kulsian to find Nilzwurn's plan amusing. "You think you are safe behind me? *Me?* Who is already dead?" She threw her head back and laughed. "You and your satrap dogs killed me over half a year ago in Imsurmik."

Nilzwurn glanced at her as if she might be mad, a ghost, or both. "Fool: that was when Imsurmik *fell.*"

"So it did...and so did my boy, Suukamanu, reclaiming it from you bastards." She threw her arms outward, beckoning to the wastes. "Shoot! Shoot now! Kill them!"

Benreka hadn't known what she was hoping for when she began approaching the old woman alone. She had nothing more than a vague notion that the scouting team was already surrounded and that her only chance of survival was to differentiate herself—and her attitudes—from the other surveyors. She'd had a fleeting vision of throwing her lot in with the tribals and, if the fates were kind and the Death Fathers' collective gaze did not fall upon them, she and Lanunaz might be reunited. Maybe she could travel with the locals long enough to find a way to escape, make her way back to Downport, and thence spaceside. Or maybe she'd remain with the tribes and find a way to get word to him, to flee to an appointed place in the wastes when he finally made planetfall. Or maybe some other ploy might present itself; it hardly mattered. Seeing Lanunaz again was the only thing that *did* matter in this benighted solar system.

It was that faint tendril of an uncertain and formless hope that now propelled Benreka to her feet, arms out to either side of the old woman as she turned toward the quarter from which most of the gunfire was coming.

"Are you mad?" Nilzwurn shouted.

"No. We won't all get out of here, but as long as I'm near the woman, the tribals will hold their fire."

"Not if you don't have a weapon out."

"They won't take the chance of missing me and hitting her. Meanwhile, the two of you can make it out, maybe ransom me." *Please don't.* "And I do have my knife." She actually had more than that: a small hold-out pistol and a razor slipped into a thin slot along the back of her left boot. But none of that mattered. All that mattered was getting the two surveyors moving toward their vehicle and saving Issikoffa's life.

"They'll skin you alive," Nilzwurn called over his shoulder as he released the woman and Oblonil helped him hobble away.

"If they do, they do," Benreka yelled back. What she didn't add was that she doubted the tribals would mistreat her. There had been only a few reports that the so-called barbarians actually tortured their captives, and all but one of those remained unsubstantiated. Surveyors had certainly found executions, but only of security teams and they'd been carried out swiftly.

Keeping a hand near her sheathed knife, Benreka turned to the old woman so that any tribals behind her could not see if she had drawn it or not.

But Issikoffa's initial surprise had not turned to gratitude. Instead, hair wild, eyes wide, she leaned into Benreka's face and screamed, "Why could you not let them shoot me? Why did you have to keep me alive? I did not lie. I am dead to this world: dead to anything that mattered. The only thing I want is to take as many of you with me as I can!"

"Is that why you volunteered to draw us here?"

Issikoffa blinked. "You knew?" When Benreka nodded, her eyes began calming. "Yes, of course you did. You knew to ask those questions." She frowned. "Why? Why have you sacrificed yourself this way? You're a Kulsian. A master of a distant world and often a master of this one. Do you truly hope to be ransomed?"

Benreka shook her head. "No. I hope to be free as I could never be on my homeworld."

Issikoffa peered at her as if another face had leaned out from behind Benreka's head. "What do you mean?"

"I mean that not all Kulsians are the masters you suppose. Those who come from south of the equator are held no better than...well, than R'Baku. We Families of the north have so little regard for them that they are said to exist beneath the heels of our boots."

"So," Issikoffa breathed, leaning back slightly. "They were right."

"What do you mean?"

The old woman nodded slowly. "You are Benreka."

She blinked. "How...how do you know my name?"

"You are why we are in this region. I did not think it possible that the star people could know of the comings or goings of surveyors here on R'Bak. But they did, for here you stand. And if the one you call Lanunaz is right—that you care for him as much as he cares for you—you will help us. Even against your own people, your own Family."

Benreka struggled through waves of shock, then disbelief, and then finally joy to accept that these R'Baku not only did know who she was, but that they also knew of Lanunaz, knew he was in space, and knew of their carefully concealed love.

She shook her head. "These surveyors are not my people," she said. "They, like my Family, once were. But not any longer."

Issikoffa nodded. "Because you met Lanunaz, who is from the south, and you were with him."

Benreka blinked hard against tears she refused to shed. "We could not let anyone know what existed between us. I am not sure who would have been punished worse, him or me. At least he would still have had a family to go back to. Mine would have been forced to reject me." She shrugged. "Not that it would have bothered them very much."

Issikoffa raised her hands slowly, then let them settle gently on Benreka's shoulders. "You are safe now, child."

As if that gesture had been a signal—and it probably was—the gunfire resumed. Benreka glanced briefly over the old woman's narrow shoulder.

In the distance, the uneven and dusty progress of Nilzwurn and Oblonil came to an abrupt end.

Chapter Twenty-Five

The Hamain, R'Bak

Cutter watched Issikoffa top the nearest dune, Benreka beside her. They were flanked by fire team Alpha. Bravo had remained behind to police the area and remove any sign of the ambush. "Welcome," he called to them.

Benreka raised a dubious eyebrow.

Cutter replied to it with a rueful smile. "Well, ma'am, you wouldn't be here at all if you hadn't agreed to your parole."

The Kulsian woman shrugged and nodded. "What do you need me to do?"

"Well, first of all," Cutter drawled, looking at the darkening sky, "you're going to come along for a little ride with us."

She looked around. "Right now? In what?"

Cutter smiled, led her over the dune behind him, nodded to the squad huddled around a small rocky outcropping that protruded from its base.

They pulled up a sand-colored, and sand-covered, tarp concealing a Huey in a small stony notch that broke up through the otherwise smooth slope of the dune.

Benreka's eyes widened. "We—our satellites—didn't see *this*? How is that possible?"

Cutter smiled again. "Oh, that's very possible, Miss. You wouldn't *believe* how possible that is. But you're gonna find out."

He gestured toward a rock that was the right height for sitting. "It will take a few minutes for the crew to ready it."

"Do you have no fear of being spotted while you fly?"

"Well, we're waiting for dusk and we'll be flying without lights. And I don't suppose it's telling you anything you wouldn't figure out soon enough, but you surveyors don't have a bird overhead right now. Won't for another two hours. So we'll have scooted to our next safe location long before anybody could see this spot, much less guess what was here."

"And our sand-runner?" she asked, glancing over her shoulder to the approximate location of her team's large, four-tracked ATV.

"Oh, that handy little land-ship has already been parked in the shadow of a wadi. Come the next gap in your satellites, it's going to be far away and no sign of its tracks. Not to worry; it won't be found, and it's not as though we don't have good use for it elsewhere."

Cutter gestured for her to rise. "Now, you'll want to stand back, Miss. I know you surveyors have your own rotary birds... but this model? Well, she does kick up a lot of sand when she gets herself going."

The Ashbands, R'Bak

Three hidden refueling caches, two brief naps, and eighteen hours later, the Huey veered north over a dried riverbed and into a box canyon. Two other helos were already there, hidden under scrub-covered tarps. Nestled under an overhang at the back of the canyon was a partially deflated dirigible that had started out in satrap hands.

The groomed landing area meant the helicopter didn't raise its usual tornado of dust, which gave Benreka a chance to scan the compound. She was particularly looking for other individuals like Cutter, who was a mystery in all but two regards: he clearly had not grown up speaking the native language, yet was clearly connected to the pilot of the helicopter whose language was related to Kulsian but markedly different in several ways. The pilot was not only thin, but evinced the skeletal attenuation that Benreka associated with children born in Kulsian orbitals.

But as the helicopter settled on its skids, she still hadn't seen other troops like Cutter. None shared his complexion, his uniform, or even the way he moved. Everyone else was a native of R'Bak, and at least half were Sarmatchani, she guessed.

Cutter, who the others called "Captain," saw her assessing gaze before she could look away. He raised an eyebrow and shook his head with a small grin. "I know you're full of questions, Miss, but I can't answer them. At least not yet."

Benreka sighed. "I know. That's why I'm staying silent." She leaned back as the security team hopped out, ducking low as they exited the still-gyrating craft.

Cutter nodded. "I saw you peering out the side door just before we crossed over the river bed. Looked like you recognized something."

She nodded. "I saw the ocean on the horizon. And I recognize the shape of the river. I've never been down in the ravine it follows. And now there's every reason not to, given how much better the natives' guns are. But our own pilots use the river as a navigation reference." She pointed her chin northward. "If I remember correctly, beyond the canyon and the massif behind it is a larger river that doesn't dry up. It empties into the sea, not too far to the west."

Cutter nodded. "That's where we're heading next." The Huey's rotors were gradually slowing.

"To the sea?" she asked. He nodded as the fuselage finally stopped rocking. She shook her head. "Just one thing I don't understand." Cutter's eyes invited her to explain. "Why show, or tell, me anything? Why not keep me in a dark room?"

The captain's smile was a little crestfallen. "Oh, that's coming, Miss. You'll probably live that way for quite some time. But it's important that you see how much control we have on this planet."

"You think that will scare me into helping you?"

"No one thinks we need to scare you. Not if everything we've heard about you and Lanunaz is true. We're showing you all this because we want you to realize that getting back together with him isn't just some fairy tale. It's something that could happen, could be the life you live from here on. If you help us now."

"And you need to show me the ocean for that?"

"Not the ocean," said Cutter, "but what comes out of it." He led the way out under the helo's languidly turning blades. "Keep your head down. We'll be moving toward that APC parked next to the dirigible." He noticed her assessing stare. "Looks to me like you recognize the model."

"I've been in one a few times," she said with a shrug. She didn't bother to specify that "a few times" was actually well over fifty hours. "But how will we get to the river on the other side of the mountain? There's no connection between it and this tributary, at least not this far downstream. The nearest confluence is back the way we flew in, almost forty kilometers to the east." She glanced up at the canyon walls hemming them in, noticed Cutter's wry grin. "As I said, I know this area."

"You certainly do," he agreed, "but as you also said, you know it from the air." He nodded at the troops who had collected just beyond the stilled blades of the helicopter. "The Sarmatchani know this region from the ground." He glanced at a sun-seamed woman carrying a Kulsian bullpup carbine: better than anything issued to surveyor scouting teams. "Glafali, please escort Ms. Benreka to the vehicle." He paused. "I assume that you no longer wish to be addressed by your surveyor rank?"

"You assume correctly, Captain Cutter."

They were clearly expected at the APC. Its electric motor was already emitting a faint hum and the driver's forward hatch-half was open. As soon as Benreka climbed into the passenger compartment, she noticed that the top exit hatches were both open as well. "For fresh air?" she asked.

"For your edification," Cutter corrected as he closed the side door and the vehicle glided smoothly forward. It drove along the sagging flank of the blimp, headed for the back wall of the cave. When it accelerated, Benreka grabbed the sides of her seat. "What are you—?"

Two guards standing near the wall hauled up a rock-patterned canopy; the APC rolled into the much smaller cave opening it had concealed. Benreka exhaled as she looked up through the nearest top hatch: the low, rocky ceiling rose away gradually, faint in the reflected light of the vehicle's headlights before it abruptly vanished upward into darkness.

"Barely a meter clearance on that opening," she commented, swallowing.

"You've got a good eye," Cutter said. "The overhead gets closer again, but don't worry, it's a short ride."

He hadn't exaggerated. Within three minutes, the headlights shut off. Thirty seconds later, the ceiling descended back toward them—and then the APC was suddenly in open air again, beneath the rapidly darkening sky. A moment later, she heard the sibilant whisper of fast-moving water. "Well, you've got us to the river," she allowed. "But this bank gets as narrow as a footpath in places, and we're still east of the ocean."

"Just a few kilometers," Cutter replied, "but that's not a problem." He smiled. "We've become very familiar with your vehicles."

The APC slowed as it eased down a gentle natural embankment that led to the river's edge. The driver buttoned up, but the commander stood higher in the top hatch as the wheeled vehicle's wedge-shaped nose kissed down against the water. A moment later, its hydraulic jets coughed to life.

For a moment, it felt like the APC couldn't decide whether to roll along the riverbed or start floating. Then its long, wide chassis heeled slightly; as the driver began angling the jets to port, its nose came around to point downstream. The current helped turn it in that direction until it had slipped all the way around to push against the rear doors, and so helped drive it toward the sea.

After a few minutes, Benreka looked up at the other top hatch, let a questioning gaze drift sideways to Cutter. He shrugged and nodded. She stood on her seat and straightened her legs.

She rose into the gathering night, enjoying the freshness of the air, the smell of the sea... as she surreptitiously kept an eye out for other signs of insurgent activity.

There were none. Behind them, the now-distant cave mouth from which they'd emerged was invisible under its own overhang. Whatever forces the natives had dedicated to watching over the river were well hidden as they motored downstream.

When she finally turned back to face west, the first of R'Bak's natural satellites had risen, revealing that the banks grew farther apart as they reached toward the sea. By the time Benreka caught sight of the distant waves, the river had become a wide channel that bisected a crescent-shaped beach of wet, moon-dappled scree.

"We had no idea that you had aircraft or controlled his area," she muttered down toward Cutter. "And that tells me that what I'm seeing is just one of scores of other similar operations that we've never detected or even suspected."

Cutter shrugged, teeth shining in the faint moonlight that came through the hatch. "I can neither confirm nor deny and et cetera, et cetera, et cetera."

She nodded, almost smiled back, noticed a hand-swung light waving from side to side approximately three hundred meters ahead. Its side-scatter glow bounced up against—and so, was covered by—an overhead tarp.

The vehicle commander produced a simple flashlight and responded with a similar gesture.

Benreka nodded at the signal's source. "I take it that's our destination."

"It is," Cutter replied without needing any description of what she had seen. "And I'd be much obliged if you'd step down again, close the hatch, and take your seat."

"You don't want anyone mistaking this for a surveyor vehicle?"

"They wouldn't," Cutter replied. "But it's protocol that you shouldn't have an opportunity to see the inlet's watch posts and ambush points as we pass them."

She sealed the hatch and settled onto the hard, small jump seat, upward-revising her estimate of just how many troops and operations like this were operating throughout the Ashbands and possibly the Greens.

Before she could come up with another question that was conversational but might also lead to some additional information, the APC bumped up on the right and then dipped slightly to the left: the starboard wheels had come into contact with the bank. Another few pulses from the jets pushed the vehicle in that direction until the left wheels also grabbed the lower extent of sloping riverbed.

The jets shut off, the engine revved, and the vehicle sped upward at an angle. The chassis leveled off as small rocks spatted against its light belly armor; the APC had reached the flat expanse of the scree beach. When it stopped a few hundred meters farther on, Cutter opened the side hatch and led her out.

Underneath the blackout tarp she'd seen on their approach, half a dozen men and women were staring out to sea. Clothed in black and faces covered in charcoal, they were watching as two dark figures labored to wrestle something out of the surf.

"Good timing," Cutter commented over her shoulder. "Might as well go take a look."

"At what?"

"At why we brought you here."

By the time they'd joined the group under the tarp, the

pair in the waves had dragged out what might have been a seal. But as they hauled it up the beach, she saw no extremities or movement. Curious and eager to see what it might be, Benreka nonetheless managed to keep herself from leaning closer until the object was under the tarp: it was a smooth, black oval, possibly some kind of container.

It was laid before Cutter and a younger man who'd joined him. "Any problems this time, Tanavuna?" the captain asked.

The fellow—possibly Sarmatchani—shook his head. "No, not this time." He nodded to one of the group that had been waiting under the tarp. She moved forward, produced a small toolkit.

Cutter shook his head; Tanavuna quickly put out a hand to block the woman, who was not equipped as a soldier: a specialist of some kind.

"There's a self-destruct package on this one," Cutter explained. He glanced at a short man standing beside him. "Disarm it."

The man crouched at the rear of the object. Craning her neck to follow the motion of his hands, Benreka noticed it was fitted with small propellers. Hidden between their housings was a small access panel that the man had already opened. He inserted two different tools, performed a set of quick manipulations to whatever was inside.

He stepped back. "The unit is secure."

The woman who'd started toward it initially reapproached. She, too, adjusted unseen controls in the rear of the unit until a dorsal section just aft of the nose rose up slightly.

Cutter leaned over, pulled a sealed plastic package out of the recessed payload compartment, and held it up in front of Benreka. "This is why you're here."

She frowned. "What is it? Operation orders from surveyor command?" Cutter didn't respond. "Entry codes for a secure facility?" Cutter only smiled, so she pushed at the limits of plausibility. "Or are those instructions for some mission that requires my ID and retinal scan?"

Cutter shook his head. "It's just some light reading. Mostly about Kulsis, but also about the surveyors and Harvester fleet."

Benreka almost laughed until she realized that, despite his smile, Captain Cutter was dead serious. "You mean, it's in code?" She shook her head. "You don't actually think that I can crack the cipher code of a different surveyor unit, do you?"

"No. It's already decoded."

Benreka tried to keep her voice level. "Then what in the name of fate do you need *me* for?"

Cutter shrugged. "To tell us where the lies are."

Cutter was staring after the armored car in which Benreka was being taken to safety when Tanavuna came up alongside him. The rangy Lost Soldier smiled at his friend and trusted lieutenant. "Good to have you back, Tanavuna."

"It is good to be back," the other replied, glancing up as the stars began emerging from the velvet black of the new night sky. "Why did you transfer her in one of the electric vehicles?" he asked, jutting his chin toward its silhouette.

"Less thermal signature," Cutter explained. "Also, it's low enough that it can run straight into the secure cavern network where she'll be hidden."

"Not far from the signaling ravines, I take it?"

"Correct, my friend. Now, tell me how you were received at Ikaan-tel?"

The Sarmatchani warrior shrugged. "There is little to tell. Their gratitude remains strong. The woman Salsaliin has a child that I presume is the issue of Lieutenant Thomas.

"She was quite polite, although the desert dwellers have different customs. However, when I passed her the letter you gave me, she absented herself. Very abruptly."

Cutter smiled. "Understandable, don't you think?"

Tanavuna shrugged. "I suppose so."

Which is all the reaction you can muster, you poor young fellah. Tanavuna's wife Kesteluni, the healer of Nuthhurfipiko, had been killed—brutally—in the battle for Imsurmik. He'd grieved and rebuilt some semblance of a life, but the wound was still too raw for him to be gentle with himself. Or anyone else. "And so, when she came back from reading the letter...?"

Tanavuna pursed his lips. "She was friendly but also...erratic. I assume that the letter was from the lieutenant, but I could not tell if she was made happier or more frustrated by reading it."

Cutter sighed. "I suspect she wasn't certain herself. Did she introduce you to the village hetman, and did he agree to what Murphy requested?"

Tanavuna smiled. "No introduction was needed; he was there

when she received me. She has become the *Atii* of Ikaan-tel and keeper of the Daaj. It is a great honor to become one so young, but she was deemed 'well-aspected'—however that is determined.

"On my return journey, I visited the command tents of all the Free Bands—eh, battalions—between here and Imsurmik. The chosen troops have been moving through the tunnels to the coast somewhat more slowly than we hoped, but without major incident. The full complement should be gathered to embark on schedule."

"Well done, Lieutenant," Cutter murmured fondly, clapping a hand on the younger man's shoulder. "The same is happening up north in the Greens, I understand."

"There are fewer tunnels there. It must be difficult."

"Not so bad, actually. Most of the infantry is coming from the Ashbands; the Greens are supplying most of the vehicles and crews."

Tanavuna crossed his arms. "I still do not understand why they have that honor. We Sarmatchani showed great skill using vehicles in the campaign against the satrap towns."

"You did, but that's one of the reasons the colonel wants to leave your vehicles and their crews here. Murphy needs you to keep the remaining satraps cowering behind their walls, as well as picking off any surveyors who stray too far from their base camps.

"Also, vehicles can't move through tunnels, but they can move from copse to copse in the Greens, all the way to the coast. And most of those are newer vehicles from caches, with crews that have used them since the start of the uprising." He nodded toward the west. "The two forces—riflemen from down here, tread-heads from up there—will give the Kulsians a thing or three to think about."

Tanavuna nodded slowly, stole a glance at the much-taller American. "Do you not regret having to remain here when the greatest battle will be elsewhere?"

"Firstly," Cutter chuckled, "don't let God or Fate or Whatever hear you assuming you know where the 'greatest battle' is going to be. That's a fine way to make sure it lands in your lap. But as far as working here in the south?"

Tyree Cutter shrugged, blew out a long breath. "I hate knowing that some of my former soldiers are likely to be taking a greater risk than me. But our jobs here could prove just as crucial. Just not so soon." He smiled at his young friend. "In the meantime, want to get a drink? Some of the tribe that Harry Tapper first contacted have started brewing beer."

"Brewing what?"

Cutter chuckled and put an arm around Tanavuna's shoulder. "Better I show you than tell you, son. Now come on, before it's all gone."

Chapter Twenty-Six

Spin One

"Okay, everyone, stop!" Bowden exclaimed, pausing the combat simulation. As the trainees leaned back from their consoles, he spent a moment composing himself. *Stay patient, stay calm.* "Lakglurm, I ordered you to move forward to support Burg."

"But by so doing, you are making me take actions which will almost certainly lead to my annihilation."

"No, I'm not. You are supporting Burg, and he will be supporting you in turn." Bowden looked at him without blinking. "I've spoken with Murphy about this, and losing people is the absolute *last* thing we want...besides losing the entire battle, that is."

"I am not about to sacrifice my life for a SpinDog or one of you Los—" He stopped himself.

"I'll finish that for you. 'Or one of you Lost Soldiers.'" Bowden nodded. "I understand how you feel. I've felt the same way myself, sometimes. I've worked with allies in Africa on our world who I would have been just as happy to attack—happier, maybe, in some cases—than our mutual enemies. People who were more worried about personal gain than doing the right thing or helping the team win.

"But going it alone is *not* how you win battles. We're not individuals, or even Family loyalists. We are a fleet. We *will* fly and fight as one. To do otherwise ensures that they will cut us to pieces. There are more of them."

"I thought your wondrous tech would ensure we prevail."

"That 'wondrous tech' will *help* us achieve victory, but it can't do it all by itself. That tech was designed with this kind of discipline and cooperation in mind. Each one of us complements the other, so that we make a whole that is much, much greater than the sum of its parts. And anyone of you who can't fly that kind of mission—or who *won't* fly like that—needs to leave this compartment right now and tell your Family that you are not fit for service with our fleet. Because this commitment to working as a team, as an integrated unit, is the foundation of every other skill you bring with you. Without that foundation, you are not merely useless to the fleet, you will be the weakest link in the chain...and far too weak to fly with us."

Bowden paused and stared at the offender. "So, Lakglurm, what are you? Are you weak, or are you strong enough to do what must be done to protect your family—even if it involves listening to a Lost Soldier or counting on a SpinDog to protect your back?"

Lakglurm—who was a bear of a man—took a deep' breath and let it out slowly. "I am the strongest one here." He glanced uncertainly toward the ever-present Kaminski, almost invisible in the shadows of the bulkhead behind Kevin. "I am certainly strong enough to listen to a Lost Soldier." He nodded, muttered, "And strong enough to come back and kill you if you break that trust."

Bowden smiled. "Fair enough. That's a start." He looked over to Fiezel, who was running the simulator. "Let's start it from the top."

Reetan Taregon's simulated corvette, along with his two remaining wingmen, sliced out from the formation at full burn.

"What are you doing?" Targ J'axon called. "Get back in formation."

"Not this time, SpinDog. You've stolen all the glory the past two engagements. These are mine." He flipped off the "radio" button that allowed him to hear and speak to the SpinDog group that was located in a different but nearby compartment.

Reetan's force advanced on a group of five cargo ships, firing missiles from medium range, and then closing to finish them off with their railguns and lasers. As they got close to the formation, the farthest enemy ship launched six missiles one after the other. The missiles passed between the other cargo ships as they accelerated, then their rocket motors went out.

"Find them!" Reetan said to the other pilots in his formation, who were sitting near him on the simulators. "Find those missiles!" All his pilots zoomed in on the space in front of them, searching.

"Got them!" one of them exclaimed. "They're coming at me!"

The ship fired its point defense systems, destroying two of the missiles, but the other four closed on it, their motors reigniting for the final burn. The missiles maneuvered wildly as they reached their terminal phase, and all four slammed into the corvette. Its icon dropped out of the link on the simulator.

"More for us!" Reetan yelled, and the remaining ships of his force swooped in on the now-defenseless cargo ships, destroying them without any further losses. "Who's next?" Reetan asked as he zoomed out his link picture.

"Oh no!" one of the pilots muttered.

"What?" Reetan asked.

"Look at J'axon's force."

Bowden smiled grimly. While Reetan had been off killing the mostly unarmed merchants—and, ironically, losing one of his group to them—an enemy task force had attacked. The numbers would have been fairly even if Reetan's battle group had been there, which would have given the advantage to the Hound-Dog force, but their absence had given the edge to the Kulsians, and they were being ground down by the Kulsians' superior numbers, even though their technology and coordination was better.

Bowden sighed as the military aphorism was proven yet again. *Quantity has a quality all its own.*

The RockHound force boosted back toward where the action was taking place, but even they could see they were going to be too late. Both of the Aegis corvettes, including J'axon's own, had been destroyed, and the others were being methodically cut to pieces. Reetan's force arrived at the same time as another Kulsian force—probably looking for the glory of being involved in the combat action—also showed up. Once again, the Kulsians had the advantage of numbers and destroyed the RockHound force out of hand.

"Bah!" Reetan exclaimed, pushing back from his console. "That was rigged against us."

"No," Targ J'axon said from the doorway, "the battle was ours to win! Only your incompetence and refusal to follow orders allowed—"

"I'll kill you for that!" Reetan yelled, jumping from his seat. The other RockHounds jumped up to follow their leader, while the rest of the SpinDogs flooded the room to back their leader.

Bowden raced to cut Reetan off and shoved a hand into his chest. "That's enough!" he roared in a voice that would have made his OCS gunnery sergeant proud. "Get back in your seat, Reetan!"

"No!" the RockHound cried. "He has insulted me. That is a dueling offense."

"And I say no!" Bowden yelled. "We don't have time for your macho bullshit."

"Did you hear what he said to me? He said—"

"I heard what he said," Bowden replied. "*And he was absolutely right!* If you had stayed where you were supposed to be, rather than running off in search of personal glory, together, you would probably have beaten the first Kulsian force, and then the one that followed it. Instead, you were defeated in detail." Bowden shook his head. "All of you Hound-Dogs better get your shit in one sock, or we're going to get our asses kicked."

"I do not understand," J'axon said. "How is putting excrement in a sock—?"

"It's a Terran saying," Bowden said with a touch of frustration. "It means to have everything figured out."

"But excrement—"

"I don't know *why* that's the saying; that's just the way it is. Don't dwell on it. The only thing that's important is that you need put away your fucking egos, *or we're all going to die.*"

Reetan held up a hand. "Did you just call us Hound-Dogs?"

Bowden blew out his breath all at once. "Yes, I did."

"I find that offensive," Reetan said, "as I'm sure the SpinDogs do as well."

"Well, honestly, I don't care that your poor little feelings got hurt," Bowden said. "You just got your asses kicked, *and you're dead!* Dead people don't get to *have* feelings. Besides, I said that intentionally to make a point. There isn't any time left for this whole SpinDogs versus RockHounds thing. Do you think the

Kulsians are going to analyze each ship they come to and decide whether to fight it based on who's crewing it?" *So much for remaining calm. Might as well let them have it with both barrels.*

Bowden put a whining, childlike pitch into his voice. "Oh, look! It's a SpinDog crew. We'll let this one go. Oh, a RockHound? Shoot it!" He glared at Reetan for a second, before resuming in his normal voice. "The Kulsians are coming with one intent, one thought in their minds: to kill *everyone* who gets in their way of raping R'Bak and destroying everyone they find in space. They don't care who you are; you are *all* unworthy in their eyes. RockHounds, SpinDogs, Lost Soldiers: to them we're all—what's that phrase you use?—'lesser beings.' So they will happily kill you—kill us *all*—regardless of which little group you belong to.

"The bottom line is that there is no longer time for 'us' and 'them' among our ranks. We are *all* Hound-Dogs—yes, even the Lost Soldiers—and if we don't fight as one, we'll all die. Separately and without hope. Is that what you want?"

"Well, no. I want—"

"You know what?" Bowden raged. "I don't give a *shit* about what you want! Glory, this. Dominion, that. I don't give a fucking shit! I'm sorry I even asked." He pointed to the door. "Get out."

Reetan jerked back as if he'd been slapped. "What?"

"Get out! Get out of my fucking simulator. We don't need you. I'd rather have twenty-eight or even twenty corvettes flown by people that I trust—people who can act like a *team*—than have a bunch of prima donnas doing their own thing." He pointed to the door again. "Just get out."

"I cannot—"

"Oh, yes, you can. You just stand up and walk across the deck, and boom! Out you go. Easy as that."

"No, I mean I cannot return to my Family and tell the Legate that I have failed. I just...I cannot."

"If you're not going to go tell your daddy dearest that you've flamed out of flight school, then you have to rise above this SpinDog versus RockHound bullshit. As in, right this second. Because we're all in this together. Several hundred years ago, when my country was trying to get out from under the thumb of an oppressor, there was a saying: We must hang together, or we will surely hang separately."

Bowden sighed when he saw the blank faces looking at him.

"Sorry, that didn't translate, but it has to do with two different meanings for the word 'hang.' The first involves sticking together; the second involves dying by strangulation. Basically, it means, 'We need to stick together, or we'll all die separately,' with a little play on the words used. That's basically what just happened here." He waved at the simulators. "You all just died separately."

"I understand the meaning, if not the actual saying," Reetan said. His shoulders slumped. "I also see its applicability here. We need to fight together as a single team."

Bowden nodded. "We do," he agreed, his voice losing a little of the steam it'd had. "We are going to be greatly outnumbered, and we're going to need to fight as one to be successful. More importantly, we need to trust each other to be successful. We need to know that you—or anyone else—isn't going to go off seeking personal glory at the first opportunity, leaving us in the lurch. We absolutely *can* beat these assholes, but we can only beat them through the use of the tactics I'm trying to teach you." Bowden tilted his head and looked penetratingly at Reetan. "Can you do that? Can you put aside all this petty bullshit and be part of the team?"

Reetan swallowed once, then he nodded his head. "I can."

"Good, because *we need you*. You're a great pilot, and we're going to need all our best pilots when the Kulsians get here."

"Major Bowden?" Burg called.

"Yeah?"

"We just got a priority message. Colonel Murphy needs you in his office."

Bowden nodded, then he looked at Reetan and Targ. "Do it again," he said, "and this time, do it *together*." He turned to Fiezel as he made for the exit. "I'll expect a report afterward, assuming I survive whatever Murphy has in store for me."

Chapter Twenty-Seven

Spin One

"Welcome back from parts unknown, sir," Bowden said from the hatchway. "You wanted to see me?"

"I did. And more accurately, my travel was to parts *undisclosed*." Murphy waved him in and to a chair.

Bowden sat and looked at his boss expectantly.

After a moment, Murphy looked up from something on his desk. "It's done, I think. It looks like the Trzgarth Family—along with their allied Families—is going to throw in with us."

"That's great news, sir!"

"Well, it will be, assuming we can conclude it."

"What still needs to be done?"

"They would like you to go and brief them on all the technology that they're going to get for agreeing to what they called 'this stupid plan.'"

"Go, sir? Where am I supposed to go?"

"To their autofabber. The primus and his scion will meet you there. They want a brief on the tech and how the plan is going to work out. Assuming what you tell them is the same thing that the intermediaries did, they say that they will join us."

"Wouldn't they like to come to the conference room? I really don't want to go there again. Not without an army behind me."

"You're allowed one other person. Kaminski can go with you, but no one else."

"Does this seem like a setup to you, sir? Because it sure does feel like one to me."

Murphy shook his head. "No, I don't think so."

"I'd feel a lot better if you said you knew it wasn't, not just that you thought it wasn't."

"The primus has pledged your safety upon his personal honor, witnessed in front of a number of intermediaries who were in attendance."

"Were they from Anseker?"

"Oh, no," Murphy said with a chuckle. "Family Otlethes would never allow itself to be perceived as requiring cooperation or assurances from Family Trzgarth. Nor could Anseker ask someone to do it directly in his name."

"Well, how did it get done?"

Murphy shrugged. "Speaking as the primus among several of his lesser allies, Anseker 'just happened' to mention how much he wished the Trzgarth would join the tech-sharing effort. That ally mentioned it to someone who was nominally neutral toward both families, who in turn mentioned it to an ally of the Trzgarths.

"That ally related Anseker's statement to the primus of the Trzgarth Family, who mused that he could foresee an exchange that would actually make joining the effort acceptable to him. Word of that response went back through the same chain and Anseker approved the deal, which resulted in a gain for the Trzgarths."

Bowden scratched his head. "If it resulted in a gain, why didn't they take the deal right away?"

"Because they were holding out for better terms, which, under other circumstance, they might have gotten." Murphy shrugged. "But at the end of the day, Anseker never had to lower himself to dealing with them directly, the Trzgarths got what they wanted, and now they are genuinely interested in joining us." Murphy stopped, but didn't end on a tone of summation.

Bowden sighed. "Okay, what's the catch?"

"The Trzgarth Family can't come to us to join and coordinate. That would signify they are lower in stature, almost supplicants. So we have to go there and beg them to join us to keep their honor intact."

"*Beg* them?" Bowden made a sour face.

"Strongly implore them to join?"

"That's not much better." Bowden sighed. "Still, if that's what it takes to get them to join, I can do it."

"I'd hoped so, because they have four corvettes waiting to join your fleet. Well, after they're specced up to the new template and change whatever else needs to be swapped out."

"Okay, you got me. I'll do it. I needed to go out on an inspection run today anyway."

"Inspection run?"

Bowden nodded. "One of the midsize Families is cheating. Burg went onboard one of their Family corvettes, and it had better technology than what they ponied up for the template." He shook his head. "These people. Always looking to get an advantage over each other, even if it means the death of everyone."

"It's a snake pit, to be sure. Just be glad you don't have to deal with it every day like I do."

"No kidding." Bowden shrugged. "Okay, so I know we were running behind in production. Where does the addition of the Trzgarth ships put us?"

"At the moment, I have promises for a total of twenty-nine corvettes by the date you've told me you need them to start moving into position, upgraded to the latest template, of which seven will have the full C4I suites. Plus crews to fly them."

Bowden winked. "My Aegis cruisers."

Murphy nodded.

"Let me see," Bowden said, doing the math in his head. "That makes... three groups of two Aegis and six regular corvettes."

"That's only twenty-four; I said you'll have twenty-nine."

"You promised me twenty-nine, but what are the odds that I'll really have that many?"

"Pretty good, I think. I used an awful lot of competition between the Families to get those promises, and the heads that don't live up to them are going to lose a lot of face if some of the others do."

"That worries me."

"Why?"

"I need these ships to *work*. I don't want them slapped together at the last minute just so some Hound-Dog can say he or she met their quota."

"Then I guess the smart Admiral would make sure he—or

someone from his staff—stays very hands-on in the final portions of their assembly to make sure everything is put together correctly."

"Because we have that kind of time," Bowden said, then he shrugged. "Still, it beats getting a crappy product, so we'll keep ourselves involved in the process, so they don't give us shit."

"What are you going to do with the extra five ships?"

"The plan calls for a rear guard that I can use as a reserve force in case something unexpected happens. The five remaining ships—four normal corvettes led by an Aegis—are my reserve. And, if I have to fill slots when I don't get all twenty-nine that I've been promised, I'll draw from there first."

"So you're all set?"

Bowden laughed. "Not hardly. That's a great start, though. What about the small craft I asked for at the start of this whole messy process?"

Murphy leaned his head into a hand that almost started trembling with fatigue before he began rubbing his temples. "Small ships? That may have slipped through the cracks. Refresh me."

"I need a small squadron of little, really fast boats—call them packets—that, once the attention of the bigger Kulsian hulls are fixed on us, can get in and knife them in the throat. Launch a flurry of missiles and get back out again." He smiled hopefully.

Murphy did not look up. "So, the equivalent of World War Two PT boats."

"Exactly. I was thinking we might be able to modify some of the RockHounds' existing craft to hold a missile rack or two?"

Murphy looked up. His face looked gray. "Anything else?"

Bowden smiled. "Well since you're asking..."

"That was facetious."

"Oh."

"Look," Murphy said, "I'm glad you're focused on this battle. It's brought out a spirit I haven't seen from you in...well, that I've never seen from you. There's just one problem."

"What's that?"

"So far, you've only been looking at the battle; you haven't been looking at what else will be going on during, and after it."

"I figured it would either be a matter of picking up all the pieces we could and regenerating combat forces, or we'll all be dead and not have to worry about it. I was kind of hoping for the first."

"There's a lot more to it than that. As part of this attack, in addition to your corvettes, all of which need trained personnel, you are also now asking for fast support craft—with missiles. You will also need recovery crews standing by to 'pick up the pieces' as you noted. I'm sure you've also thought about chaser craft to make sure none of the Kulsians make it out of the ecliptic to send back a report to Kulsis. You'll also need people to work as trainers."

"That's—"

Murphy held up a hand. "I'm not done. That's what *you* need. I also need some landers."

Bowden swallowed. "To deal with the Kulsians still on R'Bak." He nodded, remembering the initial planning sessions with Murphy. "Mostly surveyors and mostly in the northern hemisphere. But I thought they'd be dealt with after the Harvester fleet was defeated."

Murphy shook his head. "The more Bo and Cutter have looked at the ground situation, the more we realize it's imperative to hit them right after the spaceside battle is joined. Concurrently would be best."

"Sir, not to be impertinent, but... what's the rush?"

"The rush is to hit our enemies before they can react or consolidate in response to what's going on in space. Specifically, that means being in full readiness to launch counterstrikes against any planetfalls the Harvesters make into or near our allies' towns and cities. We also have to be prepared to exploit any openings in the southern hemisphere: to hit whatever units the Kulsians already have in place, or may try to land, there.

"All those missions require landers and air support elements, fully manned and ready to go within minutes, or at least hours, after you engage the Kulsians." Murphy shook his head ruefully. "And, if any of our personnel are double-tasked for both combat and combat support, we'll need to have replacement rosters for when we take combat casualties."

Kevin nodded somberly. "You need to know who'll jump into the saddles before any of them are emptied." He drew a deep breath. "That's... that's a lot of shit, sir. I also just realized I'll need a combat support staff on one of the spins—probably Outpost—during the battle." He sighed. "More people."

"See?" Murphy said. "It's a lot of requirements, and I need your help figuring it out."

Bowden nodded. "We're undermanned, compared with what Kulsis is sending now and what they could possibly send in the future."

"We are. They have a whole planet to draw from. We just have the spins. Given a few more years, we could train up a lot of people from R'Bak, maybe match them body for body. But for now, we don't have anywhere near the sheer number of people they can throw at any problem that arises."

"Every one of our lives is worth several of theirs," Bowden noted. "Every life is important and can't be thrown away on a whim."

Murphy chuckled. "I don't imagine you would do that anyway."

"No, I wouldn't." Bowden shook his head. "Still, we have to do what we can to minimize losses. Hmmm..."

"What are you thinking?"

"We may need to readjust our battle plan slightly."

"How so?"

"Well, as cool as it may be to go charging into battle, launching wave after wave of missiles, we may need to tweak our loadouts."

Rather than repeat himself, Murphy raised an eyebrow.

"Our corvettes need railguns to supplement our missiles, sir."

"Wait: now you want to go back to the original Kulsian design? A keel-mounted railgun?"

Bowden nodded slowly, thinking it through. "Yes, sir. Putting a laser in its place has been our goal, but it pulls way more energy. And it still won't be as good a ship killer. Not by a long shot."

"So you're saying you want to change the corvette template *again*? Do you know what I went through to get the Families to agree to what you asked for last time? We're already going have to add the Trzgarth optical trackers, and you want more?"

Bowden chuckled. "I deal with the Families every day—I just had to deal with the son of the RockHound Legate as a matter of fact—so I have a very good idea what you went through. As far as, do I want to? Hell, no, sir: I don't *want* to keep wrestling with them, but it's not like we have a choice.

"Besides, we need more point defense fire in our fleet, make them as close to invulnerable to enemy missiles as possible. That way, our corvettes can stay at a medium or long range while our *improved* missiles pound their ships into junk. That's why we're still looking for a better laser for our point defense."

"You're *still* trying to come up with a suitable laser?"

"Not so much 'come up with' as modify one that already exists. It's the same problem we faced when we were thinking of a laser for the main weapon: we didn't have the time or resources to build one from scratch."

Murphy nodded. "So, you've been trying to find something that's already on the shelf."

"Right, and we haven't yet. But we're getting close. Since the laser's purpose isn't to kill ships but intercept missiles, we've narrowed it down to two candidates. If we can convert one of them into a high-pulse laser that puts a beam on target for 0.1 seconds with a hundred megawatt per second energy deposition rating, the mission kill percentage would be almost as great as the original point defense railguns. And the intercept percentage increases exponentially."

"Who *exactly* is bird-dogging that conversion?"

"Well, it's way outside my skill set, but Malanye Raptis was always interested in using a modified mining laser in place of the main railgun, so I had her do some research into it."

Murphy chuckled. "Okay, that's more believable. But why has she been the persistent advocate for lasers?"

"It's all about the RockHound proclivity to hide," Bowden replied. "When you're looking at counter-targeting risks, lasers aren't visible unless you're looking right down their barrel or their beams refract as they pass an atmosphere or gas cloud—which aren't present in space. But if you use railguns for point defense—which was in the current template—you end up with streams of radar-detectable projectiles which the enemy can use for counterfire targeting." Bowden chuckled. "And those free targeting solutions are *not* what we want to give the Kulsians, since their sensor and computing limits are their single greatest disadvantage.

"Besides, with lasers, we free up all the hull volume we'd have had to set aside for the railgun ammo. That gives us room for more capacitors, which in turn allows us to beef up the energy to the main-battery railgun. And that extra power would give it another combat role: a way to cold-launch missiles."

Murphy shook his head. "I beg your pardon?"

"In the battle we're anticipating, there will be a lot of material flying around at very high velocities and temperatures. But a dormant missile launched out a railgun at lower velocity? Those might get missed, or presumed to be mines or sensor drones. With a larger railgun we can not only deploy all those packages the Kulsians expect, but also some missiles moving more slowly toward projected areas of engagement."

Murphy nodded. "Which, when they are very close, could be activated and guided remotely. No sensor signature until they home in for terminal intercept."

"Sounds like you're starting to get the hang of ship design, sir."

"I am not, but *you* seem to have it well in hand." He nodded. "Figure out what you need to finalize the corvette design. Just be aware that these modifications—or any others you might have in mind—are going to cause more complaints and more delays in production. You might not have all twenty-nine corvettes ready by your jump-off day. Or some might not be re-specced in time, leaving you with nonuniform hulls. Which you swore you would not tolerate."

"I understand," Bowden said. "But if you can get me the ships, I can live with a mix of capabilities. The only thing I'd be lacking then was a squadron or two of fast attack craft..."

Murphy shook his head. "I'll see what I can do"—he smiled— "you damned greedy squid."

Bowden replied with mock umbrage. "That's Admiral Squid. Sir."

Murphy chortled. "That will hang on you like a starving tick, Kevin. All the more because it came *from* you."

Bowden suppressed a groan, already regretting his one moment of ill-advised jocularity.

Mostly.

Chapter Twenty-Eight

Spin One

"And you are quite sure about this, sir?" Kaminski asked as they approached the Trzgarth autofabber entrance. His Polish accent was stronger than usual: a sure sign that he was on edge. "You know, in the bible, it warns about dens of vipers. This is surely one."

"You're not wrong," Bowden said, wondering if he'd overheard Murphy's comment on their destination. It was the longest sentence he'd heard yet from the taciturn Pole. The scion was waiting for them at the hatch, in addition to the guards. "Still, this is something we have to do."

"I don't know," Kaminski said, shaking his head. "I have a bad feeling about this."

Bowden did, as well, but whether that was because of the way he'd been treated on his first visit or something new, he didn't know. He stopped and held up his hands. "Permission to approach?" he asked, not knowing what to say and not wanting to be shot.

"You can come up, Bowden," T'Barth said. "I see you."

"And my companion?"

"Yes, him, too." T'Barth's tone took on an annoyed tone, but Bowden had wanted to make sure no mistakes were made.

The Terrans approached, and one of the guards opened the hatch. T'Barth stepped through and motioned for them to follow.

219

One of the guards growled something under his breath, but Bowden decided to let it go. Kaminski looked like he was going to stop, and Bowden said in English, "Ignore him."

Having passed the first hurdle, they followed T'Barth down a short tunnel and into the autofabber bay. It wasn't as big as the Otlethes', but was easily a match for those possessed by most of the other families.

"Impressive," Bowden said with a nod, trying to start out on a good foot.

"You are the first non-Trzgarth to see it in some time. We do not let anyone who is not Family in here."

Bowden bowed. "I appreciate you making an exception for me."

"We also do not share our technology, as I told you the last time you were here."

"Believe me, you made your point very clear."

"And I don't want you here."

Kaminski shifted and Bowden shook his head before smiling at T'Barth. "That is another point that was made abundantly clear. I'm glad you changed your mind. I—"

"I haven't changed my mind."

"Then why am I here?"

"Because my father has decided to join in the stupid course that you have convinced the others to participate in. If we're all going to die, he wants to make sure that we have a say in the nature of our demise."

"With all of us acting together, I don't believe that this will be the end, but a new beginning of prosperity."

"You have convinced the others of this, but we remain doubtful. Explain to me how your plan is not the worst thing to ever happen to us."

"Perhaps if you told me what you already know, I—"

T'Barth frowned. "Assume I know nothing."

"In short, we are making a fleet of corvettes which will, supplemented by an auxiliary force of smaller vessels, meet the Kulsian force when it arrives. We will attack when their ships begin to descend to the planet and are too low on fuel to maneuver efficiently. By striking by surprise, we will destroy them."

"I have heard that there are many ships in the approaching fleet, and it is unlikely that we'll have more than thirty of your corvettes ready to fight them."

"That's true. We will make up for our inferior numbers by having superior technology—especially your outstanding optical trackers. We will also use a strategy that they have never encountered before."

"I want to lead the attack. If you get our trackers, my price is to be the leader."

Not only no, but hell *no: I am not going to follow* you *into battle.* But Bowden only smiled. "I'm sorry, but that's not possible. We will be using strategy and tactics derived from those of my homeworld. You will be as unfamiliar with them as the Kulsians. Consequently, I will be leading the assault."

"How do we know that you won't run when the first missile is fired?"

"I was involved in the capture of the corvette we're using as the template. I didn't run in the attack on the Kulsians then, and I won't now. I have seen plenty of combat"—a vision of a little girl impaled on a fence flashed through his mind, and he stifled a shudder—"back on my planet." He chuckled wryly. "More than I wanted, probably."

"I remain unconvinced," T'Barth said. "Is that all you have to—?"

"Death to the Terrans!" a voice yelled off to the right.

"Stop him!"

Bowden spun as a rifle fired, and someone punched him in the chest. He tried to yell out but couldn't muster the breath to do so. The horizon tilted, and he fell. He lay on the ground, his chest on fire. People ran past, yelling. Bowden couldn't raise his head, turned it weakly as he tried to figure out what had happened and, more importantly, why he was unable to breathe.

Something flashed in front of his eyes. He blinked, then he realized it was someone's booted feet. He rolled his head to follow the boots, discovered they were worn by T'Barth. Kaminski had the SpinDog in a chokehold and had turned slightly to put his adversary over his hip. T'Barth's face was purpling as he flailed, unable to reach the Polish sailor or get a breath.

There was a reason not to do that, Bowden knew, but he had a hard time focusing enough to remember why. His vision began tunneling. *No. We need him. All of them,* a small voice finally whispered in his mind.

"No!" Bowden breathed, his lack of air preventing him to shout as he'd intended. He flung an arm out and hit Kaminski in the leg. The sailor looked down. Bowden twitched his head back and forth, mouthing the word, "No."

The sailor frowned, surprised and uncertain.

Bowden tried again. "No—" he murmured.

Then his vision narrowed to a pinpoint and the lights went out.

Fiezel looked up from the simulation as Kaminski staggered into the simulator control room. The Pole looked lost, his eyes searching for something, but not finding it. It looked like one of his eyes was blackened and shut, his clothes were torn, and his uniform was missing its left sleeve. After a second, Fiezel realized that the red on the man's front wasn't paint, but blood. A lot of it.

"Oh, my God!" Fiezel yelled. "What happened? Where's Bowden?"

Kaminski's mouth opened and closed, like a fish out of water, then he finally gasped, "Shot."

"He's been shot?" Fiezel exclaimed. "Where? How?"

"Trzgarth."

The sailor looked like he was about to collapse, so Fiezel got up and steered him into the chair. Kaminski collapsed into it. The metal groaned as his bulk hit it, but held.

"What do we need to do? Where is he?"

"Medical. I take to medical."

Fiezel started to run out, but the Pole reached out a massive hand and grabbed Fiezel's arm, stopping him in his tracks.

"I've got to go see him."

"Can't," Kaminski muttered. "Kicked out. Not go back."

"The medics are working on him?"

"Tak." *Yes.* "Medics trying to save life."

"What happened?" Fiezel asked. "You went to visit the Trzgarth, and they shot him?"

"We...we went to Trzgarth fabber," the Pole said, his vision focused somewhere else. "Were talking to asshole son. Want to punch in throat. Then man appeared with gun. Shot Bowden through chest and ran." He shook his head.

"Okay," Fiezel said, "what happened next?"

"Choked asshole son like wanted all along. Bowden made me stop."

Too bad. If anyone needed to die, it was T'Barth.

"Then what happened?" Fiezel asked when Kaminski didn't continue.

"What's going on?" Burg asked, walking into the room. "The simulator just failed and everyone's trying to contact you. I was just about to kill a—" He stopped as his eyes hit Kaminski. "What's going on?"

"That's what I'm trying to find out," Fiezel said. He motioned to Kaminski. "Bowden was shot when he visited the Trzgarth. Finish the story, Kaminski."

"Guy with rifle ran. I pick up Bowden to take to medical, but asshole son tell me to stop. I tell him to go have sex with mother. Asshole son not like that. Ten, maybe twelve, men jump on me, take Bowden from me." He looked down at his right fist. It was bloody and torn. "I kick five, maybe six asses, then get hit in head from behind. Wake up to find Bowden and asshole son gone. Men say they take him to medical. I go there and ask. They say they have him but can't see him. He have…trauma." He sniffed and a tear ran down his cheek. "I failed Bowden. Not keep him safe."

"It's not your fault," Fiezel said. "Were you expecting to jump in front of the bullet?"

"*Yes!*" Kaminski roared as a tear ran down his other cheek. "Was my job, and I fail. I too focused on asshole son. Not see shooter."

"If he's in medical, I'm sure he'll be okay," Fiezel replied. "The drugs they have on the planet below are incredible."

"What do we do?" Burg asked. "If T'Barth killed Bowden, especially after they gave him their oath that he would be protected…how will the Lost Soldiers answer that?"

Fiezel shook his head and swallowed. "I don't know, but we're going to cancel the rest of the simulators for today." He motioned to Kaminski. "Get him cleaned up. He got hit in the head, so he probably needs to go to medical and get it looked at."

"What are you going to do?"

"I'm going to go find Murphy and let him know. Then I'm going to do whatever I can to help…especially if it includes killing T'Barth."

After stopping by his berth for his pistol, Fiezel went to Murphy's office, only to find that the colonel had already heard about what had happened and gone to medical. As Murphy hadn't left any instructions—or said what the response would be—Fiezel followed him to the medical section.

The first thing he saw on entering the space was T'Barth talking to two of his goons. Without conscious thought, his pistol appeared in his hand as he stalked toward them.

"No," Murphy said softly as he intercepted Fiezel, grabbing his arm and turning him away from the SpinDogs.

"What do you mean?" Fiezel asked through clenched teeth. "It's just like the damned VC all over again. Hide in plain sight and kill us when we're not looking."

"It's not their fault," Murphy said urgently, his voice low as he tried to tug Fiezel away from the SpinDogs, who had heard the commotion and were now looking at him.

"What do you mean it's not their fault? They promised he'd be safe and then they shot him!"

"That's just it," Murphy said. "They *didn't* shoot him."

"Then how did he end up here? And who beat the shit out of Kaminski?"

"Kaminski was curb-stomped by the Trzgarths. They tried to take Bowden, to get him here faster than Kaminski alone. He misunderstood and went berserk." Murphy jerked a thumb farther into medical. "Four members of the Trzgarth Family are in there being treated for the injuries Kaminski inflicted, and there are apparently a few more sporting wounds and contusions." Murphy chuckled. "Kaminski gave a lot better than he received."

"Who shot Bowden, then?" Fiezel asked.

"Lakglurm Glarzhen," T'Barth said harshly, walking over with his two cronies.

Fiezel turned to Murphy. "And we're supposed to believe them? Lakglurm was in the pilot training program to run one of the corvettes."

"You will need a new trainee," T'Barth said with a harsh cough, and Fiezel realized the SpinDog wasn't talking hoarsely on purpose; that was all he was able to do.

T'Barth continued, "My men caught him as he tried to flee. He put up a fight, and they had no choice but to kill him—"

"Of course they didn't."

T'Barth frowned. "I had told them to bring him back alive so we could question him prior to putting him out an airlock without a suit."

"Oh." Fiezel thought a moment and shook his head. "But why would Lakglurm shoot Bowden? And why do it there?"

"Apparently, he was hoping to get away and have the blame fall on the Trzgarth," Murphy said. "As for why he did it...are you aware of where Bowden was going after meeting with T'Barth?"

"To go inspect one of the Families' fabbers for cheating."

"Do you know whose?"

"It was—" Fiezel winced as it came to him. "The Glarzhen Family."

"The primus of the family has already disowned Lakglurm and blamed him for all of the cheating that went on with equipping their corvettes."

"So that's it? Lakglurm's dead, Bowden's shot, and we all live happily ever after?"

"That's it; end of story." Murphy looked at T'Barth. "I will take it from here. Thank you for your help."

The SpinDog nodded curtly, turned, and walked out of medical with his goons following him.

Fiezel shook his head. "I can't believe they just get to walk away."

"What do you want them to do? They had intended to join us, anyway. Bowden's meeting with them was only supposed to be a perfunctory bit of political theater. They were already 'in.' Still, they had taken an oath to ensure Bowden's safety, and they failed to provide it. They killed the attempted assassin, who was disowned by his father. They only other thing they could do is declare a blood feud against Lakglurm's Family, which no one wants."

"I might."

"That's enough," Murphy said sternly. "Even if we wanted that, we can't afford it. We need everyone working hard to prepare for the Kulsians, not carrying out a vendetta. Especially one that might drag in a lot more Families once it started." He shook his head. "It's far better for all involved to let this go."

"Even if Lakglurm's primus knew all about it and is just using his son as a scapegoat?"

Murphy nodded. "He probably did know, at least about the cheating, although Lakglurm might have tried to kill Bowden on his own."

"He might have." Fiezel sighed. "Early on in training, Bowden challenged him. Lakglurm probably bore him a grudge from then."

"Perhaps so," Murphy said. "And, assuming that Bowden pulls through, this may work in our favor."

"How so?"

"Hopefully, this incident will be a unifying event that brings everyone together. Not only that, but the Trzgarth Primus has promised to put all of his autofabbing capability into producing corvettes and attack packets for us."

Fiezel clenched his jaw rather than allow it to fall open. *How can you be so bloody minded, Murphy?* he wondered. *Probably because he has to,* he answered himself after a moment. Fiezel sighed, letting it go. "What *is* the prognosis for Bowden?"

"Good. Naliryiz, the SpinDog healer, is in there with our medics. Apparently, he was shot by a small-bore carbine: a Kormak model that compensates for the spins' coriolis effect. He'd be dead if the round hadn't been a discarding sabot; not much more than a needle.

"Still, he has a collapsed lung and lost a lot of blood. The good news is that they say he's going to pull through. The bad news is that you're going to be running the training the next two or three weeks."

"Doesn't recovery take a lot longer for that?"

"If we were back home, yes, but Naliryiz tells me he should be back on limited duty by then. He'll still get tired easily, though, so you'll have to help carry the load."

"Yes, sir," Fiezel said. "I will."

Bowden's breath caught, and a wave of pain washed across his chest. "Ow."

"Well, hey! Look who's awake."

Bowden knew the voice but his addled thoughts had trouble placing it. He winced and tried to open his eyes. Although he only managed to achieve a half squint, recognition occurred. "Hi, Mara," he gasped.

"Well, hi yourself, sailor," she said, her voice sweetness and light. "How are you feeling?"

"Like an elephant is sitting on my chest," Bowden managed, a little more normally. "I guess—" He coughed and tried again a little softer. "At least I can talk again."

She smiled. "It's probably a lot easier without a collapsed lung."

"I reckon so. Anyone get the license plate of—?" He broke off again and coughed weakly.

"The car that hit you?"

"No, the bus."

"Well, yes, they did," Mara said. The sunshine left, and her voice turned wintery. "They caught the guy that shot you. He didn't let them take him alive, though."

"Too bad." Bowden chuckled weakly, trying to walk through what he remembered last. "Did...T'Barth—?"

"Yes, he's alive and owes you a debt, despite Kaminski almost killing him. He's also firmly in our court now, and the Trzgarths are doing everything they can to help us."

"Good." He inhaled shallowly a few times, enjoying the feeling of breathing again. "Who shot...me?"

"Lakglurm Glarzhen."

Bowden coughed. "Fucker."

"Apparently, he was behind the Glarzhens' cheating on their equipment. At least, that's what his father said when he disowned him. The bottom line is that justice was at least partially served, and things are moving forward as smoothly as they can." She shrugged. "Around here, anyway."

"When can I...get up?"

Mara chuckled. "Not anytime soon."

"Have...a battle to fight."

"I know. A battle to regain your health."

Bowden shook his head. "Kulsians."

"You need to get better first." Her lips thinned. "You almost died. Hell, you *were* dead when T'Barth brought you in here. They had to revive you. You were drowning in your own blood. That was four days ago."

"T'Barth brought me?"

"Yes, even after almost getting choked out, he made it his mission to get you here."

"Wow."

"No kidding." She chewed her lip a moment. "Now, go back to sleep and get some rest. Dave Fiezel was here before you woke up, and he said he would be running the training until you were better."

"He doesn't know AWACS."

"No, he doesn't, but guess what?"

Bowden lifted an eyebrow.

Mara winked. "It turns out that *I do*, and I've been helping him with a few things. And Makarov has been catching up fast, bringing along his young protégé nicely."

"Timmy Uggs?"

"Murphy's adjutant in training and all-around boy wonder," Mara grinned. "Makarov was pulled into the Soviet army from the civilian Academy. Seems he's one of their few products who actually is a good teacher. With us handling the AWACS elements, Fiezel's got the training restarted, and he can work on coordination, if nothing else, until you're up and about again."

Bowden smiled. "Thanks," he whispered.

Mara started to reply, but a snore cut her off, so she smiled and left.

Chapter Twenty-Nine

Spin One

Although Janusz Lasko was a big man with long legs, even he had to increase his pace to keep up with Colonel Murphy's long strides.

As they entered the evidence locker, Murphy warned, "We don't want to spend a lot of time in here."

Janusz blinked in surprise. "Why, sir? Is the air bad in this compartment?"

"No, but my whereabouts are clocked. So if we're here too long, and somebody gets access to my locator records, they could wonder if we're on to them."

"'On to them'?" Janusz repeated helplessly.

"Starting about half a year ago," Murphy explained as he began checking the labels of the numbered boxes lining the grillwork shelves, "Vat started monitoring Lost Soldiers who displayed significant increases in wealth."

"But sir, we have no money. Only goods."

"Yes, but if you've dropped by any of the floating poker or crap games, you'll see that there are always some people who can stake big pots with high-value goods."

Janusz frowned again. "I thought that was just what they'd already won."

"Eventually, yes, that's how they line their pockets. But those

229

pockets had to be deep enough to make their first big bets. We need to know why they had more to start with."

"Sir, with all due respects, though I am not a gambler, I know this: by every report, it is Vat himself who has always had, as you say, the deepest pockets."

Murphy smiled. "Indeed he has. And still does. That's why he's been the best person to watch the others. He's got his hands in a lot of shady deals, and even more I'm sure I don't know about. But either way, if it involves wealth, he hears about almost everything sooner or later."

"So, you are setting a thief to catch a thief?"

"Something like that. Besides, Vat owes me. But none of the others who have those deep pockets owe anything to anyone... so far as we can tell. And that makes them a threat to our operations."

"In what way, sir?"

Murphy shrugged. "Gamblers tend to have a high toleration for risk. Most seek it out, whether consciously or not."

Janusz shook his head, perplexed as to the colonel's point.

Murphy stopped checking the boxes and turned to face him directly. "Janusz, a person who's willing to bet away the few goods they own is also more likely to take loans to fund those gambles."

"Ah: you are worried that there are loan sharks among us."

Murphy turned his head slightly—not a complete rejection of Lasko's conclusion, but it foreshadowed a major caveat. "I'm not worried about loans among the Lost Soldiers; we could always control that if we have to. My concern is that some may be accepting help from the SpinDogs."

Janusz let out his breath in a slow, taut sigh. "So, you are worried that one of the local factions might have, er, leverage over some of the men. Could pressure them to work as informers."

"Or, conceivably, as saboteurs."

Janusz frowned. It seemed impossible. He knew all the Lost Soldiers. Granted, few were devout, and fewer still had lofty consciences. But traitors? He shook his head. "Colonel, I find that hard to believe." *Or maybe my father was right: that I am too idealistic. Or as* babunia *said while patting my head, I am a good Catholic boy. But still...*

Janusz straightened. "There is not one of them who would stoop so low as to betray us." He frowned. "Except for Vat, maybe.

He is very clever, but he is also very..." Jan struggled to find a tactful word, but gave up. "He is very selfish. And he often lives beyond the edge of our group because of his, er, preferences."

Murphy stopped checking the contents of two of the boxes against the list he held. "You have a problem with Vat's 'preferences'?"

Janusz shrugged "His body is his business. I did not grow up thinking that way, but over the last several years—well, nothing else makes sense. So, no, sir. My only concern is this: How do you know Vat doesn't build his wealth by taking things from this very locker?"

Murphy smiled at the younger man. "This is why I wanted you here, Janusz: because I knew you'd understand that if Vat is intentionally filing things here in misnumbered bins, those could be goods he's impounded while investigating possible black marketeers."

"But who are these black marketeers?"

"That's need to know, Janusz."

"Understood, sir. Where do we begin?"

Before they left the evidence room, Murphy had rummaged through most of the boxes and pulled contents from six of them. Janusz dutifully loaded the goods into the two duffel bags he'd brought for that purpose.

It was an odd assortment. Three weapons with copious amounts of ammunition but all of different types and calibers. There were also long-duration rations and jewelry that had originally come from the towns and even bodies of both R'Baku and surveyors. In one case, Murphy took an entire backpack filled with odds and ends ranging from compasses to mountaineering equipment to old magazines that went back as far as World War II. Janusz thought it a pity that the magazines would not last long; the paper on which they were printed had been aging rapidly ever since being liberated from the "super cosmolene" that had kept them intact for over a century and a half.

Murphy also pulled four—or was it five?—suits of cold weather survival clothing, one more suited for the desert, various sizes of web gear and boots, two different kinds of flares, six cartons of cigarettes, and an array of dried pharmaflora that were all reputed to increase one's speed of thought, hands, and limbs.

Murphy frowned deeply when he discovered almost a dozen ampules of morphine. They had probably been taken from torpedoed Liberty ships that the Ktor had kept afloat long enough to ransack.

"This is very strange, sir," Janusz said, glancing from one duffel bag to the other as they retraced their steps.

"How so?" asked Murphy as they reached the lockup's secure hatch.

"Well, sir, black marketeers usually do not bother with individual items. Their profit is in securing a few large lots of identical goods. What you have taken is all very different and all in small numbers. How does Vat, or anyone else, expect to make a profit?"

Murphy nodded approvingly. "First, this is just a sampling to confirm or disprove the possibility of theft from this locker. But if anyone had contraband in that kind of bulk, they'd be very obvious. I suspect that the culprit has smaller lots and is selling individual items periodically. No one transaction generates a great deal of profit but, over time, that constant trickle could put a lot of wealth in someone's pocket."

Janusz lifted one eyebrow. "'Someone'? So Vat isn't the only suspect."

"Not at all."

Janusz frowned. "How many suspects are there?"

"Well, let's see...Roughly how many Lost Soldiers are there right now?"

"I do not know exactly, sir, but not more than one hundred twenty."

Murphy nodded. "That's a very good guess. So, that makes about sixty suspects."

"*Half* of the men might do this?" Janusz breathed, amazed and horrified.

"No: half of them *could* do this. We just don't know which one, or ones, are behind it."

Janusz shook his head. "I am very glad I do not have to think through all these details the way you do, Colonel Murphy."

Murphy smiled. "Well, there *are* perks. Now let's close up and get out of here. I have a meeting with our number one suspect in half an hour."

✦   ✦   ✦

Murphy rapped his knuckles against the coaming of the recovery ward's hatch. He leaned in with a smile. "I'm told the professor wants to speak with me?"

Vat was sitting up straighter in the bed, only a few bandages still plastered on his face. "Yes, but before we get to that, I want something."

Murphy folded his arms. "No promises, but I'm all ears."

Vat looked off into the distance, as if he could see some grand vista. "I want you to call me 'Indy' from now on." He turned his head slightly so that his chin was at an oblique angle.

Murphy squinted before he discovered what he was supposed to see: a scar, almost *exactly* where Indiana Jones's had been. "Well, I'll be damned!"

"Well, you *might* be, but I certainly *am* damned to live with this face from now on. However, I'll admit that, despite the rest of the carnage, this one little flaw is acceptable."

Murphy shook his head. "I'll only call you Indy if you change your name. Legally."

Vat dropped the multiple folders he held at the ready. "Are you kidding me? You can't even give me *that*?"

"I can, if you change your name."

"Yeah...but damn it, my name isn't Vat, either!"

"No, it's not. So are you saying you want me to go back to calling you Victor Allen Thom—?"

Vat recoiled, palm upraised. "Okay. All right. No 'Indy.' Damn, you drive a hard bargain, Colonel."

Murphy shrugged, moved to stand alongside the bed. "So what do you have?"

"A whole hell of a lot more than you did." Vat had clearly not forgiven Murphy just yet. "There are, in point of fact, *seven* different character sets, two of which have major variations— enough so that you could almost call them separate languages."

Murphy nodded. "I knew you were the guy for this job."

"You didn't know *half* of it," Vat said, proud but also a little dismissive. "Do you care to guess how many *languages* are here?"

"I don't dare," Murphy replied.

"You're damn right you don't!" Vat exclaimed. "*Ten!* Ten different languages, each of which is represented or transliterated in at least two different character sets. One shows up in five!"

"How the hell did you even figure that out?"

"See," Vat sighed, "this is why they don't allow line grunts—even those wearing metal doodads on their shoulders—to get near the really important and complicated things. Like intelligence."

"Vat," Murphy said calmly, "intelligence was my subspecialty."

"*Very* 'sub,' I'll bet," Vat quipped.

Murphy raised an eyebrow.

"Okay, okay! Look, Colonel, think of me as a leopard. All my snark? Those are my spots. And I don't always manage to hide them."

"Apology accepted," Murphy said his eyebrow creeping even higher. "This time."

Vat clearly didn't find any reassurance in Murphy's largely unchanged expression, so he turned to the documents. "Getting back to how I figured everything out: you don't want the full answer to that, Colonel—believe me. The short version is that after many very frustrating hours I came to the realization that three of these character sets mean the same things but are pronounced differently."

"You mean like Mandarin and Cantonese?"

"Huh!" Vat exclaimed, genuinely surprised. "Maybe they *do* teach you something in intelligence school, after all." He put up his hands in response to Murphy's resurgent frown. "Sorry, sorry—that came out before I could call it back."

"Then you'd better develop faster spot-hiding reflexes. Right now." Murphy had no trouble maintaining an icy tone.

"Yep. Yes, sir. I get it. So anyhow, I then realized that some of the other character sets are ideograms and that what look like variations were later attempts to recover lost languages. Or at least what people during some eras *thought* were lost languages because they didn't have access to all of the different scrolls and ancient tomes that I have."

He stared at the folders and binders piled high around him. "I gotta tell you, Colonel, this is like some kind of archaeological mother lode, here. Who had the intelligence...Excuse me: who had the *inspiration* to make sure all this got saved, instead of being burned or turned into rolling paper?"

"Captain Cutter."

Vat nodded soberly. "Not surprising. He's a levelheaded guy. Slightly archaic ideas about sexual identity and choice but, for his time, pretty broad-minded. Anyhow, we owe him a huge debt of gratitude, because all this is laying out a story that's pretty wild. Hell, I hardly know where to start."

Murphy grabbed a chair and sat. "How about this: you start at the beginning."

"Sir, I am *not* being a smart-ass...but I'm not sure where the beginning is, just yet. And I sure as hell don't have the whole story. I'm not sure I ever will. That's what happens when you're working with languages where you only have a smattering of what was written in them, filled with forgotten references and layer upon layer of emendations.

"But this much is clear: there wasn't just one group—eh, Exodate—of Ktor who came here. There were three. The last, which landed on Kulsis, was roughly six hundred and fifty years ago and their descendants are its current ruling class. Before that there was a much smaller group that came to R'Bak instead, because the First Exodate had turned Kulsis into an industrial powerhouse with comparable technology. In short, it was too strong for the Second Exodate to conquer."

"Any indication when the First Exodate arrived?"

Vat shook his head. "See? The further back you go, the fuzzier it gets. As far as I can tell, it could be as little as twenty-five hundred years ago, or as much as five thousand. Maybe more. Maybe *a lot* more. But here's the crazy thing: in every account, there are already humans on both Kulsis and R'Bak when the first Ktor arrived. And those native populations had already been here for a really long time."

"At least you seem certain of *that*."

Vat nodded. "Because that's where over half the languages come from: back in those bygone days. There aren't many details—mostly map fragments, references to other maps, things like that. But R'Bak had empires that rose and fell multiple times before the first Ktor ever set foot here."

Murphy stared at the array of documents Vat was shuffling through: all completely incomprehensible to him. "Any idea how those first humans got here?"

Vat shook his head. "That's another poser. From what I can tell, those native humans believe they *came* from here. Well, most of them did. But some of the really early scholars weren't so sure. And they had good reason not to be."

"Last time, you asked me to be more direct. Now, it's you who's being oblique."

"Guilty as charged," Vat snapped, "but when I do it, we call it 'coy.' And besides, it looks better on me." He surveyed Murphy briefly. "Well, everything does.

"Anyhow the early scholars spent a lot of time referring to other races. I think they believed the whinaalani were intelligent."

Murphy nodded. "That's pretty much the vibe a lot of our guys got while working with them."

"Yeah, but these old sages were convinced it goes beyond high animal intelligence. Way beyond really clever dogs, or even dolphins or apes."

"Why do you say that?"

"Because, according to the oldest documents, the whinaalani were called the Rememberers."

"Sound like the pre-Ktoran humans used them as some kind of memory banks."

"That's as good a guess as any. But I don't think it was the early humans who gave them that name. There's another group of intelligent beings that are referred to and I don't think they're simply another alien race. They're called by several names, but the two most frequent are 'the Watchers' and 'the Visitors.'"

"So . . . ancient astronauts came to R'Bak?"

"No, Colonel. I think these aliens were the first beings that lived here. But they always remained apart from the others."

Murphy started at Vat's unequivocal use of the plural. "How many races are we talking about?"

"I'm not sure. In some documents, you can't tell whether the author is talking about an intelligent or nonintelligent species. But that's not the case with the Visitors, which suggests that even they weren't native to R'Bak. And it seems they were called the Watchers because that's what they did; they observed the other species."

"Okay, but why?"

"Colonel, with all due respect, I'm doing a pretty good job as an amateur translator of ancient alien documents. But I'm no soothsayer; hell, I don't even have a crystal ball. Because that's what I think I would need. Although this"—he held up the sheet that Ogweln had left behind with Murphy—"has been the next best thing. Particularly when it comes to the Exodates."

"So," Murphy sighed, crossing his arms, "now that you've told me how much we *don't* know, tell me what you *do* know about these three Exodates."

"Well, actually, the Ktor have visited one or both of 55 Tauri's stars at least four times. There may have been others, but if so, they weren't mentioned. But one time wasn't an Exodate: it was a pogrom."

"What? Why?"

"You know how the Hound-Dogs are always warning about the all-wise and all-knowing 'Death Fathers'?"

"Yes."

"Well, that's just what they are. But they're real." Seeing Murphy's uncertain frown, Vat held up a hand. "I'll explain that soon, but let me put the Death Fathers in order with the other Ktor arrivals, okay?"

Murphy nodded.

"So, 'in the beginning,' there were humans here and on Kulsis. They had a hard time getting beyond the Bronze Age, apparently, because back then even more and larger rocks got shoved in-system when the two stars approached periapsis. However, they'd clawed their way up to something approaching World War One technology when the First Exodate arrived here in a slower-than-light colony ship.

"My best guess is that they arrived between four thousand and three thousand years ago. They went straight for Kulsis and took it over in a matter of years."

"Not hard to do when the people on the planet beneath you can't reach you to fight back."

Vat nodded. "That pretty much sums up what happened. A lot of the bigger cities got smacked with space rocks and the smaller ones cried 'Uncle.' Pacifying the locals and establishing their 'dominion' took a few centuries, though. And then they had a bunch of inter-Family wars—just because they're Ktor, I guess.

"So it took a long time for the First Exodate to sort out who was in charge, which was necessary before they could redevelop their space tech to the point where it was practical to explore R'Bak. It's unclear when they first got here, but it's very clear when they discovered the almost magical pharmaflora."

"I'm betting that made it into all the history books, both as an economic driver and a source of trade wars."

"Intelligence school for the win, Colonel. And at some point those wars boiled over and they blasted themselves back to something like the Renaissance. They recovered pretty quickly, but once again, it was a long, hard climb back up to space.

"Sometime after they achieved that—say, between eight hundred and a thousand years ago—the forerunners of our very own Hound-Dogs show up."

"The Second Exodate."

"Yes, but it's much, much smaller than the first one. Either that or not as many survived. At any rate, it seems they spent a while reconning the planets around Jrar and decided to avoid the rebooting shit show there."

"Interesting choice," Murphy mused.

"Yeah. On the one hand, it's pretty clear they were far less numerous and had little, if any, technological edge. Reading between the lines, I'd say they were hoping to boost their tech to hold off the Kulsians. But something went wrong and less than three centuries after arriving here, the core Families of the Second Exodate either left R'Bak voluntarily, were pushed out, or some combination of the two.

"Meanwhile, back on Kulsis, the race to achieve dominion led the Families to start ignoring the Death Father edict never to use any technology that generates inter-system radio signatures."

"Enter the Death Fathers," guessed Murphy.

Vat touched his nose with his index finger. "It took about two centuries for them to show up, and it seems the Death Fathers don't come to punish violators personally—they send their young-turk sons and daughters. Who descended like a school of marauding space-sharks on both Kulsis and R'Bak.

"Apparently, they didn't use many nukes, if any, but they destroyed every political entity worthy of the title, and left just before the Searing that had been approaching. Which, in the absence of industrial era organization and mitigating technologies, finished the job they started."

Murphy held up a hand. "Back up. What happened to the Second Exodate?"

Vat smiled. "Excellent question. Answer: not really sure. It was small, so maybe it was missed? Or maybe that's where the Hound-Dogs learned to be so good at hiding?"

"Or the only ones who survived were those that already had those skills?"

Vat nodded. "Or the ones dirtside got whacked and the ones spaceside got overlooked. Frankly, it's not entirely clear how much time separated the Death Fathers' pogrom from the arrival of the

Second Exodate. But at the end of the day, both systems were left in bad shape and Kulsis didn't resume Harvesting until about eight hundred and fifty years ago.

"Two centuries later, the Third Exodate arrived. They had a decent population and an overwhelming edge in technology. They also brought a renewal of actual Ktor culture and genetic know-how, so they became the new nobility of Kulsis."

"A little like the Mongols taking over the Chinese Empire."

Vat nodded. "They reinitiated the Harvester fleets, built power, and promptly started waging war on each other. However, this bunch let the old local lords—their 'satraps,' now—shed most of the blood. After a generation or two, the descendants of the Third Exodate stabilized their power in the form of the oligarchic club known as the Overlords: the heads of the Families that prevail there today. Or so documents left behind by earlier Harvesters indicate. And thereby hangs the tale."

"And it's quite a tale." Murphy nodded respectfully. "Thank you, Vat."

Vat ran a hand through his hair. "Like I said, I'm still trying to get more than a basic understanding of the prevalent languages and a crude timeline assembled. Other than that, you now know just about as much as I do."

"I doubt that very much," Murphy said as he stood. "Which is why I'm going to get Timmy Uggs in here with a recorder before the week is out."

"What for, sir?"

"So you can dictate everything down to the last detail, along with annotations indicating how confident or not you are of your different translations."

"Why? Are you afraid I'm going to hold out on you?"

"No," Murphy said. "I think this could prove to be crucial intelligence even to the people who left us here, including the Dornaani. If they had any of this data, it certainly didn't shape how they prepared us for surviving in this system, and they were pretty damn serious about maximizing our chances. So I doubt this is general, or even restricted, knowledge among them. So it's too important not to be recorded. Just in case."

Vat nodded. "Ah, so you're afraid that I'll have an untimely demise."

"Vat," Murphy sighed, "I live every day fearing that fate is imminent for every single one of us. And now, for the SpinDogs and RockHounds as well."

Vat's eyebrows straightened and the facetious lilt went out of his voice. "Yes, sir. I'll help Uggs every way that I can."

"Thank you, Vat; I'm counting on it. Before I leave, did you turn up anything useful regarding contemporary R'Bak?"

Vat nodded, shuffled through his folders, extracted one. He extended it toward Murphy. "It seems there's one other permanent dirtside facility besides R'Bak, but it's not clear if it's actually controlled by the Kulsians. It's located on the narrowest part of the isthmus that connects the large northern and southern continents. It also provides direct access to both the Great Eastern and Great Western oceans. Being equatorial, it's kind of like the Panama Canal meets Straits of Malacca. We heard it mentioned while we were in Ikaan-tel, and my Russian pal Artyom dubbed it Novy Malacca, which stuck.

"The heat there is punishing at the best of times and deadly during the Searing. The jungle around it grows like a thatch of giant weeds. It's never been fully explored, and there are very few native tribes. Some are said to have devolved to the point where they're no longer fully human."

Murphy reached for the folder, but Vat held up his hand and imitated a late-night product hawker. "But wait: there's more! As in: ruins. Really old ruins with deep caverns. There's speculation that at some point, the Kulsian built a base down into them. Sure would make the Searing more livable. What's less clear is who's in control of it now—if anyone."

He let the folder slip into Murphy's hand. "Sir?"

"Yes?"

"Every once in a while, could you please call me Indy?"

Murphy shook his head slowly, walked to the hatchway, turned back. "Sorry, but I can't do that . . . Indy." He left.

As he passed the sentry that was Vat's current guardian, he heard a muffled exclamation from the recovery ward behind him.

It sounded a great deal like, *"Yesssss!!!!"*

Chapter Thirty

Spin One

Two weeks to the day after he'd regained consciousness, Kevin Bowden convinced the medics that he was able to stand and walk unaided. After a brief discussion, they decided to allow his release, on the condition that he kept things light for the next week. After promising to do so, he put on the uniform he'd had Fiezel bring him a week prior—it had taken that long to get his feet back under him—and confidently walked out the door.

At which point he'd collapsed against the bulkhead, catching his breath. After resting a minute, he'd continued down the passageway to the refectory. It was between breakfast and lunch, but he was hoping for something a little more solid than the medics had been giving him. After putting together a quick meal and eating it in blessed silence, he was up again and managed to make it to the conference room in time for the second simulator of the day.

Everyone was listening to Fiezel give the mission brief at the front of the room, so he slid into a chair in the back next to Raptis.

She glanced over and her eyes widened. "Are you supposed to be up?" she whispered sharply.

Bowden nodded. "Light duty only, but I figured I'd come watch a simulator before I went and took my mandated afternoon nap."

241

"Your face is very white," Raptis noted. "You don't look well, yet."

"I'm getting better every day, and I wanted to come see how things were going." His eyes scanned the room in front of him...and met those of a head turned backward in his direction: Targ J'axon.

Who jumped to his feet and shouted, "Attention! Admiral on deck!"

Despite some initial confusion, the full complement in the compartment stood. Most offered the prolonged, deep nod that was the Hound-Dog acknowledgment of a superior officer. A few actually made a fair showing of a genuine salute. Whether the courtesy was spontaneous or indifferently rehearsed was unclear—and made no difference to Bowden. He stood as steadily as he was able, face grave as he pushed down the small lump trying to rise into his throat. He returned a slow salute, then nodded. "As you were. Carry on, Major Fiezel."

When he had eased himself back into his seat, he leaned toward Raptis. "Am I still on too many painkillers, or is that T'Barth over there to the right?"

She smiled. "It is. He showed up the day after you got shot, despite the bruises on his throat, and said he was here to do his part. He wanted a leadership slot, as befit his status, but would take whatever we gave him."

"Seriously? He said that?"

Raptis nodded slowly. "He said he owed you a debt."

"So what do you have him doing?"

"Leading a section of missile packets."

"Missile packets?"

"Yes, Murphy told Dave that we would have some packets with missiles mounted to them."

Bowden's eyes widened. *Out of it for a short while and everything changes.* "How many?"

"We don't know yet. Maybe ten, give or take. We have them in two groups. One led by T'Barth and one led by Teseler."

Bowden's jaw dropped. "The two of them? Working together?"

The RockHound chuckled. "They are decidedly *not* working together. That is why they are each leading a section of missile packets—one on each side of the formation. T'Barth's Family is fabbing about half of the modifications to the original frames—mining craft—and the Otlethes Family the other half; it only made sense to put them in charge of the platforms they'd made."

"How is it going with them?"

"Poorly at the start, but it has gotten better. They are both excellent pilots and leaders—"

"T'Barth is a leader?"

"A very good one. His people would follow him to Kulsis if he asked."

"Wow." Bowden shook his head. "Who knew?" he muttered.

"Anyway, there were some difficulties at the start as each of them tried to outdo the other for bravery—what you called macho bullshit—but they have settled down now, for the most part. I think each has a grudging respect for the other."

The pre-mission brief finished, and the pilots stood and began heading to their individual rooms. T'Barth lagged behind the others, detoured toward Bowden. "It is good to see you," he said. "I am sorry about—"

Bowden held up a hand. "They told me about what happened, and I don't hold you accountable. I'm just happy to have you here as part of this."

"But I am accountable. I gave my oath that no harm would come to you in my space, and yet it did."

"It wasn't your fault," Bowden said, standing. "I hear you're an excellent pilot. It's good to have you here. We need all the pilots we can get."

"I see that. Your way of war is...even more different than I thought it would be, and it took some getting used to." He looked around to see who was behind him, then continued, "But if Teseler can do it, so can I, and better."

"It's not a competition," Bowden said. "The only way this works is if we all do our parts. No one is the hero unless we all are."

T'Barth nodded slowly. "They have been saying that the whole time. I didn't understand it at first, but I'm beginning to. It is strange...but like a complicated dance, when it all comes together, it is a thing of beauty."

"Exactly." Bowden smiled. "And just like the dance, you can't have one person doing what he wants. It will only mess it up for everyone else."

"I know." He looked down. "It is hard to temper the urge to rush in, sometimes, and claim the glory of making the kill. To be the one to wield the most sought-after *fethshern* at the Acclamation." He paused. "That is our celebration of victorious heroes."

"I understand," Bowden said, "but I suspect that there will be enough kills to go around."

"You wanted to see me, Boss?" Bowden asked from the door.

Murphy looked up with *What now?* written all over his face. When he saw Bowden, his jaw dropped, then he stood and waved him in. "Come in and have a seat before you fall down. Do the medics know you're out of bed?"

"Yes, sir. I got out of the infirmary this morning, and they said I could resume a light duty schedule. When the message came for Fiezel that you were looking for him, he was running a simulator. I figured that coming to talk to you was within the restrictions of light duty, so I shambled on down here to see what we could do for you."

Murphy winced. "I'm not sure you're ready for this."

"I'm not sure I like that intro, but I feel better than I apparently look. What's up, sir?"

"We just got imagery of the oncoming Kulsian fleet from one of the microsats. It mostly confirms what we guessed: five ferrying frames—two fusion, three nuclear. Between them, they probably carry between forty corvettes and sixty dedicated security ships. Some of the others can also serve in combat roles, of course."

"And just how many of these 'others' should we expect?"

Murphy's jaw might have twitched. "Normally, those ferries could collectively carry in three hundred lighters, tankers, shuttles, and robotic haulers of various marks." Murphy smiled. "But I don't think we'll see quite that many."

"Why?" Bowden asked, determined to focus on even the smallest scrap of good news.

"SIGINT suggests that the loss of the coursers—the Kulsian officers often refer to them as 'bush-beaters'—has disrupted the uniformity of purpose and politics among the Overlords. While the main nation or family collective—Syfartha—remains fairly unified in its objectives and politics, the others of the northern hemisphere seem a bit restive. The good news is that as they were rushing to get the fleet moving, a lot of them were still bitching and pointing fingers. It's unlikely they got all the logistics lined up for a maximum complement of smaller craft."

Kevin knew Murphy's tone. "And the bad news?"

"The Syfarthan Combine has decided to show the rest of

Kulsis that they are deadly serious about settling any problems that might exist in this system."

"Sir, exactly what do you mean by 'deadly serious'?"

"Do you really want to know?"

"Sir, quit stalling and show me."

"Fine. You asked for it," Murphy said, tossing a series of pictures onto Bowden's side of the desk. "Take a look. These were taken right before they flipped over and began their insertion burns."

Bowden scooped up the photos and flipped through them. A cold sweat broke out across his body, and he knew it had nothing to do with his health. *I knew there would be a lot of them, but this...* "Damn," he finally said. "That's more than a lot." Bowden shook his head. "These pictures aren't very good for identification—"

"You do realize how far away they are still, right?"

Bowden shrugged. "A long way?"

"A very long way."

"Okay, tough to recce their types, but it's easy to see how damned many there are."

Murphy nodded. "The analysts say there are over a hundred in the lead element, based on the long-range ESM and IR imagery."

Bowden winced as he sat back in the chair. "A hundred? Surely those aren't *all* combatants."

"No, they're not. But the numbers are much higher than Yukannak led us to expect."

Bowden looked up. "They're scared."

"Yeah. But they still don't grasp the full severity of the situation. If they did, there'd probably be more warships. Maybe even a whole fleet of them preceding the Harvesters."

Bowden nodded and looked back at the photos. "What's this in the lead here? One of their corvettes, followed by a number of their chase vessels?"

Murphy came around the desk and pointed at the ship in the lead. "That isn't a corvette." He scoffed and moved his finger to one of the smaller ships alongside the one in the lead. "*That* is one of their corvettes."

"Oh," Bowden muttered. "Damn." He shook his head again. "That's a big son of a bitch."

"Yeah, it is." Murphy rubbed his chin. "SpinDog analysts say it's a frigate-sized ship. It's going to take a lot of killing."

Bowden's breath whistled through his teeth. "I'll say it is," he muttered. He squared his shoulders, and then muttered, "It is what it is."

"What is?"

Bowden chuckled. "I always hated that saying: 'it is what it is.' Never really understood it. Still, it's applicable here. The fact that they have a frigate, and we don't, only means that we have to figure out a way to take it down." He shrugged. "There isn't any other option."

"Can you?"

"Sure. If I had twenty-nine corvettes, and I sent them at it all at once, there's no doubt I could kill it. Piranhas kill big mammals, after all, and there's a Chinese torture based on death by a thousand cuts. Can I do it that way? Sure, but I'm going to end up with a lot fewer corvettes in the end. There's also the fact that I don't actually *have* twenty-nine corvettes to send at the moment."

"You don't?" Murphy asked. "I was told this morning that the official count was twenty-nine."

Bowden scoffed. "Not even close."

"How many do you have?"

"There may be twenty-nine hulls, but there aren't anywhere close to that many that are fully functional. Burg went and looked at them this morning, and there are only twenty, and that's if you use the term 'fully functional' pretty loosely. It's probably more like sixteen or eighteen, which is a far cry from twenty-nine. I've got three more being outfitted today with equipment coming from the fabbers, and another six that are done but having issues in one form or another. Weapons systems malfunctions and low performance in their propulsion systems, things like that."

"You don't have much time."

"If they're already in their entry burns, no I don't." He tapped his watch. "For those of you scoring at home, this is about a week less than I was promised."

"Don't talk to me; talk to the Kulsians."

"Oh, I *will* talk to them," Bowden said, getting up. "I'll scribble some messages on the missiles I'm going to send them, just like we used to do in the Mog." He started shuffling toward the door.

Murphy's voice turned serious. "Are you going to be able to get everything done in time?"

"We'll get done what we need to," Bowden said. "To do otherwise means we don't survive this."

"A frigate?" Burg asked, looking up from the imagery. "It can't be done. Not with what we have, anyway."

"Don't let the Hound-Dogs hear you say that," Bowden said. "I finally got them believing we can do this and working together."

"But this? This changes everything." He pointed to the ship. "Not only is this going to have more weapons and armor, it is also going to have better electronics and will serve as an Aegis system for *their* fleet. It may not be as capable as our Aegis ships, but it will be able to provide their fleet with a communications-and-control capability that is vastly better than what they would have had without it.

"This is, as you say, a game-changer for them. Not only are we not going to be able to kill it, the frigate is also going to make the rest of their fleet far harder to defeat as well."

"Nothing is unkillable," Bowden said as he reached out and put a hand over the imagery Burg was holding. "Nothing. Everything has a weakness, and the appearance of this ship doesn't change anything." He smiled. "Except for maybe how we allocate some of our defenses."

"What?" Raptis asked. "New strategy? Use everything we have on the frigate?"

"That's called the dog-pile approach," Bowden said with a smile, "and it's exactly what we're going to have to do." He shook his head. "We need to get it away from all the other ships, though, or we're going to get dog-piled by the rest of their fleet."

"How many ships do they have?" Burg asked as he started flipping through the photos.

"Enough for us to need a new plan," Bowden said. He reached over and took back the imagery. "Let's go over our inventory again. What do we have that isn't already gainfully employed?"

Chapter Thirty-One

The Greens, R'Bak

Just as Lieutenant Hax Uruns of the Second Mechanized Cavalry Band had expected, the freighter's crew rose above the gunwale, axes poised to hack through the hawsers securing it to the dock's sun-bleached bollards.

"Engage!" he shouted down into his own turret as well as his radio's headset.

Commandeered Kulsian machine guns chattered from the external ring mounts of three nearby APCs. The heavier, hammering sound of a Lost Soldier .50 cal joined them a moment later, the chassis of the light ATV upon which it was mounted tremoring down against its rear shock absorbers.

Three of the crewmen fell, one with a chest wound that sent up a brief spurt of blood, some of which cleared the weathered gunwale. Twice as many of the freighter's deckhands ducked down.

Uruns nodded, satisfied. "Check fire," he ordered, not just using Harry Tapper's words, but managing a fair imitation of his tone. "Three track?" he called into the headset.

"Three track here."

"Keep your weapon trained on the superstructure. Aim away from the bridge but watch for shooters. You are weapons free. Confirm."

"Roger that, sir." The response sounded strange in a North

Greens accent, but it was part of the legend of the Lost Soldiers. It was also a reminder of how profoundly their grim fortunes—as well as those of their brothers fighting in the Ashbands—had reversed and improved as a result of Harry Tapper and his comrades. *But still, what is "Roger"? Or maybe . . . who is "Roger"? Wait: isn't Colonel Murphy's first name Roger?*

Track Three's commander was back on the tactical channel. "Are ammo protocols suspended, sir?" His words were fiercely eager; he'd lost family to the satraps and his vehicle—almost a tank—mounted a comparatively rare, and murderously effective, Kulsian rotary gun. Its projectiles were identical to those used by the majority of rifles taken from caches, and its withering deluge of fire was likely to break the morale of any opposing force, native or Kulsian. But the weapon devoured its precious ammunition as greedily as fang-frogs gulping down their own newly hatched fry.

"Negative, Track Three," Uruns replied. "Ammo restrictions remain in place."

"You are a miser, Hax."

"That I am, Waals. Six out."

No sooner had the comm channel snicked off than smoke gouted out the freighter's stack. It could try to pull away from the dock while still lashed to the bollards, but doing so would not be a swift process and the ship itself was likely to sustain considerable damage. However, since its surveyor crew was now trying to flee for their lives, anything was possible.

Uruns brought his binoculars up and tracked down along the side of the vessel to the waters behind it. Two lateen-rigged dhows were rapidly approaching its stern. Rifles bristled out over their gunwales, but what still remained unseen were the Kulsian man-portable rocket launchers that would put an end to any escape attempt. They would not destroy the freighter's propellers or their housing, but would likely damage them enough to convince the surveyors that they would never be able to get away in time. At the very least, it would take the crew that much longer to either snap the hawsers or pull the bollards out of the dock. And more time was exactly what the surveyors lacked.

The bridge's weather-hatch opened slightly, but then leaned closed again without anyone appearing.

Uruns smiled. Prudent: instead of leaving the bridge upright, someone had crawled out, staying beneath the solid rail of the exterior walkway ringing the bridge. "Track Three—" he started.

"I see them," Waals muttered.

To his credit, the surveyor who'd crept out had the good sense not to pop up near the door itself. And, fortunate for Uruns and his mechanized cavalry company, the crewman was apparently crawling away from the bridge, aftward along the superstructure. Sensible enough, since collateral damage to the helm might make it difficult or impossible to pilot the ship away from the docks. But it was also lucky for Uruns that neither the freighter's officers nor crew had any reason to anticipate that their attackers' greatest desire was to take the bridge intact, along with the rest of the ship's primary operating systems.

Consequently, it was both a relief and good fortune when the would-be sniper popped up well behind the bridge, his long-barreled weapon suddenly tilting down over the solid rail.

Hax saw the glint of a scope, saw the muzzle turn in the direction of one of his APCs.

But the first sound of gunfire was the whirring roar of Track Three's rotary machine gun. The first several rounds went low and wide. But before the sniper could duck back down, he, the railing, and the two portholes immediately behind him were thoroughly riddled. Faint maroon puffs dotted his torso as he fell from sight.

In the quiet that followed, Uruns gauged the stillness of the ship, imagined the loud and desperate debate taking place on the bridge, and judged that the time had come to call attention to his next step, just in case the surveyors had been too busy to notice. "Flare gun," he called down into the compartment of his APC. The bulky pistol-shaped discharger was placed in his hand. He checked to make sure the flare's coding was white not red and then fired it in a high arc, one that would be clearly visible from the bridge.

And also, to the dhow approaching the freighter's stern.

The flare soared up, a bright speck that was the only moving part of the tense tableau. Several seconds later, a throaty cough and white rearward plume came from the foremost of the two dhows. Although Hax couldn't see the impact, he heard water geyser up as the rocket struck the low swells just off the freighter's free aft quarter.

He handed the flare gun back down. "Load red," he ordered and watched the ship, but particularly the bridge.

He was still watching when the flare gun's hinged breech

snapped closed beneath him and its handle was placed back in his waiting palm. It would be a shame to damage the craft, but it had just received its last warning shot, albeit across the stern not the bow.

"How long do we wait?" asked his XO in Track Two.

"Not long." And as if underscoring the predictive truth of Lieutenant Uruns's reply, partially seen figures began moving hastily and furtively back and forth atop the superstructure.

"They're readying another attack," muttered Waals in Track Three, his tone exuberantly savage.

"Possibly," Uruns said, "but I don't think so." Once again, he was proven correct; the radio tower's flag line shook briefly and then tautened as it hauled a white flag aloft.

"Well, bugger them!" exclaimed Waals.

Hax spoke softly. "You have no reason to be disappointed."

"Haven't I? Those bastards killed my family. And I mean to kill ten for every one that they took from me."

Uruns nodded, even though no one could see him do it. "And now that we have this ship, that's exactly what you'll be doing before too long. Have patience, my brother. We have acquired the greatest possible instrument for your vengeance." He waved for Track Two to break squelch when it could do so safely.

"I don't see how an old, modified surveyor ship could be used to avenge my family," came Waals's answer.

Which is as it should be, Uruns thought.

Until the time is ripe and the hour is upon us.

Spin One

Murphy turned off the rudimentary and very clunky SpinDog datapad. "Uruns just reported. As suspected, the freighter at Kaladar Reef is one that some earlier Harvester wave converted to a vehicle transport. That makes three we've grabbed."

Bo Moorefield had seen the report over Murphy's shoulder. "Uruns will load his Band there?"

Murphy nodded. "And two other mech cav units that will converge on Kaladar, now that we hold the port." He smiled. "Is that enough for you, Major?"

Bo smiled back. "That may be more vehicles than we've got room for, Commander."

Murphy's eyebrow quirked. "'Commander'? Have I been cross-posted to the navy and no one told me?"

Bo shook his head. "No, sorry, sir. It's what they're calling you, these days."

"They're not using it around me, whoever 'they' are."

"I think it started with some of the RockHounds that Kevin's training up. Spread to the SpinDogs and then to some of our folks who work with them. Seems to have particular significance to the locals, sir. I think it's a more respectful title than Sko'Belm, but I haven't asked about it." He shrugged. "I get the feeling I might not get a straight answer, either."

Bo was surprised when Murphy didn't ask more questions; that was his standard operating procedure when presented with a mystery. The colonel just nodded. "How are the infantry numbers looking?"

"Again, probably more than we can transport, sir."

Murphy smiled. "Some little birds have been telling me that all the tribal officers have to do is whisper your name and 'Imsurmik' in the same sentence, and they get more volunteers than they know what to do with. There are whole columns of them moving overland and along the rivers to get to the coast."

"I'm sure that's an exaggeration, Comm—er, Colonel."

"I'm sure it's not, Major. Cutter's XO, Tanavuna, was quite specific about how it was your star-power that swelled the ranks."

Praise, particularly of such a sustained and determined variety, had made Bo blush as a kid. He was worried it might happen now, so he pushed abruptly into the topic concerning him the most. "Colonel, you said you expected local intel on the target two weeks ago. Has it come in yet?"

"Mostly, but the physical signaling—our 'rock-comms'—have a pretty slow data-rate. We're still compiling details, but I believe I've got enough to help you start finalizing your OPORD."

Moorefield nodded. "That's a relief, sir. For a lot of my cadre, this is the first time they've been in senior leadership positions. Up until now, we've been able to use the Lost Soldiers as warrant officer/advisors for the R'Baku. But this operation will require their technical competencies in dozens of command positions. So it will help my cadre if we can start talking about operational specifics."

Murphy nodded. "Which is why I'm reading you in. Some of

the tactical intel is still in flux, so I may have to correct some of it later. But the logistics are pretty much set in stone."

Bo folded his arms, looked at the maps and sheets on the planning table. "I'm ready to copy, Commander. Oh, damn. I mean—"

Before he could correct the slip, Murphy waved it away with a smile.

Moorefield saw genuine warmth behind that expression—something that Murphy rarely allowed to slip through—and his instinct told him this was a moment when he could ask the one question that might become thorny. "Rodg, just one question before we dive in."

Murphy seemed to welcome the informal address; he just nodded.

Bo uncrossed his arms. "Why didn't you make me part of the planning from the time we got word the Harvesters were coming early?"

Instead of frowning or acting uncomfortable, Murphy smiled. "Well, the planning actually started when we were still on R'Bak. And if I had read you in then, you would have wanted to stay behind. And if I had done that, I wouldn't have survived."

"What? Why?"

"Because your lady-wife Aliza would have killed me."

Bo laughed. "Okay, I can't debate that."

Murphy's face became serious. "Also, you needed to be up here. As you just mentioned, this is where your cadre is. And this is where you can be protected. We don't have anyone with your experience and gifts—and now reputation—as a field commander."

Murphy tilted his head in the notional direction of R'Bak. "Down there, it's the Wild West. And now, outside the tribes themselves, we have no HUMINT worth a damn. The satraps that remain aren't letting anyone into their towns; traders and merchants have to make their exchanges almost a kilometer beyond the walls. And what little intel we do get is relayed by methods that make tin cans joined by a string look high-tech.

"But the most important factor was that if we'd left you down there, the Hound-Dogs would have been idiots not to read the writing on the wall: that we had plans for a counterattack."

"And what would have been so bad about that?"

"Too many primae would like to see the Otlethes Family not

just fail but flame out. Some might even be willing to turn to the Kulsians."

"That's suicide."

"You know that, and I know that. But not all of the Hound-Dogs can—or are willing—to believe it. There's too much bad blood and too much fear that Anseker could evolve into an arch-autocrat. Besides, we needed to keep you safe up here, where you could build your staff."

Bo smiled ruefully. "You mean, running almost all our ground-pounders through a slap-dash equivalent of OCS. Or, for the NCOs, a basic leadership course." He frowned. "But keeping me safe? I could have hidden in the tunnels with the locals. That would prob-ably have been safer than up here."

"I'm not talking about the risks from the surveyors and satraps. I'm talking about saving you from yourself, Bo."

"Whoa. Back up. You think you know me better than *I* do?"

"No, but it might be easier for me to foresee some of the consequences. Which I'll prove right now. Let's say you were hiding out planetside and the surveyors started a pogrom against the warriors you worked with—against their towns, their families, their kids. Maybe shipping them off as slaves, even. Tell me, Bo: Would you have been able to sit—secret and serene—in some cave while that went down?"

Moorefield looked away, detected—and stopped—an impulse to shift uneasily from foot to foot.

Murphy nodded slowly. "I'm glad to see you're still a straight shooter, Major. Because I've seen—and admired—that you can only put up with so much injustice, so much brutality, before you *have* to do something. Your moral compass has a very active internal voice, so much so that when it begins talking the talk, you are compelled to walk the walk."

Moorefield stared at the floor, hands on his hips. "Damn it, Rodg: I hate it when you're right. Okay, point taken. So, you wanted to start with logistics?"

"Yes, although this is going to be a wave-tip overview; you'll have a lot of reading to take away." Murphy nodded toward several spreadsheets on the table. "Most of the dirtside logistics are well in hand. Locals are provisioning the infantry from the Ashbands and mechanized cavalry from the Greens as they arrive at their holding areas near the coast. They're also adding to the campaign supplies, although the new equipment is pretty much a mixed bag."

"Don't I know it. But do we at least have decent weapon standardization?"

Murphy nodded. "All small arms are SpinDog remanufactures or autofabs. There's more ammo than you could shoot through in half a year for the M14s and M60s. Good amount of grenades and .50 cal for the M2s. But beyond that...?" Murphy put up his hands. "It's the same come-as-you-are party you threw at the gates of Imsurmik."

Bo frowned. "I thought we were going to have enough Kulsian knockoffs to equip a few elite shock units."

Murphy nodded. "So did I. But when the Harvester fleet launched early, almost all the Hound-Dog autofabbing had to be dedicated to Kevin's corvettes. That left damn little extra capacity, and what we had was diverted toward either replacing all the shuttles we lost during the first year, or landers modified to carry assault teams down from orbit. And since there was no longer enough time to train anyone on the new, and more advanced, Kulsian gear, the entire 'shock unit' concept got tabled."

"Also keeps the logistical tail a match for what we've used thus far," Moorefield added philosophically. "What about more helicopters?"

Murphy nodded. "We got a few additional ones built before the corvettes devoured all the remaining autofabbing capacity. But we really couldn't use any more than those."

Bo scanned the maps of R'Bak. "Respectfully, I beg to differ."

"No, Major. I agree that we *need* more of them. But we can't *use* more, because we don't have enough qualified pilots and crew. A few stragglers are still finishing their simulator training, but after that cohort, anyone with the right aptitudes got pulled into crew slots for the corvettes. So there won't be a lot of extra Hueys chopping the air on R'Bak. I'm just glad that we pushed the SpinDogs to overproduce them before the Harvester fleet became an issue."

Moorefield pointed to the largest map on the table. "I'll bet that has the biggest file of all."

Murphy crossed his arms and nodded. "R'Bak Island is by far the toughest nut to crack on the whole planet. It's not just the center of the Kulsians' dirtside power; it's the gateway and final collection point for almost all the Harvesters. Over eighty percent of what they gather is boosted spaceside from its downport."

"Defenses?"

"Not many; they've never had to worry about attacks. It's distant from any of the major landmasses and, so far as they've known, they were the only space-faring force in the system. They do keep a battery of two missile launchers for suborbital interception, and we know they have some shore guns, but that's all."

Moorefield rubbed his chin, studied the outlines of the R'Bak Downport. "Where are those weapons located?"

Murphy shook his head. "Back when we had assets, and commo links, on the island, those weren't intel priorities. So we don't know."

Bo frowned. "Sounds like air assault or close support is off the table, then."

"Until you locate and neutralize their missile batteries, yes. And we can't be sure of the range of their SAMs, so it's crucial to ensure that they can't threaten any corvettes that might be at the upper edge of the atmosphere."

Moorefield pointed at the city beyond the Downport; aside from three ruler-straight roads, it was a trackless tangle of narrow streets and twisting alleys. "That looks like fun."

"Sure does. There is some good news, though. That's satrap country, so you won't run into surveyors or their equipment there. Their lapdogs do have some vehicles with armor and light weapons—the locals don't have anything that could take them out, but they'd be meat for your tracks."

"Assuming the locals even want to help us," Bo grumbled.

Murphy nodded. "Some certainly do. Most are aligned with the Overlords; their bread is buttered by Kulsian money and influence, even when they're not here. But their iron fist has killed a lot of people and bruised a lot of egos along the way. So while the underground movement isn't that large, Vat's intel says it's very skilled. Has to be, to survive all the sting operations and other attempts to root them out."

Bo glanced at the global map. "And once we've secured the island?"

Murphy shook his head. "That's going to be shaped by what Cutter learns. As soon as you've taken R'Bak Island, he's going south. Way south. Eventually, we'll be putting some of our effort there."

"Before we've finished consolidating the Ashbands and the Greens?"

Murphy shrugged. "If the satraps have no support from the Kulsians, the local Free Bands and irregular militias are eager to take matters into their own hands. I suspect our biggest challenge in those regions will be to make sure that their enthusiasm doesn't become vengeance." The colonel's eyes lingered well south of those regions before he looked up with a small grin. "Now, it's your turn to update me." When Bo responded with a puzzled start, he clarified. "The whinaalanis—what have you learned?"

"Not as much as I'd have liked, sir. I dropped the file off with Makarov as I came in, but it's pretty thin." Moorefield frowned at the deck. "The one thing that I hadn't known, but maybe should have, is that they actually don't like to use what we'd consider 'handy' water sources."

Murphy nodded. "Explain."

"You know how they can climb, right? Almost like spiders, when they're on short, vertical surfaces?" Murphy nodded again. "Well, I saw them get to water that way once, and now that I've talked to the other riders, it seems commonplace. They seem to prefer springs or other sources in high-altitude locations almost inaccessible to any other creatures—or us. Probably for safety, but those high-altitude spots are usually springs that don't dry up during Searings.

"Two of my guys also noticed something that what we initially thought was food sharing. Whinnie adults feed their young pretty much the way some birds do: with food stored in a reserve gut. We thought it was odd when we saw adults share with each other, but these two riders discovered it wasn't food they were exchanging—it was water. Seems the whinaalanis have some kind of sac that works a bit like a camel's hump."

Bo shrugged. "You put those two things together and you've got animals that can cross extremely arid areas by going from one permanent water source to the next, and are able to store reserves for the distances between them."

Murphy nodded vigorously. "Which suggests that they must remember the routes between those water sources."

Moorefield pointed to the map of R'Bak. "Combine that with the tunnel network that stretches across the continent and you've got a network to project and sustain extended offensive or defensive operations: either to outflank the Kulsians or to hide from them."

Murphy studied the map, shoulder almost against Bo's. "I've got to admit, I'm curious about those tunnels." He straightened, smiling. "Hell, I might go there myself, one day."

"Didn't take you for the sightseeing type, Colonel."

"You're right, but I might make an exception for this. Are those the highlights of your report, Major?"

"They are, sir."

"Then I won't keep you from the singular treat of reading the full dossier on R'Bak Island."

"I can hardly wait, sir. I'm sure I'll have questions, though."

"And I'll look forward to you dropping by with them. See you soon, Bo."

Moorefield saluted. "You will, sir." After Murphy had lowered his own hand, Bo slipped back out the hatchway and bumped into—or, more accurately, off of—Max Messina.

The big bodyguard leaned down. "Colonel in a good mood, today?"

Moorefield nodded, whispered, "Yeah. A really good mood. You think he's okay?"

Moose saluted Moorefield. "I'll report back on that, sir."

Bo chuckled, breezed past vinegary Makarov, and checked his chrono before leaving the ops center. With any luck, there would be enough time for him to catch dinner with Aliza.

Max slipped into Murphy's office. "Hi, Boss."

"Hi back at you, Moose. What's the good word?"

Messina started. "You find a lost footlocker full of Twinkies, Colonel? You seem in fine spirits."

Murphy waved away the big man's perplexity. "Life's too short to worry too much. What brings you by, Max?"

Messina held up a pausing finger, turned and drifted the hatch backward until it leaned against the coaming but was not shut. "Colonel, are you sure you don't want me back on bodyguard duty? I mean, I understand why you sent me on the mission to grab the corvette. But that was months ago now, and . . . well, the tensions are running pretty high around here." Murphy's brow slipped toward a frown. Moose hurried to strengthen his case. "I mean, I know Janusz is a great guy—loyal, big as an ox, and absolutely uncorruptible. But . . ." Max stopped as Murphy's hand rose slowly.

"I do want you to return to bodyguard duties, Max. But not for me."

Messina tried not to look crestfallen. "Then who, sir?"

Murphy pointed back out the hatch and beyond the ops center. "Major Moorefield?"

Murphy nodded. "Bo is going to be heading back dirtside into a very hot situation. I need someone there to keep him alive while he kicks the Kulsians' collective asses. And I can't think of anyone better for the job."

"But sir—"

"Thing is, you need to get there ahead of him."

"There? You mean, R'Bak?" Max frowned. "Wait—*ahead* of him? Does that mean I'm gonna have to ride down in one of those reentry pods like Captain Cutter?"

"It does indeed, and there's only one window left when we can get you in behind some debris. How soon can you be ready?"

Moose Messina sighed. "Whenever you need me, sir."

As if you didn't already know that.

Chapter Thirty-Two

Spin One

"Okay, folks, if I could get your attention, please," Bowden said to the assembled pilots and crews in the large conference facility just over the line in SpinDog country. He was getting some of his strength back, although the day's events were beginning to take their toll.

He smiled at the group, which, for the first time, was somewhat comingled. Gray sat with black in some places—not all, but it was a whole lot more than at their first meeting—and the feeling of accomplishment warmed Bowden. *This may all work, after all.* As soon as he'd had the thought, the corollary presented itself. *Until the shit hits the fan, anyway, and things start falling apart. That's when the imperative to do things as "us versus them" will want to take over again.* Bowden cleared his throat and continued, "I'd love to have more time to practice this, but we're going to have to go with what we have right now."

"Why is that?" Targ J'axon asked from where he was sitting next to Reetan Taregon. Interestingly enough, the two had become... if not "friends," per se, then something very close to it, based on the mutual admiration of each other's skills as a pilot and leader.

"Because the Kulsians are inbound. They are currently in their retro-burns, and we need to get into our positions before they turn around and begin looking at the planet again."

"Why are we here, then, and not in our ships?" Reetan asked. Targ nodded and started to rise.

"Seats!" Bowden ordered, as many of the crowd started rising to follow Targ's lead. "There has been an...issue that we need to address, which we've had to accommodate by tweaking the plan slightly."

"It was a good plan," Targ said. "I may not have liked it when you first proposed it, but I have come to see the value in it. What has changed?"

"The lead ship of the Kulsian force is a little bigger than their standard corvette," Bowden replied. He'd destroyed the imagery of the ship after his staff had seen it. When asked why, he'd replied, *"So none of the pilots see it. It's better if they don't know ahead of time. They will either be all-in when they see it, or they will run. As running means dying, I'm hoping they will be all-in."* He didn't feel good about the decision—it was too much like lying for his taste—but he'd stood by it.

"How much bigger?" Targ asked, obviously sensing his reluctance to talk about it.

"Quite a bit," Bowden replied, not wanting to lie, but also not wanting to scare them. "But—like I said—we've come up with a new strategy that we will use to defeat it with, without having to go toe to toe with it where our ships will get hammered."

"I see," said Reetan with a smirk. "And will you be briefing us on this wonderful strategy of yours?"

"Absolutely," Bowden said. He flipped over the first piece of butcher-block paper on the easel next to him. "I like to call this new strategy Operation Bait and Switch."

"So, that's it," Bowden said, thirty minutes later after he'd explained his plan and everyone's parts in it. They hadn't been what he would have called "wildly supportive" of it, but they'd at least seen the necessities involved and had decided it was probably the best use of their assets. "Are there any questions?"

Reetan cleared his throat. "I'm sorry, but you didn't mention me. You have this huge plan with lots of 'moving pieces' as you called them—which I remember you saying were 'bad things'—and yet you did not mention the part you wanted me to play in it."

"That's because I wanted to talk to you privately to discuss your part."

"Why not in front of everyone? Are you still mad at me? I have come to respect even Targ here"—he patted the SpinDog on the shoulder—"and I have done everything you've asked me to. I am widely acknowledged as one of the best pilots we have, perhaps even better than Targ... Why am I not part of the plan?"

"You are part of the plan, just not a part I've discussed yet."

"And what part is that?"

"I want you to lead the reserve force. It will be made up of an Aegis corvette—led by you, Reetan—and four regular corvettes." He named the four pilots who would be with him.

Reetan shook his head. "I still don't get it. What have I done to offend you?"

"Nothing."

"Then why are you marginalizing me?"

"Marginalizing you? Nothing could be further from the truth. You have the most important job in the entire fleet. In fact, it was the position that I was going to claim for myself, until we had to implement the bait element."

"It is more important than leading the vanguard of our fleet into battle and crushing the Kulsian fleet into its component atoms?"

"Yes, very much so." Bowden smiled. "You have heard me say, 'No plan survives contact with the enemy'?"

"More times than I care to remember. You said it was one of Colonel Murphy's laws."

"Exactly," Bowden said, "and the corollary is 'anything that can go wrong, *will* go wrong,' especially in combat." Bowden nodded. "I expect that something will go wrong in this attack—something unexpected will occur, equipment will break, or the enemy will decide not to go along with our plan. And you, Reetan, *you* are the *only* thing I have to recover from that when it happens."

"What do you mean?"

"At some point during the battle, something is going to happen that could alter its outcome. It doesn't matter what battle or where it takes place, there's always something that happens with the potential to turn a loss into a stunning victory, or a victory into a humiliating defeat. It's your job to act when that opportunity presents itself. I'm trusting you because you have the experience to recognize when that thing is occurring and the courage to act decisively when you do."

Reetan frowned, obviously not believing what he was being told.

"I'm counting on you more than anyone else," Bowden said. "I'll be at the front of the attack. Odds are, if—no, *when* you're needed—I'll probably be out of comms, likely dead, and you're going to have to use your best judgment on where and when to intervene. I'm counting on *you* to be the glue that holds this whole thing together.

"You will have to act independently, without my advice or consent, and use your best judgment. You ask why we're not using your skills in the other portion of the plan. That's because I'm betting everything I have that you will make the right decision at the right time, and you will save us all."

"You sure about this?" Fiezel asked as everyone filtered out of the briefing room.

"The plan?" Bowden asked. He shrugged. "It's as good as we can make it with what we've got."

"That's not what I meant. Are you sure you want to be on the corvette? You could handle it just as easily from Outpost, and I could take your spot on the ship. We've still got some time before we get underway; I can get up to speed."

Bowden shook his head. "No, I've got this." *And no, there isn't enough time left.*

"But are you well enough for it?"

"I am," Bowden said with more confidence than he felt. "Besides, I need to be close to the battle to make sure the comms work out." He raised a hand when Fiezel opened his mouth. "I know the Dornaani comms will work just great, but I've been in too many battles to expect comms to work perfectly."

Fiezel chuckled. "In the goo, over Hanoi...that's always where the radios always went out, and you prayed that your wingman wasn't going to run into you coming off target. The missiles coming up at you were bad enough; running into an ally would have been far worse."

"Exactly," Bowden said. "And that's why I'll be on the corvette, and you'll be on the Outpost."

Fiezel nodded and turned away. "Whatever you say, Admiral."

"What was that?"

Fiezel laughed. "While you were lazing around in your hospital bed, I had plenty of time to talk to Murphy. He told me how much you liked that call sign." He smiled with a twinkle in his eye. "Don't worry, I won't tell anyone."

Bowden sighed at the certainty that everyone *already* knew. But at least Murphy hadn't passed along the full title: Admiral Squid.

Bowden frowned. *At least, I hope not...*

Chapter Thirty-Three

Spin One

Naliryiz glanced at the candles, smiled over the quivering tongues of flame at Murphy, who was still chuckling. She smiled and, looking into his steady eyes, realized she no longer felt awkward after what had been a most embarrassing faux pas.

Rodger Murphy's invitation to dinner had come as a surprise, given his apparent desire to avoid her except when she was the mandatory witness at his debriefing of a Kulsian. However, as they only occurred when there was new intelligence, the intervals between seeing each other were highly irregular. One time, there had only been a two day gap; at another point, they did not see each other for twenty-one days. Not that she was counting.

So when his dinner invitation arrived without any change in the frequency or nature of their contact, she had hardly known what to make of it. So she did what any forthright, logical, and dominative member of the Otlethes Family would do: she secretly contacted the human female who was her de facto sister-in-law, Mara Lee.

However, Lee herself was increasingly busy preparing her helicopter crews for operations on R'Bak and had not been much in contact with Murphy herself except to provide him with brief updates. She had, however, shared an insight on the colonel's multiple sclerosis, something of which Naliryiz, though a healer, had been unaware. After all, there had never been a documented case of the affliction among any SpinDogs, so their knowledge of the disease was quite limited.

That new insight and their long separation might have been why she was not entirely composed when she arrived at Murphy's quarters. She greeted him affably...which elicited, of all things, a small, rueful grin. She also noticed a number of rather enticing aromas emanating from an array of pots and pans perched on his quarters' small cooking unit. She looked around for plates and utensils...but discovered that they were already laid out on a table that had evidently been brought to his rooms for this purpose. There was a cloth—a bedsheet?—under them, which puzzled and even worried her. Why obstruct the presumably washable surface of the table with an easily stained expanse of linen? Was it some strange test of her ability with the decidedly impractical Terran utensils?

Of which, she had never seen so elaborate a collection—several sizes of spoon, two different forks and knives, and several different cups. Although puzzled, she leaned eagerly toward the cooking smells while politely admiring the items arrayed on the table. Whatever else that signified, the arrangement had required time and precision to lay out. She decided that was a positive sign and remained standing where she was.

Only then did she realize that Murphy had left her to attend to one of the pots on the cooking unit. She wondered where the cook, presumably an orderly, had gone. Surely Murphy, Sko'Belm (or, increasingly, Commander) of the Lost Soldiers was not responsible for tending to the meal in his orderly's absence! When she inquired after that matter, he stared at her for a moment before explaining, with a small but reassuringly warm smile, that no, he had prepared the meal himself.

She hardly knew what to say. It was not merely peculiar, but somewhat arresting. She was surprised she had not noticed such a strange custom before, but then again, the only times they had shared meals or beverages were public occasions. And of course, meals with Mara were no different from meals with her family— except they were far more boisterous, and even amusingly bawdy.

When the food was ready, Murphy did not call her over to the cooking unit but, instead, brought several pots and pans to the table, from which he drew small portions that he placed on the smaller plates. She managed not to frown; it was a strange ritual, that a leader should behave like the lowest of servants. But even so, she was not prepared when he invited her to sit and then quickly moved to stand behind the chair she had selected. Presuming she had misunderstood—that the chair was, in fact, his—she hastily moved to the other chair. But he followed, indicating that now, she should stay where she was. Smiling, he drew forth the chair, and still holding it, bade her sit.

She was so confused that she did the only logical thing she could: she complied. Whereupon he sat and they began eating not the main meal, but small rations of other foods.

It was between the strange delicacies he called cashews and the ones that succeeded them—olives—that she realized that none of his preparations or solicitude was some strange shedding of dominion. Nor was it one of the rare circumstances in which a far more powerful person took ritual steps to put an inferior guest at their ease. No, this was simply his culture's way of showing esteem and, possibly, appreciation that she had accepted his invitation to dinner. Or what he had called a "home-cooked meal." On reflection, that alone should have warned her how strange this dinner would be; after all, where else would one cook a meal but at home?

However, her greatest disorientation—and abashment—occurred when she finally thought herself oriented. After a pleasant conversation regarding their respective siblings, Murphy rose, opened a bottle of wine, and served the main course: an unusually symmetric block of blended meats served with a sauce rendered from R'Bak citrus fruits. Perhaps it was the heady aroma—part salt, part spice—that distracted her just enough to step wrong.

Leaning over, he brought forth the small igniter the Lost Soldiers called a Zippo lighter and lit two low candles she had not noticed until that moment.

Naliryiz gasped. "I am sorry. I had not heard! I did not know this was a commemorative feast!"

"A what?" Murphy asked, a small frown curving down toward his small smile.

"A death feast. Who died?" She gestured toward the candles.

Murphy stared at her, then at the candles, and then burst out laughing.

Naliryiz was so confused that she was only fully aware of one thing: she did not like being laughed at by Rodger Murphy. Not that she enjoyed anyone laughing at her, but certainly not him. She was preparing to stand and depart, when he reached out and squeezed the wick of first one candle and then the other. She blinked as wisps of smoke rose from them; was he disavowing honored dead? What could it mean?

His next words were her answer. "No one has died—although you haven't eaten my cooking, yet." He chuckled; she frowned and looked at him sideways. It sounded like a quip, but—

He waved away his words and her faux pas. "Among my people, most cultures use dim light—candles especially—to signify that they are defining the space within the glow as their own. That they wish privacy so they can get to know each other better."

"This is—this is an invitation to intimacy? Rather than thoughts of grieving?"

Murphy considered. "Well, in some cultures, candles could be present in either situation. But when it's just two people, we usually understand it as . . . well, yes, an invitation to intimacy."

Naliryiz felt herself mentally step back from the misunderstanding, and almost laughed. "I am sorry, but this was . . . quite amusing, in a way."

Rodger Murphy smiled widely; his teeth were every bit as straight as the most Elevated SpinDog. "I found it amusing, too. Now, would you like some wine? I'm told that 1939 was a very good year for Bordeaux."

"I do not know what that means," Naliryiz replied as the ruby red liquid began filling her glass.

"Actually," Murphy said, smile still wider, "neither do I. Let's eat."

"This wine—Bored Doe?—is the most wonderful libation I have ever tasted," Naliryiz breathed toward Murphy. "And the meat—the Spam? What creatures is it made from?"

Murphy looked sideways. "I'm not entirely sure. And you wouldn't have heard of them."

"The sauce is *agdajhay*, is it not?"

"I don't know that word, I'm afraid. It's a fruit my soldiers have nicknamed jalapineapple. It's pretty spicy."

"Delightfully so!" she exclaimed, surprised at how loud and voluble she had become. She leaned away until her spine touched the back of her chair. "Murphy..." she started—and then did not know how to continue.

"Yes?"

Well, that's *not a very helpful response, Rodger Murphy*. She sighed. "I am from a plain-spoken people so I lack the art of approaching a matter sideways—obliquely, is your word?" He nodded. "Then here is what I must ask: I do not understand why you must be present on R'Bak for the battles there. Certainly Tapper could do what you intend to. Assuming that Moorefield and Cutter are not sufficient."

Murphy looked slightly surprised. "Yes, but if anything goes wrong, either dirtside or spaceside, Tapper, second only to Mara, is the Lost Soldier most respected by all the Families, both Spin-Dog and RockHound. And, between the two of them and Kevin Bowden, they have the knowledge and skills most needed by my people—and yours—for surviving whatever might follow."

"You think like a primus." She sighed. "Better than them, actually." *Although right now, I would welcome impetuosity!* She pushed that thought away. "More like a Matriarch."

He smiled. "I don't have the legs for a dress."

She frowned, then understood. "Ah. No, I make the comparison to matriarchs because they do not have the luxury of indulging their spleen when making decisions. Nor do you. Nor is it so firmly embedded in how your culture seems to raise males."

He tipped his wineglass toward her. "There's actually a lot of variability in that regard. But no, very few of us are raised the way your, er, males are."

She nodded, studied the wine. It was safer than his eyes. "Murphy."

He smiled. "Yes?"

"I regret having caused you to extinguish the candles. Would it be an imposition to ask you to relight them?"

He did so before replying, "Not. At. All."

Naliryiz studied the tongues of flame through the wine; they made it look like blood. Not the blood of a kill, but of hearts, of life... "I miss the light, Murphy. Down on R'Bak. I miss going there as a liaison."

He nodded. "Yes, the lights on *Spin One* are a bit cold. I expected they'd be different in the hydroponics core, more like what the plants would receive in their natural environment."

"The scientists say it is optimal for them. Better than the sun's own rays." She sighed, resisting the strange urge to pout. "And here in the corridors, the lights are optimized for activating vitamin D, maintaining alertness, preventing depression, and of course, lowering costs." She smiled at the candles. "But I like the flame. It is warmer. It is not so predictable. And your people are right: it seems to radiate as much intimacy as light." She rushed on before she could think the better of mentioning what Mara had revealed to her. "I think that a major part of intimacy is truth...so may I share a truth with you, Rodger Murphy?"

He seemed unable to speak, as if he was staring at her and had not quite heard her words. "I would be honored if you would share a truth with me, Naliryiz."

Well, we shall see if you do. "I have spoken with my adoptive sister-in-law, Mara."

Murphy smiled. "You speak with her quite a lot, I'm told."

"I do. And about all things. Such as you."

Murphy sat slightly straighter. He did not appear disturbed, but possibly a bit wary. "I'm not sure what to say." He smiled. "Should I be flattered or embarrassed?"

"Neither, for I am in earnest." She leaned far over the table. "Your disease, what you call multiple sclerosis: you know we have never seen it. So I have been unaware of...of many of its symptoms. Its consequences. Upon the most intimate parts of your life."

Murphy's smile didn't so much fade as it changed; it was sad, but also...relieved?

Naliryiz wished the table was not a hundred kilometers across. "Rodger Murphy, know this. I understand that this may trouble you. A great deal. That it might keep you from...from expressing all your feelings. But know this as well: it does not trouble me. Not in the slightest." She leaned back. "That is the truth I have wanted to speak...for a very long time." She had no idea what would happen next, which seemed to be why she was having trouble drawing each breath that punctuated the silence that followed.

He looked down for a few moments, and when he looked up again, his eyes were bright and very clear. "Naliryiz, this is a very important conversation for me. It is probably the most important personal conversation I can imagine, sitting right here, right now."

Her heart felt like it was rising up in her chest.

"It is so important that I cannot imagine having it in the

shadow of all the unknowns before us." He drew a great breath and released it as a long sigh. "We have to get through this time, first. There is so much that will happen, so much that could change all our lives forever, in the next two weeks. And almost none of the outcomes, or their consequences, can be foreseen."

Naliryiz lifted her chin and spoke another truth: the truth that made it possible for her to remain where she was, neither running out the hatch nor to the other side of the table. "I presumed you would say this, Murphy. You are a Sko'Belm and yes, a Commander. You could do no less."

He leaned toward her. "I won't—can't—say all the things I'm feeling right now, Naliryiz. If I did . . . Well, here's what I *do* know: right now, what we do, how we behave toward each other, is scrutinized. Many among your people would use it to tear apart the fragile bonds of cooperation and trust that have been forged between the SpinDogs and the RockHounds. We cannot risk that. I cannot risk that. However much I might want to—and damn, do I want to."

He leaned back sharply, as if he'd surprised—even scared—himself. Then his expression became hard with focus, determination. "Naliryiz, once we have control of R'Bak, where beyond the lands we've already searched would it be best to seek healers or shamans who might know more about the cure that's mentioned in your archives?"

Her heart may have missed a beat. "I do not know, and I cannot ask the older healers, or those of other Families, for they would readily guess the reason for my inquiry. But I can ask to access their archives. And it is also likely that the healers—the ones who call themselves alchemists—on R'Bak will have better records." She shook her head. "I am sorry, very sorry, that I am not more knowledgeable."

"No, no, that's fine." Murphy reached across the table and took her hand for a moment, then let his fingers slip aside. "That's a good start. And it's something I can . . . I can hope for." He raised his glass toward her. "To the future, whatever it may hold. May it be what we wish."

She raised her glass, smiling, but wondered if his smile was so wide that it was forced. "Promise me that you will be careful, Murphy."

His smile became calmer, warmer. "I promise. And here's another promise: when I return, things will be different." He paused, and his eyes grew shiny. "One way or the other."

PART THREE
Attack

Chapter Thirty-Four

Aegis corvette **Hornet,** *approaching R'Bak*

"That's the last one," the tech called from outside the ship as he released the towline to the missile pack. "I have good communications with it."

"Very well," Bowden said. "Come on back inside; we need to get out of sight as soon as possible."

"Everyone else is complete with their loads," the comms officer reported. "They are all moving to their positions."

"Thanks," Bowden replied with a smile. He turned to the Rock-Hound actually flying the corvette. Even though Bowden knew he could technically fly the ship, it was in a lot better hands with someone else at the controls, and it was a lot more important for him to follow the "big picture" of what was going on, rather than getting involved with the stick and throttle stuff of actually flying the craft. And—if the truth was known—he still wasn't a hundred percent. He consoled himself with the thought that, with his experience, his ninety percent was more important than anyone else at a hundred.

And, in spite of all that, the Hornet pilot in him wanted to be at the controls—to be the one firing the guns and missiles, destroying the enemy, rather than the one sitting back and directing the individual actions of the battle.

Bowden sighed and shook his head. *I guess this is just what admirals do. They sit and make important decisions that decide the outcome of the battle.* He watched the rest of the crew, who were busy with crucial hands-on tasks to make the mission happen, while he did nothing more than watch. *Yeah*, he thought to himself, *this admiral shit is vastly overrated.*

The craft raced forward as they sped back to their hiding place on the other side of the planet. There was no telling when the Harvesters were going to turn back around again, but he knew it would be soon, and they had to be well hidden by then.

Aegis corvette Hornet, off R'Bak

"We're here," the pilot, Kelebar said, sitting back in his seat. "Now what?"

"Now we wait."

"I know *that*," Kelebar said with incompletely suppressed irritation. "I was at the brief; I know it will be a while before the next phase begins, but I want to be doing something now. It is not in my nature to wait, but to act. You said you've done this before. How did you get through this part?"

The same way you are, Bowden thought. *By wishing time would jump ahead.* Bowden sighed. "The waiting part is always the hardest. Back home, the plane I flew didn't carry as much fuel as we would have liked, so once we launched, we'd go hit the Texaco station while we waited."

"What's a Texaco station?"

"It's a tanker aircraft. You would follow it, and they would extend a hose with a basket on the end. My aircraft had a plug that I would insert into the basket and then they'd transfer fuel to extend my flight time."

"Sounds dangerous."

"It could be, but it was something that we practiced a lot and got good at."

Kelebar nodded. "Then what would you do?"

"We'd go and orbit somewhere and wait for the attack to begin, sort of like we're doing now." *And pray no one did something stupid that pushed back the target time and made us go to the tanker again.*

"But what did you do to pass the time?"

"We'd review the plan, over and over, so that we were sure of our part in it—"

"I've got that," Kelebar said. "Our job isn't that hard."

"—then we would review everyone else's jobs, so we knew where our allies were, and when they'd be there, in case we needed assistance."

"You weren't the preeminent force?"

"We were," Bowden said. "We had the strongest military on the planet."

"Then why would you need assistance?"

"It's one thing to have overall superiority and another to have local superiority. For example, we thought we knew where the enemy forces were. Where they'd stationed their fighters and missile systems. But what happened if they'd moved some without our seeing it? They might have more in a given place than we did. If that happened, you might need to call in some of your allies to join you."

"Did that ever happen to you?"

"No. The people I fought didn't have much of anything."

"Doesn't sound like much of a challenge."

Bowden sighed. "We weren't outnumbered, but the conflict that I was in, some of our allies looked like the enemy forces. Hell, on any given day, some of our allies could *be* the enemy forces."

"So what did you do?"

"The best we could."

"Was that enough?"

"Not always," Bowden said, blinking back a tear. He swallowed to clear something in his throat. "Even when you tried your hardest." He smiled as he put the memory out of his mind. "Happily, we don't have that problem here. We know who the enemy is: the Kulsians. All we have to do is kill them before they do the same to us."

Aegis corvette Hornet, off R'Bak

"*Hornet*, Outpost," Fiezel's voice called a few hours later. "The Harvester fleet has arrived and is in position. It's time for the rabbit to run free."

"Very well," Bowden said. "We're on our way." He met Kelebar's eyes. "Take us out, and let's get this started."

"Yes, sir, Admiral!" the pilot exclaimed. "Right away, Admiral!"

Bowden's eyes narrowed. "Did Captain Fiezel put you up to that?"

The RockHound looked over his shoulder and grinned. "Maybe," he said, then he turned back to his controls.

Bowden shook his head as Kelebar advanced the throttles, and the craft started forward.

Surveyor snoop satellite 17624, above Shex's ecliptic plane

The satellite continued on its mission, listening for anything that shouldn't be there. Although there'd been small hits of communications, they hadn't lasted long enough—or the satellite hadn't been in the main beam of the transmission—to lock in on where the transmission had originated or to gain any real intelligence from it.

The majority of the—admittedly random and stray—intercepts it had received, though, had seemed to originate in the spinward Trojans asteroids in the third planet's orbit, and it had stationed itself nearby in order to assess whether there was anything of value to be picked up there.

Because of this, it was very well positioned when a signal arrived from the third planet, beamed on a lascom directly to the collection of asteroids, from a ship that was on the other side of the planet.

It captured the data, packaged it, and transmitted it in the direction of V'dyr.

Frigate Harvester One, *approaching R'Bak orbit*

"Harvester Fleet, *Harvester One*," the comms officer said over the radio. "Cargo ships should begin preparations for insertion and landing at Downport. We have a contact on our sensors that we are investigating. It may be the corvette that we were told to watch for, the one suspected of having gone rogue."

Ebis'qupoz Barogar nodded as his instructions were acknowledged, then he felt himself being pressed back into his command chair as the frigate's engines began a burn to chase down the corvette they had found.

"We don't have a lot of fuel remaining," his navigator warned. "If the corvette maneuvers or leaves orbit..."

"Then we will fire our missiles and destroy it," Barogar replied. "This is the only target we've seen so far, and I am not going to give up the honor of catching it or, if need be, wiping it from space."

"Lord, I am getting a signal from the second planet," the comms officer announced. "Surveyor packet *Kunsheft* is calling."

A ship of no consequence, but still... "And what does its master want?"

"I'm waiting to hear back, Lord. The communication delay is about a minute and forty seconds each way. His last communication mentioned something about a signal they had received—wait a minute, I am receiving him now." The comms officer listened for a few moments then said, "Lord, the ship we are chasing made a lascom transmission to the spinward Trojan asteroids, which was picked up by a snoop satellite he had positioned there in case the rogue corvette made an appearance."

"Interesting," Barogar replied. "He's not headed toward the asteroids, is he?"

"No," the tactical officer replied. "He is heading toward the planet's small moon."

"So he's going toward the moon, yet talking to someone on the asteroids..."

"Yes, Lord."

"He's obviously trying to draw us away from the asteroids."

"Shall I turn toward the asteroids?" the navigator asked. "We don't have fuel to do both."

Barogar considered. "No, I have no intention of letting the corvette get away, although I'm curious what is hiding from us in the asteroids. Did *Kunsheft* say what was intercepted?"

"It was in a foreign language or some kind of code; they were unable to determine the message. However, the fact that there was a lascom signal..."

"Tells me that the ship we're chasing isn't something the aboriginals here strapped together on their own. The ship must be the reaver corvette that went rogue. Also, it appears there are more of the rogue force hiding in the asteroids." He paused for a moment, thinking, then said, "Comms, call and detach two divisions of corvettes to take a look at the asteroids. Whatever they find there, tell them to destroy it."

"They also won't have a lot of fuel for maneuvering," the navigator warned. "Perhaps even less than us as they had to burn more in transit."

"I know that," Barogar replied, "but they should have enough. It's not like there's a fleet of ships hiding out in the asteroids that they'll have to fight a battle of maneuver against."

Aegis corvette Hornet, off R'Bak

"*Hornet*, Outpost. You've been seen!"

Bowden nodded as the comms officer acknowledged the call. They'd been watching the frigate at the front of the formation—*of course they had! Where else would they have been looking?*—and they'd seen the engines on it go to full throttle. It was definitely coming for them.

"Um..." the pilot said. "Shouldn't I...shouldn't we be running from it now?" Conditioned to run and hide his entire life, Bowden could see the sweat beading on Kelebar's forehead. To intentionally tweak the Kulsians' collective noses was something that went against the grain of any Hound-Dog's psyche. Reetan had recommended the pilot as being "stalwart," but even that had its limits when you were being chased by a craft three times your size.

"Wait for it," Bowden replied. "We're fat, dumb, and happy—"

"Speak for yourself," the SpinDog running the comms muttered, although Bowden didn't know which part of the statement he was referring to. *Probably all three.*

"—just out for a ride...not suspecting a fleet to show up..." Although Bowden tried to play it cool, this was just the first of many things that could possibly go wrong with the plan. If the frigate didn't give chase—or if it broke off, once it was chasing—they were hosed. They had to keep it engaged, so they needed to get close enough to it to really pique the Kulsians' interest. Of course, the only thing worse than having the frigate not pursue them was actually having the frigate catch them, because then they'd be dead and of no use. The line between too soon and too late was razor's-edge thin.

"Sir..." Kelebar said.

"Not yet."

"They're getting awfully close."

"Not yet..."

"We're not going to be able to get away..."

"Go!" Bowden ordered finally. "Run!"

Kelebar's hands were already in motion as he jammed the throttles forward and skew-turned the craft away from the oncoming nightmare. Bowden was shoved to the side, then back into his seat by the gees as the comms officer made the call to Outpost that they were running away, which was the signal for the Hound-Dog force to begin their assault. For good or bad, his plan was now in motion. They were either going to win… or they were all going to die.

"We're in missile range of the frigate," the tactical officer advised, looking at the link signal that Outpost was sending them.

Bowden nodded brusquely. "Can you go any faster?" he asked the pilot. "I thought this craft was faster than the frigate."

"It is," the RockHound replied with a grunt, "but our momentum was headed toward the frigate while they were accelerating toward us. I'm out-accelerating them now, but their velocity is still greater than ours." He then muttered, just loud enough to be heard, "You waited too long." The pilot slapped the dashboard as if he were riding a horse and could urge it to go faster with a little physical encouragement.

"The Kulsian frigate is calling," the comms officer reported. "They have identified themselves as *Harvester One*, and they say they are going to fire on us if we do not cease our acceleration and allow them to board us."

"I don't think I want them to do that today," Bowden said, "as I doubt that meeting would go very well for us."

Bowden stared at the plot, unable to pull his eyes away from it. He knew there were other things he was supposed to be doing, like coordinating the movements of the fleet, but the fact that he was in missile range for the first time in hundreds of years had captured his attention, and he was unable to break away. The distance between the ships continued to shrink, but he could see the rate at which it did was slowing as the corvette out-accelerated its larger kin. He breathed a sigh of relief as the distance began to increase.

"*Harvester One* says that this is our final chance," the comms officer said, his eyes wide. "We can either allow them to board, or they will fire on us." Bowden nodded once in acknowledgment. "Should I reply to them?"

"No. Don't say anything."

"But—"

"We're not stopping."

"Missile launch!" Outpost called as he saw several blips separate from the frigate on the tactical plot. "Missile launch from the frigate."

"Damn it," Bowden said under his breath. *I did wait too long.*

FOB "Outpost," spinward Trojans of R'Bak

"Go!" Dave Fiezel urged as he watched the link from the Dornaani microsat. No matter how hard he implored them, though, Bowden's craft continued toward the Kulsian frigate.

"They're going to have a hard time staying out of missile range if they wait any longer," the RockHound standing next to Fiezel said. "Maybe you should call them again."

"He knows what he's doing," Fiezel said with more confidence than he felt. A lifetime of flying in-atmo tactical jets hardly gave Bowden the experience he needed to fight a space battle... not that any of them had any more experience with space battles than Bowden. *Please know what you're doing. Please... Please...*

"They're finally turning," the RockHound noted. "He waited too long," he added with the flat tone of, "and I know what I'm talking about." Confirming his opinion, the ring around the frigate showing its likely missile range reached Bowden's ship and marched past it, putting *Hornet* well within range.

Sweat trickled down Fiezel's back, but there was nothing he could do. Bowden was committed. *No*, he realized, *there is something I can do.* "Call the fleet," he said. "Tell them to hurry."

"Tell them to hurry?" the comms officer asked. "What do you mean?"

"Tell them to go as fast as they can," Fiezel clarified as missiles began firing from the frigate, "or there isn't going to be anything left of the Admiral when they get there."

Frigate Harvester One, off R'Bak

"They are in range, Lord. Should I fire?"

"No, let us give them a chance to surrender, first. The corvette will make a nice trophy, but only if it is not destroyed. Call them and let them know that we will fire on them if they do not stop and let us board."

"What will we do with them if they do?"

"Hopefully we will gain some intel on their organization."

"What if they won't talk?"

"Then we will start throwing people out an airlock until they do. I would like to know where they have hidden their goods. It is not too late to call off the attack on the asteroids, if that is where they are. Ultimately, they will all go out the airlock, and I will take possession of the corvette that they stole from us."

"They do not appear to be stopping, Lord."

"No, they do not, and they are beginning to get away from us. Fire missiles one through four. If they will not stop, then we will bring them to heel, ourselves."

Chapter Thirty-Five

Great Western Ocean, R'Bak

The shuttle's pilot turned away from her instruments long enough to shout, "An open window is confirmed; no surveyor satellites in line of sight. We're heading down fast...and no promises for a smooth ride." As she turned away, she grumbled. "I hate flying these winged barges: about as responsive as a rock."

Bo Moorefield swallowed back the urge to recommend that Captain Hadraysa might want to consider projecting a calmer—or at least more reassuring—command presence. Instead, he began a final recheck of his gear.

Before he could move on from the snorkel and rebreather, the shuttle banked sharply. Flung forward against the five-point restraint, his surprised grunt came out so forcefully that it was almost a gasp.

"Apologies, Major," Hadraysa shouted from the cockpit. "Randomized radar sweep from an offshore surveyor ship."

"Is that typical? Were we illuminated?"

"'Yes' to the first, 'no' to the second. The surveyors keep many freighters in storage between Searings, mostly for gathering the Harvests. But they also equip some of them with high-power radars to run unscheduled sensor sweeps, particularly along the approaches to R'Bak Island." She banked again, cursed under her breath. "They're usually not this far out, but they may be noticing the increased maritime traffic up north. There are more seaplanes in local hands than they're accustomed to."

As the shuttle leveled off, Bo finished checking his flight suit. "Damn, I expected these things would be more comfortable."

Hadraysa's chuckle became a dark mutter. "Looks can be deceiving, Major. But other than putting you in a vac suit, that was the only reasonable option for this mission."

Bo nodded, although neither she nor the other two persons in the craft—the copilot and the crew chief near the fuselage door—were looking at him; they were too busy with their own tasks. "How long, now?" Moorefield shouted forward. He'd never admitted to or mentioned his misgivings regarding the mission profile, but as they dropped lower, he discovered he was occasionally wiping beads of sweat away from his temples.

"No more than fifteen minutes," she called back. The glow that had crept up along the edges of the cockpit glass faded rapidly; its nose was dropping out of its positive-pitch reentry angle. The sky darkened ahead.

"Heading into clouds?" Bo asked.

"No," Hadraysa replied. "We are moving across the terminator. Descending into the dark." As she spoke, the cockpit lights dimmed to one-third intensity and the nose of the craft disappeared against the black into which it was flying. Painted a charcoal-blue slate, it was reasonably camouflaged for any but the brightest of ocean conditions.

Bo had just become accustomed to the steadiness of the deceleration and new vector when his inner ear alerted him to a very faint bank to the right.

"Coming around slowly," the captain called into the comparative quiet. Then, turning toward her copilot: "Tilt nacelles: lowest thrust."

"Not zero burn?" he asked.

"There could be more surprises. I don't want to rely on lateral mode reignition. So, no: keep the nacelles hot."

Once again, Moorefield began to relax; the faint banking of their slow turn remained consistent and slow. He had almost begun to smile at his own anxiety when reality gave him an immediate and abrupt reason not to.

"Vent me!" the copilot shouted. "Satellite contact! Polar vector one-two-seven true."

Hadraysa emitted several now-familiar RockHound curses and rolled hard, flaring back the other direction with a quick pulse of the thrusters.

"You're dropping us out of the profile," the copilot warned.

"I must," she snapped. "If that platform lights up an active array..."

As if summoned by her trepidation, two red lights flashed on the sensor console; a rippling klaxon filled both the cockpit and the rear compartment.

The laconic crew chief's question was as sharp as a dog's bark. "Do they see us?"

"Working on it," Hadraysa snarled back. Two tense moments passed, then: "No; its active sensors just happened to switch on while it passed overhead. We managed to get outside the down-look footprint. Barely."

"I thought there weren't any satellites in line of sight," Bo said quietly.

The copilot answered. "There weren't forty-eight hours ago, but the surveyors have been getting nervous ever since our warships appeared. They must have directed the satellite into a new orbit when it was on the other side of the planet."

Hadraysa nodded tightly. "Yes. Still, I'm surprised the Dornaani microsats didn't pick it up."

"They can't be everyplace at the same time," said the crew chief. "Think it was luck or the surveyors detected the microsats?"

The captain shook her head. "It would be a minor miracle or a curse of the Death Fathers for them to even spot one of those little birds. And I don't know if they'd be willing to give away having learned of their presence simply to illuminate a shuttle that's now at least six hours away from R'Bak Island. They'd save that surprise for something more decisive." She half turned toward the payload bay. "Are you all right, Major?"

"Never better," Bo lied. At least the craft had straightened out again, but it was diving at a steeper angle than before—far more than the mission profile specified. "Why the hurry if the surveyor platform didn't see us?" he asked in as casual a voice as he could muster.

"There's no reason to suspect it did, but the only way I could be *sure* is if I had been staring over its operator's shoulder. So I'm following the fast-descent contingency, just in case they know but intend to keep us unsuspecting as they scramble assets into our area."

"Which means...?"

"Which means we are going to complete this mission immediately. Chief Hrekul, help the major."

"I'm sure I can manag—"

"Help the major *now*, Hrekul!" Hadraysa shouted.

The crew chief almost leaped from one side of the fuselage to the other. "Major Moorefield," he said loudly, reaching for Bo's arm, "we were going to complete your insertion after several minutes of level flight. We do not have that luxury anymore.

"We will dive to our safety limit and will then execute a hard rotation and full thrust from the nacelles to achieve hover. You must deploy very quickly; we cannot remain at the target zone for more than twenty seconds. We will shear off on a vector that puts us behind the satellite that just went overhead and will allow us to stay beyond the sensor cone of the next one that will be on station in eighteen minutes."

"Understood," replied Bo, swaying up to his feet.

That was when he realized that the deck of the shuttle was actually slipping and bucking very slightly. Hadraysa was delicately tweaking the shuttle's attitude as it cut through thermals and wind currents that, on a regular descent, it would simply have gently bellied through.

"Tell me when you have eyes on target," Hadraysa ordered her copilot.

The crew chief made sure that Bo was standing in front of the still-sealed side door before fixing the flotation ring around his waist. "Major," he said, "tell me what you've learned about deploying in this gear."

"I hop forward. Both feet. I pull the tab on the ring with one hand while I hold the mask against my face with the other. The ring should inflate. If it does not, I activate the backup pressure canister and check the ring's integrity. The pickup team should reach me within thirty seconds. I remain as stationary as possible. They throw a line. I attach it to the harness. They reel me in and tow me toward a reef just outside the drop zone."

"You have it, sir," the chief confirmed as the deck rose sharply; they were swooping up, Hadraysa lifting the nose to cut their dive.

"Objective in sight," called the copilot. "We're coming in a little hot, Captain."

"I know, I know," Hadraysa hissed impatiently. "Ready back there? Secure yourselves; there will be a sharp retro-blast." The thrust from the nacelles almost cut out as they rotated into vertical attitude and then flared back to life.

The craft seemed to buck backward; Bo felt like he was in the head of a prizefighter rocking back on his heels after a pop to the chin.

"Ready to deploy?" called Hadraysa.

"Ready, aye," replied the crew chief.

"Count me down," Hadraysa shouted to her copilot over the roar of the thrusters.

"Twenty-seven meters...twenty meters...fifteen meters..."

"Door open!" Hadraysa shouted back into the compartment.

Bo didn't even hear the ten-meter altitude call. The sudden blast of the ocean winds and the throaty roar of the now vertical thruster nacelles drowned out every other sound until his ears became accustomed to the competing howls.

"Five meters!" the copilot shouted.

"Retrieval sighted?" Hadraysa yelled.

The crew chief stared into the heated vapor roiling up off the ocean swells below. "Scanning...scanning...There! Thirty meters to the southwest!"

"That's awfully close," Hadraysa called after a moment.

"Retrieval is at safe distance," the chief yelled at her. "My call."

"Acknowledged. Dipping to three meters." Hadraysa twitched her hands across the controls. Bo saw the brightness reflected from the thrusters diminish slightly.

"Stand in the door!" the chief called. Bo did. "On my call: big jump, both feet. Hold, hold—Go! Go! Go!"

Bo jumped out, hand on his mask, realizing he had left the other on the coaming to steady himself. He snapped it over quickly to the inflation activation tab; the sudden sideways motion tipped him out of a vertical entry into the water.

He felt the float ring cinch him hard around the waist the same moment his boots hit the risers at a slight angle. The chop rolled him to that flank but the buoyancy of the ring straightened him out.

The shuttle, poised above him like a fire-breathing dragon with two mouths, angled away and then began rotating its nacelles into lateral flight mode, It sheared off, slowly building altitude.

Bo caught a small riser in his face, shook the water off his mask, squinted around, eyes still adjusting to the much darker ocean, now that the glare of the thrusters had receded.

"We like Ike!" yelled a heavily accented voice from almost directly behind him.

Trying not to laugh, he responded with his code name—"SHAEF!"—and paddled to turn himself.

An outrigger ketch was drawing up to him, a small, primitive electric motor pushing it the last few meters.

The crew tossed a line; Moorefield affixed it to his harness. The boat motored slowly around to head away from the drop point as its crew raised a small lateen-rigged mast and chocked it in place. Perhaps a kilometer away, a low, rocky mass rose above the swells. Beyond it, the silhouette of a narrow-hulled ship, crew busy with its much larger spars, was readying to set sail.

A gray smudge was just limning the eastern rim of the ocean when a call from the lookout paused the deckhands. As if in response to that cry, a sea-monster growl rose from the south.

Shortly after, a strange beast appeared above that part of the horizon, rushing toward the ship at great speed, wings spread, belly almost skimming the risers. When it finally lowered enough to touch the swells, it raised a spray that hit its whirling propellers and was flung away like an unruly cloud of steam.

The boat-bellied seaplane bumped once again, then faintly a second time before its hull settled into the water. As it motored toward the xebec, the captain turned to the tallest and fairest of his small crew. "Major, as I've heard Lost Soldiers say, 'your ride is here.'" He gestured toward a waiting skiff as the hatch in the side of the seaplane opened.

"I like Ike!" called Max Messina's voice from the black hole in its fuselage. It sounded a great deal less amusing without the incongruous accent.

"SHAEF," Bo shouted in return. "Coming over now. Do you have an update, Moose?"

As Moorefield stepped down into the pitching skiff, the outline of Messina's head emerged into the dove-gray light of predawn. "Two of them, sir."

"How long to R'Bak Island?"

"Four hours to reach the boat that will take us in the last five klicks."

"Fast sitrep?"

"No such creature exists, sir, but expect a long brief on the ride."

Bo smiled. "Looking forward to it," he called over the sloshing rhythm of the risers as the feeling of arrival finally rose up in him.

Chapter Thirty-Six

Aegis corvette **Hornet,** off R'Bak

Bowden watched as the missiles tracked toward him on the plot. One of the best things about being on one of the Aegis corvettes was the connectivity. As long as they had lascom with Outpost, they were connected to the satellite network and were able to see—to a good extent, anyway—what was going on. But that came at a price. When someone was shooting at you—like now, when there were missiles inbound—you also had situational awareness of that, which was far less cool.

"Maybe they'll run out of propellant?" Bowden asked.

"Unlikely," the tactical officer replied with a shake of his head.

"Any chance of outrunning or outmaneuvering them?" Bowden asked the pilot.

"If I maneuver now, we'll just help them catch up quicker and complicate the targeting solution for your point defense lasers," Kelebar replied.

Bowden looked over his shoulder. "How's the point defense coming, by the way?"

"Just waiting for them to come into range," the tactical officer replied. "Stand by . . . Firing!"

Bowden watched the plot as if his life depended on it—which it did—as their weapons began firing. His corvette—like many due to the slew of last-minute changes—was nonstandard in that it had both a laser and a railgun for point defense.

The missiles raced toward the *Hornet*, but unlike back home, where the missiles would have come fairly close together, these were spaced apart, giving the tactical officer—maybe—a chance to stop all of them. It also helped that they were running straight away from the frigate when it fired. Not only was the closing velocity lower than it might otherwise have been, but the missiles were also coming straight toward them without any sort of terminal maneuvers.

"Got it!" the tactical officer exclaimed as one of the lines dropped from the link. "Switching to the second."

The second missile was already close, Bowden saw, and the third was in range, too. It had taken too long to kill the first one. The second track continued to close as the weapons realigned and then slowly—*too slowly!*—began firing.

Finally—within a second of it hitting the corvette—the laser finally scored on the missile, and it detonated, close enough aboard that pieces of it went *Ping! Ping! Ping!* as they struck the aft end of the corvette. The tactical officer swung his weapons in search of the next target, but both of the missiles began gyrating rapidly. "The missiles are maneuvering!" he called after a second. "I can't lock them up."

"Got it!" Kelebar exclaimed, his face a mask of concentration. With the point defense unable to hit the weapons closing on them, he was free to maneuver, and he threw the craft back and forth, rolling it over and yanking it down and then back up again, all the while firing off chaff from the craft's countermeasures stores like he'd been taught.

Bowden nodded in recognition. *In another time and place, he would have made a good Hornet pilot.*

The third missile merged with them on the plot, and Bowden grabbed hold of the arms of his chair, but the explosion never came. The missile went past them on the plot; the chaff had either distracted it or the pilot's maneuvering had defeated it—*either way, it had missed!*

Bowden looked for the fourth missile but couldn't find it on the plot. Then something slammed into the craft, there was a flash of light, and everything went dark.

Corvette **Taregon's Pride,** overwatch off **R'Bak**

"*Hornet* has been hit, and we aren't showing any signs of life from it," Fiezel said, calling from Outpost. "It's even money on whether the Hound-Dog fleet or the Kulsian fleet will reach him first."

"I was watching, too," Reetan said from his overwatch position halfway between Outpost and where the battle was happening, "and I am aware he has been hit. That said, the Kulsians are not a fleet; it is just one ship."

"I need you to go and help him," Fiezel said.

"No," Reetan replied, looking at his tactical plot. The frigate hadn't seen the fleet coming from behind the planet yet, and it was proceeding even farther from the safety of its fleet. Both forces—the Hound-Dog fleet and the frigate—would end up near Bowden's craft at nearly the same time. Whether there was even anything worth saving hadn't been determined yet. "Bowden said that something like this was possible. He served his purpose as the bait. He got the frigate to follow him and separate itself from the rest of the fleet. Now, it is up to Targ to save him and to destroy the frigate while he's doing so."

"But they are both going to converge on Bowden, and it's likely that there will be a battle around him. If you were to swoop in from your current position, the frigate might turn away from Bowden and head toward you."

"Perhaps," Reetan said. In looking at the plot, he decided that possibility was actually quite likely. The frigate *would* turn away, but it would also bring it back closer to the remainder of the fleet. He felt the pull of every spacer not to leave a comrade alone in the black . . . but at what risk? He shook his head. "The answer is no," he radioed. "Bowden said that there would be a time to use the reserve, and I would know when it was. This isn't it." He pursed his lips as he looked at the plot. "Yes, I might get the frigate to turn, but that might also get the rest of the Kulsian fleet to rejoin with it before it is supposed to. Bowden stressed the importance of fighting the frigate alone and hitting it by surprise. If I intervene, that might change. Unfortunately, Bowden is on his own. Reetan, out."

Corvette J'axon's Revenge, *off R'Bak*

"Outpost just called," the comms officer reported.

"What did they want?" Targ J'axon asked.

"They said Bowden's craft has been hit."

"Is he okay?"

"They don't know. The ship isn't responding. They want us to go faster."

Targ studied the plot for a few seconds. "We're going to arrive at the wreck of his ship at about the same time as the frigate, if we continue at the same speed we are. The frigate will see us coming well in advance of their arrival and will either turn back or engage us instead. Bowden should be all right." *Unless they fire at the ship again, just out of spite. They are Kulsians, after all, so it isn't just possible... it's more than likely. But there isn't anything I can do from here.*

"Outpost is worried about both sides firing missiles past Bowden's ship."

Targ tilted his head as he looked at the comms officer. "Do they not realize we have a repeater of the tactical plot?" He motioned to it. "I can see the geometry of the situation every bit as well as they can. I probably understand it better than someone who doesn't have a life's worth of time flying in the black."

Targ glanced at the plot again and shook his head. "They have lost sight of the situation. We're fighting for the lives of everyone in this system. Bowden knew the risks of being the bait—*he explained them to us!* He would not want his sacrifice to be meaningless." He shrugged. "Tell them we will try not to shoot Bowden's craft as we pass it, but I *will* take every opportunity to kill the frigate and make Bowden's plan a success.

"Are you ready for the second phase?" Targ asked his tactical officer.

"I am."

"As Bowden would say, then, lights out."

Frigate Harvester One, *off R'Bak*

"Got him!" the weapons officer exclaimed.

"One hit out of four missiles fired isn't something to get excited over," Ebis'qupoz Barogar noted wryly. "Nor is it particularly cost effective. Still, the ship *is* dead in space, which will make their capture easy. Hopefully, they were wearing suits and won't all die on us before we can get there."

Barogar relaxed back into his command chair. "Navigator, you can slow to a more fuel-efficient speed."

"Yes, Lord."

"Lord!" the tactical officer exclaimed.

"Yes?"

"I have signals...No! Two sets of signals. There are ships coming from around the moon the corvette was heading toward, and there are others coming around from the back side of the planet!"

"How many ships? What type?"

"I'm not sure, Lord. It looks like many of them—at least ten in each group. The long-range telescope indicates that the group from the moon are more of the corvettes like the one we were chasing. Stand by... The ones from behind the planet are also corvettes. I make it at least twenty corvettes coming toward us. There are also a number of what look to be smaller ships in company with the group coming from the moon."

"Navigator, flip us and then full thrust. Get us out of here."

"Lord..."

"I don't want to hear about the fuel state! There are twenty ships coming! *Get us out of here now!*"

"Yes, Lord."

"Comms officer, call the fleet and have them meet us on our way back. Don't let them whine about fuel states or having to climb back out of the gravity well. I want them here *now!*"

"Yes, Lord," the comms officer replied as the ship started maneuvering. After a few moments, he asked, "Lord?"

"Yes? What is it? I don't want to hear that they can't make it; I want them maneuvering *immediately!*"

"There's a problem, Lord. Our comms aren't working; I can't get a signal through to either group. The communication satellites don't seem to be working."

"What? How is this possible?"

"There appears to be some sort of static. The only time I ever saw this before was when I was being jammed in the last conflict back home...but that isn't possible, is it? The locals don't have a comms-jamming capability, do they?"

"No," Barogar replied with a grunt. "Not unless the rogue operatives have given it to them."

"It is more capable than anything the rogues would have had. I can't get a signal through at all. Perhaps when we are back within line of sight of the fleet I can get a message to them, but at the moment, I am unable."

"Navigator, we need to go faster!"

The minutes required to get back to within line of sight of the rest of the fleet were the longest of Ebis'qupoz Barogar's life. "Are we within sight yet?" he finally asked when he couldn't wait any longer.

"One more minute, Lord," the comms officer replied. "Perhaps less."

"Missile launch!" the tactical officer exclaimed.

"What?" Barogar asked. "Where? The ships are too far away." He scoffed. "They're desperate. There's no way they can hit us from there."

"No, Lord. Closer. More missiles now!"

"From where?"

"Some of the trash in orbit, Lord. They must have hidden missile launchers in the garbage!"

"Destroy them! Destroy them now."

"Trying, Lord. There are at least twelve missiles inbound."

"If nothing else, we won't go alone. Fire six more missiles at the corvette we disabled before we're out of range."

Corvette J'axon's Revenge, *off R'Bak*

"The frigate is turning to run," the tactical officer noted.

"He is afraid," Targ said. "Be prepared for anything; this is when he will be the most unpredictable."

The crew watched as the frigate spun and brought its engines to full, working to kill its momentum. Before long, it was accelerating back away from them.

"He started the maneuver a little before we had planned. If the fleet goes to full throttle, they will be close to the frigate before we can catch up to it."

"Then maybe we should slow it down. Fire the orbital missile packs as they come in range."

"Yes, sir," the tactical officer replied. Three minutes later, missiles separated from two of the non-maneuvering icons on the plot, and they watched as the missile icons raced toward the frigate. The icon blurred slightly as it used its jammers and countermeasures, then missiles started launching from the frigate in response.

"Does the ship have antimissile missiles?" the tactical officer asked.

"Not that I am aware of," Targ said.

The missile sped out from the frigate, but then turned and raced back along its path.

"*They're going to kill the admiral!*" the tactical officer exclaimed in horror.

Targ shook his head. "There's nothing we can do. Maybe Burg can stop them, but we're too far out of range."

He turned back to the plot in time to see one of the missiles approaching the frigate drop out of the plot, then a second. Targ bit his lip. They needed the missiles to hit. Everything was predicated on taking out the frigate first. In the simulations they'd run, the results were usually catastrophic for the Hound-Dogs if it wasn't taken out before the fleets joined, which is why they'd prepositioned the missile packs. They weren't much...but the missile packs were all they'd had left over. A couple of the ships were each short a missile, as they'd had to pull some from the fleet to have enough to fill the launchers.

A third missile from the group approaching the frigate dropped out of the plot, then the icons for the missiles merged with the frigate. Two more continued past it, clean misses. Targ continued to stare at the plot. Did they really get seven hits on it? More importantly, *would it be enough*?

"I have hits!" the technician manning the long-range telescope yelled.

On the plot, the frigate's acceleration began dropping.

"We've got you now," Targ said to the frigate's icon.

"But what about the admiral?" the tactical officer asked.

"It's all in Burg's hands now."

Corvette Hound-Dog One, *off R'Bak*

"Sons of motherless whores!" Burg Hrensku said vehemently as missiles left the frigate and bent back toward the admiral's ship. "Throttles to maximum! Comms officer, tell our group, flank speed ahead!" He could feel the sweat—formerly of anticipation, but now of horror—running down his back. There was no reason to shoot at the admiral's ship, other than pure malice. *But it* was *the Kulsians they were talking about.*

He smiled as Raptis's group alongside his also went to full speed, and the missile packets leaped forward ahead of the group to chase down the frigate. Burg didn't know if he could get to the admiral in time to save him, but he was damn well going to try.

"Sons of motherless whores?" his tactical officer asked. "What does that even mean?"

Burg chuckled. "I have no idea. It's something the admiral

says when he's frustrated. You can ask him about it, but first we have to save his ass." He stared at the plot as the missiles raced toward the *Hornet.* "Contact Raptis's tactical officer. Our group will take the first three missiles. Her group can take the last three."

"Yes, sir."

Hrensku chewed the inside of his lip. Once they saved the admiral—not if, but when—they'd have to slow down slightly to keep from arriving at the frigate piecemeal; the sudden burst of speed was ruining their carefully planned timing. He shook his head. The shots were going to be long ones; hopefully the missiles didn't have any terminal maneuvering capability. If they did, the Hound-Dogs were going to be screwed, as Fiezel would say. The angle was good and the targeting information they were getting from the Dornaani satellites was solid; the missiles were coming right at them, making the shot as easy as it could be.

Aside from being right at the upper end of their point defense lasers' effective range.

He didn't have long to worry about it as the missiles covered the space between the ships quickly. "Weapons free," Burg said as he'd been taught.

"Ships are all linked," the tactical officer said, looking at his screen. "Good lock... Firing!"

Corvette **Hound-Dog Seven,** *off R'Bak*

Malanye Raptis nodded her head as the first missile blew up short of *Hornet.* As tempting as it would have been to have her crews join in on the first missiles, she wanted them concentrating on the ones they'd been given responsibility for. She had six ships and there were three missiles; there were two ships for each missile.

The second missile dropped out of the plot, destroyed, then the third, then her ship was firing. The only indication was the whine from the equipment over her head.

"We got ours!" her tactical officer cried jubilantly.

"Keep firing at the others!" Raptis ordered. If two ships firing was good, three or four was better.

"Fifth missile down," the tactical officer said, his voice now full of concentration. "Weapons failures from *Eleven* and *Twelve!*" he called. "Now the missile is maneuvering, too. Gods! *Eight* through *Ten* are all firing..."

The icon for the missile gyrated wildly in its final approach to the *Hornet*, then merged with the admiral's ship.

"Did you get it?" Raptis asked.

"I don't know." The tactical officer shrugged. "I think we hit it right before it hit the *Hornet*, but I can't promise anything."

"Comms? Anything from the *Hornet*?"

"No, ma'am," the comms officer said. "I can't reach them on the radio."

Good luck, Bowden, Raptis thought as her corvette raced past the icon of the *Hornet*. *We'll come back for you after the battle... if we can.*

Chapter Thirty-Seven

The Hamain, R'Bak

The shuttle's tilt-thruster nacelles ignited and began throttling up as Cutter and Tanavuna led their handpicked team into the payload section of the emergency shuttle. Those familiar with the procedure began strapping in. The others, most of whom had never been in a vehicle of any kind, were assisted by the Spin-Dog crew chief and mechanic. Along with the pilot, they were the only off-worlders who'd remained behind on R'Bak when the surveyors arrived, except for two helicopter pilots.

Half of Cutter's section had been chosen because, of all the bands in the Hamain, they had the most familiarity with the high desert and regions south. However, they had never flown before; nor had half of the others. So when the thrusters roared and the shuttle rose straight up, they flinched and stared nervously at Cutter.

He simply nodded at them. They nodded back and sat at attention, agreeable smiles on their faces, but their eyes wide and unblinking. When the craft shuddered, buffeted by a crosswind, one of them swallowed audibly but all their eyes remained fixed on the opposite side of the fuselage.

Cutter had believed himself beyond surprise at anything that might happen in a shuttle—until he heard Colonel Murphy's voice speaking to someone in the cockpit. Or, as the shuttle jockeys

301

insisted, the bridge. "Egret Three, say again your ETA at Point Break One."

"Ten mikes, Glass Palace."

Cutter almost rolled his eyes. "Glass Palace" was Murphy's code name, typically when he was on *Spin One*. The creative, even fanciful, names preferred by the post-World War II Lost Soldiers were far, far too fancy for Cutter's taste. *Lord, give me the old days when it was just Apple, Baker, Charlie.*

"Roger that, Egret Three. Update on Roro Zero?"

"Secure at wharfside, ramp ready. Waiting on SHAEF."

"Inform when SHAEF arrives Roro Zero, Egret Three. Glass Palace out."

"Good copy all, Glass Palace," came the reply before the radio connection cut out.

The pilot's voice sounded concerned. "Turbulence ahead, Commander Murphy. Move with care."

There it was again: a Hound-Dog calling Murphy "commander." What the heck was that about?

If the colonel had acknowledged the pilot's warning, it must have been a nod, because his next words were over the intercom. "Chief, is there a spare jump seat?"

"Two, Colonel," replied the crew chief.

Cutter realized he was frowning as Murphy came back from the cockpit. "Why did you come along for the insertion, sir?"

"Wanted to talk to you, but not over the radio." Murphy strapped into the seat the chief had folded down and locked in readiness for him. Normally sure-footed, the colonel almost tumbled into it.

"Talk about what, sir?"

"We'll get there. First, can you think of any last-minute needs we left out of your TOE?"

Cutter frowned, shook his head. "No, sir. We've got everything that's worth the weight to carry. And, assuming the supply caravan from Ikaan-tel got to the oasis at the south edge of the Hamain, we'll have mounts and consumables waiting for us there." Tyree made his caveat a statement, but he ended it in the tone of a question.

Murphy nodded. "The caravan signaled its arrival at the oasis about thirty hours ago, Captain Cutter. I presume you've had a chance to show our orbital mapping to the locals who traveled to Novy Malacca before the Searing?"

"I have, sir."

"And do you stand by the last time estimate for your team's arrival there?"

"I do, but I've still got serious doubts about how reliable any ETA will prove, sir. There are a lot of assumptions built into it. The biggest is that the weather won't kick up and give us monsoons and high water to contend with, to say nothing of what you call super-saturated humidity levels. And since the only meteorological records we have for the area fall someplace between received wisdom and hearsay, any projections are little more than guesswork. We only have what we've observed going into the Searing and what the locals tell us—none of whom were alive for the last one." He paused, then lowered his chin and his voice. "Sir, is there anything else I should know about Novy Malacca?"

Murphy glanced sideways at him. "Why?"

"Because my guys aren't scared of much... but they're scared of this. Almost no one travels down there, even in the best of times. But during the Searing?" Cutter shook his head. "Tanavuna asked if there was a classified objective I'd withheld. Made me wonder myself, sir. Granted we've had tough missions, but it's hard to square up the danger of traveling there now with the lack of any obvious, immediate need."

Murphy nodded slightly; his reply was barely above a whisper. "That's what I wanted to talk to you about in person. Vat found indications that Harvesters go there occasionally. No indications of how many or how often, but it's possible they have a base in or around a city called Kanjoor. Assuming it's not abandoned during the Searing, it could have a population partially or wholly descended from Kulsians who were either stranded or 'went missing' there during earlier harvests. If so, and if some of the surveyors know its location, or just rumors that it exists..."

Cutter nodded. "Then any that can't get to R'Bak might risk heading down that way."

"And if they do, we need to know."

"You want us to intercept them?"

Murphy shook his head. "You are not going to that region to engage the enemy, Tyree. Your primary mission is observe, report, and—if there are approachable locals—make contact with any population you might find in or around Kanjoor."

"But if we see Kulsians, sir?"

"Assuming that 'Admiral Squid' Bowden has prevailed upstairs, then you break squelch. We will reply with the code set for further comms and you'll give us their coordinates. You might have to keep the Kulsians in sight for a while, but I have no intention of putting any of you in a rainforest firefight. Pick up the pieces after we deliver a strike package, maybe, but no more than that.

"Hell, I regret having to send you farther south at all. I wish we could have put this off until we get a look at the data the Harvesters maintain on R'Bak from one Searing to the next. But most of that will come from any of their ships that are salvageable after the fleet action. Unfortunately, if we waited that long..." Murphy concluded with an eloquent shrug.

Cutter smiled. "Yeah, that would kind of defeat the whole purpose of getting ahead of any Kulsians who might be south-ward bound."

Murphy smiled back. "Yes, it would."

Cutter sighed. "I always seem to get the real sweet assignments, the vacation spots. In this case a tropical isthmus." He chuckled. "I'm hoping to put in some time at the beach, but I think I'm gonna skip the sunbathing."

As if agreeing with his precaution, the combined light of 55 Tauri's two suns came through a small porthole in the seaplane's fuselage. The rays were so strong that it felt like a beam weapon hitting Cutter's arm.

"Of course," he added, "if there's a flood or a monsoon, any of the terrain maps from the Dornaani microsats could be damn near useless. Our line of march could get washed out either behind or in front of us in a day or two. Then we'll have our hands full just surviving."

Murphy nodded. "Then you follow the OPORD: you break squelch on the frequency of the day. Supplies would have to be dropped. If you need to be evacuated, we should be able to pull you out with a Jacob's Ladder. But given the elevation of your route, there's little chance of conditions getting that bad."

Cutter nodded. "Roger that, sir. But I also know how weather can change and radios can break and about a dozen other ways that simpler plans than this one can get fubared. So I'm just thinking ahead to our worse-case scenarios."

"*Worse* case?" Murphy repeated. "Never heard it put that way."

Cutter grinned. "Sir, I'm just superstitious enough that I refuse to call any imagined foul-up a *worst*-case scenario, because—sure as shooting—fate will prove me wrong."

As Murphy nodded agreeably, Tyree scanned his men's gear. Almost all of them were carrying the ubiquitous M14 rifles that had been produced on the spin habs. The rest of their equipment was a mix of Lost Soldier spares, castoffs, and local clothes made for hot, swampy environments. "I figure we'll do just fine the way we are. I just wish we knew more about the languages down there."

Murphy nodded. "I have a little more information about that, too. According to Vat, all accounts of merchants who claim to have journeyed to, or from, Kanjoor, speak a fairly understandable hodgepodge of R'Bakuun and Kulsian."

"Roger all that, sir. Anything else?"

"Just one thing." Murphy smiled. "How about a home-cooked meal?"

Cutter started. "What?"

Murphy smiled and nodded to the crew chief, who pulled a thermal blanket off a hotbox lashed against the payload section's aft firewall. At a nod from the colonel, he and his assistant began distributing sealed containers. Wisps of steam escaped along with the aromas of a rich stew.

Murphy nodded at the meals. "Might be the last time you see real food for a while."

Cutter rolled his eyes. "Don't remind me." He glanced at the colonel, making sure that the briefing had truly ended.

Murphy smiled, shook his head against the possibility of further needful conversation, and nodded at the misting container in the captain's hands. "Mind the turbulence," he warned.

Cutter nodded and dug into the food.

The last of his team lagged behind by almost as much as two seconds.

Chapter Thirty-Eight

Missile packet **Trzgarth One**, *off R'Bak*

"And now you are mine," T'Barth muttered as the missiles hit the fleeing frigate. Its acceleration dropped off noticeably, and the two missile pack swarms—his and Teseler's—seemed to jump forward at it on the little monitor that Bowden had called "the plot." He was still unsure about the technology involved in creating the view he had, but the tactical edge it gave him was well worth the frisson it sent down his spine when he thought about it. Not that he would ever show it, of course.

"*Otlethes One* is requesting we slow slightly as we are getting ahead of them."

T'Barth smiled. *The engines may be the same, but I have the best mechanic on the spin.* He glanced back at the plot and smiled. He *was* pulling slightly ahead of the Otlethes swarm and a little voice inside him urged him to redline the engines, to get there first and claim the honor of being the first to savage the frigate.

But I gave my oath to follow the procedures laid out by the Terrans. The Terrans had also explained that by making the attack run together, it made it harder for the defenders to target any specific group, and easier for all the attackers to get free again once they'd made their runs, but that was less important to him. He would have far rather braved the enemy's missiles by himself to claim the honor of the kill.

But I gave my oath.

"Pilot, slow five percent," T'Barth said.

"*Slow* five percent?" The pilot's voice mimicked the little voice inside him. "Do you not mean to take the frigate ourselves?"

"No. I mean to do this as we practiced. Slow slightly so the Otlethes swarm can catch up with us and we can attack it together. If all our missiles go in together, we overwhelm the frigate's defense."

"Aye. Slowing five percent."

The Otlethes swarm caught up to his, and he stared at the plot, waiting to see if they would run past him to try to claim the honor of first launch, but they didn't.

"We're with you," Teseler radioed. "We will fire on your command."

T'Barth shook his head. *Teseler ceded the honor of giving the command to fire? Maybe he isn't the worthless idiot I thought him to be.* The Otlethes swarm pulled even with his group, and then split into attack formation when the Trzgarth swarm did, giving them twelve missile packets in a line abreast.

"Stand by to fire," T'Barth radioed. "Fire!"

The missiles rippled off the launchers down the length of the line, racing forward to claim their victim.

"Pilot, skew turn one eighty degrees," T'Barth said. "There's no sense getting any closer than we have to."

Frigate **Harvester One,** *off R'Bak*

"The little ships are firing?" the weapons officer said, his surprise turning the statement into a question. "Those can't be all *real* missiles, can they?"

"It appears they are," Ebis'qupoz Barogar growled. "Flip the ship and defend it."

The pilot turned to look at him. "But if we do that—"

"Just do it!" Barogar shouted. "There are dozens of missiles coming after us."

"Yes, Lord."

Barogar looked at the plot. The rest of the fleet was coming, but they wouldn't be able to help with the mass of weapons headed toward them. And, even though he had the best crew and self-defense weapons in the fleet, he also knew it wouldn't be enough. With the number of missiles they had coming toward them, they *were* going to take hits. The only thing he had a say in was where those hits occurred. Already down one engine, he couldn't afford to lose the other. It was better to sacrifice the equipment on the bow—and the people stationed there—to protect the remaining motor and the combat center from which he commanded the ship. Positioned in the middle of the vessel, it was the best protected from damage.

If they could weather the missile storm, they still had the other motor and might be able to escape to the safety of the fleet afterward.

But we have to limit the number of hits we take. "Full power to the jammers," Barogar ordered. "Fire all countermeasures. Use them all if you have to. Point defense weapons, *fire!*"

The missiles continued to track inbound, although some spun away, victims of the ship's defenses. Not enough, he could see. *This is going to hurt.*

Corvette J'axon's Revenge, *off R'Bak*

"The frigate is dead in space," the tactical officer said.

"Very well," Targ said. The fight with the frigate had gone better than it ever had in the simulator. With the loss of one of its motors in the missile packet attack, and the abuse it had taken, the frigate had lost the power to run most of its missile systems, and the corvettes had swarmed it "like a pack of piranhas" as they'd been taught. He had no idea what a piranha was, but if the creatures were as deadly to people as the corvettes had been to the frigate, he hoped to never meet a pack of them in real life.

All twenty-four corvettes had fired a single missile simultaneously, overwhelming what was left of the frigate's defenses and pummeling it into scrap. The few missiles it had fired had all been intercepted by the groups' Aegis-networked fires.

They'd destroyed the corvette without losing a single ship— the bait ship didn't count, since it technically *could* have gotten away if it had turned sooner—which was something they'd *never* done in practice. *Maybe there actually* is *something to this technology,* Targ thought as he broadened out the scope to look at the incoming Kulsian fleet. *Maybe computers really do have a place in society.*

He shook his head at the thought. Two months ago, he never would have believed it. *Funny how things change ... when they need to.*

"I can't believe how easy that was!" the tactical officer crowed. Targ frowned. From the tone of the tactical officer's voice, if they'd had gravity, he would probably have been jumping up and down, clapping his hands like an uncultured child.

"The first battle is over," Targ said gravely, making eye contact with him, "but the war is only starting." He nodded toward the plot. "The fleet is almost here, and we're going to be outnumbered five to one ... maybe more. We need to get the ships back into formation." He raised an eyebrow. "That is your job. Shouldn't you be doing it?"

"Oh!" the man exclaimed, looking at the mass of icons approaching them. "Yes, sir. Right now, sir."

As the tactical officer began making calls and maneuvering the ships back into formation, Targ studied the plot, looking for the opportunities that Bowden and Fiezel had taught him. He didn't have missiles to waste; he needed to find openings in the Kulsian fleet he could exploit.

He changed the range on the plot and re-centered it, then he smiled and laughed a couple times.

"What is it?" the tactical officer asked, looking back toward him.

"Two things. I can tell that the Kulsians are planet dwellers, and that—perhaps without the frigate—there is no one in charge of the fleet."

"Why is that?"

"They do not think in three dimensions. They are moving toward us in a long line abreast of about thirty ships, with three more similar lines following the one in front of it. There are also gaps here"—he pointed—"and here, where it looks like there are different groups that are not used to working—or flying—together. We need to speed up, then I want you to maneuver our fleet this way..."

Corvette Taregon's Pride, off-R'Bak

"Interesting," Reetan said as the clusters of Hound-Dog ships reconfigured their formations, going from a line-abreast formation to something more like a sphere. There was a front ship, then four following it in sort of an X shape, then the Aegis ship following the X at the same distance as the X followed the first ship. The second Aegis group under Targ's command pulled in behind him in a similar formation, while the two Aegis groups under Burg Hrensku's command shifted into a similar formation.

The maneuver was finished as they approached missile range to the Kulsian fleet, and it was performed as smoothly as only people who'd lived their entire lives piloting ships in space could have done.

"What are they doing?" Reetan's tactical officer asked.

Reetan pointed at the plot. "They are going to drive wedges down the gaps in the Kulsian formation here and here." He pointed and chuckled. "The Kulsians are all lined up like land armies, and they're going to get some shots in from range, but the closer he gets, the fewer are going to be able to shoot at him without fear of hitting their allies. Then, once he's through, the first line is in danger from the missiles of the second line, and so forth. Basically, the way the Kulsians are spread out, he can get local superiority." He shrugged. "Assuming he survives the initial maneuver, that is."

He tilted his head as he looked at the display. "One thing is for sure."

"What's that, sir?"

Reetan smiled. "It will be interesting."

Corvette Festal's Folly, off R'Bak

Festal Lantrax laughed as his ship moved to the lead position of their "sphere" and closed up on Targ J'axon's ship.

"What is so funny?" his tactical officer asked. "This is the dumbest formation I've ever seen. We've never even practiced it!"

"No, we haven't, but if it works, I'm going to buy Targ's first drink when this is over."

"You don't even like him."

"No I don't, but this idea is brilliant...as long as we don't get destroyed on our approach."

"Why is that?"

"Once we're joined with the enemy, only a few of them will be able to fire at us at a time; meanwhile, all our ships can fire outward at them. Like I said, it's brilliant...assuming we survive to get in close."

Festal jerked his chin toward the plot. "Look at the Kulsians. They have no idea what they're doing." He laughed again. "They've never flown together in formation; that much is obvious. Now, as they all try to figure out what Targ is doing, and they maneuver to try to counter it, they are all getting into each other's way. They're also all trying to be the first ones to fire on us, so they are all charging toward us, rather than turning sideways to unmask all their weapons systems." He shrugged. "Land warriors playing at space battles."

"There are, however, a *lot* of them," the tactical officer said as the Kulsians began launching missiles.

"There are. Perhaps you could do something to thin them out some. And maybe destroy some of those incoming missiles."

Corvette J'axon's Revenge, *off R'Bak*

The tactical officer was working hard to keep everything under control and defend their formation as the missiles intensified, but Targ could see he was quickly becoming overwhelmed. Caught up in missile, railgun, and laser allocation, the officer had yet to expend any of their countermeasures. Targ fired off some chaff and flipped on the radar jammers, then he made a call to have the other ships do the same. Some of the missiles headed toward them spun off, distracted, but others continued inbound.

The only thing keeping the tactical officer up to the task was the fact that the Kulsian attack was a complete mess. Their formation alone prevented over half the front line of battle from firing, and the way some ships raced forward while others hung back probably masked another quarter of their launchers, especially since most of them seemed to only be using their chase armaments as the approached. Targ shook his head. *Idiots*. Still...the ones who could shoot at them were, and if even a small portion of the massive fleet fired at a time, that was still a *lot* of missiles. Especially if you were on the receiving end of them.

"Damn it!" the tactical officer exclaimed as one of the missiles he was working to destroy was hit by the group behind his as they came in range.

"Isn't their help something to be welcomed?"

"Yes, but I *had* that one."

Targ nodded. The lack of coordination between the groups was...inefficient, a term he would never have used for battle until recently. Working together—rather than trying to be the one with the most glory—was an interesting concept, and he could see how it was helping them, while the lack of coordination was hurting the Kulsians.

"Festal, Targ," he called over the radio.

"Kind of busy," the RockHound replied. "What?"

"We need to work together better. We'll focus our efforts on the missiles to port; your group can take the ones to starboard."

There was a long pause, and Targ could almost see Festal working it through his mind. The RockHounds had been the most reluctant to adopt the new tactics. *Revenge Two*, the lead corvette, took a missile, and he winced. *We need to do this better.*

"We will defend the starboard side," Festal finally agreed. "Do not make me regret this, SpinDog."

Targ laughed over the radio. "Only if you'll do the same for me." He nodded to the tactical officer. "The missiles to port are your responsibility."

The tactical officer squared his shoulders and took a deep breath. "I will do my best."

FOB "Outpost," spinward Trojans of R'Bak

"I can't believe that worked," Dave Fiezel said as he watched the Hound-Dog corvette formations pass through the Kulsian force. It had cost them seven of their ships, although all seven of the Aegis corvettes were still in service.

"Whatever the Kulsians expected," Specialist Steve Wisniewski said, standing next to him at the plot, "that wasn't it."

He didn't know what to call the two double-sphere formations—*dumbbells, maybe?*—but the only thing that was harder than naming the formations was the Kulsians actually having to deal with them. As the two dumbbells lanced through the Kulsian lines of battle, each succeeding line fell further and further apart. By the fourth line, the Kulsian line had become a giant sphere of its own as some of the captains went high to avoid their allies, while others went low. Missiles flew everywhere, with the Aegis corvettes defeating a majority of the ones coming at them.

All the Kulsians succeeded in doing was pummeling their own ships as many of them ripple-fired all their missiles, only to have an allied ship cut in front of them and intercept them.

Some of the cargo ships obviously had been pressed into service and had a missile or two mounted on them. They were the worst of all, as they didn't appear to have any sort of targeting system, and they fired their missiles in the general direction of the Hound-Dogs, before turning away and running. Very few of those missiles turned out to be a threat to the Hound-Dogs.

"Where's that guy going?" Wisniewski asked, pointing at the plot. "That one, too... and that one."

"I've got no idea," Fiezel said, shaking his head. The three ships Wisniewski had pointed out were continuing out in the direction of... well, nothing that Fiezel could see. They were just cruising along, non-maneuvering, and he didn't think that they'd been hit, as they hadn't been very close to the Hound-Dog force. "Maybe they're fleeing or took damage?"

"No—I watched that one," Wisniewski said, pointing at one of the ships. "That one was on the end of the formation; it never got hit."

It couldn't be fleeing, either, Fiezel saw, as it wasn't accelerating to "get away." It was just coasting off into the black. And then it hit him. "They're out of gas," he said with a touch of awe.

"Gas?"

"Well, whatever they fuel their craft with. I'll bet if you pulled ESM on them, they'd be dark and unpowered. They've run out of gas, just like we figured they would!"

"So they're just going to..." Wisniewski's jaw dropped. "We've got to help them."

"Didn't take long for enemies to turn into something less... I don't know. Antagonistic, maybe?" Fiezel asked with a chuckle.

"I don't care who they are," Wisniewski said. "No one deserves to die out in the black like that."

"We will try to rescue them afterward," Fiezel replied. He pointed back to the battle. "But right now, we're still greatly outnumbered, and going to play fetch at the moment is somewhat contraindicated."

"What are our ships doing?"

"Something that ancient mariners would have appreciated," Fiezel noted. "They're crossing their 'T.'"

"They're *what*?"

"Crossing the *T*. Also known as 'capping the *T*.'" He pointed. The first ball of the two corvette formations turned away from the other group and made a line perpendicular to the Kulsians, who were turning back to engage. The second balls turned toward each other, filling in the gap between the first two formations. The result was a single line, seventeen ships long, facing the oncoming Kulsians. "They just made a line where they can all use all their weapons against the Kulsians, while the Kulsians can only use the chase armaments located in their bows."

Fiezel laughed. "If the Kulsians had done this at the start, we wouldn't have stood a chance."

"But..." Wisniewski's head tilted as he thought. "But this is space. Couldn't they get going in one direction, and then just spin their ship so they're going through space sideways and accomplish the same thing?"

"They could," Fiezel said with a nod. "The question is... will they?"

Chapter Thirty-Nine

Corvette J'axon's Revenge, *off R'Bak*

"We're almost out of missiles," the tactical officer said. "Before much longer, we'll be down to just lasers and railguns."

"And at that point, we'll work on a different formation," Targ said. "Until then, keep hitting them as they approach. They're out of missiles, too, most of them, so we don't have to worry about that."

"What about if they finally organize and rush us en masse?"

"Then we will maneuver away from them. Do you seriously think that bunch of dirt-pounders can catch us if we don't want to be caught?"

"Of course not," the tactical officer said, with a bit of hurt pride. "Still, without more missiles, this is going to take longer than it has to."

"If nothing else," Targ said with a chuckle, "we have plenty of fuel to escape them if we decide to leave." He indicated a couple of Kulsian ships at the periphery of the plot. "They're out of fuel. There's going to be a lot of salvage for us after this battle." He smiled. "And the longer it goes on, there will be more and more Kulsians who run out of fuel. Those ships will be easy to pick up in a few days."

"But wouldn't it be more *efficient* to finish them now?" the tactical officer asked, using one of Bowden's favorite words. "We'll have to chase some of them to the outer system to recover their ships."

"What did you have in mind?"

"The reserve force isn't doing anything, and they have full missile loads. If they came in now, it would break the spirit of the Kulsians and would finish them off more quickly."

Targ stared at the plot for a few moments, looking for flaws in the argument. He didn't see any. In fact, he was disappointed that he hadn't come up with the strategy himself. He smiled. "I think you're right. It's time to end this."

Corvette Taregon's Pride, *off R'Bak*

"*Taregon's Pride, J'axon's Revenge.*"

Reetan's ears perked up. He'd become absorbed in watching the battle on the plot. Some of Targ's maneuvers were nothing short of "inspired," and he wondered how things would have been different if Bowden was still in the fight. He didn't see how things could have gone much better...and they certainly could have gone a lot worse.

"*J'axon's Revenge, Taregon's Pride.* Go ahead."

"Hey, Reetan, how about a little help here? Some of our ships are starting to run low on missiles, and we could use some fresh ships. If you were to join us now, I think we could break the spirit of the Kulsians."

Reetan surveyed the battle on his tactical plot. More of the Kulsians were turning around to make a run on the Hound-Dog formation, but not enough that he thought the Kulsians would actually overwhelm them. Get in some blows? Maybe...but the battle appeared won unless Targ did something grossly stupid. Not impossible, but unlikely, based on what Reetan had seen so far.

While he watched, another of the Kulsian corvettes dropped out of the link as it was pounded to scrap by three of the corvettes under Malanye Raptis's control. It had gone exactly as Bowden had told them—they didn't need to have more ships than the Kulsians, if they could use the tactical knowledge given to them by the Dornaani microsats to achieve local superiority.

It was a game of maneuver and maintaining that local superiority, and, so far, J'axon was winning it. Throwing in Reetan's five ships wouldn't vastly change the state of play, although he could pick off some of the ones at the back of the formation that looked like they were holding out to see which way the battle was going to go, before recommitting themselves to the attack. If things continued to go against them, they'd probably run. But, if Reetan's reserve force swooped in from behind them, there'd be nowhere for them to run to; they would be forced to fight. To hear the SpinDogs who'd been down to the planet tell it, there was nothing that fought harder than a cornered *batang*.

Bowden had a saying about not sticking your private parts into a meat grinder; if he were to hit the formation from behind, he might very well be doing that, and to very little gain.

"Sorry, Targ, but it looks like you have the battle in hand. The glory for this battle is yours—as it should be. We will continue to monitor it, but for now, it doesn't look like you need our assistance."

"Roger, out," Targ replied, sounding a little annoyed, and Reetan smiled. There really wasn't much else Targ *could* say. He really *didn't* need Reetan's support, after all; he just *wanted* it to make his life easier. And, when it came right down to it, Targ *would* bask in the glow of the accolades at the end of the fight, a prospect that would advance his cause mightily among the SpinDog Families. Assuming he didn't fuck it up, as Dave Fiezel warned them while doing simulators.

Having decided his services were not immediately needed, he went back to monitoring the battle as he had told Targ he was going to, and as Bowden had instructed him. As Bowden had explained, Aegis was the shield of the gods, and the forces in the battle were the Aegis for their people on the habs. Every good warrior needed a shield, though, and Reetan was the shield of the forces in battle—the Aegis's Aegis, as it were. It was his job to sit in overwatch and ensure nothing snuck up on them that would turn the battle.

He broadened out the link picture to see if anything *was* sneaking up on Targ by going around the planet. After a moment, he shrugged. If there *was* someone sneaking up on Targ, they were doing it so quietly that the satellites hadn't noticed their presence.

As he re-centered the picture around his location, though, he twitched back in surprise. "Hey, Stellan," he said to his tactical officer. "What are these ships?" He pointed to two groups of ships approaching the asteroids in which Outpost was hidden.

Somehow, the ships had snuck around behind him—the person who was supposed to be watching for just that sort of thing. "They can't be ours, can they?"

"No," Stellan replied. "Ours are all engaged in the fight, except for the four with us...and there are more than four there."

"I see that," Reetan replied with a growl. Frustrated and knowing he had little time—the ships were almost to Outpost—he rewound the scenario as Bowden had shown he could do with the technology. He tracked the ships back in time to where they'd split off from the Kulsian fleet at about the time the frigate had gone charging off after Bowden.

Everyone had been so focused on the frigate, they hadn't watched the fleet, and no one had missed them when their attention returned to the fleet for the battle to come. By that point, the task force approaching Outpost was already gone.

Reetan stared at the plot with one question in mind: *Why?* Why had they split off all of a sudden and gone on a direct course to Outpost? They couldn't have known it was there, could they? While he had no idea *how* the Kulsians had known about Outpost, there was no reason for the ships to be headed in that direction if they hadn't. None. A cold shiver went down his back.

Somehow—and it didn't matter how—but *somehow, the Kulsians had found Outpost.* And they were on their way to destroy it.

In an instant, he knew this was the possibility of which Bowden had spoken—the one thing that would allow the Kulsians to snatch victory from the jaws of defeat. Their frigate was destroyed, and their fleet was soon to be nothing more than next week's meteor showers in R'Bak's sky, but the Kulsians were going to win, because they were going to kill all the Hound-Dogs' leadership, including all the Lost Soldiers who were in the forward operating base, helping to manage the battle.

And, having allowed such a thing to happen, none of the locals—neither the SpinDogs nor the RockHounds—would trust each other or the Lost Soldiers...ever again. Things would go back to the way they were, with the Kulsians exerting their dominion over everyone in the system.

Reetan was tired of living in fear of them, and—having been given the most important task of the whole battle by Bowden—he was *not* going to fail in his mission.

"All ships," Reetan called over the frequency his squadron

was using. "Max thrust. Outpost is under attack, and we have to save them."

FOB "Outpost," spinward Trojans of R'Bak

"What the hell did Reetan just say?" Dave Fiezel asked.

"I didn't hear anything," Specialist Steve Wisniewski said.

"Are you listening to the Reserve Squadron comms channel?"

"No. I don't think so, sir. There's nothing going on with them, so I turned it off. They were just talking about stupid shit, and it was getting annoying."

"Well, here's something really annoying: Reetan just told them to go to max thrust because Outpost is under attack."

"We're not under attack. I think we'd know if we were under attack, sir."

"Why would they think we were, then, if we are not?"

Fiezel took control of the tactical plot and re-centered it around Outpost. "Fuck," he muttered under his breath as the picture re-built.

Wisniewski was louder. "*Where the hell did those guys come from?*" he exclaimed, pointing at the two groups of ships making a beeline toward them.

Beyond the Kulsians and off to the side, the Reserve Squadron was streaking in, but they had a lot of space to cross, and the Kulsians were almost upon them.

"Doesn't matter; they're almost here!" Fiezel said. He looked around; a number of people were already looking at them due to Wisniewski's outburst, but he raised his voice so all would hear. "Everyone! There are Kulsian raiders who are almost upon us. We have to go dark and quiet. Let everyone on the habitat know."

Corvette Taregon's Pride, off R'Bak

"Can't this thing go any faster?" Reetan asked.

"Sure," his pilot said. "How fast would you like to go screaming past them?"

Reetan growled, although he knew the pilot was right. He hadn't really wanted an answer to the question; he was just voicing his frustration at having failed. He'd been given the most important part of the plan—according to Bowden, anyway—and he had failed. The only good thing out of Bowden's death at the hands of the frigate—if indeed Bowden was dead—was that Reetan wouldn't have to explain his failure to Bowden and endure his shame. Several weeks ago, he never would have thought that meeting and exceeding Bowden's standards was a goal to be sought after, but, somehow, along the way, it had become one.

And he had failed.

No, he saw as he continued to watch the plot, he hadn't failed yet, although he was going to have to endure a lot more personal danger—for both himself and his squadron—in order to avoid doing so. He chuckled to himself at the irony. The very thing he had railed against Bowden for—potentially throwing away the lives of RockHounds—he was now going to do intentionally. And willingly, too, when it came right down to it.

Bowden, if you could only see me now.

There were four major asteroids in the loose cluster, and their one chance was that, even though the Kulsians knew there was a habitation in the asteroids, Reetan doubted they knew exactly which asteroid it was on, so they would probably have to take a little time to figure it out. They probably wouldn't just come in and waste missiles indiscriminately on the asteroids; they would only want to target the one with the people on it. They might even want to negotiate with them for their surrender.

If so, there was an opportunity to strike them from behind, with minimal losses to his force. Even if the Kulsians didn't negotiate first, they still had a chance. It was far riskier to himself and his forces, but that was a chance he was willing to take.

Kulsian corvette Pillager, *near R'Bak*

"Did Barogar say which of the asteroids was the one with the rogue group on it?" the navigator asked.

"No," Marksa said. "He failed to mention that before his untimely death."

"There are four asteroids large enough to support people," the navigator said. "How do you want me to prioritize them?"

"Well, we're almost out of fuel, and I have no intention of joining the slaughter that's going on. We need to take care of this as quickly as possible so we can escape to the planet before... whoever that is comes looking for us, too." He pursed his lips. "The quickest way to do this is to have someone fire a missile at each of them to see what happens. I suspect that when the rogues find out that we're here, they'll contact us quickly to prevent us from wiping them out."

"Do you want me to fire on them?" the tactical officer asked.

"And waste our missiles?" Marksa laughed. "Not hardly. We'll be lucky to turn a profit at all with this fiasco, much less if we go spending missiles for no real reason other than expediency. Tell Stanax to have each of the ships in his group fire a missile at one of them."

FOB "Outpost," spinward Trojans of R'Bak

The room exploded into action as people ran out the door, while others used the habitat's communications systems to warn Outpost's inhabitants of the imminent attack. Interior pressure doors were shut, and exterior systems were checked to ensure they were off. Hangar bay doors were closed and left in vacuum in case of breach. As the Kulsians approached, there were no exterior signs that anyone was inside the asteroid.

Fiezel hoped.

The Kulsians slowed as they approached the asteroids. Fiezel had no idea how the Kulsians were aware of their presence, but they wouldn't have sent ten ships to the area without a really good reason. Perhaps there was a snoop satellite in the area that had caught some of their comms; that might have caused this reaction. The Kulsians stopped just short of the asteroids.

"They don't know which one we're on," Fiezel muttered.

"Shall we fire on them with the railgun?" the SpinDog charged with the defense of the station asked.

"No!" Fiezel exclaimed, sharper than he meant to. A hush had fallen over the operations center, and his outburst caused everyone to look at him. In a hushed whisper—more appropriate to the environment—he added, "They don't know where we are, and we don't want to give our position away."

The SpinDog was a mixture of anger and frustration. He wasn't sure of what he wanted to do, but he wanted to do *something!* Fiezel chuckled to himself. A couple of months ago, all the Hound-Dogs had wanted to do was run and hide. Now, when the situation actually called for hiding, they wanted to mix it up with the enemy fleet. It was funny how times—and people—changed.

When the SpinDog continued to stare at him while tapping a toe on the ground, Fiezel finally took pity on him and explained his rationale. "Reetan and his squadron are coming. Why don't we let them do what they're here for—our defense—rather than getting into a fight with ten armed corvettes, when all we have is a single railgun, and one that's been modified for package delivery, not war."

"That makes sense," the man said.

"It does," Fiezel said with a smile.

"God damn," Wisniewski breathed, looking up from the plot. "They're firing at us."

Chapter Forty

With alarms howling and people either fleeing from or into the city, one more motor ketch entering Downport Bay attracted less attention that it would have normally. It certainly attracted less than the seaplane that had appeared well to the north an hour before. Indeed, most of the panicked, pointing fingers had been quickly swatted aside by the dockhands who recognized the aircraft as a frequent regular in the port. As if to prove just how unwarranted the concern had been, the big-bellied craft—recognizable as Umaren's *Loklis*—dropped beneath the rim of the land, apparently landing someplace slightly out to sea.

Consequently, when the small ketch motored up to one of the freighters tied up along R'Bak Downport's busiest—and now, most frenzied—wharves, no one even noticed the two figures that clambered up the cargo netting hanging over its bayward side.

Bo Moorefield was only halfway up when Max Messina paused him with a raised palm. "Me first, sir."

Bo didn't like having a bodyguard, was impatient to get aboard, and disliked remaining aloft on a flimsy grid of ropes, but Moose was no doubt obeying Murphy's orders. Moorefield nodded.

With surprising alacrity, Messina was up the rest of the netting in a three-count and pulled himself over the gunwale.

Resolved not to obsess on feeling like the last target standing

325

at a carnival huckster's popgun booth, Moorefield used every interminable second to survey the soon-to-be battlefield.

The big ship immediately behind the freighter had been purpose-built as a roll-on/roll-off cargo hauler. As such, it carried the attack force's heavy armor; designated "Roro One," it had the ramps and heavier hull to not only get its vehicles off quickly, but stand up to moderate punishment while it did so.

By contrast, the ship to which Bo was affixed like a flimsy barnacle had been dubbed "Roro Zero." Mostly, that was because it wasn't a true roro; it had started out as a conventional freighter. However, at some point, surveyors had converted a relatively small, hull-side cargo door into a full-sized ramp that lowered out of its side like a drawbridge.

Bo had no nautical inclinations, but even he knew that the transformation was either an indication of dubious intelligence or downright desperation. It was wrong in so many ways that brevity was best served by listing what was right about it. All of which reduced to the fact that, although it shouldn't have, it worked. The violation of its hull integrity had either inspired its masters to be exceedingly cautious, indicated their phenomenal luck, or a bit of both. And on reflection, Bo's own reason for choosing it to carry his first echelon of AFVs may have been the rationale for its conversion in the first place: unlike a genuine roro, it was much smaller and easier to maneuver. Which meant it also attracted less attention.

However, the latter consideration was proving to have been unnecessary. The docks were filled with panicked workers, mariners, merchants, and surveyors roiling like the population of a freshly kicked ant's nest: much motion without any apparent coordination. However, several began waving to a seaplane—half the size of Egret Three—as, feathering its props, it began drifting toward a debarkation float. Moorefield smiled, recognizing a fanciful marking on the starboard vertical stabilizer, or "fin," of its twin tail: *one of ours.*

"Major!"

Bo looked up; Max's broad face was smiling down at him. "Everything in place, Moose?"

"I wouldn't quite put it that way, but they are definitely ready for you, sir."

Mystified, and with a sinking feeling in his gut, Bo resumed scrambling up the cargo netting.

✧   ✧   ✧

"Stop," Bo said sharply. He resisted the urge to rub his suddenly throbbing temples. "I need you to tell me *precisely* what was happening when the ATV got hit."

The captain—young for the role and chosen as much for reliability as skill—also proved confident even when called on the carpet before the very, very frustrated officer in charge of the entire operation. She nodded curtly. "The vehicles were crewed and their engines were on lowest idle. When we reached H-Hour, I followed the protocol for contacting the port authorities."

Moorefield regretted having to ask the question, but it was necessary. "Captain, were *you* the one who initiated the contact?"

"No, sir. As per your orders, I put my XO on the line to handle the exchange." She nodded at a man older than Bo, with a scar that crossed his eye and left it a murky gray orb.

And not the faintest hint of being offended that we had to go with an older male, given the misogyny of this place: she's a great find. He turned toward the XO. "Was there anything atypical about the exchange?"

The older man grunted out what might have been a dismissive laugh. "Only that they didn't even ask the most basic questions about us. Just accepted the credentials we presented when we put in yesterday and today they jumped off the wireless like a cat on a hot stove."

"Did they accept your offer of assistance?"

The man shrugged. "Barely acknowledged it. They were still in a panic about whatever is happening in space." He gazed upward. "Don't suppose you can tell us anything about that, sir?"

Can I? Sure, but: "That is need to know." He shifted his gaze back to the young captain. "So, there was no sign that they suspected this ship was carrying armored attack vehicles or troops?"

"None, sir."

"What did you do next, Captain?"

"We waited until we got the signal that Umaren's *Loklis*—uh, Egret Three—had landed outside the bay. We counted down the ten-minute delay and then began lowering the vehicle ramp. Before doing so, I personally confirmed that the lead vehicle—the only that would be visible when the ramp was lowered—was the civilian ATV with the hidden grenade launchers. Other than the driver, there were only four troops on it and they were lying on the floor of the passenger compartment so they could not be seen.

"Again, as per the operation orders, we did not fully lower the ramp until we had word that your ketch had been spotted. As soon as we did, there was a loud blast—a cannon, we later learned—and the vehicle was hit as it moved out on to the ramp."

"Was the driver rushing or maneuvering evasively?"

She shook her head sharply. "No, sir. He was edging it out, as instructed. Nothing that would appear suspicious." She drew in a tense breath. "He reversed, but the cannon shell apparently hit the left-side track; it starting running off the road wheels. He made it back into the hold before he died."

"Fragments?"

"Concussive shock, sir. Internal injuries."

So, a pretty big gun. "And there were no further attacks?"

"None, sir. But port authority contacted us."

"With what instructions?"

"None, sir. It was to inquire if the ship had been hit and if there were casualties." She paused. "They weren't speaking to us as if we were enemies. It was more as if they were worried about someone ashore having made a mistake for which they might be liable."

"And since then?"

She clenched her jaw before answering. "We knew you were near, so I waited, sir. With a vehicle disabled at the head of the ramp and no further fire from the shore...well, sir, knowing you'd soon be aboard, I felt it likely that you would wish to revise our next steps, rather than activate the 'fast exit' contingency." She glanced sideways at her XO.

Who rolled his eyes.

"You feel that was a mistake, mister?" Bo asked sharply.

The old mariner started. "I—I do, sir. We were found out. We needed to act quickly. We lost the initiative."

Or your captain kept them calm during a pivotal moment of uncertainty. Bo looked back at the captain. "You did the right thing, Captain. It seems they were, and have remained, unconvinced that this ship is a hostile. With the events in space causing panic here, I suspect they've already got their hands full and don't have the time to deal with a situation that doesn't seem threatening."

"Why do you think they fired on us, sir?"

Bo shrugged. "Confusion is a much greater force on battlefields than most people realize." He stared out the bridge's landside windows. "Did anyone see where the shore gun—?"

"Sirs," the helmsman's mate interrupted nervously, raising a hand and index finger, "I think—"

The thick thunder of an M2 machine gun rose over the low roar of the crowds. Bo leaned sideways to look past the captain's shoulder.

The twin-tailed seaplane that had motored up to the float two berths in front of Roro Zero had popped a side hatch and was firing up at surveyor-suited figures crouching behind the bollards. It wasn't clear who—

—and then Bo found himself pinned low against the bulkhead at the rear of the bridge. Max smiled down apologetically. "We gotta get you away from all these windows, sir." He shouted a more blunt warning to the others, half of whom had the good sense to crouch down; the other half were gaping at the sudden firefight in the bay.

Bo shook Max off. "I've been under fire before, Sergeant."

"Yes, sir, but with all due respect, you've never been the commander-in-theater." He smiled. "It's why you got code-named SHAEF, after all."

Moorefield would have argued—if he could have.

A shore gun thundered; the glass shook. "That's not a high-velocity tube," Bo muttered as a water-muffled explosion geysered up someplace out in the bay. "A one-twenty, at least."

"At least," Max agreed.

Crouching, the captain waved them toward the stairs that led down to the chart room directly below. Bo wondered if, by the time they looked out its safer portholes, the seaplane would still be there.

They were peering out a porthole when the third shell took off the seaplane's portside wing, engine and all. The vehicle listed hard, righted, but the cockpit was a webwork of shattered and missing glass.

"Probably more than one hundred twenty millimeter," Bo murmured. "How the hell did we miss them?"

"You never see everything, sir." Messina sighed. "And from the look and sound of it, they must have tucked the guns in empty warehouses just beyond the dock's landside berm."

Bo nodded. "No other way to have hidden it." Beyond all reason, the seaplane's waist machine gun was still cutting into the security team that had apparently been unfortunate enough to be on hand and to ask for credentials when it pulled up. No other surveyors or their satrap-furnished auxiliaries had shown up yet, but that was just a matter of time.

Bo leaned away from the porthole as a grease-covered grandfather shinnied up the ladder into the chart room. "Report from the hold, Captain!"

She turned, nodded. "Quickly."

"Aye. That blasted ATV just burst on fire, ma'am." In response to her surprised frown, he shook his head. "I know, I know; fooled us all. Shrapnel must have cut through the chassis and hit a fuel line. We got it under control, but it's diesel and it's still smoking. Choking the crews and troops, Cap'n. We need to get the smoke out. Can we relower the ramp?"

Before she could answer, Bo stepped forward. "Does the hold have evacuating fans?"

The old salt blinked. "Aye. But they won't get out all the smoke."

"We don't need 'all.' Just enough."

"Enough for what, sir?" asked the captain.

"To get this offensive moving." He gestured back toward the seaplane. "The surveyors are alert now. But they're also distracted. So we get the vehicles out: now."

"But sir, the guns—"

"The guns are going to be there until *we* do something about them. And the best time to do that is while they're busy. Better yet, for a few crucial moments, we can make it appear that this ship is on fire—and can use that as a brief smokescreen. Chief," he turned to the grimy engineer.

"Just a mate . . . but aye?"

"Take me to the vehicle bay. Captain, I need your radio operator to start patching through to the command tracks below."

She swallowed but nodded: a job they'd planned on having thirty minutes to accomplish now had to be done in seconds.

He smiled at her determination and grit. "You're going to be our comms center, until you can hand that off to Roro One. As soon as you have, get a sitrep from them."

"Sitrep on—?"

"Spaceside operations." He waved the engineer's mate down the ladder.

✧   ✧   ✧

The last five rungs down into the cargo-deck-become-vehicle-bay was like descending into a level of hell that Dante had left out of *The Inferno*. At least it wasn't on fire, but the smoke was as black and acrid as anything he could have imagined. Sullen, coal-colored clouds hung low around the extinguisher-frosted ATV.

Bo took a moment to assess the obstacle. The left front of the vehicle resembled twisted modern art, and the roadwheel just behind the drive sprocket had been blasted clean off. That quadrant of the chassis was sagging toward the deck and about a tenth of its narrow gauge tread had spooled off. It would have been an easy job for a tank recovery vehicle, but on R'Bak, more basic methods would be required.

The crewmen of the other vehicles and their troop comple-ments were staggering around through the smoke and the noise of their own shouting and coughing, calling to find anyone who knew who was in charge. Or at least someone who had any rea-sonable idea of what to do next.

Bo ran down the vehicle load in his head, glancing around as he did—and found the vehicle he was looking for: a small armored car with double-quad grenade launchers on either side of its tiny turret. He had a momentary impression that he was approaching Dumbo as he put his hand on the hood: it was electric, making its idle unusually subtle. And with the noise around him, and the vibration of at least a dozen diesel engines running through the deck, he had to look up toward the vehicle commander, who was talking to someone in the vehicle behind his.

"Hey!" Bo called. "Is this thing running?"

The vehicle commander turned abruptly, squinted through a billow of black smoke. "Who wants to know?"

"Your commanding officer, Major Hubert Moorefield." He jumped up on the glacis plate. "Remember this voice and this face," he shouted, as much for emphasis as clarity. "They're the ones you're going to take orders from."

"Sir! Yes, sir!" The commander nodded sharply: the local salute. *He hasn't served with one of us before; no Terran salute, but instant respect.* For once, Moorefield was glad for his Lost Soldier accent. Initially, reactions to it had been suspicion or even prejudice. But right now it got him the reflexive authority and compliance he needed.

He scrambled up to grab a handhold between the clustered

grenade launchers. "Give me your handset." He nodded at the psyops speakers, which had been the other reason he'd sought this particular vehicle. "Angle the speakers wide to either side." As the vehicle commander complied, he switched the handset to public address and held down the send button.

"This is SHAEF." His voice boomed back at him from the corners of the cavernous bay. "Those of you with command priority three or above should be familiar with that word: it's the codename for the commander of this operation. I am Major Hubert Moorefield. You will be taking orders directly from me until further notice. Combat teams remount immediately. We are moving out." Baffled faces turned toward him; two senior sergeants pointed to the intermittently guttering ATV blocking the ramp. Bo shook his head, bellowed. "Stand by. Freighter hands to the ramp controls. Vehicle commanders: I will guide you out."

Bo was able to cover the handset before the armored car's commander could sputter out a startled "S-sir?"

"Just follow my orders." He smiled. "I've done this before." He toggled the handset. "Track five, next to the bay door. Wave if you can hear me." The commander in the very small turret of that very large APC crossed his arms vigorously several times. "Excellent. Ram that wreck out of the way."

"Sir?"

"You heard me: ram it out of the way. Clutch out, rev your engine, then clutch in and hit the ATV in the side. Keep pushing until it's clear."

"But, Captain, that will push it into the recce car just across—"

Bo had already waved the small team in that recon vehicle to abandon it. "Do it, son. Right now. We have two choices: we get out of here or we die in here."

The big APC seemed ready to shake apart as its engine spun up. Crews and troops alike covered their ears against the roar-and-whine of its turbine.

Which abruptly became an enraged squealing of heavy treads as the vehicle leaped forward. It wasn't moving very fast when it hit the much lighter ATV, but its engine's RPMs kept the APC moving forward. As its commander had predicted, it drove the wreck straight into the abandoned recce car.

But access to the ramp was clear. The APC reversed to its prior position—a few road wheels squealing—as the ship's fire crew charged toward the two mauled vehicles, ready to douse new flames and smother new smoke.

Because Bo had pored over his order of battle so often, he knew all the vehicles in each of the three transports carrying his attack force. He leaned toward the pale, sweaty face of the armored car commander. "Where is track three? No: that's Kaladar Six, now. Any idea?"

Almost timidly, the fellow pointed at the vehicle just behind them. "Right there, sir."

Bo glanced at the vehicle to ensure that it was the same as the description from the TOE roster. Similar to the one Moorefield had commanded during the Battle of Imsurmik, this one was slightly more modern. The main gun only had a seven-centimeter bore, but was fitted with a thermal sight and a coaxial hypervelocity autocannon. The meanest beast in the bay.

He extricated himself from the double-quad grenade launchers. Max stood ready to help him down. Bo shook his head, glanced back at the armored car's commander. "When I give the signal, you're going to take this vehicle over the ramp straight onto the dock. Not racing; prudent speed."

"Me, sir? This little vehicle?" He looked at the humble machine gun that was the turret's main armament. "The first?"

"Correct. And once you're off the ramp, you are to turn hard left and head down the wharf with the throttle wide open. Warn civilians out of the way, but *do not stop.* You have only two objectives: don't get hit, and dispense smoke every twenty meters. I want the shore gun's crew trying to zero in on you, but after the first two smokes, your vehicle will be screened. And remember: shore guns that big can't track with you." *And given that no one has ever attacked this port, I'm betting that they don't know how to lead a target, either.*

"Sir," the commander gulped, saluting. "As fast as we can drive: yes, sir."

Bo nodded, climbed over the back of the engine deck, Max following him with a hangdog expression.

Bo hopped over to the glacis of Kaladar Six. Senior Lieutenant Hax Uruns smiled at him from where he stood in the commander's hatch. "It is a pleasure, and an honor, to meet you in person, Major."

"Likewise, Hax." Bo glanced at the smoke dischargers on

either side of the gun mantlet. "Are you loaded for smoke or antipersonnel?"

"Both, sir."

"Can you select?"

"Yes, sir."

"Set for smoke, and prepare to move out." Moorefield managed to keep the order calm and firm, rather than the whoop that it wanted to be.

Max positioned himself directly in front of Kaladar Six. "Sir, I believe your orders are to remain in the CP. Which, right now, is this ship."

Bo's forehead became a rage-hot band of sweat. "The CP is wherever I am, Sergeant Messina."

"Sir, that's not the colonel's understanding. Or intent."

"Sergeant, are you trying to countermand my orders?"

"No, sir. I am very respectfully reminding you that the colonel issued extremely specific directives on this. Perhaps given all the activity, you've forgotten the exact phrasing."

But I'll bet you *know it by heart.* Bo leaned forward, spoke in a broad Southern accent that usually made him impossible for R'Baku to understand. "You're not here as just my security. You're here to make sure I don't violate Murphy's 'rules of engagement' for his command staff."

"Sorry, sir. Those are my orders."

"No doubt. But do you see anyone else here with my skill set, Sergeant?"

"No, sir."

"And what's Murphy's first priority: keep me alive—or take Downport?"

For the first time in Bo's knowledge of Maximiliano Messina, the big man did not have a ready answer. "Not sure that I know the answer to that, sir. But given all that's at stake . . ." He sighed and grumbled, "Lead on. You're going to do what you have to, anyway. But I'm going to stick to you like glue."

"Glad to hear it. Besides, I'm not long for this world, anyway." Max raised a puzzled eyebrow. "Murphy will have my head—and my ass—for this."

"No, sir," Max said, displaying an easy familiarity with how best to hang on the back of a turret during an armored assault. "It's not the colonel's style to punish someone for demonstrating the kind of initiative that gets the job done. But if something happens *to* you?" Max shook his head. "My ass will be grass and Murphy's the lawn mower."

Bo turned back to Hax Uruns, fighting a grin. "Main tube load?"

"I just changed it to smoke, sir."

"You read my mind, Lieutenant. Signal the ship's crew to lower the ramp and reverse the evacuators; let's blow smoke in the Kulsians' faces. While they're arranging that, run a quick comms check. Confirm that the formation is to follow your track in the original order. If there's a snag, AFVs have priority."

Moorefield dropped down into the observer's hatch, tilted the feed from the thermal scope so it was level with his eyes. "Stand ready to fire as I direct." He popped his head over the hatch ring and shouted at the armored car commander. "As soon as the ramp is down, move out!"

He settled lower to get the best view of the thermal imaging screen. It was nowhere near as good as what he'd been used to in an Abrams, but was comparable to second-tier NATO systems.

The armored car rolled toward the ramp. Hax Uruns held his driver in check for a two-count before following toward the bright square that marked the opening in Roro Zero's hull. As they accelerated through it, the armored car's tires squealed as it hung a hard left and raced south along the wharf, kicking out one smoke grenade as it did.

Kaladar Six had just begun bumping across the ramp when a shore gun's report almost deafened Bo and a long jet of light bloomed in his thermal sensor feed: the shot had gone well behind the armored car.

"Twenty degrees right!" Bo yelled. "Fire two rounds smoke!" Then he hastily added, "Cheat short!" Used to the eerily precise weapon stabilization and target tracking system of the Abrams, he wanted to make sure that if the main gun's two rounds didn't go true, its smokes landed in front of, rather than behind, the shore gun.

The good news was that the first round was so accurate that it might actually have hit the gun itself. The bad news was that Bo had to fling around for, and find, ear protection just as Kaladar Six thumped down onto the wharf and its gunner sent the second round downrange. Even half deafened, Bo knew that it was old-school ear-pro: no smart filter to kill the audio peaks. No surprise, though, given the Kulsian avoidance of digital anything.

But at least it was patched into comms. "Roro Zero, this is SHAEF, over."

"SHAEF, this is Roro Zero actual. Go."

"Report effect. Report other guns."

"SHAEF, Roro Zero reporting first target smoked in. Other fire indicates at least one more gun, southwest your—"

A blinding hot circle appeared in the thermal sensor.

Bo jerked back—pointlessly—as Kaladar Six shuddered and the thermal sight seemed to fail—but then cleared.

"What—?" began Hax, who'd never yet been in a fight with an enemy equipped with comparable weapons.

Bo interrupted. "Incoming hit the berm." Which was only six meters away. "Discharge threw dirt at our sensor. Cleared. Acquire and fire! Two smokes!"

In the next ten seconds, Hax Uruns demonstrated why Tapper had recommended him as the best native tank commander. He calmly talked his gunner on target, got one shot away as he directed the driver to follow the berm down the wharf, and sent off the second round as he guided Kaladar Six into a hull-down position.

He glanced over at the Lost Soldier of legend. "Now, what, Major Moorefield?"

Bo smiled, pushed himself up out of the hatch.

"Sir!" Uruns shouted, alarmed as the commander of the entire invasion force started back over the deck.

Bo called back toward him. "Get me a pair of road flares." As Hax complied, he nodded back toward the freighter's ramp; it was visible but dim. "The breeze is pushing our own smoke back at us. I'm going to guide the other vehicles off Roro Zero."

Max opened his mouth.

"Not a word, Sergeant. Just do whatever you can do to keep me safe as I make sure our tracks don't crash into each other and block the wharf. Hax, hold this position. Keep yourself smoked. Pull an infantry team from an APC to provide local security. You've got two jobs; keep those shore guns blind and keep our people moving down the wharf until they reach the freight marshalling area. As they make that run, they are to discharge smokes to landside. If the surveyors put out foot teams with rockets or heavy weapons, they're going to try to pick our vehicles off as they go past single file. So, never the same interval. Got it?"

"Got it. But if they disable a track?"

"The next track with enough power pushes it over the edge."

"Sir, the crew—!"

"We could lose a lot more crews if we get jammed up on a one-lane road with no way off. Carry out your orders."

Flares in hand, Moorefield ran down the center of the deck; the heat of the engine made it feel as if he was running across a just-doused grill. He hopped off between the radiators, popped the first flare, and ran toward the big vehicle that was gingerly feeling its way down the ramp: the now noisy track five. He waved the flare wide and slow.

The silhouette of the commander called for a halt and then dipped down—probably to give the driver a directive kick.

Like a bull seeing a cape, the heavy APC came forward quickly. Bo waved it left as soon as its rear drive sprocket was no longer over the water. It pivoted sharply and roared down along the wharf toward the jagged skyline of the ancient city that poked above the flat buildings of the downport.

Bo smiled, used his flaming wand to summon the next armored demon into daylight with the large gestures and couldn't help but think:

SHAEF wasn't the right code name. Because here I am, directing traffic—just like Patton at the Bulge.

Chapter Forty-One

Corvette Taregon's Pride, *off R'Bak*

"The Kulsians are firing on the asteroids!" the tactical officer shouted.

"I see that," Reetan acknowledged grimly as he studied the plot. A single missile launched from four of the ships in the first group, with each missile going toward a different asteroid. "They don't know which one is Outpost..." he mused, then he sighed. "I wish we could have gotten closer, but we can't let them keep banging on them.

"Stellan, did you see which one did *not* just fire?"

"I did."

"I want four missiles into that one. Two missiles for all the rest."

"It's a long shot from here..."

"But they don't know we're coming, and they aren't maneuvering much. Besides, I want their attention on us, and this is the fastest way to get it." He gazed at his tactical officer a moment, and when Stellan looked up, he asked, "Ready?"

"I am," the tactical officer said with a nod.

Reetan winked and switched to the radio. "Reserve Squadron. On my command, execute fire mission Alpha. Stand by... Fire!"

Four missiles ripple fired from the *Pride* and two of the other corvettes in the squadron.

"Is there some reason that only two other ships fired?" Reetan asked. "This was our chance to hit them when they weren't ready."

"Both ships are indicating they had launch malfunctions."

"Launch malfunctions? We need those missiles! We're outnumbered two to one, and we just kicked over an *astakos* nest. Tell them to get them online *now*!"

FOB "Outpost," spinward Trojans of R'Bak

"That is the weirdest attack plan I've ever seen," Wisniewski said as the missiles from the Reserve Squadron began slamming into the Kulsian corvettes. "Any guess what Reetan was thinking?"

"I really don't have a clue," Fiezel replied. "I think his ship fired four missiles at the one ship in the group that hadn't fired. No idea why."

"That's the leader of that group," the SpinDog said. He hadn't left after being told not to fire the railgun, but instead had stayed to watch the missile attack on the plot.

"How do you know? Wouldn't the leader want the glory of leading the attack against us?"

The SpinDog chuckled. "As you said, they didn't know which one we're hiding in. So, rather than incur the expense of a wasted missile, he had the ships under him fire." Three of Reetan's missiles slammed into that corvette. "I think he just eliminated their leader."

"What about the other ones, then? Only two of his other ships fired, with two missiles at a couple of ships in the first group, and two each at two ships in the second group? How do you explain that?"

The SpinDog smiled. "The RockHounds build shitty ships?"

"What do you mean?"

"With surprise on his side, I expect he tried to hit all of the enemy ships. It looks like two of his ships had difficulties firing their missiles—like I said, shitty ships." The SpinDog shrugged and pointed to the plot. "Either way, it looks like he's gotten their attention off us."

On the plot, the seven remaining Kulsian ships began accelerating and turned to take the new threat under fire, and within seconds, missiles raced away from them in response.

"I hope their point defense systems work," Wisniewski muttered as the missiles neared the reserve fleet.

Corvette Taregon's Pride, *off R'Bak*

"Well, you wanted their attention," Stellan said.

"No, I wanted them dead. I did not want them coming after us, and I definitely didn't want them shooting at us." He sighed as the Kulsians began firing missiles. "And here they come. Three missiles each on two ships from the second group."

"Which ones?"

"I don't care. Whichever you think is the leader and one more. Who fired first? Hit that one and one of the others."

The reserve force released chaff and turned away from the threat, giving the oncoming missiles as small a target as possible and reducing the closure rate, while still allowing the aft lasers to target them. The only problem was that if they didn't destroy all the missiles, the weapons would hit in a vulnerable place. One of his ships—*Four*, one of the ones with an operable weapons system—was hit in its motor and dropped out of formation.

Reetan called for a turn back toward the Kulsians and found that his missiles had been successful. Only five Kulsian corvettes were headed toward his four ships. Of course, only one of them, plus his own, had operable weapons systems...

"Comms officer, where are *Three* and *Five* with getting their weapons working?" Reetan asked.

"One rebooted his system and is waiting for it to re-initialize. One has an electrical failure they're working on. Both need time to finish troubleshooting."

"They realize that's the one thing we don't have, right?"

"They're working on them."

"Time," Reetan muttered. "Pilot, right forty-five degrees, comms, tell them to stack on us."

The other ships shifted formation moving up "above" the *Pride* compared to the Kulsians, who fired another round of missiles. The tactical officers worked furiously, but two missiles hit *Two* and *Three*, and both dropped out of formation.

Suddenly, *Five* came to life, and three missiles leaped out toward the Kulsians, and two more dropped out of their formation, leaving three Kulsians against his two ships. As the two ships began turning back to the Kulsians, he thought furiously, looking for an edge. He'd never been a fan of the new technology, but he really hoped it wouldn't let him down now.

FOB "Outpost," spinward Trojans of R'Bak

"Now what do you suppose they're going to do?" Wisniewski asked as the Hound-Dog ships skew-turned back toward the Kulsians. "Laser and railgun duel with the Kulsians?"

"Looks like it. I think all the ships must be out of missiles." The remaining ships made a run at each other, but it was impossible to determine if any of them had been hit.

As the Kulsians extended away from the firing run before turning back toward the Hound-Dogs, there was a *Thump!*

"What the hell was that?" Fiezel asked.

"That felt like they just fired the railgun," Wisniewski said. "Hey, where'd that guy go?"

Fiezel looked around but didn't see the SpinDog who'd wanted to fire the station's massive railgun. Built to launch small craft and drones from the station, as well as to send material between Outpost and the habitats, the railgun was mounted in the center of the asteroid and normally fired large tubs several meters long.

On the plot, a blip fired out from Outpost, before turning into a number of smaller targets, which then disappeared. *Thump!*

Fiezel spotted the man bent over a console across the room with a headset over his ears, and he ran over to him. "What are you doing? You'll give away our presence!"

"They're going to lose without our help," the man said. "I'm doing what I can to take away the Kulsian advantage."

"What are you firing?" Fiezel asked.

The man chuckled. "Anything they can find and load. I think we're going to need a lot of office furniture when we're done. And kitchen utensils. They're leaving the tubs unsealed, so whatever's loaded will spread out after launch. It's not very likely to hit them, but more so than if we used a single slug."

"Basically, like a giant shotgun," Fiezel said.

"Whatever that is," the man said. "We have to do what we can to help them."

Fiezel stared at him for a second, thinking, then he nodded. "Okay, go ahead."

"Fire," the man said into his microphone. *Thump!*

Kulsian corvette Pillager, *approaching spinward Trojans of R'Bak*

"Next pass, we both fire at the one in the lead," Marksa said. "That one tore the *Reaver* to shreds on the last pass."

"There are two of us and two of them," his tactical officer said. "Surely their technology isn't as good as ours."

Marksa pointed to one of the long holes in the overhead where the ship was open to space. "Theirs is obviously good enough to do that! Thankfully, it didn't hit anything vital."

Pink! Pink! Pink! Pink!

A number of hard objects hit the skin of the ship like metallic rain.

"Pilot, what was that?"

"Must have been some asteroids or debris from the missiles that have been fired."

"I don't think so," the tactical officer said. He held up his arm, from which a piece of metal was sticking out.

"What is that?" Marksa asked.

"I think"—the man sounded confused as he looked at the splinter of metal, then he pulled it out and slapped a hand over the three small holes in his space suit—"it's a fork?"

"Where did a fork come from?" Marksa turned back to his console. A steak knife protruded from the bulkhead. *"Pilot!"* he yelled. "One of the asteroids is firing at us. Figure out which one!"

"We got hit when we went past the last asteroid in the formation," the pilot said. "That's probably where they're firing from."

"Pillager, Reaper," a voice came over the radio before Marksa could act on the information. "We have repaired our damage and have three missiles operational. Do you want us to shoot them at the ships you're fighting?"

"No," Marksa said. "We will deal with these ships. One of the asteroids is shooting at us, though. Coordinate with my pilot and tactical officer, and use your missiles on the asteroid."

Corvette Taregon's Pride, *off R'Bak*

"Missiles!" the comms officer exclaimed. "Outpost says there are missiles headed toward them!"

"What?" Reetan asked. "Where did they come from?" He

broadened the view of the plot and saw the missiles heading from one of the Kulsians he'd previously thought destroyed. "Damn!" There was no way he could get into range to intercept them in time. The new technology was good, but it was easy to get too focused on your little battle and lose the big picture, as he noted...yet again. All three missiles slammed into Outpost.

"It's time to end this, *Four*," Reetan said over the radio. "We've got to kill these two before that last one does anything else to Outpost. Join on us and follow the targeting I send you." The new technology had allowed them to mass their fire on the last pass, destroying one of the Kulsians and damaging one of the others. He'd marked that one; they'd finish it first, and then the other, then they'd go kill the one launching missiles, hopefully before it launched any more or did anything else to Outpost.

Four moved into position alongside the *Pride*.

"Here we go." Both ships started forward at the same time the Kulsians accelerated toward them, almost like a medieval jousting tournament that had dual riders on each side, not that Reetan would have understood the reference.

The Hound-Dog ships spread slightly so they could maneuver, as the Kulsians' railguns had an edge in range. It was, however, easier to make it miss by maneuvering. While the Kulsians could also dodge the Hound-Dogs' railguns, they couldn't dodge the Hound-Dogs' lasers, beyond trying to keep from being accurately targeted. Movement didn't help the damaged Kulsian, as *Four* speared it as soon as it came in range, and a lucky railgun round gutted the cockpit. It began tumbling in a straight line, and Reetan's next rounds finished it off.

Despite being told to keep maneuvering, though, *Four* maintained a constant course for a few seconds. Whether that was to give his system a stable platform for targeting the Kulsian corvette, Reetan would never know. *Four* opened up on the Kulsian at the same time a railgun round smashed through the front of it, then a second one ripped through it.

"No!" Reetan exclaimed as his tactical officer found the range, ripping open the last Kulsian. Something inside it exploded a second later.

"Comms, call *Four* and see if they're okay," Reetan said. "Tactical, let's go kill the corvette that just fired on Outpost."

"I'm not getting anything from *Four*, sir," the comms officer said.

"Nor am I showing anything on the plot," the tactical offi- cer said, confirming what Reetan had already seen. "They just dropped out. They're gone."

Reetan nodded once, adding the pilot of *Four*—a cousin of his—to his list of people to grieve for later. Right now, though, there were some Kulsians he could still take out his anger on. "Let's go get that last one. Full speed."

Kulsian corvette Reaper, off R'Bak

There was no escaping the rogue corvette chasing them down, the *Reaper's* commanding officer knew. Their power plant was only able to get about sixty-five percent, and they had no more operational missiles. Their railgun had also been damaged when they'd been hit by the missiles at the start of the engagement. They couldn't outrun the rogue corvette, nor could they outfight it ... but they could reach back from the grave to ensure the leaders back home found out what happened, so that they sent more forces next time.

"Comms officer, use the snoop satellite to send back a message to Kulsis. Here is what I want you to tell them ..."

Corvette Taregon's Pride, off R'Bak

The final Kulsian ship blew up as Reetan's ship hit its propellant tanks with his railgun. The threat was over, but Reetan didn't feel any sense of achievement. Outpost had been hit with four missiles, and the last corvette had gotten a message off, probably to Kulsis. While he hadn't "failed" in his job as leader of the reserve force—he'd destroyed the force sent to eradicate Outpost without allowing them to achieve their goal—he'd lost his force doing so, which left a bad taste in his mouth.

While preventing the Kulsians from getting a message off hadn't been a mission goal, Reetan couldn't imagine anything good coming from it, if indeed the message made it back to Kulsis.

Reetan sighed, opening out the tactical plot. The battle for R'Bak was still going on, although both sides were considerably diminished. He only had one ship, but it was mostly operational. He smiled. It was finally time for the reserve force—such as it was—to join the main battle.

Corvette J'axon's Revenge, *off R'Bak*

"What do you think?" Targ asked as he surveyed the plot. Even though he knew it was impossible for him to smell smoke inside the enclosed environment of his shipsuit, that didn't stop traces of it from tickling his nose. The Hound-Dogs were down to nine functional craft, and all of them had sustained damage, including the railgun round that had gone through the *Revenge*, missing him by only six inches. Raptis's craft and his were the only two Aegis ships remaining, but they still had a good picture of the battle from the Dornaani satellites.

"I think we're hanging on by a thread," the tactical officer replied. "We've lost over half our force, and the ships we still have are in bad shape."

"As badly as it hurts to be us, it has to hurt even worse to be them," Targ replied. "They've lost over three-quarters of their frontline warships, including their frigate, and they only have a handful of corvettes remaining, supported by a few up-armored cargo ships. It's become a matter of wills—who wants this more." He smiled. "And that person is me."

Targ changed to his radio. *"Hound-Dog Seven, J'axon's Revenge."*

"J'axon's Revenge, Hound-Dog Seven." Malanye Raptis coughed over the radio then said, "Go ahead."

"I think they are done. They cannot have much left."

"We don't either, though. What are you thinking?"

"I think that if *we* attack *them* for once, it is going to break them. I think they're going to run."

"If they don't, we will be outgunned by them in close."

"We will, which is why I'm asking for your concurrence."

There was a long pause, but then Raptis's voice came over the radio. The touch of doubt was gone. "Bowden once said that it doesn't matter who's against you; what matters is who's beside you. I'd be honored to fight alongside you and take the battle to them for once."

Targ nodded to himself. SpinDogs and RockHounds fighting together to rid their system of the Kulsians. *As they should.* A picture Bowden had shown him once of ground combat on his planet came to mind. A group of men mounted on beasts that looked nothing like whinaalanis, dressed in armor with wings on their backs, riding out against overwhelming odds to save their city from a horde of marauders. "Form a line abreast on me," he said over the common channel so all the remaining captains would hear. As the ships slid into formation, he made one final transmission. "Charge!"

Corvette Taregon's Pride, *off R'Bak*

The charge was a thing of beauty to behold, Reetan thought as his corvette eased into the line of battle racing toward the enemy. Not because the line was perfect—it wasn't; several of the ships had damage and lagged slightly—or because of the magnificence of their vessels, which were beaten to shit, but because for the first time in system history, the SpinDogs and RockHounds were working together willingly.

He took a handful of seconds to savor the moment, then he studied the opponents waiting for them a short distance away. Targ had aimed his ship at the core of the Kulsian forces—a group of four corvettes that seemed to be leading the force, as much as any group actually "led" it. Throughout the battle, the Kulsian attacks had been uncoordinated at best, as a handful or two of ships would try to rush one end or another of the Hound-Dog line. They would get in some shots before retreating, usually with fewer of their own ships remaining.

The other Hound-Dog ships closed in on Targ, and he raced forward, creating an arrowhead aimed at the heart of the Kulsian resistance.

The Kulsian corvettes began moving, spreading out to give themselves room to maneuver. The other Kulsian ships went into motion, too, but it was quickly apparent that many of them were fleeing. Almost all the cargo vessels ran for the safety of the planet, and Reetan shook his head. Some of those craft weren't made to land on the planet, and others had damage that would make reentry perilous—at best—without repairs. Even with them, he expected many would still experience fatal burn-throughs.

As his attention returned to the main combatant forces, he saw their motion hadn't ceased, nor had they turned to aim their weapons at the approaching Hound-Dogs. They'd all separated, *and they were running, too!*

The Hound-Dogs, committed to the maneuver, raced through where the enemy had been, with only a few ships actually getting shots off at the handful of Kulsian ships that'd waited too long to flee. His tactical officer drilled one on the periphery of the formation, and the *Pride*'s lasers sliced open a thinly skinned cargo ship and vented most of it to space.

"Should we chase them down?" Raptis asked.

"We'll go after the corvettes in teams of three," Targ said. "The cargo ships are no danger. Allow anyone that wants to surrender to do so; kill anyone who refuses. Hurry, though; there are a lot of ships that will require assistance."

"Are we assisting the Kulsians?" one of the captains asked.

"Of course we are," Targ said. "Right after we ensure the safety of our people. If they expire in the meantime, that's just more spoils for us."

Aegis corvette Hornet, *off R'Bak*

Burg Hrensku worked the controls of his maneuvering unit and slowed himself as he approached the derelict ship. A sense of foreboding came over him as he surveyed it from up close. No signs of life or power were in evidence, not even the emergency lighting. The crew's shipsuits would have lasted three hours or so...but it had been over five since the ship had been hit and gone dead. Having flown past the aft end of the ship as it tumbled slowly through space, he could see why. The missile that had hit the motor had blown away a large portion of the engine and had mangled the parts that remained; it would need to be replaced before the ship would fly again. Not repaired; replaced.

He worked the controls on the airlock and entered. Unlike many ships, there was no window into the ship, so he had to wait to know more until he could manually shut the exterior door and cycle atmosphere in from the ship. At least the interior was still pressurized. That was something, although it had to be getting cold inside. Very cold. And it wasn't like you could light a fire to stay warm, like you could on the planet below.

Five people waited for him inside. "Burg!" Bowden said as he entered. "Good to see you. What took you so long?"

"Well, there was this matter of fighting a desperate battle against incredible odds, as I heard you explain it to Dave Fiezel."

"And...?"

"And what?"

"Did we win?"

"Well, Outpost got hit—"

"What?"

"It got hit by several missiles before Reetan could kill the attacking Kulsians. Outpost received significant, but not catastrophic, damage. The Kulsian fleet, though... their damage *was* catastrophic." Burg paused and squared his shoulders. "You asked if we won. Yes, *we* did." Burg smiled his biggest smile. "Spin-Dogs, RockHounds, and Lost Soldiers, all fighting together. We won it. Together."

Bowden reached out to steady himself with the nearest handhold. "Send that message. Along with sitrep code 'alpha.' Tight beam to *Spin One* and Pakir Station. Also... uh, to the dirtside relay microsat." Bowden sounded sleepy, or perhaps groggy with exhaustion and relief.

Burg secured himself with his left hand so that he could lift the other in a slow, but very precise Lost Soldier salute. "Aye, aye, Admiral."

Chapter Forty-Two

The Hamain, R'Bak

"Priority message, Commander Murphy." The pilot turned, eyes wide. "Routed through the orbital relay, sir."

Murphy carefully replaced the binder he'd just extracted from his briefing folio and nodded. "Go ahead." He put his worries aside, cleared his mind of every thought and task, purposely let his eyes lose focus: all so that he could just hear the words without distraction. And hopefully, concentrate enough to overcome the tendency most likely to push him out of the present: his reflex to analyze every event and word in the context of securing the Lost Soldiers' future.

He succeeded, more or less. He listened carefully, nodded when the copilot/comms operator finished, asked him to read it back very slowly. No reason not to be sure that he had, in fact, remained attentive to each word.

The copilot glanced sideways at him and complied.

At the end, Murphy nodded again. "Thank you."

"Wonderful news," said the pilot, but his tone ended on the rising tone of a question.

Murphy kept his voice and his face calm, composed. "Yes, it is wonderful news." He turned to face the copilot directly. "Please tell the chief that I need my main pack. Be certain that he handles it carefully when he removes the lashings."

The copilot stared at the hatch behind him, saw that Murphy

did indeed mean for him to oversee the chief's compliance personally, popped his straps and slipped back into the payload bay.

Murphy turned toward the pilot. "Change of flight plan, Captain Essklur. I need to go to Ikaan-tel."

"Ikaan-tel, sir?"

"That is what I said, Captain. I need to convey this news personally to some of our contacts there."

The pilot looked at his plot. "How long do you plan to be there, Commander Murphy? I will need to apprise security that your ETA has changed."

Murphy shook his head. "I will be at Ikaan-tel for at least a day, possibly longer, and as this is currently our only planetside shuttle, we can't afford to let it sit on the ground. If I recall, you're due to pick up a combat team for insertion near the coast, so you will not be changing your ETA."

The pilot looked sideways. "Sir, given the protocols for your security... Commander Murphy, are you sure about this?"

Murphy smiled. "Well, Captain, you could speak to the CO about enforcing those protocols." The pilot's eyes revealed the instant he remembered who he was talking to. "But I think we can be pretty certain regarding the outcome of that conversation."

"Yes, sir."

"However, after you've dusted off from Ikaan-tel, I need your comms officer to send a signal back to the microsat. Routing is to Crystal Villa, aboard *Spin One*."

The pilot raised an eyebrow. "Crystal Villa, sir? I have never heard that code name."

"And you shouldn't have. The message is a single character: 'delta.' I will also need you to keep checking for my recall signal; there's a slim possibility I could be done within a few hours. Either way, top up your fuel tanks every chance you get, because when you return, I will probably not be your only passenger. Assume you'll be loading at least six other individuals, about eight tonnes of equipment, and possibly a small vehicle."

The pilot stared at him. Murphy shook his head. "I can't tell you what's going on. But since it supersedes our survey of western coast's port traffic all the way up to the Greens, you can guess the comparative priority."

The pilot nodded. "I think I do, sir. Changing heading for Ikaan-tel. ETA: twenty minutes."

Murphy nodded and stared down at details among the dunes which, given the shuttle's speed and altitude, scudded by like frozen white waves.

R'Bak Island, R'Bak

Bo hated admitting that Max Messina had been right.

Which was made harder by the fact that if he hadn't insisted, one Major Hubert Moorefield would have been KIA at the Battle of Downport.

Well, actually the Battle for R'Bak city. Once the two guns had been smoked in—and ultimately taken out with thermally sighted counterfire from Kaladar Six—the wharf became the invasion force's secure highway. Meanwhile, the really big tracks—and whole Free Bands—swept across Downport's expanse with little opposition. The few surveyors and locals that fought back learned, in the hardest possible way, not to try cases with machine-gun-armed APCs, surging with impatience to discharge scores of vengeful, M14-toting R'Baku.

But the strategy for taking the city was necessarily more measured. Bo, ringed by almost a dozen Lost Soldiers who were either company and troop leaders or staff for his mobile CP, had explained the plan to the locals, none of whom had been read in. R'Baku were loyal, but as locals, they were always subject to extortion of the most cruel and abhorrent kinds.

"We are not fighting to take the city," he began. "We are making a very focused strike into the northwest quarter only." He pointed to the location on a hastily improvised sand table. "It will be a fast armored assault, spearheaded and well-flanked by infantry. Right now, we do not care about the rest of the city, so we are avoiding it."

A local had raised his dark, tattooed hand: a tribal from the eastern extents of the Hamain. "But how can the attack succeed if we do not control the whole city?"

Bo smiled. "Oh, we will. But we won't have to fight for it." He pointed to a square in the approximate center of the northwest quarter. "We are going to take and hold the power plant. If that falls, all the other surveyor infrastructure in the city collapses. That is why we are not going after the surveyor stations, or the satraps, or the puppet government. We are going for the electricity upon which every Kulsian advantage depends.

"The tactics are simple. Infantry secures the moving column: front, flanks, rear. Local intel multiply confirms that the Kulsians have never brought portable antitank weapons to R'Bak, because they're the only ones with tanks. Other explosives are possible, but between infantry on point, and local sympathizers—of whom we have many; watch for red armbands and a white hat or sash—we should have no significant opposition getting to the power plant."

A woman Band leader in Sarmatchani garb stood. "I mean no disrespect, Major SHAEF"—a strange permutation of which Bo was growing fond—"but how can you, who are not from here, know if some who approach us as friends are only pretending to be?"

Bo remembered smiling. "Firstly, we gathered some very good local intelligence on the city starting a year ago. We will also be met by a dozen proven friends who will travel near the infantry that is on point or guarding our flanks. And *they* will know if those dressed as sympathizer are impostors.

"The only factor that may delay us are the satraps' crowd-control vehicles—er, big machine-gun carriers built by the surveyors for putting down disturbances or protests." The R'Baku who had encountered the upgunned versions of SWAT tactical vehicles muttered grimly. "If any are encountered, you are ordered to fall back to the head of the mechanized column. The guns and armor of our vehicles are more than a match for those machine-gun carriers." Which was almost a comical understatement, as the locals would no doubt discover.

The plan was simple in concept, and its execution did not ask the Free Bands to perform any actions they weren't already familiar with: move-and-fire leapfrog advances, supporting armored vehicles, and pinning threats in place until superior firepower could arrive. But as Bo was climbing into the hatch of his chosen command vehicle, Max had appeared alongside him and looked at the rooftops ahead. "So, this thunder run of yours—"

Bo grinned. "I see I'm not the only one reading through some of the history we've missed."

The big man nodded but did not return Moorefield's smile. "I have, sir. Enough to look at this culture and say that the chance of running into IEDs that could take out our tracks are pretty slim."

"But...?"

"Sir, you can take your mobile CP wherever you want—*but* buttoned up. The whole time."

"You do know we're going to have air support within the hour?" With the defeat of the Harvester fleet and the seizure of the downport, Mara Lee's Hueys were dusting off from their staging base near the same southern cove that Ulmaren had favored when he was still carrying cargos and smuggling on the side.

Max shook his head. "No one is happier to hear the whup-whup of an inbound slick than me, sir. But they can't look in windows, and they can't stop thrown bombs. They can get payback, sure, but that's not really the point here, is it, sir?"

Bo sighed and stared at the quiet bear of a man. Messina had watched his commander's six throughout the entire unloading of Roro Zero and probably had several litters of kittens while doing it. And damn it, the man knew his craft from Vietnam, so...
"Okay, Max: no open hatch."

So it was with a chill like the one Bo's grandma called "walking over your own grave" that Hubert Moorefield saw one of the two vehicles that had been lost to second-story Molotov cocktails. The blackened body slumped over an open hatch's weapon ring could easily have been his own. He swallowed thickly as the image dropped beyond where he could see it through the bulletproof observation ports of his own vehicle's sealed commander's cupola.

As the already-battered Track Five drove its bulk through the perimeter fence of the powerplant, surveyors and local troops scattered in all directions.

Finally deemed safe enough for "Major SHAEF," Bo emerged just as the first four of Mara's choppers began orbiting, their door gunners cutting down ambush teams waiting on roofs or lurking around blind corners. For every enemy they hit, half a dozen broke and ran.

Max Messina was, of course, right behind Bo. Who sighed.
"Moose, you're a bigger man than I am."

"Very obviously, sir."

"I mean big in character: for not saying, 'I told you so.'"

Moose just shook his head. "Those locals back there, the ones who burned to death doing their duty? I'm not about to crack wise or make quips in the shadow of their bodies, sir. We may be from Earth and they may be from R'Bak, but we fought side by side.

"Maybe I've got the charity of spirit you think I do, sir. Who knows? Maybe I do. But today, I couldn't tell you. Because with their ghosts all around us, I'd be a bastard to do anything other than hold my peace in respect."

As they watched, smoke grenades were popped inside the compound. A rich, violet plume reached up and, as if summoned by it, four Hueys came in hard and low.

"Purple haze," murmured Max with a tone between longing and melancholy as the slicks lifted their noses and slowed.

Bo nodded. He'd only heard the phrase in films; Maximiliano Messina had lived it and had lost brothers while wreathed in the same-colored fog that was even now dissipating.

With the Hueys still a meter off the deck, Chalmers and Jacks jumped down, leading their teams toward red-and-white-wearing locals who'd infiltrated the plant the night before.

"Major?" Sergeant Renaldi called from the RTO's seat in the AFV that was Bo's CP. "Am I cleared to signal objective taken?"

Bo looked at the power plant, the downport, and finally the blue sky beyond which their fates had been decided. "Yes, Adam. Send that SHAEF reports, 'Omaha is open.'"

Spin One

"Major Tapper," Timmy Uggs called from the main room of the operations center. "Coded sitrep coming in."

"Source?"

Harry heard the comm operator's nervous swallow all the way in Murphy's office. The keyboard that Makarov had increasing ceded to Uggs clattered briefly. A long pause. "Code alpha, sir! Bowden won! Or, as the message says, they all did."

Tapper leaned back in Murphy's chair, pushed back the irony that the man who'd orchestrated so much of the day's desperate gambles wasn't here to see them pay off. Assuming, of course, that all of them did...which was a pretty big assumption.

"New code coming in, sir!"

"From dirtside?"

"Aye, sir. It's from Major Moorefield." Timmy whooped. "He sends, 'Omaha is open'! And, eh, he adds that he is presently consolidating control of Downport. He estimates it will be an hour before he can clear landers." His head poked around the coaming of the secure hatch. "Damn, sir: two victories in one day! Can you believe it?"

Frankly, not really. Harry Tapper had learned to expect that some hitch, some mishap, some loss invariably came along with every operation—and the greater the success, the more certain that fate would insert a sufficiently sobering counterpoint. *C'mon*, he thought at the overhead, *get it over with. Drop the other shoe, already!*

His stomach plummeted when Timmy jumped away from the hatchway in response to yet another of the pings that indicated an incoming signal.

Still staring at the overhead, Tapper felt a bead of sweat forming on his hairline. *No: I didn't* really *want anything to go wrong. I was just being a cranky SEAL. I would never—*

"Sir..." Happily, Timmy's voice was not dark with grief. But it was...baffled?

"What's the signal, Mr. Uggs? Is there a problem?"

"No, sir. I mean, I don't think so. But this is...well, it's a strange signal. And it was routed here but to a call sign I don't recognize."

Tapper stood. "What's the call sign?"

"Crystal Villa, sir."

Tapper frowned as Timmy reappeared in the hatchway. "What or who is 'Crystal Villa,' sir?"

It's me: the home-plate backup in case Glass Palace goes offline. Which is to say, something may have gone sideways with Murphy. "Who's the sender?"

"Pulling that up, now, sir. It's...huh?"

"Report, Mr. Uggs!"

"Sir, I—yes, sir, but it doesn't make sense. Sender is Glass Palace, sir."

What the fu—? "What's the signal, Mr. Uggs?"

Timmy had rushed back to the computer, answered in a loud, aggravated mutter. "It's double-encrypted sir. Cracking now...produces day code 'delta.'" Uggs may have cursed under his breath before calling out. "Sir, since it's a single Greek letter spelled out, it should refer to one of our fast sitrep or instruction presets. But 'delta' is not in the code list."

Tapper discovered that his mouth had become dry. "Enter it." He walked to the hatchway to watch as Uggs processed the signal.

"But, sir, the system will reject any unrecognized code."

Yes, but you *don't have the clearance to see the full menu of codes resident in the system, Timmy.* "Just enter it."

"Aye, aye, sir." Uggs blinked when the screen started scrolling through the security handshakes. "Hey, it's processing! You were right, sir!"

Wish I wasn't. Tapper managed to wait a whole second before pressing, "The message, Mr. Uggs?"

"Oh, right, sir! Uh...the message is 'Lawful Lawless. Check files.'" Timmy looked up, brow furrowed in perplexity. "Does that mean anything to you, Major?"

Harry frowned. "It does, Timmy. I need the ops center for a few minutes. Shut the hatch. I'll dog it behind you."

The Hamain, R'Bak

The young Atti of Ikaan-tel, Salsaliin, waved her two guards out of the yurt-hut. The village hetman, Bafguur, rose. Murphy did as well.

Salsaliin held up her hand: a gesture of request, not command. "Why do you leave, Honored Bafguur, first of our tribe?"

He bowed to her. "Because soon, the colonel's questions will no longer concern tribal matters." He smiled toward Murphy. "Since telling us of the defeat of the Kulsians and the health of your daughter's sire, his questions increasingly touch upon the whinaalanis and the tunnels below. Soon he will ask of the Daaj or things very close to it. And that is not for my ears."

Bafguur grinned. "Of course, they are not for his, either. But when dying, Atti Ooshwelo trusted Vat to carry her to the place of which we do not speak. So I suspect his commander must already know more than I do."

Murphy nodded slowly and deeply. "I thank you for understanding, Hetman Bafguur. Your wisdom has spared me the rudeness of requesting privacy: a rudeness that no guest should ever show to a host. Particularly the leader of a community."

Bafguur's smile widened, revealing several gaps where teeth should have been. "You have been our friends from the first, you and your Lost Soldiers. Because of you, we may never need to take refuge in the tunnels again. It is a small thing, giving you the space to ask your questions."

After the flap closed behind him, Salsaliin mused, "He believes he is seeing the great wheel of fate finally coming full circle. Legend has it that men from the sky ruined the world, hunted whinalaanis, and behaved as do the Kulsians. It is only fitting that now, other men from the sky undo their works and are friends to the whina-laanis, just as our ancient forebears were said to be. So although it is we who keep the whinaalanis' shelter safe and guard their water source, it is you whom they seek out and bear upon their backs."

Murphy nodded, decided to take a chance that might move things along quickly; every minute counted, now. "When you speak of the whinaalanis' water source, I presume you refer to the butte beyond the mountain you call Mount Whinaalani, just to the north."

Salsaliin sat very erect. "How do you know there is water at that butte? That was not even revealed to Va—Lieutenant Thomas."

Murphy shrugged. "In the course of freeing large towns from the yoke of the satraps, we found many ancient records, most of which they had forgotten."

Salsaliin sniffed. "I am not surprised. The satraps care for nothing but money and the power it brings."

Murphy nodded. "We, on the other hand, consider knowledge the greatest power and, if used wisely, a path toward much that is good within and between people."

"These are close to the words of the Daaj." She paused. "Perhaps the essence of the Daaj has sent you here."

Murphy heard the tone: half curiosity, half trap baited to catch opportunists and megalomaniacs. He smiled and waited.

She smiled back. "That is the last time I shall try to be sly with you, Colonel Murphy."

He shrugged. "A leader cannot neglect any tool that might protect their people. But if I am here at the will of the Daaj, I assure you, no one would be more surprised than me."

She chuckled softly. "So, these ancient writings told you of Whinaakanut?"

"The butte?"

"Yes." She frowned. "You know of it but do not know its name?"

"That is correct. It was referred to, but not by that name—if it was named at all. However, the information allowed the machines that watch from above to locate it and peer deep into the crevice that can only be reached from its top. Except for birds . . . and, of course, whinaalanis."

"So you know of their preference for water in high places."

Murphy shrugged. "It is embarrassing we did not foresee it. Their ability to scale rock should have told us that for them, every inaccessible water source is what a high-walled oasis is to humans. Particularly those where the water never runs dry."

Salsaliin frowned. "Your eyes in space could show you all of what you say...except that the water of Whinaakanut is always present, even in the height of the Searing. Yet I see in your eyes and hear in your voice that you are quite certain of this. How?"

Murphy set aside all the measurements and projections and models made possible by the Dornaani satellite, found the story-skein that ran through them all. "The eyes in space do not just see light; they see heat. And when a surface reflects light differently—such as when wet rocks shine—it shows that, too.

"We noticed that when night falls, the rock surfaces that line the inside of the crevice cool much sooner than the others. The water that collects on them runs down into a pool that, once they saw it, our space eyes revealed to be fed by a spring as well. Between those two sources, the water collects until it reaches the point where it is vaporized by the suns. We think a measure of it also runs off more slowly in underground caves and"—Murphy glanced at the ground—"to other subterranean structures."

Salsaliin reclined with a sigh. "According to the few who have ever scaled Whinaakanut, all is as you say. And your unspoken guess is correct; the water from the crevice which we call Ajat-huk—the Well of Deliverance—sustains the refuges of the Daaj. It also feeds Ikaan-tel's village well, but in the Searing, it does so slowly or sometimes, ceases altogether."

Murphy nodded gratefully. There was no reason to mention that he had not had to guess that the Daaj's reservoir was sustained by the Well of Deliverance. Maps from various sources showed that it was the only subterranean water source within a hundred kilometers and that the aquifer that spread out from it was the only reason Ikaan-tel had a well at all.

Salsaliin considered him. "As Bafguur remarked, you have asked many questions. But I cannot help but wonder if they are preludes to a request."

"They are."

She frowned. "When Ooshwelo allowed Vat to behold the Daaj, she was in dire need. He was the only one present with enough strength to carry her to the place where her mothers were sure to find her spirit, and where she knew I would take the first step of becoming the next Atii. Unless your need is as dire as was hers, please do not request that I bring *you* to the very place I am sworn to keep secret."

Murphy shook his head. "That is not my request."

Salsaliin sighed, relieved, but puzzled also. "Then if not that, what do you wish?"

Murphy pointed north. "It is written that there is an entrance to a smuggler's tunnel halfway up Mount Whinaalani's windward slope. Do your people know of it?"

She nodded. "Yes, but it has not been used in many decades."

"By humans, you mean?"

Salsaliin smiled. "So, is it whinaalanis you seek or tunnels?"

Murphy smiled back. "Both. They are part of the same mystery."

She leaned forward. "Which is...?"

His smile widened. "Now it is I who must ask you not to ask after a secret that I may not divulge."

She laughed. "You are quite pleasant. It is strange that your men think you so severe and humorless."

"Well, they do see a different side of me."

She chuckled. "That, too, is true." She stood. "I know of this tunnel and shall summon two hunters who can show you the way. But you will arrive only a few hours before dark. If that. If you wish, I can arrange for you to stay with—"

Murphy stood and shook his head. "I am grateful, but I must decline. I have promised to be on my way before the sun sets."

Salsaliin frowned. "To whom did you make this promise?"

Murphy shrugged. "To myself." Which was the simple truth. "I have a journey to undertake, and I am the only one who may undertake it. So to start at once is one of the promises I must keep." *"And miles to go before I sleep"—in one fashion or another.*

Salsaliin was nodding slowly. "This sounds much like our Trek of Self. Vat said it was very similar to the vision quest of some of your native peoples."

Murphy nodded. "Similar. It's actually probably closer to what some of the peoples of a place called Australia do: something called a walkabout. But both must be done alone."

Salsaliin began heading to the flap of her ritual home. "I—*we* understand that. Our Trek of Self is just that."

Murphy stopped, she turned. "Then you will understand that,

if others come seeking me, I ask you one further favor: that you do not mention what we spoke of here. Although they might be my friends, and might mean well, they might also try to find me—and that would be the end of my walkabout."

Salsaliin nodded solemnly. "I shall respect your wishes. Now, come: if you mean to make it to the tunnels before dark, we must move quickly. Once inside, your friends could search the four points of the compass and not find you."

Murphy nodded and, as she turned to lead him out, smiled sadly. *That was the plan, after all: scatter them across the whole system.*

As they must *be, if they're to remain safe.*

Chapter Forty-Three

R'Bak Island, R'Bak

Chalmers wasn't sure how to react to what had just emerged from the radio.

Apparently, no one else was either. When the silence dragged on for a three count, Tapper's voice returned. "Is everyone there?"

Moorefield, who'd been called from a "situation" he was handling in the downport, mumbled, "Affirmative."

Jackson was so distracted he responded by nodding, then remembered that only Mara Lee and Chalmers could see it. He leaned close to the big tactical set that had been secured to the deck of Mara's command bird. "Jackson here."

"Chalmers." He looked at Mara, who'd grabbed him away from a perfectly good card game when the all-hands call had come in.

Now, her eyes were shut tight and her face was alarmingly red. She was breathing as heavily as a prizefighter between rounds. She stopped abruptly, sucked in a lungful and yelled, almost shrieked, "*What the* fuck?"

Tapper's voice was unusually cool. "I could ask you the same thing, Major."

Her eyes opened sharply: hurt, surprised, angry. "What the hell does that mean, Harry?"

But it was Vat—apparently on the same shuttle as Harry—who screamed back. "Just when were you going to tell us that Murphy has *fucking* multiple sclerosis, Mara? I thought we were *friends*."

"We are. But I made a *promise* to that other friend to keep my mouth shut. Which seemed like a pretty good idea, what with him working 24/7 trying to keep all of us from getting pushed out airlocks. And then..." She drifted to a halt. When she resumed, it was in a disbelieving, even horrified whisper. "Damn it, this is about him looking for a cure, isn't it?"

Tapper's voice had not warmed up much. "So you knew about that, too?"

"Jesus, Harry: if Murphy's gone hunting for a cure down here, how the hell do you think he got the intel except through *my* 'family connections'?"

"So Healer Naliryiz knows, also."

"Yeah, and so did the first Matriarch, Kelrevis, who saw it almost right away. Her sister Shumrir and Naliryiz have been working in secret to unearth an old pharmaflora remedy. Frankly, it was looking pretty grim; everything in their archives just pointed back down here—and Murph was fighting to hold it together."

"How bad were his symptoms?" Moorefield's voice sounded broken with—what? Regret?

"So bad that it was only a matter of months, maybe weeks, before someone tweaked to it."

Vat seemed to be spitting at the audio pickup. "Yeah, and then the SpinDog genetic purity league would have thrown their hands up, accused Anseker of having known it all along—which he couldn't deny without throwing Naliryiz under the galaxy's biggest bus—and we'd be lucky to avoid a civil war."

Jackson nodded. "Yeah, and even luckier to make it alive out the other side." His voice had a slow, graveyard pace.

Chalmers let the silence run to a three count before asking, "Major Tapper, you sound like you're pretty close to R'Bak. Hardly any delay."

"Grabbed Vat and got on this bird right away."

Moorefield's question was almost clipped. "Where's Bowden?"

"Still recovering. He was tilting toward hypothermia when they finally got to his ship and his wound hasn't fully healed yet. He's holding the fort with Makarov. Which buys us some time: the Hound-Dogs are deeply impressed by victors who return bearing scars and tales of imminent death. So they won't press Bowden too hard on why the rest of us are ganged up near R'Bak. While we're taking attendance, any news of Cutter's whereabouts, Bo?"

"Nothing useful. So far no signals for emergency supply or extraction. And Murphy gave him orders for radio silence and to break squelch infrequently, except if at need."

"Of course he did," Vat muttered. "That way the guy who saw him last, and who we can *trust*, is the one guy we can't talk to."

"And since R'Bak Island hadn't been secured yet," Bo added, "it made sense. Hell, we still have no track on almost a third of the surveyors we know were planetside when the shit hit the fan."

"Okay, but what do we *do*?" Mara said loudly, before glancing at Chalmers. "You're a damn good investigator, I'm told. Where would you start looking for Murphy?"

Chalmers sighed; he knew he'd have to say it eventually, but he'd been in no rush to do so: "With respect, Major, I don't think that's the right question."

She glared at him, then must have seen the regret in his face. "Okay, then what *is* our first question?"

Chalmers mentally girded his loins for the shitstorm he was sure to summon. "The first question we have to ask is, 'what happens if we *find* Murphy?' And everything about how he pulled this off tells me that he *wants* us to ask that question: first, last, and foremost."

Tapper's voice was serious, collected, slightly encouraging. "That's an interesting question, Chief. So what do you think was going on in the colonel's mind, if that's what he wanted us to ask?"

Jesus, isn't it obvious? But Chalmers calmly replied, "The best way to understand what the colonel was thinking is to step back and look at what he did—what he actually *did*—while setting this up."

Moorefield sounded uncertain. "You mean arranging to be in a shuttle that we couldn't find immediately?"

"No, sir," Jackson answered before Chalmers could. "The chief means that since the day we came back from the mission to grab the lighter, everything the colonel has done was to make his disappearing act possible. From the moment we arrived back at *Spin One*, he knew that unless someone found a cure for his MS, he wasn't coming back."

Mara shook her head. "Are you saying he's been lying about everything? That he was spinning some kind of fantasy for us to believe in?"

"No, ma'am," Chalmers jumped in, fearful that Jacks was

close to corking off. "I'm saying he did everything with not one purpose, but two. And he took steps to make sure we'd never notice that." *Although maybe if* I'd *been in the inner circle...*

Vat saved him the trouble of being tactful by being painfully blunt. "Look: hindsight makes it pretty clear what he was doing. He had all of you running around like long-tailed cats in a room full of rocking chairs. Bowden had a fleet to build so he could go fight the Harvesters. Major Moorefield was assigned an extra-credit project on the whinaalani while also confabbing with Mar—Major Lee on the ground campaign. Of course, that's when she wasn't keeping the Otlethes Family onside. Major Tapper here was working on his super-secret project to handcraft our very own new and improved Constitution under the secure file 'Lawful Lawless.' And when he walked into my recovery room he was there to dangle the bait of an ancient mystery in front of me—and in five minutes' time, I'd taken it hook, line, and sinker and began figuring out a dozen dead languages in the deepest dive of my life.

"Of course, it didn't stop there. He had Bowden recruit Makarov into becoming an AWACS artiste, with Timmy Uggs as his loyal, red-haired sidekick. He sent Cutter and Moose planetside—different times, different missions—as we started coming down to the finish line. Hell, he even got his bodyguard Janusz to outfit him from the goddamn impounded goods locker by convincing him that he was gathering evidence for a hush-hush investigation into black marketeers. With my name at the top of the list, no less."

Vat sighed. "Murphy not only kept us all crazy-busy, but kept us working on separate tasks, because that way, we'd never catch him out."

"What do you mean?" Moorefield muttered.

Chalmers stepped in before Vat went too far and tempers flared. "Vat means that Murphy kept maximum control by interacting with us one at a time. And if any of us worked on related tasks, we never had to meet the colonel in a group."

"Yeah," Vat summarized, "that way, he only had to manage one con game at a time. Mark of a promising amateur: he avoided his weaknesses and played to his strengths."

Chalmers heard Moorefield mutter irritably. *Time to save you again, Vat.* "It was a pretty clever plan, actually, particularly since he was able to conduct his own part of the charade not only in plain sight, but because with the exception of the trip to the evidence locker, everything he did was something that *had* to be done."

Jackson's patience once again ran thin when Chalmers's explanation met with uncertain silence. "Damn it, it's just like every assignment the colonel gave all of you; every action *he* took was a logical step toward our greater objectives. That was the elegance of it; there were no extraneous activities, no unexplainable actions. Everything that he did was actually necessary for what we all accomplished three days ago. He just found a way to build his own preparations into them. Seamlessly."

Lee nodded. "But by gathering all the information he needed to go on this suicide walkabout, he's also left a trail of clues that tells us where he's trying to go, and maybe why. That should give us a way to follow him, or at least pick up his trail."

Chalmers sighed, shook his head. "I'm not sure it does, Major. See: Murphy didn't gather *just* the information he needed; he gathered *all* the relevant information for every one of the operations he was overseeing. He assessed all the ports, all the tunnels, all the whinaalani trails and watering holes, all the rumored sites of alchemical knowledge. And because he did, we can't even begin to guess which of the various pieces of information he actually used."

Lee flung up a hand—not at Chalmers, but at the impossibility of the situation.

Moorefield's voice was flat and devoid of patience. "Look: we've got everyone we need to mount a search either here on R'Bak or inbound. We're the ones who know Murphy best, who knew exactly what he asked us about. If anyone can reconstruct the full scope of the deck he's playing with, it's us. And with your shuttle, Harry, we've even got our own, very private ride. We should start looking for him right now, before the trail gets any colder."

"Except..." Mara's slow start indicated she was conceptually pivoting even as she spoke. "Except that brings us back to Chief Chalmers's first point: about Murphy wanting us to ask these questions and to realize that he *doesn't* want us to go looking for him."

Chalmers nodded.

Moorefield was clearly working at keeping his reply less than extremely clipped. "Okay: I'm listening." He didn't succeed.

Mara felt her way along, Chalmers agreeing with his eyes.

"Murphy knew that if we stayed down here, the Hound-Dogs would want to know why."

"Yeah," Vat muttered, realizing where Lee was heading. "And half of them will be convinced that this was *our* play all along."

Jacks nodded. "I've gotta agree. They're likely to figure that we planet-born folk were looking to become the new masters of R'Bak. Wanted to turn the tables so that all the space folk have to kowtow to us. But especially the SpinDogs, since they're the ones with the most to lose, genetically."

Moorefield scoffed. "They can't be that stupid."

Tapper sighed. "Actually, that line of thinking probably doesn't come from being stupid as much as from being panicked. Consider: if Murphy, the very embodiment of all our gambles *and* theirs, doesn't show up, that will be bad enough. But if *we* don't show up to tell of triumph and lead the conga line at the victory dance? *Then* what might they think?"

Moorefield's even greater sigh indicated he'd seen the way the dominoes would fall. "They could think all sorts of things, particularly the ones that hate us already. Maybe they'll figure that Murphy was in earnest about working with them but we bumped him off to grab the brass ring of planetary control. Or that he's alive and well and we're faking his disappearance and maintaining close security so no Hound-Dog operatives can find and liquidate the mastermind who orchestrated their now-inevitable fall from 'dominion.'"

Vat muttered. "Great. Screwed no matter which way we face. So what do we do?"

Mara looked at Chalmers and they nodded in slow unison. "We do what Murph realized we'd have to do for the safety of all the Lost Soldiers. We go back and report him missing. Some of us come back to look for him." Her eyes seemed to swim with light. "And either we find him cured and he's a homecoming hero...or what we find doesn't come back with us, ensuring that his MS is never revealed."

Jackson leaned toward Lee with a sudden rush of compassion. "Don't you blame yourself for saying that, Major. You're just following the script Colonel Murphy wrote. It's pretty clear it wasn't just his plan to get us to head back to the spins. He gave us zero trail to follow quickly and left us in a bind where we can't ask too many questions without tipping our hand." Jacks shook his head. "He made sure that there was no way that staying behind would do any good. And that would spare us having to decide between that and going back—which he knew we'd have to do for the good of all the Lost Soldiers."

Chalmers nodded and hoped his eyes were not, as his mom had said, gateways to his soul and his thoughts. *Because by the time we get back, Murphy will either have found a cure or died on the search.*

And he knew—and intended—that, too.

High Desert of the Sub-Hamain, R'Bak

Rodger Murphy came to another forking branch in the tunnel that led away from the first oasis into which he'd emerged. The one advantage traveling underground in the desert was that the passages were a comfortable temperature and unusually dry, compared to other caves.

Not surprisingly, other creatures had learned to take advantage of its respite from the lethal heat of the surface. Most of them fled the moment they saw his light, particularly when he held it high. Of the two species that had proven more aggressive, the most active resembled beetle-spiders about the size of a lean dachshund. Called *zartzhu*, they were actually mammals and individuals were barely more dangerous than a large rat. Unfortunately, they usually appeared in what the ancients had referred to as clutches. Fortunately, they were both very stupid and very flammable and having read about them, Murphy had taken special care to have a reasonable supply of willie petes and camp oil.

The other dangerous species was a reclusive creature that resembled a hybrid between a snake and a millipede. Happily, it was reclusive and only wanted to be left alone to hunt its rodentine prey in peace. Less happily, its hide was natural camouflage in the tunnels and its venom was usually fatal—which was why Murphy had equipped himself with a sawed-off shotgun that had been cut-down to the size of an overlarge pistol.

Checking both branches before entering the T-intersection, he spied sigils on the far wall. Murphy hurried to study them—and barely caught himself against the rock as his left leg spasmed and failed to respond, even though he could still feel it. The MS had been getting steadily more pronounced, but if he could just get into the deep desert where the alchemists were known to gather the chyrsalises of Catalysites, then maybe—

He felt metal under the hand holding him up. As his leg began responding again, he staggered back from the wall and shone the light full upon it.

A map, its key points marked by knob-headed metal spikes. It was surrounded by the initials and advice and graffiti of untold millennia-worth of wanderers, black marketeers, and seasonal traders who had hazarded this very path.

He pulled the first copy of his binder out of his knapsack and commenced to reproduce the map in detail. With any luck, the stylized trees clustered off to the left, or east, indicated that the same passage would lead him to the second oasis. If not directly, then, eventually.

Rather like his search for a cure: a winding path without any surety of survival at its end.

Murphy repacked the binder, checked that only one of the gun's two hammers was cocked, and set off toward the east and whatever fate awaited him there.